Praise for

When Every Breath Becomes a Prayer

Boundless material for contemplation, that will keep readers busy long after they turn the last page. Highly Recommended.
Columbia Review

"Susan Plunket writes eloquently of the soul."
Kirkus Review

A sumptuous and beautifully crafted novel, *When Every Breath Becomes a Prayer*, is not only powerful in its clinical acu͡r   ͟t deeply moving in its portrayal of a family find͡: transcendence, through heartache, la͡͡
Monica L. Creelman, PH.D., Clin

This magical book speaks eloquently   ͟͟visible miracles in our midst.
Charmayne Kilcup, PH.D., Soul healer and author

The kind of novel that stays with you long after you turn the last page, this beautiful book about love will catapult you into a new awareness of what it means to be human.
Meadow Linn, Co-author of The Mystic Cookbook

When Every Breath Becomes a Prayer dives deep into the heart of love, life and relationships. How do you move on, heal and live a life of joy? Susan Plunket will guide you along the path.
Debra Oakland, Founder of Living in Courage and bestselling co-author of Unwavering Strength

As a spiritual healer, I study and teach about concepts bright and beautiful: the soul, light, divinity, love, the inner planes, the matrix, unity, energy, and more. It's easy to intellectualize these ideas, reducing them to "mental constructs." In this box, they can't scare us, but neither can they empower or guide us. In her amazing fictional book When Every Breath Becomes a Prayer, Susan Plunket employs textured and rich writing, poetry, really to follow the lives of several all-too-real characters who are able to integrate these truths into their life journeys. As they learn to follow their dreams, we, too, are able to peer around the corner into our own possible futures. As they embrace their sufferings, wringing the light from them, so do we. In summation, Plunket expertly shows us how this curiosity called "life" is itself a spiritual gift.

Cyndi Dale, Renowned intuitive consultant and author of multiple bestselling books including The Subtle Body, Energetic Boundaries, The Complete Book of Chakra Healing and The Intuition Guidebook

A vividly rich novel you can just sink your whole being into, and characters you can get comfy with, who are willing to reveal their inner worlds, to remind you that, "you don't face off with the dark, you find the light in it."

Pollyanna Blanco, Educator, Dancer, Author of In Rhythm With Your Soul

At once a heart wrenching and heart soaring story, this wise tale of grit and grace, offers a gentle hand to draw you forward, toward that hallowed space of love beyond love.

Carrie E. Ruggieri, M.A., Clinical Psychologist

Susan Plunket's breadth of knowledge as a Jungian psychologist, her words as poetry, and her presence as a spiritual being, shine through on every page of this novel, about the power of suffering to transform our lives.

Christen Daniel, M.A., Intuitive healer and psychotherapist

Journey deep into the heart of the feminine psyche with Jungian psychologist, Susan Plunket. Feel the scorching truth of Jung's words, "Love is not a choice. You're captured." Travel the landscape of heartbreak and betrayal, accompanied by a wise, funny and loyal sisterhood, to arrive at last, on a luminescent shore.
Nancy Fleisher Johnson, PH.D. Clinical Psychologist

A captivating book that tenderly explores how the raw pain of human suffering can lead us to the knowledge of timeless truths.
Jo-Anne Brown, Holistic Wellness Practitioner and co-author of The Nurtured Woman Book Series

This is not a book for the self-help shelf, but self-help you will receive, if ever your heart has been broken. Susan Plunket's expertise comes through every page, in the most compelling form: story.
Tammy Letherer, Intuitive healer, author of "Hello Loved Ones," "My Health in My Hands," and "Real Time Wreck."

Mission
from Venus

Mission
from Venus

Susan Plunket

COSMIC EGG
BOOKS

Winchester, UK
Washington, USA

JOHN HUNT PUBLISHING

First published by Cosmic Egg Books, 2019
Cosmic Egg Books is an imprint of John Hunt Publishing Ltd., 3 East St., Alresford,
Hampshire SO24 9EE, UK
office@jhpbooks.com
www.johnhuntpublishing.com
www.cosmicegg-books.com

For distributor details and how to order please visit the 'Ordering' section on our website.

ISBN: 978 1 78904 170 5
978 1 78904 171 2 (ebook)
Library of Congress Control Number: 2018947809

A CIP catalogue record for this book is available from the British Library.

Design: Stuart Davies

UK: Printed and bound by CPI Group (UK) Ltd, Croydon, CR0 4YY
US: Printed and bound by Thomson-Shore, 7300 West Joy Road, Dexter, MI 48130

We operate a distinctive and ethical publishing philosophy in
all areas of our business, from our global network of authors to
production and worldwide distribution.

Contents

To all those who know we're not alone in the universe

Part One

The Call Across the Universe

Chapter 1

Venus

The sky was pink, streaked with gold, as Ederah and Bereh, two natives of Venus, walked along in the throng heading toward the archway into the temple. Green skinned and gold toned beings, some no more than four feet tall, walked beside black, brown, red and white ones, some standing more than fourteen feet high. Those with eyes like melting gold embraced those whose eyes resembled drenched violets. Many were bipedal, but scattered through the crowd were tri-pedal and quadrupedal beings as well. Some had tentacles and sensory spots, rather than eyes and ears, with which to perceive their worlds. But all of them had come to Venus for the same purpose. A call had come out across the universe from the Council of Nine, asking for volunteers for a mission to Earth. Tonight, Lady Master Venus and her twin flame, Sanat Kumara, the Lord Hierarch of Venus, would address them about the mission.

Although the throng approaching the temple in the soft golden light was magnificent in its physical diversity, they had one other thing in common. Each of them had passed beyond duality, beyond judgment of self or others. They all honored the Law of One, which states that all beings are One, and love for all must be constant, no matter what happens. For them, there were no "others." They had each traveled beyond longing, into the infinite sea of light. No desire remained but the desire to serve. Like Ederah and Bereh, they had all volunteered for the mission to save planet Earth from the dark lords, and to help humanity make the leap into the fourth dimension.

Though natives of Venus, and well-traveled galactically, neither Ederah nor Bereh, had ever been to nearby Earth. They'd recently been serving the Confederation out near the Pleiades, where they'd grown close with another twin flame pair, Maepleida and Heipleido, who would also be joining the mission to Earth. Ederah stretched her long neck to try and spot them in the crowd and caught the delicate fragrance of a flowering fruit tree carried on the breeze. Bereh watched as the breeze ruffled Ederah's long golden hair.

Like all those native to Venus, Ederah and Bereh were over twelve feet tall, slender and delicate, with gold-grey eyes, long necks, faces the shape of a perfect oval and quiet hearts. Known for their love of beauty, Venusians incorporated it into everything they touched. The temple they were about to enter was no exception. Made of light colored stone, which looked like pearl, the outer walls reflected different colors as the light from the sky changed throughout the day.

Ederah and Bereh, as is common with Venusians, were more given to conciliation than to war. And because of this temperament, evolution, up through the dimensions, had been rapid on Venus. The planet had now evolved up to the sixth dimension and could support life forms in every dimension vibrating below that. Venusians could perceive, as can much of the galaxy, Earth in its current third dimensional state, as well as in possible higher dimensions. But Earth beings, now only in the third dimension, know only a third dimensional Venus with an atmosphere of sulfuric acid, inhospitable to life as humans know it. Earthlings have no idea of the many different dimensions in which Venus exists in different forms. The third dimension is a challenging one, because it is the only dimension which cannot perceive the higher dimensions. Most of the volunteers approaching the temple in the evening light were fifth dimensional. Many of the masters coming to prepare them for the mission were sixth dimensional and beyond. Venus in the sixth dimension is a serene and beautiful planet.

Ederah stood and gazed up at the temple dome, a dazzling sphere soaring to the heavens, which at the moment reflected various shades of pink as it shimmered above them in the evening light. When she lowered her gaze again, Maepleida and Heipleido were standing beside her and Bereh. Natives of the Pleiades, Maepleida and Heipleido were even taller than their Venusian friends. They stood nearly fourteen feet high, with emerald eyes, black skin and great intelligence. Although the Pleiades is known for the wise counsel of its people, the Pleiades is also a place of pleasure and joy. Not only in early education, but even at their galactic university, all teaching is done using only games, in order to enhance the joy of learning. So, although he looked imposing, Heipleido was a playful being, much given to joking and fun. The moment he saw Ederah and Bereh, Heipleido drew his lips back in a big smile, momentarily flashing the almond whiteness of his teeth, before tilting his black marble brow and bowing deeply to acknowledge the divinity residing within them. Maepleida stood beside him, decked in her eternally youthful beauty, her ears small and flattened to her head, her lips soft and full, her long dark hair reaching to her waist. She lowered her head slightly, and Ederah and Bereh, returned the compliment.

The four friends walked together beneath the arched entrance into the vaulted temple. Inside, it was like a small town, ringing with anticipation as they all awaited the details of the mission to planet Earth. Maepleida glanced down and saw that a different mandala, designed as a circle within a square, was worked into the floor under each of the temple's six vaulted ceilings. Several of the mandalas held images of sacred geometry. In one, the flower of life was depicted, in another, the tree of life. Several others displayed the symbols of creation. The interior walls were decorated with scenes from the history of Venus, including many paintings of the Ra group, highly evolved beings, who had created the pyramids on Earth. Various panels also depicted life on current day Venus among the peace loving Hathors, one of the most advanced groups of light beings in the same solar system as Earth. Other panels showed Venus as it had been in previous dimensions.

As the four friends made their way deeper into the temple, they saw that there were seats of various shapes made of many types of crystals: amethyst, rose quartz, emerald, topaz, aquamarine, lapis lazuli, tourmaline, sapphire and diamond. Some beings were already using their intention to shape the crystal seats to suit their height and shape. Everyone understood that each type of crystal could imbue the one seated on it, with its particular gifts.

Ederah chose a rose quartz seat which she knew would enhance her feelings of love. She refashioned it into the shape of a lotus, with an oval center on which to sit, in the hope that love, as the strongest force in all universes, would help her to defeat the dark lords and to save many humans on Earth. Bereh, desiring to polarize as much positive energy as possible for the mission, chose an amethyst, which he reshaped into a seat with a back and arms, which encircled his sides, surrounding him with amethyst which has the ability to transmute negative energy. Maepleida was drawn to a large sapphire, shaped like a small throne. She chose the sapphire with the intention that it might align her will to the will of the Divine. Heipleido debated between a healing emerald chair and an amethyst. He, like Bereh, chose the amethyst. The four friends requested their crystals, which are first dimensional beings known for service, to group together, and when the crystals had obliged, sat down on them to catch up and to watch the waves of beings from around the universe pour through the temple archway.

When the temple was nearly full, a bright light appeared and materialized into two, tall, bipedal beings, each with a head, two arms, two legs, eyes and ears. Lady Venus and Lord Kumara stood before them. All present understood that those who view the universe as one being are able to proceed from one location to another and to assume any form they choose using thought

6

alone. Still, it was dazzling to witness Venus and Kumara materialize out of light and a hush fell over the group at the sight of them. The two stood in silence for a moment, gazing out at all those seated before them. Light emanated from them. Few of them had ever before seen Venus, Goddess of Love. Her perfectly symmetrical form shimmered, giving off a pale blue light. Such was her gentleness that simply standing there, it felt as though she was reaching out to wrap each of them in the wings of love. She had long ago chosen as her mission the job of amplifying the radiance of love in this solar system. It was challenging, not only because several of the planets had beings more given to war than love, but also, because those beings who served the dark side were ever seeking opportunities to enslave those serving the light. Nevertheless, she worked to teach all beings how to become masterful in the wise use of love. Having united with her twin flame, Lord Kumara, twenty million years before, together they served the path of light.

Kumara stood silently beside her as all the volunteers gazed at the radiant feminine beauty of Venus. He understood that the time for the re-ascendency of the power of the feminine on Earth had come, as it had many eons ago on Venus. He knew also that it would be Venus, along with the other feminine deities, who would open the portals to Earth, and direct the influx of cosmic rays, which would transform consciousness on the blue planet. So, he stood in silent respect, supporting her, his long purple robe just brushing the floor. Both Venus and Kumara wore pendants made of amethyst and gold in the shape of a star tetrahedron. The pendants were created of two, three dimensional tetrahedrons, one inverted into the other, the one facing upward representing the male, and the one facing down the female. All present understood the significance of this, as there is a star tetrahedron field, made of both masculine and feminine energy, around every being in all universes.

Finally, Venus spoke. "Welcome dear ones. Let me tell you

how very welcome you are." Her smile radiated love. "You have come from all over the universe in answer to our call to help the humans on planet Earth. There are sixty-seven million planets in the Milky Way Galaxy alone. You could have offered your services to any of them. Yet you have chosen this mission. For that choice, we thank you." Here she paused, as if determining a direction, then gathering momentum she continued. "Kumara and I have just returned from the rings of Saturn, where we have been meeting with the Council of Nine responsible for governing this solar system. We have now finalized plans for your mission to planet Earth. As you know, the council convenes in Saturn's rings and governs from there. It reports to our confederation of five hundred planets in this corner of the Milky Way. Know that the Council, and the whole confederation, support your mission to Earth."

Hearing these words, a cheer went up from the many beings assembled before her. Venus and Kumara exchanged a look as they enjoyed the vibration of the cheer. Venus gathered her thoughts before continuing.

"All of you who are seated here tonight are beings of the fifth dimension, where harmony, compassion, telepathic communication and the ability to create reality directly from your intention are the natural order. You understand that the true reality is Oneness. By working to serve your fellow beings you have traveled the path from the first dimension to the second, to the third, and the fourth, and the fifth, always gathering light and love into your being as you proceeded. In each successive dimension you mastered new skills, until you could truly be called creators. You understand that the mechanism of creation works by wielding the energies of light and love. Were any of you to walk on Earth in your present state, and to display your abilities, you would be thought a god. However, for this mission, you will go to Earth with none of your powers beyond those which any human of the third dimension possesses. For this mission, you will be born on Earth, as a human infant, to human parents. Your human parents will not know that you come from a higher dimension. And, once born, you yourself will not remember that your true home is in a higher dimension. No doubt this news comes as a shock. And you may question how you can be of help if you are only third dimensional yourself once you incarnate. Search your heart. Ask yourself if you are willing to make this sacrifice in order to help planet Earth and her people."

Bereh reached for Ederah's hand and she turned to gaze into his grey-gold eyes. They had not known that they would be asked to give up all they had achieved and be born as third dimensional beings as a condition of this mission. But as they looked into one another's hearts, each understood that the other was willing to make this sacrifice. Heipleido found himself even more excited about the mission now that he knew of this added challenge, but Maepleida couldn't easily swallow the idea, and choked as if she'd gulped too much water at once. Heipleido turned and reached for her hand as an involuntary shudder rippled through her.

When Venus felt she'd afforded them the necessary moment to absorb this news, she continued.

"Should you find the condition of regressing to a third dimensional consciousness for this mission unacceptable, you are free to leave at any time. There are plenty of other opportunities throughout the galaxy where you can serve the Light."

Both Venus and Kumara looked up to see how many would choose to depart. No one moved. Both bowed to the group in acknowledgement of their courage. Then Venus continued.

"Though humans are capable of great compassion, there is still much disharmony among the peoples of Earth. It is our wish that the disharmony not lead to the destruction of their beautiful planet. Our hope for averting this destruction lies in you."

She raised her hands as if to embrace them all, and her ring, made of many gems, flashed in the light.

"At this time, most humans are third dimensional beings, with some moving toward the fourth dimension, so they are limited in their knowledge of how the Divine works. Despite this, remember that the Divine resides in every cell, even in every atom and electron of every human being. Yes, the Divine pervades the heavy, chemical, physical shell that humans wear, every inch of it, from head to toe, just as it pervades your own light bodies." Venus spoke these words with infinite softness, for she loved all beings of every dimension, and also because she had long felt a special love for her human neighbors on Earth. As she spoke, a look of great compassion came over her face and she seemed to lose herself as she plunged into that well of memory she held of Earth beings. Seeing her lost in love, Kumara stepped forward to address them.

"Many of you may already know one another, either from your home planets or from missions on which you have served together. Among you are representatives from all seven solar systems in our confederation. And our numbers also include those from the star systems of Lyra, Sirius, Pleiades, Arcturus, Cygnus and Andromeda. As you are all fifth dimensional beings, you are capable of appearing simply as light, and of creating any form you choose for yourself. You can appear as the natives of your home star or planet, or you can change your form in any way you desire. We have a request, which we believe will be helpful in preparing you for this mission. If you are not already in bipedal form, we ask you to consider adjusting your form for the training here on Venus to a bipedal one, with eyes, nose, mouth and ears, placed in a head of some round or oval shape, and to reduce the number of your other appendages to two, with five digits per appendage. We ask this so that you may accustom yourself to the bipedal form, with two arms, as that will be the type of body you will have on Earth. If your native body already meets these criteria, you need make no further adjustment. We also ask, as part of your preparation, that you take on some weight, and become half-light and half-flesh, so you may accustom yourself to eating food rather than light. This is not a command, merely a suggestion to help prepare you for the third dimensional body that you will wear on Earth. In addition, though it is many thousands of years since any of you has slept, we ask that you now resume a sleep wake cycle. These alterations will make your incarnation on Earth easier."

As Kumara spoke, all of the beings seated before him who were not already in bipedal form began to alter their appearance. Tentacles disappeared to be replaced with eyes and ears, tri-pedal and quadrupedal beings became bipeds, scales and fur became skin, heads were fashioned over shoulders, and the number of arms on each being became only two. And everyone took on some flesh. They experienced all this as a powering down of their energy. These transformations were accomplished as if in an instant, for these highly evolved beings needed only to think something for it to become reality. The crystal beings on which they sat also redesigned themselves to accommodate the new forms of their occupants.

Kumara thanked them for responding to his request before introducing a new topic. "I will also tell you that among you are many pairs of twin flames. This will be a great aid to you in your mission to Earth."

Bereh turned to look at Ederah, who smiled back into his grey-gold eyes. At his glance, she felt the fullness of his love for her, that all compassionate love which demands no return. He noticed everything. He was not one of those beings who never look up into the sky, or who for weeks never look into the face of their beloved. In all their eons together, he had never looked at Ederah without seeing into her heart.

Kumara continued. "I will ask my own twin flame, the Lady Venus, to speak to you now of this sacred union." He turned to her and bowed deeply. Venus, having recovered from her plunge into love, returned the courtesy and again spoke to the group. "As you know, twin flames come from one spark, one Soul, when they first fly out from Source. They agree to split into their masculine and feminine aspects and to incarnate as one soul in two bodies."

As she said this, her hand grasped the star tetrahedron resting over her heart on its long golden chain. "Should the twin flame pairs among you succeed in reuniting on Earth, the light energy created by your reunion in the third dimension will create a pathway home for humanity. It will not be easy, as you may not even be born on the same continent as your twin flame. And twin flames, in particular, will be hunted by the dark side to prevent their reunion."

Heipleido squeezed Maepleida's hand and she turned her brimming emerald eyes to him and held him fast in her gaze. She still dazzled him, even after all the thousands of years they had spent together since their reunion as twin flames. Each time they had served the confederation, their twin flame union had benefited their mission, not only in their home in the Pleiades, but on the Violet planet, inside Arcturus and in the Rings of Saturn.

"This will be the seventh attempt to liberate the Earth beings and bring humans into the light," Venus explained. "The dark forces still remain among the humans in disguise. Fourth and fifth dimensional negative entities from Orion continue to slip through the quarantine which the council has placed around Earth, and attempt to lure humans onto the negative path of service only to self. Those from Orion are in league with corrupt planetary leaders in many countries of Earth, and they have infiltrated not only government, but the world of finance as well. Their method of controlling humanity is to blend black magic with technology to consolidate power and money in the hands of the few who are in league with them. They tempt and distract humans with drugs, sex, addictions, food, power and money. They also employ coercion through fear. Creating fear is a favorite choice for those on the negative path. You, too, will have to resist these temptations, addictions and obsessions once you incarnate as human for this mission. Search your hearts dear ones. Are you ready for this challenge?"

"So, these are the devils we must confront on Earth," Maepleida whispered to Heipleido.

"The negative entities from Orion are no match for the strength of our love," he telegraphed back. Heipleido had already proven himself fearless in battle with the dark forces many times. He was confident that this time, too, the light forces would be victorious.

After pausing so they might absorb this information, Venus continued. "Because of the strict protocol for incarnating on earth, this will be a dangerous mission. Though you sit here tonight as fifth dimensional beings with many powers, in the full knowledge that ultimate reality is Oneness, that only love is real, and only love remains, once you are born on Earth you will be subject, like any other human, to the veil of forgetting. You will no longer consciously remember anything of your mission, your origins, your past glories or your soul gifts. The veil will suppress all memory of who you are, and what your mission is. You will not know that you are wanderers from a higher dimension. This must be so, as these are the laws governing incarnation on planet Earth."

It was one thing to ask them to incarnate without any higher powers, but it would be an added burden for them to have no memory at all of ever having been higher dimensional beings, and to perhaps believe that this life on Earth was their only lifetime. Venus again paused and waited while these realizations traveled the corridors of the hearts and minds of the beings seated before her. Then, she continued. "Even the greatest avatars incarnating on Earth: Jesus, Buddha, Mohammed, Tesla, Socrates, Rumi, Thomas Jefferson, Benjamin Franklin and many others, were all subject to the law of forgetting. And although you must have your memory wiped at the moment of your human birth, there will be aids to help you remember your true identity as light beings. Your job on Earth will be to awaken as a human, with third dimensional consciousness, and to pierce the veil of forgetting and remember who you are and why you've incarnated on Earth. If you succeed in awakening, your higher dimensional powers will return to you and the battle will begin. Make no mistake. The risks are great. Should you fail to awaken, you will be trapped in the third dimension, reincarnating again and again, perhaps for thousands of years, believing that you are only a human."

Here was a new concern. None of them wanted to be trapped in the third dimension, let alone for eons.

"Courage," Ederah telepathically sent to Bereh. "We must have courage for our neighbors on Earth."

Bereh's response was a confident smile directed right into Ederah's heart. She felt it like the warmth of a thousand suns warming her, drying up her fear like so many puddles.

"Once they become aware of your presence on Earth," Venus told them, "those of the dark side will hunt you to the death to prevent you from aiding the humans. They will especially be on the lookout for twin flame pairs. But the dark side being less familiar with love, other than self-love, may have difficulty recognizing your connection. That is the good news."

"This mission gets better and better," Heipleido said, absolutely reveling in the challenges.

Maepleida tried to absorb the energy of her blue sapphire seat in order to align herself with the will of the Divine regarding this mission. She didn't share Heipleido's enthusiasm for the increased danger. Was this even her path? It had been Heipleido's idea to volunteer. But not wanting him to go on this mission without her, she'd agreed to come along. Attempting to swallow her doubt, she turned her attention back to Venus.

"Thousands of advanced souls, known as wanderers, have gone before you on previous missions to Earth. Their mission, like yours, was to lighten the vibration on Earth, save her from destruction and help her to polarize toward harmony. Inroads have been made, but many brave volunteers from higher dimensions who have preceded you have failed to awaken, and remain trapped in the third dimension. If you succeed in penetrating the veil of forgetting and in raising the vibration on Earth, you will also free these trapped wanderers to return to that higher dimension which is their home. Though you risk being stuck in the third dimension yourselves, there are ways to penetrate the veil so that you can wake up and remember your origin, and your mission. During the coming weeks of training here on Venus, you will be told how to do this and how help will be sent when called for. But, know this, even by simply living among the humans, as a human, you will lighten the whole planetary vibration. But I will not rhapsodize. This is a dangerous mission. However, if you succeed in raising consciousness in a critical mass of the population, the destruction of the planet and the captivity of the earth beings by the dark side will be averted. And should you succeed, the dark lords from Orion, who have chosen the negative path, will withdraw, the positive vibration being inhospitable to them."

At these words, again a cheer went up from the thousands gathered before Venus and Kumara. All eyes, for all before them now had eyes, were turned to the pair and looked at them with hopeful hearts. Heipleido felt his heart soar up out of his body at the idea of rescuing the blue planet and her people.

Venus scanned their faces, then glanced up at the vaulted ceilings above her, wrinkling her forehead most charmingly, as if she was considering her next thought, before continuing. "As I have said, you will not be without help once you incarnate. We here on Venus, and all those in the command center, in Saturn's rings, will assist your awakening, as will your own higher selves.

We'll be in contact with you, employing various methods which won't violate the strict laws surrounding incarnation on Earth. Among our methods for contacting you once you incarnate will be the sending of dreams and thought forms. Dreams can penetrate the veil of forgetting. Our approach will be flexible. During your infancy, babyhood and childhood, you will be protected by beings which humans call imaginary friends. Your imaginary friends will guide and advise you for the early years of your life. Your imaginary friends are actually your sixth dimensional selves, that aspect of each of you which looks out for all your lower dimensional selves. In most cases, human children lose the ability to see and hear their imaginary friends by age five. Before that time human children have magical ability. By magical ability, I mean that they have the ability to directly access their unconscious and the collective unconscious. When in contact with the collective unconscious, one can see the future as easily as one sees the past. As human children age, and undergo the process of being socialized and educated, they lose this ability to directly access the unconscious. Once this is lost, they need to use dreams to recover the wisdom in the unconscious. As you will be a human child, you will also lose direct access to the unconscious after about age five or six. Therefore, after that time, it will become more important for you to call on us, and your Higher Self, for help. If called, we will be free to assist you. But you must call out and ask, or we may not interfere. These are the laws surrounding earth."

Again, she paused to observe them. Then, as if dashing along the corridors of her mind to see if she had forgotten anything, Venus continued. "Most humans lean toward service to others. Fewer humans, are in service only to self. Those who choose this negative path of service only to self can often be found among the wealthy elite who are concerned only with what benefits them. They are generally in league with beings from the Orion group who are on the negative path and are always on the lookout for human conquests who they can enslave and bring to the path of service only to self. It will be the aim of those from Orion to thwart your awakening and your service to others. The quarantine around Earth can occasionally be breached, and those from Orion watch for opportunities to slip through in order to draw humans to the mission of the dark side, which is the creation of an elite and a non-elite. They employ racial and income differences to create a non-elite. Their purpose is ever the conquest and enslavement of the non-elite. Should the Orion group become aware of your presence, they will attempt to end your mission, even by causing the physical death of your human vehicle. But before they destroy your body, they will first attempt to enslave you and turn you to the negative path. Should they succeed, you will be trapped on the negative path for an untold time before you are able to return to the light and the path of service to others. Should this happen, remember that all beings eventually return to the path of love and light." Here Venus paused so long that some of those listening thought she had concluded. But she again found her voice and went on. "The great adventure on which you are about to embark is girded underneath by the majesty of the One Infinite Creator. So, my beloveds, my courageous ones who have come from all corners of the universe to train on Venus for this mission, I commend you for your bravery and your love of all beings as One."

Heipleido, basking in these words, reached for Maepleida's hand and wrapped his long slender fingers around its smooth elegance. How many times over the centuries had he taken this perfect appendage with its five beloved digits and caressed it, he wondered. Now, in the face of this new, challenging mission, she was even more dear to him than ever.

"These next few weeks many masters and twin flame pairs will come to prepare you for your mission," Venus told them. "You will be asked to plant seeds deep in the pineal gland of your light body, seeds, which we hope will sprout in your new human bodies once you are born on Earth in your human families. These seeds will help you remember who you are, and what you have incarnated to achieve. The time is auspicious for this mission. Earth is ending a cycle of 75,000 years. With or without the humans, Earth is moving, even as we speak, into the fourth dimension. It is the time when humans must make the jump from third to fourth dimensional consciousness, or end their cycle of incarnations on Earth. Those who do not move into fourth dimensional consciousness will have to continue their incarnations on a different planet, which is still third dimensional, in this or another galaxy, as Earth's new vibration will no longer be hospitable to them. The planet has begun the shift. If the dark lords don't destroy her, Earth will be fully fourth dimensional in a few hundred years, as they measure time. Your presence on her surface will greatly improve her chances for survival."

Bereh was still intent on what Venus was conveying, but Ederah was growing restless and shifted in her rose quartz seat in order to glance around the temple to see how the others were taking this challenge. She spotted Toomeh, sitting up straight as an arrow. Toomeh, born on Arcturus, was a good friend of Maepleida and Heipleido's. His lustrous orange-gold eyes were fixed, like two lanterns, on Venus. As a native of Arcturus, Toomeh was muscular and stood about ten feet tall. Strength, generosity and courage ran freely in him. Ederah's heart delighted when she spotted him, his strength giving her new confidence in this mission, and she felt her restlessness subside.

Venus and Kumara looked out at the beings assembled before them. Love flowed out from them and spread over the group like a warm ocean rolling up to caress the shore.

"Before we part this evening, I would remind you that each of you has a unique ability, some special talent or service to offer. Rejoice in that, and may you awaken on Earth and use your gifts to serve her and the beings who dwell on her surface.

"Tomorrow we'll begin our training. For tonight, we invite

you all to feast in the great hall where food, like that consumed on Earth, has been provided so you might get accustomed to eating again, rather than using light alone for your energy. Get acquainted with those you haven't yet met. Greet old friends from distant galaxies. We shower each of you in the light. All is well." With her last words, Venus raised her lovely arms and hands, turned her palms toward them and emitted a wave of ruby light, wrapping them in the wings of love, and bringing a feeling of joy and peace into every heart. Then Venus and Kumara once again became one oval of light and vanished.

Still awash in the beauty of the ruby light, Bereh and Ederah stood up to leave. As they made their way out of the temple, they spotted Attivio and Soonam not far off. Born and raised on the Violet Planet, they were elegant, lively, and full of fun, especially Soonam. Her eyes, deep as rain washed violets, flashed when she saw Bereh and Ederah and she rushed forward to embrace them.

"Oh wonderful, you're going on this mission, how completely perfect," Soonam gushed. "And I want to know everything you've been doing since I last saw you on the Violet planet."

Ederah and Bereh smiled and embraced Soonam and Attivio. The four old friends headed for the doorway, where Maepleida and Heipleido were standing with Toomeh. As the group made its way outside toward the great hall, Soonam glanced back over her shoulder at the temple dome. "I love all things Venusian."

Strolling beside her, Maepleida told Soonam, "Enjoy it now, because, although Earth herself is a jewel, some of the characters living on her surface are far from Venusian in their consciousness."

"So, you've been there?" Attivio asked, walking up beside Maepleida.

"Not incarnated, but yes, Heipleido and I slipped through the quarantine in our light bodies to look around before signing on for this mission."

"I'm impressed," Attivio said.

They all paused momentarily and formed a little group to listen.

"What about you, Toomeh? Have you been to Earth?" Bereh asked.

"No, but I'd like to hear what Maepleida and Heipleido observed."

"Let's fill our goblets and sit under that big tree, and we'll tell you what we learned." Heipleido said.

They settled around the tree in the peace of the last few rays of pink-gold light reflecting off the temple dome. Soonam handed around a platter laden with various fruits which they would have on Earth: star fruit, blackberries, cherries and pomegranates. Attivio tried a blackberry and declared it delicious. Heipleido bit into a cherry and spit out the pit onto his palm. "Sweet," he said.

Ederah split open a pomegranate with her mind and gingerly tasted the seeds before handing some to Bereh.

Relieved that Earth food was going to be acceptable, Heipleido began the discussion.

"I'm afraid our visit to Earth has given Maepleida second thoughts about this mission."

"Why ever?" Soonam asked.

"For starters, the majority of the Earth beings have no awareness of the many lifetimes they've had on Earth. And most have no belief that life exists anywhere else in the universe. They think they're it," Maepleida said.

"Terribly self-centered of them," Soonam teased.

"But there are some humans who do seem to know that this is a special time on Earth, the time of a shift into the fourth dimension, a quickening of the vibration on the planet," Heipleido said, "and most of them are a good sort and try to help one another."

"Not everybody is a good sort," Maepleida said, "some are only out for their own interests and they try to amass power and money and subjugate everyone else. These power-hungry types lie and put other beings, whom they consider racially inferior, or what they call illegal aliens, in prison."

"You mean they don't understand that we're all one being, that no one is inferior or illegal, since all are one?" Soonam asked.

"Of course not," Maepleida said, "have you forgotten what it's like to be third dimensional, Soonam?"

"Sounds like they need our help," Bereh said. Ederah saw that Soonam was grateful for Bereh's support and she flashed him a smile. She adored that he was so relentlessly positive.

"Quite right, Bereh, it's good we're on our way," Attivio added. Attivio was happiest when he was serving others. Like most beings born and raised on the Violet planet, he was divinely elegant and unflappable, but took little interest in his own beauty and focused his energy on being of service to anyone in need. Even though he knew there shouldn't be, there was one being he cherished above all others, and this was perhaps his only Achilles' heel. He had been trying, unsuccessfully, to get his mind around the reality that he would be parted from Soonam for this mission. He felt Soonam's violet eyes on him and pulled his mind back to the present conversation.

"As I said, most of the beings on Earth are a good sort." Heipleido smiled.

"Although there appear to be countries with boundaries, there is a wealthy elite which operates across all boundaries to consolidate money and power in their own hands, and then, there are those from Orion, who are truly dark," Maepleida added, pointing out the glistening poison on the point of the dagger.

"So, do the rest of the beings live in poverty and serve this elite?" Toomeh asked.

"There is widespread poverty, starvation and disease in many parts of the Earth," Maepleida said.

"Can't they prepare food by thought?" Soonam asked.

"Definitely not. You really have forgotten what the third

dimension is like, Soonam," Maepleida said.

"And what do Earth beings look like?" Soonam asked.

"Humans are a denser, shorter version of us, standing only five or six feet tall when fully grown. They wear a heavy, fleshy, electrochemical body which operates somewhat like a battery and they seem to be unaware of their light bodies, or of how to use light to heal themselves," Maepleida said.

"You don't sound as if you like them much," Ederah said.

"I don't know yet. I'd say I feel for their backwardness," Maepleida said.

"Is that fair? We were once third dimensional beings ourselves on one planet or another," Soonam said.

"Quite right, Soonam. I should be more compassionate," Maepleida said.

"If they can't heal themselves with light spirals, what happens when they get out of balance and fall ill? Toomeh asked.

"They have a kind of rudimentary approach to healing which involves cutting, burning and poisoning themselves with harsh chemicals which they call medicines," Maepleida said.

"It sounds ghastly," Soonam said. "Surely we can help with this simply by showing them how to use light to heal themselves."

"No, we can't. We'll be in this primitive world once we incarnate there without memory of our abilities." As she spoke, Maepleida glanced at Heipleido, who easily withstood her gaze. Her attitude concerned him, but he felt confident she would come around, for he knew the depth of her compassion for all beings, even though she tried to hide it.

"We must remember that humans, too, are a unique portion of the One Creator," Heipleido chided her.

"But Maepleida's right, soon we'll be like them," Toomeh said, "with no knowledge that we have any power, or are connected to anything greater than ourselves."

"But only until we wake up and remember who we really are," Attivio said. He looked at Soonam to reassure her. Since they'd volunteered for this mission, her innocence and simplicity, the softness in her violet eyes, never holding even a hint of judgment, had become even more dear to him. He sat beside her, dying of tenderness.

"What are our chances of waking up in the third dimension?" Toomeh asked.

"That's the question," Heipleido said.

"Many wanderers from higher dimensions have volunteered before us, and are still stuck, reincarnating again and again on Earth," Maepleida said.

"But the volunteers for the earlier missions didn't receive the training we're about to get," Ederah reminded them.

"Right, on that note, we're off to our cottage." Bereh stood up and reached for Ederah's hands to pull her to her feet. Ederah grasped his hands and looked up into his eyes. She stood and wished them all good night. By now the sky was a deep violet and the hillside, where they were headed, was black under the starlight.

Bereh and Ederah strolled hand in hand toward the grassy hillside dotted with cottages, mostly still dark, but here and there firelight lit up a window and splashed a brightness onto to the ground below it. Their cottage was nestled in among some fragrant flowering bushes. The night had grown cooler and Ederah shivered. Bereh summoned a glowing fire which appeared in the fireplace the moment they opened the door. The fireplace was flanked by two armchairs in the same type of richly woven fabric that covered the bed. Like all fifth dimensional beings, both Ederah and Bereh had the ability to change their surroundings at will. Earlier in the day, Ederah had used her intention to change the fabric on the armchairs from green to blue brocade, and to re-cover the bed in tapestries of blue and gold. They stood together a moment and enjoyed the effect they'd created. Then Bereh took her in his arms and the rose-pink of Ederah's body, now only half made of light, turned violet as she merged with Bereh's peacock-blue light.

Attivio and Soonam followed along behind Bereh and Ederah. As they strolled arm in arm under the Venusian sky, shimmering with stars, Soonam said, "I never want to forget to look at the stars. Do you suppose they will look the same from Earth? I mean different constellations will be visible, but will the stars look like beautiful jewels, as they do here, from Venus."

Attivio smiled and kissed the tip of her nose in answer. Had he ever loved, until her? Love, for him, had never held such fullness until he met the face of God in her countenance. If he could have chosen from every creature that ever breathed the face he would most love, the voice, the eyes, the touch, heart, the very Soul, it would all be Soonam. Her heart was as open as the sky. How would she survive on Earth? Reading his thoughts, she reminded him of the battle for the Violet planet. He had to concede, she had been a formidable warrior in that contest with the dark side. But they would be parted for this mission. Even if they did manage to meet, would they recognize one another in the third dimension? As he watched her gazing at the night sky he promised himself: *No matter what the odds, should she fail to awaken on Earth, I'll find her and lift her up.*

Maepleida, Heipleido and Toomeh were the last to make their way toward the cottages. They talked as they strolled along.

"Should we really be volunteering for this?" Maepleida said. "I mean it's crazy odds, and we don't even know what kind of families we'll be born into as helpless human babies."

"But that's the challenge, darling," Heipleido said.

"I know how you love a challenge. But why will we succeed when the previous six attempts to help Earth have failed?" Maepleida asked.

"Maybe that's what we'll find out during our training here on Venus," Toomeh said, coming to Heipleido's rescue, speaking in the characteristic voice of a good friend, the tone he customarily used when attempting to restore Maepleida's faith in the face of doubt. Heipleido gave him a grateful smile. "We'll say goodnight then."

Before making his way further up the hill to his own cottage, Toomeh stood alone under the stars, breathing in the delicate sweetness of the flowering bushes growing on the hillside. He thought about Heipleido and Maepleida, both from the Pleiades, and Ederah and Bereh, native to Venus, and Attivio and Soonam, of the Violet Planet, and wondered if he, too, had a twin flame, maybe someone from his home star of Arcturus. Not everyone had a twin flame. But he hoped for one, and his heart leapt at the thought.

Chapter 2

Training Begins

The morning sky over Venus was pink, streaked with gold. Soonam opened the cottage door, gazed out over the hillside, and breathed in the beauty. Turning when she heard Attivio stirring, she smiled at him. This new ritual of sleeping at night that they were all engaging in now, in preparation for life on Earth, created the unexpected joy of reunion each morning. Attivio opened his arms to her and she floated into them.

It had been so simple, from the first moment he'd seen her, at a celebration on the Violet planet. He'd caught her eye across the table, and as the evening progressed, he'd taken less and less care to hide his feelings. She'd assented to his attention with her violet eyes, which glistened and beckoned him as she bowed her golden head in playful recognition of his interest. Since that long-ago evening, thousands of years ago, they'd been inseparable, traveling the star systems together, doing the work of the confederation on many different planets. This mission to Earth would be their first time apart. Attivio didn't relish the prospect of their separation. Soonam was his one.

When we separate for this mission, half myself will be missing, he thought. Soonam read his mind and lay her head on his heart, breathing him in. He buried his face in her buttery hair, and smelled her beauty. He had never regretted for a moment following the light in the bottom of her eyes. It hadn't even been a choice. He'd been captured.

"Ready to go?" He asked her. She lifted her head and looked up into his eyes. Gazing down at her, he read the many emotions in her eyes.

Maepleida, Heipleido and Toomeh entered the dome together

for the morning training. Seeing that Lady Venus and Lord Kumara were already there preparing to address them, they summoned their crystal seats and requested that they move to be near Ederah and Bereh. Just when the last seat was in place, Venus greeted them and explained that Lord Kumara would be addressing them that morning. He stood beside her in his long purple robes, holding a wand with a large amethyst ball on the top. Lady Venus turned and bowed to him before leaving. Kumara cleared his throat, and a hush fell.

"Good morning, dear ones," he began in his powerful but kind voice. "Today we begin the training for your mission to Earth. It is an auspicious moment, because the time for the ascension of planet Earth and her surface dwellers is at hand. As you heard last evening, Earth has begun to transition into the fourth dimension. Only those humans who qualify will be able to go on living on Earth in their future incarnations. The confederation would like as many beings as possible to move up into the fourth dimension. But in order to transition to the fourth dimension, each human must be able to embody a higher intensity of light. And many have not yet learned how to embody enough light to survive in the fourth dimension."

Ederah looked around for Soonam and Attivio and spotted them just then coming in through the temple archway. Soonam caught Ederah's gaze and she and Attivio made their way to the rest of their friends and summoned their crystal seats. Lord Kumara went on speaking without seeming to notice the latecomers.

"Our first task is to prevent the destruction of Earth by those who have chosen the negative path of power, greed and self-interest. From outside the Earth, we cannot interfere directly with their activities, because that would be a violation of their free will. The free will of all beings, whether they choose the path of light or the dark path, must be respected, for free will is the law governing life on Earth. It must be born in mind that all beings serve the Creator in their own way, and ultimately, all return to the positive path for the final journey back to Source. As you know, beyond the sixth dimension there is no way forward except on the path of light. Sixth dimensional beings on the negative path see this and make the jump, at that point, to sixth dimensional positive. However, up until that point, all beings have free will, and may choose either the positive or the negative path in accordance with the laws governing life on the blue planet."

"I wonder if it'll be difficult, once we're third dimensional, to respect the free will of those on the negative path who'll be trying to enslave us," Ederah whispered to Bereh.

To reassure her, he picked up her hand and kissed the tip of each of its digits, ending with her pinky, which was spread out from the others like a small star half belonging to another galaxy.

"Although it has been several million years since any of you were third dimensional, you may remember that the third dimension is a dimension of duality, where each soul is free to choose her path. The quintessential experiences in the third dimension are about choice and love. Each human chooses to learn about love, either by loving only himself or by loving all as one. Up until the sixth dimension, both are valid choices. Each being is free to embark on either the positive path of service to others, or the negative path of service only to self. It cannot be reiterated enough that both paths serve the Divine, each in its own way. All will eventually come into the Oneness of the Light."

At the words, "all will eventually come into the Oneness," Soonam felt her heart expand out beyond her light body. Her rose quartz seat reacted to her heightened state by vibrating gently and sending a warm glow all through her. Soonam silently thanked this crystal being for its love and its emotional, as well as physical, support. Though each of them was developing a relationship with their crystal seat, Soonam, in particular, appreciated her first dimensional being of the crystal realm, and it, therefore, responded to her most sensitively. That friends and allies are to be found in every dimension of existence was something Soonam thoroughly appreciated. But she had long felt a special love for first dimensional beings, especially rocks and crystals. Attivio similarly cultivated a relationship with beings in other dimensions. His favorites were the second dimensional creatures, known as trees.

"In general, humans are unaware of the spark of the Divine within them," Kumara explained. "Your job will be to raise the level of vibration on the planet, so that humans will begin to wake up, and remember their divine origins. The difficulty will be that first you must wake up in the third density yourself, and remember your own divine origin. Search your hearts dear ones. We ask you again: Are you ready for this challenge?"

Attivio reached for Soonam's hand and again silently vowed to her: *I will find you on Earth and lift you up, if, by chance, you fail to awaken.* Soonam was stalwart in her commitment to serve and sent her heart's answer to Kumara on a ray of pink light. She and Attivio had responded at once when the call came out across the universe that earth was in need of love. At least, that's the way they heard the call. They had made plans immediately to depart the Violet planet and head to Venus to learn more about the mission. And now that the details were becoming clear, their commitment remained unwavering.

Perceiving general acceptance of the challenge, Lord Kumara continued. "As you know, there are many pairs of twin flames in our group. Your reunion in human bodies will be of much benefit to Earth. Because as twin flames, you are a perfect energetic match for one another. If you manage to find one another on Earth, your reunion will release a great eruption of light which will raise the vibration of the planet, and help to hold it in a field of love. Remember, time and space are of no matter to twin flames. They exist beyond the worldly platform, where nothing remains but an infinite sea of love. So even should you fail to find one another on Earth, and remain trapped in the third dimension, your connection in the higher realms will remain, always."

"Small consolation," Maepleida whispered to Heipleido, with a hint of distress in her voice.

"Do you not trust me to find you should you fail to awaken?" he chided her.

"Some of you have previously encountered, in battles on other planets, those beings from Orion who travel the dark path. On Earth, the dark side uses many tricks to enslave and control the humans. For example, they have perverted all organized religion by taking what was once the truth in it and distorting it just enough to use it for the purpose of controlling the populous and creating wars. They also create wars for their own profit by hiding free and clean energy sources in order to keep the populace fighting over control of oil rich lands. They fool the naïve, and use the poor as cannon fodder to profit themselves."

As he listened, Toomeh closed his eyes for a moment, and tried to imagine the challenges of life on Earth, with the dark side abroad in the land, creating strife. His eyelids grew heavy with the pain of his imaginings, and he pushed them away, and drifted off into a different reverie. As he let his mind wander, a pleasant scene came into view behind his eyelids.

A small boy, of no more than two or three, walked with his mother and father up an emerald green hillside covered with wild flowers. As the child climbed the gentle slope, he reached up to take, first the hand of his mother, a young rose-lipped woman with curly reddish-brown hair, and then the hand of his father, a sturdy, handsome chap, dressed in tweeds and brown hiking boots. A breeze billowing up from the ocean below them caused the sea of wild flowers which surrounded them to bow down and slowly stand up again. The salty breeze seemed to exhilarate each living thing it touched. As they climbed higher up the hillside, unable to avoid crushing some of the flowers underfoot, the woman sang to the boy, swinging his little arm in rhythm with her song. The boy's joyful state was intoxicating, and Toomeh felt himself merging with the child's innocent happiness.

His orange topaz seat began violently vibrating and jiggling. Maepleida glanced over to see Toomeh slumped forward, nearly off his topaz chair. But the vibrating crystal had done her job, and Toomeh jerked upright out of his reverie.

Whoa, he thought, suddenly opening his eyes, did I slip time, and see my future life on Earth? He withstood Maepleida's look of concern, nodding only slightly in acknowledgement, then thanked the topaz crystal for her care, offered her his gratitude for calling him back, and tried to return his focus to Lord Kumara's words.

"As you will be human once you incarnate, your emotions will control you at times, as is the case with all humans. It is impossible to be in a human body and for this not to be so. Be mindful, because negative emotional outbursts are food for the dark side, which feeds on negative energy to grow stronger. Do not succumb to emotional outbursts. Understand them as food for those in service only to self. Plant this seed now deep in your subconscious, so you may remember the danger of negative outbursts. In your current dimension your understanding of others is intuitive, you no longer remember the pain of being possessed by negative feelings toward others, or toward yourselves. But in the lower dimensions, negative emotions are a powerful destructive force. Be the love that you are, and that magic will shift the vibration on Earth into a higher frequency. There is always love. There is never a situation where there is no love. There are only beings forgetting that love exists."

Ederah's heart sang at this understanding of love. *"There is never a situation where there is no love. There are only beings forgetting that love exists."* It seemed so obvious now, not even necessary to imprint it, but she heeded Kumara's words and made the effort to plant the seed to remember this. She asked her rose quartz lotus seat to intensify this memory as she directed it to her pineal gland.

"This is the message that you will carry to Earth to save her, and her people, from the fate of Maldek," Kumara continued. "As you know, the planet Maldek once existed between Jupiter and Mars. The consciousness on Maldek became so predatory, so saturated with evil, greed, and hunger for power and wealth that 700,000 years ago, it blew itself up in a nuclear war. All that is left now of Maldek is an asteroid belt. We hope for a different story for Earth. You, my beloveds, embody that hope. You are the grand collective from many star systems. You will turn the tide on Earth and combat the lower vibrational forces there which keep the humans ignorant of their divine origins. It is you who will liberate humanity."

There was silence in the dome as the weight of Lord Kumara's words fell on each of the beings before him. Heipleido felt a powerful stirring in his heart, a sincere desire to save Earth from the fate of Maldek. His whole being was bent on giving this service to the blue planet and her people. Maepleida sensed this in him. It troubled her when they didn't think as one.

"And do not think the Earth beings are not worthy of the risk you take," Lord Kumara said. "Many are brave and courageous souls, who long ago answered the call for an experiment. An experiment which was created to ascertain whether True Light could find its way back to its point of origin, to Source. Each of those who volunteered to fly out from Source as a spark of the Divine in order to help determine whether they could find their way back to that Source, with no memory of it, was a courageous being. They volunteered to incarnate on Earth, and agreed to the condition of passing through the veil of forgetting, and in so doing, to forget their own divine origins. This was an experiment requiring courage equal to that asked of you now. Do they not deserve to be liberated?" A resounding cry rose up from all those assembled.

Bereh, who had been nodding off into a sort of trance, jerked his head up at the sound. They were receiving a lot of information about Earth. Maybe he needed a moment to process it all, because again, he felt himself nodding off, and jerked his head up once more, before succumbing to a sort of dream vision.

A little boy sat cross-legged beneath a flowering lime tree, enjoying the sweet fragrance of the small flowers which covered its branches. He tilted his head back, and looked up high, where a small, yellow bird sat, singing. A dark-haired, brown-skinned woman in a saffron colored sari approached him, disturbing his reverie. She said something to which the boy responded by handing her the small book sitting in his lap. She took the book and pressed it to her heart before returning to the house. The child suddenly turned his head, and looked through the green air of the garden. He smiled as if in response to the sound of a friend's voice. Bereh followed the boy's gaze and saw that the friend was a pachta, an Indian sugar-mill woodpecker. The boy and the pachta communed, momentarily locking eyes as if they shared a secret.

Bereh jerked his head up when he felt Ederah's eyes on him and he whispered to her, "I think I slipped into some sort of reverie, maybe about my future life on earth." Ederah squeezed his hand.

"It's quite possible that you did. We are still fifth dimensional and time is still unbound for us," she whispered back. "Tell me later."

"When you live among the earth beings, as one of them," Kumara was saying, "you will enliven their hearts to such a degree that enlightenment will sweep the planet. Those on the negative path will be no match for your love. They will try to thwart you by creating fear, because fear is the path to the dark side. Fear, as the tool of the dark side, is the root of all evil. Fear leads to hate, and hate to anger, and anger to revenge. But fear is no match for love. Love is the most powerful magic of all."

Soonam sighed and brought her fingertips together in front

of her lips. Her heart stirred as she thought of the joy of rescuing the divine beings caught in the third dimension on Earth. Whenever her heart was touched, her violet eyes overflowed. Attivio turned to her to see her violet eyes brimming with tears. His heart squeezed in his chest.

Lord Kumara silently blessed them all and released them for a long lunch, to relax and absorb the morning's teachings. He suggested again that they manifest and eat actual food, rather than take nourishment directly from light. As they filed out of the temple, Ederah spotted Laaroos, an old friend, and called her over to join them under the trees. Ederah introduced Laaroos to everyone, and it seemed to her, that, when she introduced Laaroos to Toomeh, a spark flew out between them. Bereh noticed it, too, and exchanged a smile with Ederah. Once they were all gathered underneath their tree, Soonam manifested a lovely cloth, designed to reflect the leafy branches above them. She spread it on the ground, and each of them created something appetizing to share and placed it on the cloth. Bereh offered fruit in the shape of stars, and Ederah, fruit curved in the shape of the crescent moon. Maepleida made a round loaf of bread, which at her direction fell apart into eight equal portions. Heipleido added slices of something similar to cheese, only more delicious. Attivio supplied the nectar and goblets. Only Toomeh and Laaroos had not yet added to the feast.

Toomeh looked at Laaroos and tried to fathom what would please her, even more than please her, delight her. And Laaroos, being new to the group, wondered what she might offer them all for their enjoyment. Then Toomeh got an idea. For celebrations on Arcturus, a sweet was often created and shared so that the Arcturians might delight in, and give thanks for, the many blessings of existence by tasting the sweetness of life. He not only created these Arcturian sweets, which looked like tiny flower blossoms, but he placed them on a most beautiful shimmering dish, in the shape of Arcturus herself. He offered the dish first to Laaroos, who blushed to a deep crimson as she bowed her head and selected a sweet from the plate which he held before her. A moment later, a vase filled with fragrant lavender flowers appeared in the center of Soonam's cloth, compliments of Laaroos. It nearly tipped over when Heipleido reached for the bread, but Toomeh quickly rescued it. Maepleida smiled, realizing that Heipleido had caused Laaroos's vase to fall so Toomeh could rescue it.

While they ate, Heipleido told them that he'd heard that during their training they would be meeting the twin flame chohans of all seven rays, as well as Earth's planetary Buddha, the Lord Gautama Buddha. Maepleida shifted her position to sit on her other hip while she listened. Soonam leaned back and nestled into Attivio as he sat with his back up against a tree. His arms naturally encircled her, and he rested his chin on the top of her head.

"My head is swimming with this morning's information," Ederah said.

"Mine too," Laaroos agreed.

"Where is your home?" Toomeh asked her.

"Arcturus."

Toomeh broke into a big smile hearing this. "I thought so," he said. "It's mine, too. When I saw your eyes, such a deep gold that they're nearly orange, I thought you must be native to Arcturus."

Laaroos allowed herself to look into Toomeh's eyes and saw reflected back at her the image of her own deep, orange-gold orbs.

"Oh," said Soonam, "but of course darlings, your eyes are the color of Arcturus herself. Many beings don't realize that there are civilizations living inside of some stars, and not just on the surface of planets surrounding stars."

Everyone smiled at Soonam. They couldn't help it. Her childlike openness refreshed every exchange. She tilted her head back and sought Attivio's face for reassurance that she hadn't intruded in Toomeh and Laaroos's conversation. Toomeh wanted to share with Laaroos the vision he'd had during Kumara's talk, of the little boy and his parents on the emerald green hillside, and describe to her his feeling that he was to be that little boy. But he knew that it was too soon to speak to her so intimately.

"Time for me to process all this morning's information," Bereh said. And he stretched out on the ground, started munching on a star shaped fruit, and promptly fell asleep in the warm Venusian sun. His last thought before dozing off was, *this is the same sun that will shine on us when we're on Earth.* Ederah brushed his lips with hers and took the fruit from his hand. Her heart was full of softness and peace, and she lay down and put her head on his chest. Soon she was drifting off into her own reverie.

An elegant woman in a white, silk robe leaned back against several down pillows in a large bed with a medieval scene depicted on its tall headboard. The woman held a newborn baby swaddled in a soft, pink blanket. She looked out the window at the thickly falling snow, then lowered her eyes to gaze at the sleeping infant in her arms. A little boy of about four or five climbed onto the bed next to her, and gently placed his little hand on the top of the baby's head. Next to the woman sat a handsome man, with a short, neatly clipped black beard. He placed his arm around the woman, and he, too, looked down at the baby with great tenderness. He was a man who never failed to see what he looked at. The little boy asked him something, and the man turned and broke into a smile as he inclined his head forward in a yes.

Bereh shifted his position, and Ederah, whose head rested on his chest, suddenly came too, wondering what she had just witnessed. Was it her future family? Was she to become the baby in the woman's arms? A few feet from Bereh and Ederah, Toomeh sat close to Laaroos, offering her a crescent moon shaped fruit which she took in her small, strong hand. Soonam noticed a kind of pink glow around the two of them. Attivio pressed his back into the tree trunk and tightened his arms around her. She whispered something to him which made him smile. Ederah glanced at Bereh's sleeping face and dozed off again herself, hoping to catch another glimpse of the little family on the big bed. Only Maepleida and Heipleido seemed momentarily out of harmony. But finally, they, too, relaxed, and silence fell over the whole group as each heart filled with peace and stillness. All thought stopped, and their minds shut down to meditate and metabolize the morning's information. The processing was accomplished through their heart chakras, as each mind bowed down before its heart. A serene hour of meditation passed quickly, rejuvenating them, for meditation was more nourishing to these fifth dimensional beings than food.

Bereh awoke from his meditation to the sound of the gong calling them back to the temple. Ederah sat up and extended her hand to help him up. They all brushed themselves off, adjusted their soft, flowing garments, banished the remains of their picnic, breathed in the sweetness of the fragrant air, and made their way back into the temple for the afternoon session. As they passed under the arch, Laaroos noticed the scent of oranges, as if from thousands of orange trees.

"Good afternoon," Lady Venus began. "I'd like to introduce you all to our guest, Adama, who comes to us from Telos, one of the inner cities of light inside the Earth. Telos was constructed inside Mt. Shasta, in a place now known as northern California. When the Lemurians learned that their continent of Lemuria would sink into the ocean, they made plans to save what they could of their holy sites and their culture by rebuilding on the safer ground of Mount Shasta. Mount Shasta is part of what is called The Ring of Fire. And thanks to the foresight of the Lemurians, much of their advanced and peaceful civilization is preserved there in the inner city of Telos. But not all of the population could be moved, and many Lemurians were lost in the deluge when the continent sank beneath the sea 12,000 years ago. Many of those who died that night remain on the surface of Earth, incarnating as humans. They carry much trauma from the destruction of Lemuria. The Lemurians in Telos want very much to free those who perished in the deluge, when Lemuria sank, from the karmic cycle of rebirth. Once you awaken on Earth, the Lemurians will be your allies, and will help you to raise the vibration of humanity and avert the destruction of the planet. Like you, the Lemurians are fifth dimensional beings with many gifts, which will be at your service once you awaken. I now give you Adama of Telos, city of light."

As Adama stepped forward and bowed to them, Laaroos noted that again the scent of oranges filled the air. About twelve feet tall, Adama had shoulder length, light colored hair and sea-green eyes. He wore a long robe the color of white sand and he spoke in a gentle voice.

"We of Telos and the Agartha network of the inner cities of light are grateful to all of you for volunteering to come on this mission. Though risks are great, and many could be lost, there will be help and protection. Once you are in human form the diamond spark in your hearts will be your gateway to enlightenment and the remembrance of who you are. We, of the inner cities of light, will be there to assist you, but you must call on us. The protocol for incarnation on Earth requires that no assistance can be given without first being requested by the surface dwellers. Once assistance is requested, every light being in the inner cities below the surface of the planet will be at your service the moment you call. You will be invited to visit us in your light bodies, during your sleep time. We live in a peaceful, cooperative society inside the Earth. Our city inside Mount Shasta is in the Pacific Northwest of the United States. Telos is full of light, gardens, groves of orange trees, and temples of great beauty. We invite you to visit and share in the comfort and beauty."

Laaroos sighed. Ah, that's why I smelled the delicious fragrance of a thousand orange trees, she thought.

Toomeh picked up her thought without responding. He, too,

had enjoyed the fragrance of the orange trees.

"We Lemurians live in harmony with all of nature, and also with the universe beyond. Many visitors from around the galaxy come to visit us. Some of the humans living near Mount Shasta have become aware of something special going on inside the mountain, and some have even seen space ships in the sky above Mount Shasta. Most of these humans are excited to see evidence of these visitors from other planets and dimensions."

Heipleido tried to keep his focus on the message, but lulled by the gentle beauty of Adama's voice, and the sweet scent of the orange groves, he found himself drifting off into a reverie.

He saw an enormous pyramid, at the foot of which stood a young boy of five or six. He wore kaki-shorts, a white shirt and brown, lace-up ankle boots. Next to the boy, holding his hand, was a delicately featured, dark-haired woman in a gossamer pastel dress with a pattern of blue lotuses on it. She reached up under her wide-brimmed straw hat and brushed the hair from her forehead, tucking it under the brim. The boy pointed to the ground beneath the pyramid and her eyes followed his finger. He told her that there were beings living underground, in a city beneath the pyramid. She smiled at what she assumed was the boy's fantasy, but rather than contradict him she asked, "What kind of beings?"

He answered her without hesitation. "Beings from space."

As he listened in, Heipleido felt certain that the child was speaking the truth, that there was a small, inhabited city under the pyramid. Still in a trance, he leaned forward in an effort to hear more of their conversation, hoping the boy's mother would continue asking him questions. But he leaned so far forward that he almost fell out of his amethyst seat, which had started jiggling fiercely. He opened his eyes to see Maepleida looking at him in wonderment, for Heipleido was a being of astounding agility, power and grace.

"As I said, some humans are aware of our presence and have even witnessed what they call flying saucers over Mount Shasta,"

Adama continued. "And many more humans are awakening to the awareness, that something is changing on their planet. When you incarnate, come to us for teachings and healings during your sleep time, and all the support you need will be yours. The window of opportunity is now. We of the inner cities of light stand with you in this battle for the souls of humanity."

Attivio looked at Soonam and sent her his thought. *We will win this battle and I will find you on Earth, no matter what happens.* When she heard his thought, Soonam turned and embraced him with her eyes alone. Even now, after all these eons, it was still as if silver trumpets resounded in his heart at her glance. For a moment, he thought he saw her as a little girl playing in a park, watched over by a man who seemed to cherish her. He shook his head and took a deep breath.

Adama was concluding his remarks. "Let me leave you courageous light beings with this information. Once you incarnate on earth as human, your heart must be opened like a door. And the key to open the door of the heart is silence. Yes, it's that simple. A period of silence every day will benefit your awakening. To rest in silent meditation each day is key. You know this now, but as a third dimensional being you must relearn it. We, from Telos, and the network of the inner cities of light, bless you and thank you for your help in this great battle."

Adama bowed to them, and again the scent of a thousand orange trees filled the air with a sweet fragrance.

Maepleida sent a thought to Heipleido. *But how are we going to remember all this once we're in the density of a human vehicle?*

Heipleido tried to lighten her mood by creating a teasing tone with his thought-reply. *Darling, my darling, most brave of all Pleiadian warriors, are you getting cold feet?*

Ignoring his playful attempt to cajole her, she shot back. *You're the one who wants this grand adventure to Earth, not me.*

Before Heipleido could offer her some reassurance, Lady Venus released them and invited everyone for evening tea on the lawn under the ancient trees. Toomeh contrived to walk out of the temple beside Laaroos, and to ask her how she knew Ederah. He used his voice, though he could read her thoughts. He decided it might be forward to already be communicating telepathically.

"I served with Ederah and Bereh in the battle of the Violet Planet against the Draconians," Laaroos answered. But Toomeh barely heard her words, his feeling of bliss was so overpowering as he gazed at her, wondering how she was so familiar and dear to him after only a few hours' acquaintance. Walking beside her, it felt to him as if all the galaxies were singing around them and moving into alignment in support of their meeting. He already loved her face, framed as it was by hair like strands of liquid amber. He decreed her face a most perfect setting for her deep, starry eyes. Leaving the dome together, side by side, they looked heavenward to see the sky above them turn from pink to transparent gold.

Maepleida and Heipleido looked at the pair with interest. Toomeh had long been Maepleida's pal and Heipleido's best friend. Maepleida asked Ederah about Laaroos, and learned that Ederah and Bereh had fought side by side with Laaroos on the Violet planet. They'd met up again more recently, while serving as guardians of the children on Arcturus.

"Well, it's not the ideal time to fall in love," Maepleida said, glancing at Toomeh and Laaroos, "when we're all about to be separated from our twin flames, and thrust into human bodies with no memory of who we are."

"Maybe we'll be wildly successful on Earth and reunite in one lifetime, lifting up all beings," Bereh piped in.

"Aren't you relentlessly positive," Maepleida said.

"We all know energy follows thought, so my plan is to be relentlessly positive."

"Right you are, Bereh," Attivio said, handing Soonam a cup of tea.

"I'm glad there'll be tea on Earth," Soonam said. "I love tea."

"Maybe you can ask to be incarnated in England. I've been studying and I learned that they drink a lot of tea there, while the Americans drink more coffee," Laaroos said.

Laaroos felt the warmth of Toomeh's smile on her face as she spoke, and she liked the feeling of his tender support. It was a new sensation for her, as she had been on her own for eons.

Maepleida strolled off a little distance from the group. Heipleido followed her.

"I still don't see how we're to remember all this once we pass through the veil of forgetting," she said.

"But that's the challenge of it, darling," Heipleido said.

"We're going for a stroll before bed," Maepleida called back to the others. "See you in the morning."

"I do love you so very much you know," Heipleido said, as they climbed the hill toward their cottage.

"I know you do," Maepleida answered.

Chapter 3

The Blue Ray

Maepleida awoke in Heipleido's arms, his breath warm on the back of her neck. She opened her eyes, rolled onto her back, and looked around. She was pleased with what they'd created in their cottage. Deep-green, restful walls surrounded their bed. The sheets were of the softest cotton, and there were lots of pillows. She adjusted her pale-blue, silk nightgown, which had wrapped around her legs. Slowly, she was getting used to this semi-dense body that they had all assumed upon arriving on Venus. But she missed the freedom of her light body. In their light-bodies they needed neither food nor sleep. Now, as hybrids of light and flesh, which were not quite as dense as humans, they needed both. Maepleida was not always sure of the etiquette involved in using this new body.

Heipleido opened his eyes. "Hello darling," he said, leaning up on one elbow to kiss her. Holding her tenderly with his eyes alone, he was struck anew by her dazzling beauty. "I want to remember you as you are in this moment forever."

"Why particularly?" Maepleida asked.

"I don't know. Maybe it's the blue silk against your black skin or the way your hair looks so wild when you first wake up, or the depth of your emerald eyes in the morning. This sleeping business at least has the benefit of seeing you anew each day."

"You're quite romantic this morning," Maepleida said, "but we should get up now."

"No. Kiss me, and call me by my name," he said, pulling her into his arms. She did not kiss him, but looked at him as if she had discovered something new in him. He saw her surprise and tenderly kissed each side of her mouth and then her lips themselves. The taste of orange blossoms still lingered on her skin, a gift of the previous day from their Lemurian visitor. Between kisses he whispered to her, "Never think you're alone. I am always with you. Somewhere I will always be holding you." At these words, she surrendered to him completely.

The roof of the temple glittered in the morning light. As they entered, Soonam pointed out the pink sky visible through the clear roof. Attivio glanced upward and felt a soft wave of pink light rush toward him. Some of the glass panels of the roof had been opened to let the air in. It flowed down over them carrying the fragrance of roses. Soonam sat next to Attivio breathing in the rose filled air, contemplating the sky. The sky could not be owned or held down by temples. It didn't suffer injury. It was a moving, expanding house over everything.

Toomeh came in after Soonam and Attivio, and was followed a moment later by Laaroos, who asked her orange diamond seat to come along and join the crystal seats of Toomeh's group. Knowing what would please her most, the orange diamond situated itself in the midst of the crystal chairs, right next to Toomeh's orange topaz chair. It would not be content to let Laaroos be some loose star out on the periphery. This choice by the orange diamond made Laaroos smile and gave her a little insight into the personality of the crystal she had chosen. Soonam, too, had noticed the orange diamond's move and was amused. Diamonds are known for their strength and incorruptibility, but this orange diamond was also a little matchmaker. Toomeh, also, did not fail to notice, and it gave him hope.

The fragrance of roses grew stronger. Sometimes when twin flames met, the scent of roses filled the air. Was this lovely fragrance courtesy of Toomeh and Laaroos meeting, Soonam wondered? It was as if the two of them were all alone, inhabiting a secret garden, two bodies, but one heart. Attivio heard Soonam's thoughts. He and Soonam, too, shared a single heart. He felt his love for her like an endless, steady stream, flowing to the sea.

Ederah and Bereh came in next and joined their friends. They both saw a glow around Toomeh which he'd never had before. Only Maepleida and Heipleido were missing. Their crystal seats sat empty. Then, just in time to hear the Lady Venus's opening remarks, they arrived and their crystals jiggled in greeting.

Lady Venus welcomed them all and introduced the shimmering deities standing beside her. Amerissis, Goddess of Light, bowed to them. She radiated such a high frequency of crystal light that it was almost impossible to look directly at her. Beside her stood her twin flame and fellow chohan of the first ray, Master El Morya. As guardians of the Blue Ray, it was their task on Earth to help all souls align their will with the will of the Divine. In addition, Amerissis ensouled a quality of light which could restore emotional balance to any being seeking her aid. Rising upward from her third eye burned a flame about six inches high. Standing still in her white robe, holding her sword, point down, she looked the formidable deity that she was.

Maepleida shifted in her sapphire seat. She had never before seen a being continually emitting a live flame from her body. Her sapphire chair jiggled, whether to reassure her or warn her, she wasn't certain. She had chosen a blue sapphire specifically to help her to align her will with the will of the Divine, but resistance to this mission was still strong in her. She looked from Amerissis to El Morya as if for an answer to an unasked question.

El Morya's piercing blue eyes were sweeping over them with the intensity of a hawk scouring the earth below him. Despite his countenance, Maepleida observed that he had the perfectly symmetrical features characteristic of all masters. Masters, like beings of the fifth dimension, were very fair to look upon. El Morya was no exception. His shoulder length brown hair was partly covered by a gold turban with a large agate set in it just above his third eye. His beard was close clipped over his bronze skin. He wore a flowing robe the color of lapis lazuli. And although light radiated from his magnificent being, Maepleida felt there was a sternness about him. The golden staff with a quartz crystal on the top, which he held firmly in his right hand, looked to her as if it was about to strike.

"Greetings, dear ones," Amerissis began. "El Morya and I come to you from Darjeeling, India, on planet Earth, where we serve as Hierarchs of the Brotherhood of Light. We represent the attributes of the Blue Ray, which are courage, faith, initiative and self-reliance. All these qualities each of you possesses, and will need for this mission. We have a great love for the Earth beings, and I hope that you will come to have a love and affection for them as well. They are a courageous and self-reliant people, and we have often lived among them as one of them, as you are about to do.

In the Fifth Century AD, El Morya was embodied on Earth as King Arthur, and headed the mystery school at Camelot. In that lifetime, he learned the hard lesson that it is possible to love another so much, that despite them breaking your heart or even betraying you, you can go on loving them, and feeling more concern for their well-being than your own. In that lifetime, as King Arthur, he was incarnated with several others in our soul group, one he adored above all, his queen, who was known in that life as Guinevere. But she fell in love with the man, of all men, he most admired, known in that life as Lancelot. At first he wanted a man's revenge for their betrayal. He loved them, and they answered him with pain. Only when he saw that their pain was as great as his own did his torment cease. Passion, dear ones, cannot be selected. This is one type of challenging lesson with which humans are faced over and over again, as they fall in love and betray one another. These lessons about love are among the strongest catalysts in the third dimension, which help humans to grow and move forward toward the fourth dimension. I will leave you to wonder what part I played in that lifetime. As she said this an enigmatic smile swept across her countenance."

Maepleida listened to Amerissis, but kept glancing at El

Morya. What she had at first viewed as his harshness seemed to melt away, like ice before the sun, leaving in its place the image of a kind and wise King Arthur, forgiving both Guinevere and Lancelot.

"Fortunately, early in that lifetime, as a young boy," Amerissis continued, "El Morya, or as he was known then, Arthur, had the good fortune to be trained by another of our soul group, known in that lifetime as Merlin, the great alchemist. Because of this training, he was able to use the experience of heartbreak and betrayal to learn many lessons, including that aggression is not strength, and compassion is not weakness. He who was Merlin is now an ascended master, Master Saint Germain, Chohan of the Violet Ray of Transmutation. He will be coming to Venus with his twin flame, the Lady Portia, to speak with you before you depart on your mission to Earth.

I'd like to tell you of one more of El Morya's Earth lives. Previous to his incarnation as King Arthur, he was embodied on Earth as Melchoir, one of the three wise men at the birth of Jesus. Jesus, who is also a member of the Brotherhood of Light, is known to us as Lord Sananda, Chohan of the Sixth Ray, The Flame of Resurrection. And he, too, with his twin flame, Lady Nada, will be visiting Venus to prepare you. Lady Nada was incarnated on Earth as Mary Magdalene. Together, they will teach you to wield the Flame of Resurrection."

Bereh and Ederah had long wanted to meet Lord Sananda and Lady Nada. Ederah gave Bereh a sideways glance and saw that he had swallowed this news in a joyful gulp.

"An unexpected gift," Bereh whispered, but then he caught Soonam out of the corner of his eye and nodded in her direction. Ederah followed his gaze, and saw that Soonam seemed to have drifted off. Her eyelids were closed, but fluttering slightly, as if she was watching something.

"She must be seeing into the Earth realm as I did," Ederah said.

A little girl and a man sat on a low, circular stone wall which surrounded a fountain. Water from the fountain reached at least fifty feet up into the air. Sun shining through the water created a rainbow which arched up over the fountain. The little girl pointed to it with obvious joy. Both the man and the child were eating ice cream cones. Pink ice cream dripped down the little girl's cone onto her small hand. The man took the cone from her and wrapped a napkin around it before handing it back to her. The child licked her fingers and smiled up at him. He looked down into her violet eyes and smiled into them. He was a man who would never forget to look at the stars.

Soonam was jolted out of her reverie when Amerissis turned to El Morya and he began to speak. But the child's violet eyes, so like her own, stayed with her.

"Many beings on Earth have had enough of life as it is," El Morya began, "and will welcome the change you bring. But before it can materialize, the change must happen first in the consciousness of each human. It is our hope that you who sit here before me will affect that consciousness, and usher in the next *Golden Age of Enlightenment on Earth*. If you succeed, you will become ascended masters. If you fail, you could be stuck for eons in the lower vibrations. It is likely that you will begin to lighten the vibration on Earth from the moment of your birth, but you will certainly raise the frequency once you awaken and remember that you are light beings from a higher dimension. As you grow from infancy into childhood in your human form, the chohans of all seven rays will begin to place thought forms and dreams in your minds to stimulate the memory of your true identity, to remind you that you are wanderers from a higher dimension."

Soonam tried to focus on El Morya, but kept wondering if she had just seen her future human form as it would appear in her childhood on Earth. Had she visited the future for a few brief seconds and seen herself with the man who would be her father? She made a mental note to ask the others if this had happened to any of them.

"And, during your weeks of training here on Venus," El Morya said, "you will be planting seeds deep in your consciousness, in the heart of your pineal gland. It is these seeds that the chohans will attempt to stir into consciousness through your dreams. Dreams are one way in which humans can penetrate the veil of forgetting.

You will incarnate in the areas of the Earth where you're most needed. Some of you will incarnate in an area called the Middle East, in countries where women are oppressed. Others of you will incarnate in Western countries, where the challenge will be to resist the pull of addictions and materialism. Each of you will face challenges in your new environment even as you try to recover your true identity. Cultivating a disciplined human personality will help you. Focus the discipline of your human personality on *acceptance of self, forgiveness of self, and the directing of your will toward service to others*. If you succeed in this, you will perfect your balance between compassion and wisdom. This balance is necessary for your further ascension into even higher dimensions, beyond what you now enjoy.

To help prepare you, Amerissis and I have devised an exercise in which you will experience yourself on Earth as a third dimensional being. In this exercise, you will each bring a message to a human that will be of great service. For the purpose of the exercise, you will be required to temporarily relinquish all your fourth, fifth and sixth dimensional powers. So, with your permission, I will return you all to your third dimensional capabilities. If anyone does not wish to surrender their will to me, you may block me, and simply observe the exercise. As you have all volunteered for this mission, and will be born on Earth within a few weeks, we have permission from our governing body in the rings of Saturn for you to travel through the quarantine around Earth and to interact with humans for the dual purposes of training and the offering of service.

When you walk out of the temple, you will find yourself instantly transported, via a large merkaba, to New York City in the present time. Rather than activating your own personal merkaba for the journey, you will all travel together in one large time-space vehicle of counter-rotating fields of light. At the end of the exercise, you will travel back to Venus via the same counter-rotating fields, which will again create an energetic time-space vehicle. When you feel the pull of the group merkaba you must return, as you will not be able to activate your own personal merkaba as a third dimensional being and will be stuck on Earth.

Each of you will be tasked, using only third dimensional skills, with delivering a message to a specific human. *Intuition* is the most powerful tool available to third dimensional beings. Use it to find the person with whom you are meant to speak. If you find the right being, and give them the message, they will awaken and embrace you as a fellow wanderer. If you succeed, you will have done a great service to another being. If you give the message to the wrong person, they will simply think you are weird or crazy. You may approach only three people in your attempt to find your connection.

The message you are to transmit is this. *Dear one, you are here on Earth as a wanderer, who has come from a higher dimension to help the Earth beings. Awake now and reclaim your higher powers as a being of light.* Remember, you have only three tries. There are eight and a half million people living in New York City, so this will be challenging. Use your intuition. Trust it.

"In fact," Amerissis added, "human intuition is so powerful that once an entity develops it in the third dimension, it can be used to access information across time, both from the future and the past. Intuition can also access knowledge of events that the entity has never even consciously processed, but which it has either recorded unconsciously, in the personal unconscious, or discovered in the collective unconscious. As you will be human in your consciousness for this exercise, your intuition will be your most powerful ally. Employ it well." Amerissis nodded to El Morya, who resumed giving instructions for the exercise.

"When Amerissis raises her sword, she will be temporarily revoking all your higher skills and powers, with the exception of one. You will still be able to understand and speak all languages. We will return your other powers to you at the end of the exercise. You may search alone, in pairs or in groups. The humans will perceive you as human, though to yourselves you will still look as you do now. You will find the necessary U.S. currency for this exercise in the pockets of your new, present day American clothes."

Amerissis raised her long sword high into the air above her and released it. The sword sailed out over all those gathered and as it passed over each of them it changed all their clothes to present day human garb, and revoked their higher powers. Repeated gasps were uttered as each wanderer felt the shock of her reduced ability to hold light.

Soonam reached for Attivio's hand. Bereh smiled into Ederah's eyes. Maepleida gave Heipleido a skeptical look. Toomeh and Laaroos stood silently side by side, not touching. None of them felt right. The third dimensional vibration was so much slower and heavier that they moved cautiously toward the temple doors. Soonam was the first to attempt a positive attitude about the third dimension.

"What fun this is going to be," Soonam said, lifting her heels off the ground in a little hop, and smiling at her new outfit which was a pink, cotton, summer dress and sandals. "We're going to visit Earth, and have a preview of what life will be like there." Attivio stood beside her in a blue, cord, summer suit and white shirt, trying to match her gracious energy.

"Spiffy," Bereh remarked seeing Attivio's new outfit.

"You're not looking too shabby yourself," Attivio countered, pointing at Bereh's beige, summer suit and blue necktie. Ederah stood next to him in a white, cotton blouse and a full skirt with a pattern of lavender flowers, and kitten heels.

Heipleido was delighted when he looked down at his feet and beheld his fancy running shoes. He was also wearing a dark-blue T-shirt and Bermuda shorts. Maepleida was less pleased with her running shoes and red workout suit. Toomeh complimented her on how becoming red was with her skin, but she brushed him off, telling him she'd rather be wearing his blue jeans and loafers. Laaroos, too, had on blue jeans, but with sneakers and a pretty blue and white checkered blouse.

As travel via a merkaba is instantaneous, almost as soon as they had all assembled outside the temple in their human clothes, they found themselves in New York City, listening to the sounds of a New York afternoon on a summer day. The sky was clear blue, not pink, as on Venus. And it was noisy. Sounds of sirens and fire trucks and ambulances and taxicab horns, dogs barking, babies crying, ice cream trucks playing their music and children laughing assailed them all at once.

"Wow, what an intense and seductive place this is," Toomeh said. He tried to tune in to how Laaroos was experiencing it, but he could no longer read her thoughts. They all stood for a moment in a group, just looking around and taking it all in with just their third dimensional abilities.

"Sensation is so strong in the third dimension," Bereh said, as the smell of hotdogs and pretzels with mustard hit him.

"I like it," Soonam half shouted over the sound of a barking dog. She looked up to read a sign on the corner which said, Fifth Avenue and Ninth Street.

"There's a fountain," Heipleido said. "Let's walk down there and get our bearings. And water generally helps intuition."

"I hope so. I feel so powerless just at this moment," Maepleida said.

"Darling, we are somewhat powerless, we've come with none of our usual abilities, but that's the fun of it," Heipleido said.

As the eight of them headed toward the fountain, Soonam spoke to a passerby.

"What area is this?"

"Greenwich Village, and that's Washington Square Park," the young woman, wearing skinny jeans and a big white shirt with the sleeves rolled up, exposing the many beaded bracelets adorning her wrist, answered with a friendly smile.

"Tourists," they heard her say to her friend with the spiked hairdo as she moved off. Soonam smiled to herself at the word 'tourists'. Humans are friendly was what she was thinking.

As the group walked under the Washington Square Arch, Laaroos shivered and stopped. A woman, who looked to be in her late twenties, dressed in blue-jean short shorts, a tank top and faded gray converse sneakers, squatted on the stone patio between the arch and the fountain. She was drawing a huge mandala, using colored chalk. Laaroos wanted a closer look.

"A shiver can be an intuition," Toomeh told her when he saw the shiver move through Laaroos again. Laaroos nodded, remembering El Morya's instruction to use intuition. The woman looked up when Laaroos approached, and their eyes locked. The others stood back observing. Laaroos squatted down next to her and asked about the mandala. The woman said she didn't know why but she was always drawing them, and had been ever since she was a child. For the last few years she'd been creating them in public places. Laaroos studied the drawing and saw what she thought looked like a representation of Arcturus in the very center. The pathways from the edges of the mandala all seemed to be trying to reach the center. Was this woman trying to get somewhere? Was she trying to get back home? Laaroos glanced up at Toomeh, but she couldn't read his thoughts.

"What's that in the center?" Laaroos asked the woman.

"It's a star, called Arcturus. I don't know why, but I put it in all my mandalas."

Laaroos shivered for a third time. "Can I tell you something?"

Laaroos said to the woman, who nodded in answer.

"Maybe that star is your true home, and you've come here on a mission, but you're really from a higher dimension. You're really a wanderer, possibly from Arcturus."

Tears began streaming down the woman's face. It was then that Toomeh noticed the woman's eyes turn a dark, orange-gold.

"I've read lots of books about wanderers, but I wasn't sure they were real," the woman told Laaroos. "Because I always feel like an outsider, I wondered if I was one."

"They are very real, and I'm certain you are one," Laaroos said, embracing the woman. A shock wave of recognition went through her as they touched, and Laaroos involuntarily said, in the language of Arcturus, "Mother."

The rest of the group watched the reunion with full hearts. Was this woman the same being who had been Laaroos's mother, and left all those years ago on a mission to Earth, and gotten trapped in the third dimension? Standing a little distance from Laaroos, as their third dimensional selves, they were all stunned. And Laaroos, in that instant of recognition, understood that nothing wider than a hair's breadth, separates joy and pain. The violence of her grief, and joy, crippled her tongue. Finally, she did manage to convey to the others that they should go on with their own searches, and that she would stay with her mother for the rest of the exercise.

"That was easy enough," said Maepleida, "I hope I'll be so lucky."

"Don't be spikey, darling," Heipleido said.

"So, what now?" Toomeh asked. "Anybody have a thought, or an intuition?"

They sat down on the stone benches around the fountain. Toomeh kept glancing back at Laaroos who was now seated under the arch with her mother. Soonam started at the sight of the spraying fountain. This was the very one she'd just seen in her reverie back in the temple. She looked around to see if she could spot the man and his little daughter, eating ice cream, but they weren't there.

"I just saw this fountain in a kind of dream, while El Morya was talking," Soonam told them. Bereh, Ederah, Toomeh and Heipleido all said they'd had images, too, of what they took to be their future incarnations on Earth.

"We can talk about these visions we've been having later," Maepleida said. "For now, I think we should each try to follow our intuition about where we should go to get on with this exercise."

"Soonam and I will stick together," Attivio said.

"Ederah and I will, too," Bereh added.

"Maepleida?" Heipleido asked.

"Yes, let's go together."

"That's me on my own then," Toomeh said, and he sagged a little at the knees.

"Maybe we should meditate a moment to see what our intuition offers as to which way to head," Ederah suggested.

Before they could even close their eyes and still their breathing, a joyful yellow lab bounced by Soonam, licked her hands, then brushed her legs as it ran to the fountain, jumped in, then turned around and peeped his head over the edge to look for his owner.

"I hope I have a dog when I come to Earth to live," Soonam told Attivio.

Once they had all closed their eyes, the noise of the gushing fountain dropped into the background and each of them focused on his breath and entered a state of relaxation.

Toomeh was the first to open his eyes and speak after the meditation.

"I'm seeing a giant statute of a woman, wearing what looks like a sari. People are climbing up inside this statue, all the way up into the crown chakra. She seems to be surrounded by water, like she's on an island. I'm going to ask someone where this is and head for it."

Soonam said she was being drawn to a large park with a lake and row boats.

"Good. We'll ask someone where that is and go there first then," Attivio said.

Heipleido asked Maepleida how she felt about a sporting event? He'd gotten an intuition of a game involving a ball and a wooden stick, going on between two teams in a large coliseum.

"Fine with me," Maepleida said.

Ederah had seen a classical looking white stone building with fountains all along the front. Intuitively she knew that inside the building there were works of beautiful art from all over the world. She and Bereh agreed to find it together.

Following Soonam's earlier example, Ederah asked a passerby for help. She chose a white-haired woman wearing a pastel summer dress and pearls, who was walking a small dog, and inquired as to how they could get to the big museum with the fountains all along the front.

"Do you mean The Met?" the woman asked.

"Yes," Bereh said, giving the woman a radiant smile. "How can we get to it?"

Sizing them up, and determining that they were from out of town and could probably afford a taxi, the woman said, "From here, probably the best thing is to take a cab and tell the driver you want to go to The Met."

"Thank you, and, can you direct us to a cab?" Ederah asked.

The woman glanced around and saw a yellow cab stopped at the light at the bottom of Fifth Avenue. "There's one," she said pointing, "but you better dash before the light changes."

"Thank you so much for your help," Ederah said again.

"You're very welcome, now run." The woman watched as the young couple dashed for the cab, and caught it just as the light was changing. She watched the cab turn left at the corner and waved back when they waved at her through the open window.

What a polite couple, she thought. I wonder where they're visiting from. Her little dog looked up at her and gave a few barks to let her know he'd like to move along now, if she was finished.

Toomeh approached a young guy with a skate board, wearing black jeans and a t-shirt with the sleeves cut out. Smiling at the young man, Toomeh asked where the statue of the big lady that you could climb up inside was located. The skateboarder stopped and looked Toomeh full in the face, perhaps amused by his description of the Statue of Liberty, before telling him to catch the subway down to the boat for Liberty Island. Toomeh thought he probably shouldn't ask what a subway was, so he stood still for a moment thinking. The guy picked up on Toomeh's confusion and said that he was going that way, so he'd walk Toomeh to the subway entrance, a block away. They walked mostly in awkward silence until they got to the entrance.

"Go down those stairs and take the one train downtown to South Ferry."

Toomeh thanked him, then turned to descend the stairs into the subway. He paused and turned back around.

"I didn't even ask your name," Toomeh said.

"Carlos," he called over his shoulder before he dropped his skateboard to the ground and hopped on it, giving his shoulders an involuntary shake as if he was releasing some weird feeling.

Soonam put her arm through Attivio's and smiled up at him.

"Now, let's find that big park with the rowboats," she said.

Attivio glanced around the fountain and saw the young woman with the yellow lab that had brushed by them earlier. Both the dog and the girl were watching the fountain shoot up into the sky. Soonam followed Attivio's gaze to the girl and her dog.

"Yes, let's ask her," she agreed.

"Do you mean, Central Park?" The girl with the long black

ponytail asked. "They have rowboats on the lake."

"Yes, can we walk there?" Attivio asked.

"It's a pretty far walk, but you can take a train or a cab, or an Uber, if you have a cell phone."

"We don't have a cell phone," Soonam said.

"Do you have a metro card?"

"We don't, so what would you recommend?" Soonam asked, then added, "I'm sorry, we didn't introduce ourselves or even ask your name."

"I'm Ana and this is my dog Obi Wan."

Soonam bent to pet Obi Wan and this time he licked her face rather than her hand. She was squatting on her heels and nearly fell backward when Obi Wan tried to hug her.

"He's lovely," Soonam said, recovering her balance, kissing him back and laughing.

"He is," Ana agreed. "I think you should take a cab, since you seem a little lost. We'll help you find one."

The four of them left the fountain and walked over to Sixth Avenue, where Ana hailed a cab for them and told the driver to take them up to Central Park.

Soonam hugged Ana, then Obi Wan, goodbye. Attivio bowed slightly before climbing into the taxi beside Soonam. Ana watched the taxi disappear up Sixth Avenue, but she couldn't get the unusual couple out of her mind for the rest of the day. They were so luminescent, so polite, and yes, so other worldly. Obi Wan looked up at her and wagged. Perhaps he agreed with her thought.

Maepleida and Heipleido left the park and strolled back up Fifth Avenue.

"We'd better not wander too far, since we don't know in which direction the arena lies," Heipleido said.

"Let's ask that man wearing exercise clothes," Maepleida suggested.

Heipleido called, "Hello," and made eye contact with a tall, young, black man in running shorts and sneakers.

"Can you direct us to the large outdoor sporting arena, where a game is underway," he asked.

The man seemed a little taken aback until he realized English probably wasn't their first language. He thought a minute.

"There's a ballgame this afternoon up in Yankee Stadium. Is that what you mean?"

"Yes." Heipleido nodded. "What's the best way to get to Yankee Stadium?"

"Take the four train at Union Square."

Seeing the confused look on Maepleida's beautiful face and fancying her himself, the man asked, "Do you know where Union Square is?"

This time Maepleida answered. "It's our first time in New York. We don't know where anything is."

She's like a willow tree, the jogger thought, as he listened to her.

"Would you direct us to the four train?" Maepleida asked.

"Happy to," he said, smiling and looking directly into her large, unusual, emerald eyes.

With help from various New Yorkers, Bereh and Ederah made it up to the Metropolitan Museum of Art. Maepleida and Heipleido got all the way up to Yankee Stadium. Soonam and Attivio arrived in Central Park, and Toomeh made it down to the Statute of Liberty. Each of them began to follow clues and to use intuition to find the person they were meant to speak to.

Toomeh climbed all the way up into the crown of Lady Liberty and stood looking out over New York Harbor. A man standing next to him, who was also observing the harbor from high up in Lady Liberty, began a conversation with him, the way a stranger sometimes will, confiding intimacies. He told Toomeh that he often climbed up here, to the top of the Statute of Liberty, because he had a special feeling for her. He felt that he'd lived in another time and place, an ancient time maybe, where there had been a statute just like this one. Although he knew that this monument had been given by the French to America, he felt that it was really a replica of one that had stood at the gates of some ancient civilization that he had once been a part of, maybe even Atlantis. He told Toomeh how he had dreams in which he saw a magnificent city of crystal and light, with this very statute at its eastern gate. Toomeh felt a tingling in his body as he listened to the man, and imagined the city of crystal and light as the man described it. The more he listened, the more certain he felt that this was the person meant to receive his message.

Maepleida and Heipleido were standing outside Yankee stadium, when a young man in plaid Bermuda shorts came up to them and offered to sell them two tickets for the afternoon game. Heipleido produced some money from his pocket. Holding the money out to the man, he asked him to take the price of two tickets.

"Oh, foreigners, don't know our money, huh. Here. This is what you pay me," he said taking eight twenties from Heipleido's bank roll. "The entrance is over there."

Inside the stadium they found their seats next to a young couple wearing Yankee caps and eating hotdogs and drinking beer. When a guy came by with a tray around his neck, selling food, Maepleida and Heipleido ordered the same thing. As Maepleida started to take a sip of beer, the man next to her suddenly blurted out, in an almost protective way, "That's not good for you, it's alcohol."

Maepleida, unabashed, smiled at him, and he hastily apologized for his remark. "I don't usually tell strangers what to do."

His girlfriend looked at him like he was out of his mind.

This man's instinct to protect her made Maepleida feel there must be a reason. Unconsciously, he must know her, or at least realize that she's wasn't who she seemed to be, and that alcohol might harm her. When his girlfriend left to go to the bathroom, Maepleida spoke to him and delivered her message. His eyes filled with tears hearing her words, but his girlfriend returned before he could speak, so he answered her only with his eyes, which told her of his gratitude for her message.

Heipleido picked up the tension between the man and his girlfriend and suggested to Maepleida they stroll about the stadium. They said goodbye to the couple and climbed the steps up to walkway. As they walked past the VIP section, Heipleido got the creeps looking through a glass window at a bunch of people drinking and eating in an unconscious way, with no gratitude. A man who was passing them on the walkway saw Heipleido staring and volunteered, "That's the Goldman Sachs box, sweet huh."

Maepleida glanced at it and shuddered. For a moment, she felt as if she was looking at a bunch of reptiles. "We have to get away from here," she said. "If they are working for the dark side, they'll see us for who we really are and we'll be in danger."

Heipleido took her elbow to leave, but it was too late. One of the men had noticed them looking into the box and was coming out, walking fast, right toward them. Heipleido felt it better to stand their ground than to look like they were fleeing. Maepleida attempted a smile when the man asked in a threatening tone if there was anything he could do for them. But her smile failed as her skin crawled at his nearness. Without her higher dimensional powers she couldn't be sure, but her intuition told her he was likely a reptilian posing as a human, come to corrupt and enslave earth beings. But how to get away? Did he perceive that they weren't really third dimensional? And if he did, what would he do to them? Someone inside knocked on the window of the box, held up a cocktail and motioned him back inside. Luckily the lure of the drink worked. Tossing them a look of distain, he withdrew.

"That man who knocked on the window, he had El Morya's eyes. No human or reptilian has eyes that color blue," Maepleida said.

"Are you suggesting El Morya took over the being's body for a moment to distract the reptile?" Heipleido asked her.

"I am."

"Come on, let's get out of here."

"What now?" Maepleida said once they were outside the stadium.

"I don't have a clue," Heipleido answered. "Maybe we should get back on the train, and go the other way from how we came up here."

Once they were seated on the train heading back downtown, the doors between the cars opened, and a man came through holding out a paper bag and asking for money. Heipleido reached into his pocket for some bills. He liked something about the man. He was old and unkempt and he didn't smell too good, but he had an angelic face. When he got to Heipleido, Heipleido slid over and offered the man a seat next to him. Surprised, the man sat down anyway, still holding his paper bag open. Heipleido emptied his pockets into the man's bag. Everyone on the train was now watching. Maepleida, observing the expressions of the other passengers, suggested that the three of them get off at the next stop and stroll together.

"Why not," the man said.

By the time they reached the top of the subway stairs, Heipleido was sure this was his person, and he delivered his message. The man appeared not to be at all phased as he listened. Then he surprised them by telling them that he knew he came from some far-off universe, which he visited in his dreams, and that even as a boy he'd known that Earth wasn't his true home, and that he'd never been able to make sense of how to get on in the third dimension.

"Maybe you're from the Pleiades," Heipleido said. The man

gave them a radiant smile when he heard these words.

"Maybe so," he said. "Is that where you're from?"

Heipleido looked at Maepleida with a question on his face. She nodded.

"Yes, that's where we're from."

Meanwhile, Ederah and Bereh were wandering around The Met trying to sense something. Ederah stopped to ask one of the museum guards a question about the giant Buddha. Listening to the guard speak eloquently of the Buddha, Bereh got a haunting feeling. Certain that this was his person, he looked directly into the guard's eyes, and addressed him in the manner of one enlightened being speaking to another. Tears filled the guard's eyes as he recounted to them the persistent feeling he had that he didn't belong, that he'd come from somewhere else in the universe, and that there was something he should remember, something he was supposed to do, but which always seemed to be just beyond the reaches of his memory. Bereh told him that he was right, that his true home was in another dimension, and that his mission was to awaken on Earth, and remember his own Divinity, and then to help others to realize that they, too, had Divine origins. The guard, whose name was Angelo, expressed his gratitude to Bereh over and over, with tears streaming down his cheeks. Angelo was reluctant to let them leave, and abandoned his post to accompany them all the way to the Met's front entrance.

It wasn't until they'd said goodbye to the guard and were standing at the top of the Met's big stone staircase that Ederah intuited anything special about anyone. Then, down at the bottom of the big outdoor stairs, she spotted an elderly woman, bent over with care and age, pushing a shopping cart piled high with empty cans and bottles. Sensing that this was her person, Edereh flew down the stone steps.

While Ederah was running down the stairs to her woman, Soonam and Attivio were strolling in Central Park, people watching. They sat down by the sailboat pond to rest and enjoy the small boats made to zoom around the charming oval pond by hand-held remotes. Soonam glanced over toward the statue of Alice in Wonderland. Several children were climbing over it and under it and around it. But there was a little girl in a wheelchair, unable to climb, sitting alone, parked in her chair, near the mad hatter. The child smiled as she watched the other children playing. Soonam walked closer and overheard the child's caregiver, who was some distance from the child, explaining that the little girl had been deprived of oxygen during the birth process and would never walk. Approaching the girl, Soonam knelt down by her side. Fortunately, the caregiver was so engrossed in her conversation that she didn't even notice Soonam engaging with the girl. The child's life was transformed from the moment of Soonam's kneeling. She accepted the information Soonam gave her with a completely open heart, as if she'd been sitting there just waiting for Soonam to appear to her to explain how the catalyst of illness works to help with awakening. Soonam slipped off the rose quartz ring she was wearing and gave it to the child, telling her that whenever she looked at the ring she would remember their conversation and her own Divine origin. The child put the ring in the pocket of her dress and laid her hand over the pocket. "I have a secret treasure box at home. That's where I'll keep it," she told Soonam.

"Yes, Soonam told the child, "let it be our secret."

Reluctantly, Soonam stood up, and she and Attivio walked the short distance from the statue to a restaurant overlooking the lake.

Attivio was so pleased for Soonam that he nearly missed his own person, even though she was serving them watermelon coolers as they sat in the Boathouse Restaurant watching the many rowboats out on the surface. A young couple with a child and a chocolate lab in their boat rowed by.

"Careful Beatrice," the mother called when the little girl

leaned a little too far over the edge of the boat. But the dog was there first, nudging the child back down onto the safety of her seat. Next Soonam's eyes rested on an elderly couple, rowing slowly but proudly, and taking obvious pleasure in the water, and at still being part of the flow of it all. Soonam felt she could sit there all day watching, but Attivio hadn't found his person yet. Then, their waitress came to present the check, and she chanced to say. "You don't seem like you're from here."

Attivio felt his intuition leap like a trout from the rapids. She might have meant they seemed like tourists, but that's not the way Attivio heard it. And it was just in time, because only moments after he spoke to her of her true origin they felt the tug of the merkaba. Moments later, New York City's blue sky vanished, and they were all once again standing under the trees outside the temple, beneath the rosy pink of the Venusian sky.

Amerissis and El Morya came out of the temple and addressed them. "Welcome back," Amerissis said. "And well done all of you. You've had a taste of current day life on Earth in a big city, in third dimensional reality. Each of you has successfully completed the task, using only your intuition. Bravo, you all succeeded without the use of your higher dimensional powers. This is most heartening for your future mission to Earth. Well done, one and all. I hope you now have a better sense of the humans, and a little liking for them. As you metabolize today's adventure let it deepen your love and appreciation for third dimensional beings. Be no lover of only higher dimensional specimens, instead be fascinated also by the wild and the weeds of the third dimension."

Amerissis lifted her sword and restored their fifth dimensional powers. A collective sigh went up from the group as their higher chakras reopened and began spinning again, initiating feelings of lightness and joy. Amerissis laughed a tinkling laugh at their relief. El Morya stood beside her tasting the sound of her laughter as if it was a cool drink after a trek across the Sahara.

After swallowing, he spoke to them. "Some of you encountered the dark lords during the exercise. Be assured, they are abroad in the land, but they are no match for the power of love," he said, blue eyes flashing. "We will leave you now, beloveds, but remember, a simple prayer from your heart will bring us to your field with our legions of blue flame angels. Call on us, and we will work to keep you aligned with your purpose and with the will of your soul. Once you are on Earth, visit our temple in Darjeeling during your sleep time. There you will be restored and supported in your mission. Amerissis and I will be your friends of light and our presence will guide you until your glorious victory. May courage and determination accompany you always." El Morya raised his staff, and Amerissis her sword. Together they blessed the group. Waves of blue light flowed out over the assembled faces and bodies, bestowing a feeling of bliss. Then the pair vanished, even before all the waves of bliss had reached the future wanderers.

Friends sought each other in the crowd gathered before the temple. Toomeh, his heart pounding, searched intently for Laaroos. Soonam and Attivio headed for their tree and found Ederah and Bereh already there. Maepleida and Heipleido arrived next. The afternoon had grown long, and the pink sky was streaked with transparent gold, by the time they all settled under the comfort of the tree to exchange stories about the humans they'd met on Earth. Each of them had had to rely on a human to find the place they sought. And in each case, the humans had been open and helpful. Soonam couldn't get either the dark-haired girl and her dog, Obi Wan, or the little girl by the Alice in Wonderland statue out of her mind. Laaroos felt an ease about her mother that she hadn't known in hundreds of years. Ederah's heart had gone out to the lady with all the cans, living such a hard life on the street. And Toomeh said he would long remember the man he'd met on the top of the Goddess Statue in New York Harbor. Heipleido imitated the big, toothless smile of the man from the underground train. Bereh felt a lovely serenity. Attivio shared how he'd recognized his person in the nick of time, just before New York City vanished. Only Maepleida seemed out of sorts. The brush with the reptilian and his hate filled look had brought home the reality of the dangers this mission would entail.

While Maepleida fretted, Toomeh's mind was full of Laaroos's luminous beauty. The sensation of sitting there, under the tree, next to her, in uncertainty was almost unbearable. *Beauty and order are heavens first law. And here beside me, is beauty incarnate. Why am I leaving heaven to go on this mission to Earth? But then Laaroos herself is going. Now, more than ever, she'll be committed.* His mind was so full of her that he didn't hear the gong which called them to the temple for the evening meditation.

Laaroos turned to him and asked, "Are you coming?"

Lady Venus awaited them in the temple. She explained that she wished them to recharge and reorient to the fifth dimension by means of a group meditation. She instructed them to use light, focusing on any ray of their choice.

"Consider all twelve rays, the seven within the body as well as the five extrinsic, in making your choice. Twin flame pairs will use the same ray as their twin flame for the meditation."

For a moment, Soonam again thought of the rainbow which she'd seen in her vision of the father and daughter eating pink ice cream by the fountain, in what she now knew was Washington Square Park in New York City. She tried to remember if the rainbow, arching over the fountain, had been seven colors or twelve, but she could no longer see it. Attivio suggested to her that they use the violet ray of transmutation for the meditation, and Soonam agreed. Maepleida and Heipleido chose the blue ray of the will of God, as they were grateful for El Morya's rescue at the stadium. Ederah and Bereh chose the yellow-gold ray of the resurrection flame. Toomeh chose the pink ray of cosmic love. Laaroos, unbeknownst to Toomeh, also chose the pink ray of cosmic love.

The gong rang three times to signal the beginning of the meditation. All eyes closed at the sound. Before long, the temple inhabitants were deep in a state of timeless bliss. Any being looking upon the scene, from a dimension able to see the rays, would have witnessed beautiful light in many colors pouring down through the open temple roof into the beings beneath it, and rising up through the floor into the soles of their feet, and swirling in spirals up their bodies to meet the down-pouring light rays. An hour passed as if no time had elapsed, when the gong signaled the end of the group meditation.

The last rays of pink-gold light caressed them as they emerged from the temple in silence, each of them still in a state of bliss. Ederah gazed up at the sky and wondered if there was light anywhere, in any universe, as beautiful as Venusian light. Bereh, who was also a native of Venus, answered her softly. "I very much doubt it, but then, as we're Venusian natives, we must be allowed our prejudice." These weeks of training on Venus were a joyous homecoming for them. Tomorrow was a free day and they planned to visit Ederah's family and to take all their friends along, including Laaroos, who had now become part of the group.

Chapter 4

The Visit

The next day dawned, like all days on Venus, warm and luscious, with a luminescent sky. Together the eight friends created a counter-rotating field of energy, of a sufficient speed to activate a group merkaba which could transport them to Ederah's parents' home, on the other side of Venus. Since transport by merkaba is instantaneous, they arrived at Ederah's parents' country estate the same moment they left the temple grounds.

Hundreds of years could go by between Ederah's visits with her parents, depending on where in the confederation they were all serving. Although time in the fifth dimension is very different from time as experienced on Earth, in the third dimension, it nevertheless felt like a while since all of them had been on Venus together. Often the mansion stood empty and shuttered. But today the large, comfortable home, made of ancient stone the color of pale gold, was open and inviting, and Ederah's parents were there to welcome them. Being reunited with her parents always had the effect of opening Ederah's heart, and when the heart opens, the mind naturally slows down. When the mind slows down sufficiently, a Buddha-like quality pervades the being. This was the state in which Ederah now found herself as she placed her palms together and bowed slightly to acknowledge the Divine resting within her mother and father. Her parents returned the bow. Then Ederah introduced her fellow volunteers, and bows were offered all around.

Over breakfast on the spacious terrace, made of the same stone as the house, they discussed plans for the day. Ederah's mother suggested a walk in the gardens and orchards, followed by luncheon under the trees, a rest, then an afternoon swim under the waterfall. And later there would be a dinner. The plan delighted them, everyone was more than ready to be only in the present moment, and to forget the mission to Earth and the looming separation from one another. Soonam listened to the plans for the day with pleasure as she gazed at the flowers surrounding the terrace. Hundreds of blue and white blossoms grew alongside the terrace walls, and climbed up to spill onto the parapet, draping themselves over it and tilting their little faces up as if to say good morning. Soonam returned their greeting. She very much loved all beings of the second dimensional world, particularly flowers.

After breakfast, eager to leave behind all desire for anything, except the wish to let the day unfold as it would, the group started toward the gardens, rejoicing in the peace of the moment. The walk was sweet relief after the intense training of the last few days. The contact with nature had the same effect on them that it has on third dimensional beings, it healed and soothed, not only their brain waves, but their souls, completely restoring them to a blissful state. Soonam remarked on the feeling. "This is so delicious that I could fly right off the ground, up into the treetops, and commune with the birds." She danced along spinning around in the tall grass.

"But you can fly up into the treetops if you wish," Attivio called after her. "Lady Amerissis did restore your higher powers after the exercise in New York," he teased.

"Yes, but to fly up there, I'd have to leave you here on the ground, and that, I'm reluctant to do."

"But you don't," Attivio corrected her, and the next moment they both found themselves high up in the tree branches, in propinquity with a small bird decked in orange and turquoise feathers, who gave out a surprised chirp in his sweet voice when he suddenly found himself in their company.

"I hope you don't mind the intrusion, little one, it's only for a moment – to say hello," Soonam chirped back to him. At the sweet sound of Soonam's voice, the little bird hopped onto her upheld palm, upon which she manifested a small, violet fruit not unlike a raspberry. To Soonam's delight, he ate it with relish and tilting his little head looked under her palm for more.

Ederah, arm in arm with her mother, strolled under the tree where Soonam and Attivio sat perched feeding the little bird. Mother and daughter smiled up at the scene in the tree.

Before Ederah's birth, her parents had volunteered for a previous mission to Earth. They had been among those of their group who had managed to awaken in the third dimension, and to return to their home dimension safely, but many of their number had failed to realize their true identity and remained stuck, reincarnating on Earth in the third dimension. Her mother hoped that Ederah's mission would succeed in lifting up these old friends so they could awaken, realize their true identity, and return to the sixth dimension. But even with this to hope for, part of her wished that Ederah hadn't volunteered to go. Ederah picked up her mother's thoughts, and gave her arm a gentle squeeze. "It'll be alright."

Soonam said goodbye to the little bird, took hold of Attivio's arm, and together they flew down from the tree and landed by a bush of peony-like flowers. Attivio picked a large, lacey pale-pink blossom and placed it in Soonam's hair.

"I wonder if they'll have these on Earth."

"I hope so," Soonam answered. "They display the beauty of infinite intelligence, so they should be everywhere, although, I didn't see any in New York City."

Attivio leaned in to smell the flower he'd placed in her hair and brushed her neck with his kiss. Maepleida and Heipleido who were nearby heard their conversation. Heipleido assured them that indeed, he had seen flowers similar to these on Earth in country gardens.

Some distance behind the others, Bereh strolled side by side with Ederah's father. They were so comfortable in one another's presence that even their thoughts were still. Her father had been pleased with Ederah's choice of Bereh for a husband. There was something undeniably decent, positive and straightforward about Bereh. Even for a fifth dimensional being, he was spectacular. And then there was the fact that he was Ederah's twin flame. Even if he hadn't approved, there would have been no stopping it.

Toomeh and Laaroos were still not quite admitting who they might be to one another. Unable to think about anything but each other, they walked along together without meaning to touch, but every so often, one or the other of them would accidentally stumble into the other, and then apologize with an embarrassed word. Toomeh's eyes remained polite, but his heart wanted to jump on her. The morning passed for all of them in a kind of rustic bliss.

Lunch, too, was a rustic affair of ambrosia, bread and cheese, vegetables and fruit, served on a long wooden table under the trees.

"Lady Venus and Lord Kumara must have you practicing eating solid food," Ederah's mother said, passing the cheese board to Maepleida, "in preparation for life on Earth." She'd noticed that Maepleida had been all but silent the entire morning.

Maepleida graciously accepted the proffered wooden board and selected a single piece of cheese before passing the board to Heipleido, who helped himself to several tasty looking hunks. Soonam leaned forward and took a deep breath over a large bouquet of the same pale-pink blossoms as the one which Attivio had placed in her hair. The blossoms graced the center of the table in a shapely amphora vase. Sunlight falling through the leaves of the overhanging branches decorated the table in a golden pattern of light and shadow. Each time the breeze blew, lifting the tree branches above them, the pattern moved across the table and then fell back into place. Ederah's father poured nectar into all the goblets and offered a toast to their mission. Toomeh opened a ripe fig for Laaroos and offered it to her. Although everyone noticed the intimacy of his gesture, no one commented, or even telegraphed a thought. But each of them was secretly happy, especially Soonam, who felt all things keenly. A more beautiful face it would be impossible to find, Toomeh thought, as he extended his hand to offer the open fruit to Laaroos. Her cheeks blushed to a color nearer to crimson than pink.

After lunch, they all lay about in the grass on oyster colored silk and velvet cushions, strewn on Persian carpets, which their hostess had materialized for them. During her incarnation on Earth, Ederah's mother had lived in ancient Persia, and had fallen in love with the silk and wool carpets from Esfahan. She often recreated objects of beauty which she had seen on Earth, such was her love and appreciation for the blue planet, and for the creativity of its people. Lying in nature under the rose and gold sky, enjoying the luxury which Ederah's mother had provided for them, there was nothing to disturb any of their thoughts, and so with still minds, they rested in the serenity of their hearts. As she lay back on a pile of cushions, Maepleida glanced to the left and imagined for a moment that she saw a beautiful lady in a long, emerald gown, which trailed behind her as she slowly walked along in the tall grass, followed by slender birds with blue-green plumes. Wondering if this was real or imagined, Maepleida lowered her eyelids, only to find another scene unfolding behind them.

It was the lady she had just seen walking in the grass, but this time she was in a drawing room full of people in elegant dress, holding cocktails. Rich paintings, both landscapes and portraits, and several busts adorned the large, well-appointed room. The woman no longer wore a long gown trailing behind her, but instead a short, ivory brocade cocktail dress and diamond earrings. She was part of a small group gathered around a man who was speaking on what appeared to be a serious topic. The woman interjected a comment, and everyone turned to her in surprise. She smiled to herself at their reaction, before gliding away from them.

Maepleida opened her eyes and the scene vanished. This must be what the others had experienced, she thought. Who was this woman in brocade? Was she to be her mother, on Earth? Maepleida didn't want to think about it. And not wanting to think about it, she exhaled, and decided to let nothing disturb her as she descended the stairway from her mind, to recline in her heart. After an hour or so of rest, Ederah's father broke the silence and suggested a swim. Maepleida was the first to get up. She threw her head back like a horse tossing its plume, impatiently trying to shake off some unwanted feeling which was trying to possess her. Ederah watched her, then stood and extended her hand to Bereh. Bereh, who was a trifle clumsy in his hybrid body, grasped her hand, and allowed himself to be pulled up. Soonam seemed to be gazing far off, as if she were watching bees among the flowers in the further field. But at a word from Attivio, she turned her large, violet eyes up to him, and taking hold of both his extended hands, leapt up. With carefree ease, they all made their way to the small lake on the other side of the estate. Fed by a waterfall, the lake looked like melted diamonds in the sunlight. At the sight of the rushing water, the little group came to a halt and watched as falling jewel followed falling jewel, and slipped into the lake.

Heipleido suggested they have a little fun and use as inspiration for their swim suits what they imagined people wore on Earth to go swimming. Using only their intention, they transformed their clothes into swimming costumes. Soonam created a one-piece swimsuit in a playful flower pattern, with large blossoms in shades of pink and tangerine. Then she added a bathing cap in the shape of a flower with petals. Ederah created a sea-green two-piece which tied behind her neck, and Maepleida chose a bright red one-piece with a heart shaped bust line. To amuse Soonam, Attivio made his trunks a playful print of swimmers under a waterfall. Bereh was sedate in navy blue trunks and Heipleido created black trunks with a red trim to complement Maepleida's red suit. Toomeh and Laaroos were still deliberating, until Soonam suggested they design something for each other. "But no pressure," she added, and everyone laughed. Toomeh focused on Laaroos for barely a moment, and presto, there she stood, looking every inch a goddess in a white one-piece swimsuit perfectly fitted to her gentle curves. Everyone applauded. Then Laaroos put her finger to her bottom lip, set her intention, and Toomeh stood next to her in matching white trunks, bearing a small emblem representing Arcturus. He took her hand and pulled her toward the waterfall. When they disappeared behind it, Soonam shot Attivio the biggest smile. Heipleido, full of energy as always, plunged in and called to Maepleida, who followed him.

Ederah's parents chose not to swim, but manifested nineteenth century English chaise lounges for themselves, and reclined to watch the others. Ederah meant to sit a while with her parents, so Bereh flung himself down on the ground with a little more passion and a bit less grace than he'd intended. Try as he might, it was hard to reconcile being separated from Ederah for this mission. And she felt the same. *He is so perfectly sensitive, so kind and decent*, Ederah thought, as she watched him nearly fall to the ground beside her.

After a little rest, Bereh started to roll some thought up and down the deck of his mind, trying to give it shape, but then pushed it overboard, and standing up, took Ederah's hands and pulled her to her feet. A moment later, they too were swimming to the waterfall. Beside her, in the water, Bereh watched Ederah's fingers pierce the surface, her great sapphire ring flashing as her fingers dipped beneath the water and rose up again, only to disappear from sight once more. The sapphire had been his mother's ring in times of old.

Heipleido manifested a ball and suggested a game similar to water polo. And they all so lost themselves in play that the mission to Earth was even more completely forgotten. Like all happy parents, Ederah's delighted in listening to the joyful voices ringing above the water. Even Maepleida seemed to forget herself, much to Heipleido's joy. Seeing her happy, he started to perform wildly for her pleasure. Among his super powers were extraordinary strength, speed and agility. He excelled not only at lifting heavy objects with his will and running nearly at the speed of light, but also at leaping to great heights. To everyone's delight, Heipleido leapt sixty feet into the air to reach to the top of the waterfall. From there he executed a perfect swan dive.

More to gain Laaroos's approval than to outshine Heipleido, Toomeh, whose super power was shape shifting, changed himself into a pale-grey dolphin and leapt about beneath the falls before offering Laaroos a ride on his back. Dolphins were native to Venus and very beloved. Dolphins, too, had been among those who had volunteered for previous missions to Earth, and many still voluntarily remained there in the oceans, attempting to raise the vibration on the planet. When Ederah remarked that riding a dolphin looked like great fun, Bereh used Toomeh's blueprint to turn himself into a dolphin, too. Attivio and Heipleido did the same. The dolphins didn't disappoint, diving deep under the water and leaping high into the air, they created much delight for their passengers.

After the dolphin rides, Maepleida introduced a game of tag, declaring herself the first to be 'it', then promptly doubled herself, challenging them to tag only the original of her. Fortunately, Soonam's superpower was psychometry and simply by feeling the aura of an object or person she knew it's entire history. She set off through the water in hot pursuit of first one, then the other Maepleida, directing the others to the original once she found it. Ederah was the one who finally tagged Maepleida, which caused everyone to groan, as one of Ederah's powers was the ability to become instantly invisible. Tagging an invisible 'it' would require a special superpower. Attivio, who was adept at time control stepped up to the challenge. Without warning, he dialed the time to the moment before Ederah had made herself invisible, and when she popped back into sight Laaroos, who was swimming next to her, reached out and tagged her.

"Bravo," Toomeh shouted, evoking a blush from Laaroos.

Spent, after all their play, the friends threw themselves down on towels to rest and sip ambrosia from lovely, tall, crystal glasses with candied rose petals floating in them. Soonam, who loved dressing up, suggested an idea for the evening.

"Let's pretend we're having dinner on Earth, during a period when people still dressed for dinner in evening clothes."

They debated which country and which time period, and finally agreed on England, in the year 1920. Ederah's mother said she would create the appropriate table setting and food, as she especially enjoyed this kind of challenge.

"When we return to the house," she told them, "I'll set the crystal in the library, which connects to the Akashic records, to 1920 in England/elegant dinners, and we can all have a look to get the general idea of the costumes, food and decor."

When the late afternoon sky began to turn a soft pink, they made their way back to the house in pairs, to prepare for the evening. Soonam particularly loved this moment of the day, when the afternoon light turned soft, and all the promise of the evening lay ahead. By the time they reached the doors of the mansion, the waning light had turned the hills violet, and the woods deep purple. Seen from the outside, the house began to light up, first one room and then another, like a small village coming alive. They gathered in the library to view the Akashic records. Each of the women delighted in the gowns and candelabra and crystals they viewed. In no time, Soonam was dashing up the staircase to get started on her gown. Attivio bounded after her. Ederah and Laaroos lingered a moment in the library, and overheard Toomeh remark to Bereh on how "women's hearts are even more intricate than their dress."

"But soo worth the effort of discernment," Bereh assured him. As they ascended the staircase to their room, Heipleido produced a bowl of rose water from behind his ear, like a magician, and offered it to Maepleida, that she might dip her fingers, which she did, like a queen. Walking behind them up the stairs, and seeing Heipleido's gesture, Laaroos said to Ederah, "How lovely to be adored as he adores her."

All were into the fun of creating their attire. Maepleida, ever elegant and sophisticated, created a sleeveless gold and silver gown which fell straight to the floor from her shoulders. A long necklace of tiny gold links, each the shape of the infinity symbol, hung almost down to her hips. Golden slippers peeped out from below her gown when she walked. She slowly executed a turn so that Heipleido might enjoy each angle.

"Magnificent," he said. "May I add a touch?" Maepleida nodded, and he adorned her shoes with small ankle straps made entirely of diamonds. He looked for a smile, which she at first denied him, then, laughing at his expectation, she gave him that which he sought. Taking hold of the tender flesh of her upper arm, to pull her closer to him, he kissed her on the lips, whispering into them, "Diamonds, to represent my incorruptible love for you."

In her suite across the hall from Maepleida's, Ederah was busy manifesting a floor length halter gown with a top made of pale-green jewels and a floor length skirt of silk in the same pale-green. Bereh came up to her in his tux and white tie, and placing her hair first behind one ear, then the other, attached an earring made of sea-green chrysoberyl to her left ear. It dangled down to rest its weight against her ivory throat. He turned her head and placed its twin on her right ear. Glancing in the mirror, her heart leapt at the beauty of the jewels. He pulled her back against his chest, encircling her with his arms, his head resting on her shoulder, the long jewel hanging from her ear caressing his cheek.

"Remember this moment, don't let it be wiped when you pass through the veil of forgetting as you enter Earth," he whispered into the secret passage in her ear.

Two doors down from Ederah and Bereh, Soonam floated across the room, stopped and twirled in a complete circle to give Attivio the full effect of her pale-blue creation in the 1920s flapper style. It fell just below her knees and plunged low in the back to a V, which reached well below her waist. Her long gloves, too, were of the palest blue, but her earrings were a deep sapphire. Attivio reached into his pocket, and pulled out a long sapphire and pearl necklace. Soonam dipped the slightest bit so he might place it over her head. He stepped back to look at her. She withstood his gaze without a blush, and spun round again with joy.

"Soonam," he began.

"Please don't," she said. "Tonight I can't think of being separated from you."

"Alright, darling, come here then, and make me forget about it."

Laaroos sat deliberating in her room, wanting to create something in white, as Toomeh had chosen white for her bathing suit, but not wanting to be too obvious. Ederah knocked lightly on her door and entered. Hearing her dilemma, Ederah told her to definitely go with the white, and then waltzed out of the room and left her to it.

When Ederah walked onto the terrace, she found her mother resplendent in a gold gown with a long, gold scarf floating off one shoulder and down her back. She led Ederah to the table to show her what she'd recreated from the image of a table in a grand English estate that she'd found in the Akashic records. The candelabras, flowers, crystal, silver and china had the effect of jewels glittering under a canopy of stars. After suitably appreciating her mother's effort, she turned to see her father and Bereh who were crossing the terrace and coming toward them, followed a few paces behind by Maepleida, Heipleido and Toomeh. They were nearly all assembled, missing only Soonam and Attivio and Laaroos.

"It's not like Soonam to be late for a party," Maepleida said.

"Finishing touches, I suspect," Heipleido countered, remembering the discussion he, Attivio and Bereh had had about the presentation of jewels.

"Oh, here they are now," Maepleida said. "We're all here, save Laaroos."

Moments later, Laaroos stepped onto the terrace where they all awaited her. At her entrance, the candles seemed to soar up and turn her skin to gold. Though she wore no jewels, and had used no artifice of makeup, she looked every inch a goddess in her Grecian style, floor length white gown of sheer silk, which draped in luscious folds about her body. Toomeh turned in time to see her entrance. At the sight of her, he felt as if gunpowder had ignited in his heart, which banged mercilessly against his ribs as he reached out his hand to receive her.

They began with golden bubbling drinks in crystal flutes, and a toast offered by Ederah's father to the unity of all beings as one. It was followed by a toast to their success, made by her mother. No opportunity for pleasure was lacking as they conversed under the velvet sky. Toomeh sat next to Laaroos and told her that sitting there beside her, he had a feeling of deep glittering peace, as if all the stars were showering them with love. Laaroos, fearful that her eyes would betray her before she was ready to speak her heart, lowered them and gazed into her glass. Had he been an ordinary man, Toomeh would have been bewildered, but he read her thoughts, and with a patient heart, accepted them.

Meanwhile at the other end of the table, Heipleido was recounting for Ederah's parents the details of the training they'd received the previous day from Master El Morya, and how he had been King Arthur in one incarnation, and how he'd told them that he had learned the true meaning of love that lifetime.

"I know the story well," Ederah's mother said. "That love triangle was a test for all three of them. Each had agreed to play a part, before incarnating, for one another's growth."

"How do you know all this?" Heipleido asked.

"I know El Morya well, and had many talks with him about the nature of love when I visited his temple in the Himalayas during my mission to Earth."

"But he seemed so cold to me," Maepleida said.

"Then you mistake him. He has a heart as big as the sky," Ederah's mother said softly, smiling at the memory of him.

After six courses under the stars, and more conversation, much of which was about their appreciation and love for the humans they had met in New York during their recent exercise, the perfect day was over.

"I hardly want to move," Bereh said, "eating food is quite pleasurable, but it tires one when you've been used to taking nourishment directly from light for so many centuries."

"Sorry, but you'll have to get up," Attivio joked, "we need your energy to create the merkaba."

Ederah bowed to her parents, not knowing when they would meet again. Everyone expressed gratitude for the day. Then they created rotating bands of energy in a star tetrahedron, sped it up, and vanished, leaving Ederah's parents standing alone before the stone mansion. Instantly, they were back on the temple grounds, still wearing their evening dress, standing under the shimmering stars. They climbed the grassy hill to their cottages, calling goodnight to one another as they walked, laughing their young laughter.

Chapter 5

Ancient Wisdom

The next morning, when Soonam and Attivio walked into the temple, they came face to face with a black jaguar and a golden goddess. As the pair stood together in the temple archway, the fragrance of cool mountain air emanated from them. She introduced herself as Shoshimi, twin flame of Lord Lanto, who at that moment was coming toward her holding his staff made of seven orbs of light in different colors, each color representing one of the seven rays. Lord Lanto, the great light of ancient China, Chohan of the Second Ray, the Yellow Ray of Illumination, shimmered with each step. He, Shoshimi and the jaguar, had arrived on Venus the previous evening from their retreat in the Grand Teton Mountains of Wyoming.

Lord Lanto spoke first. "I greet you beloved light beings with faith in your commitment to liberate mankind." All eyes were fixed on his chest as he spoke. There was a light so bright, glowing in the area of his heart, that it was visible right through his deep yellow-gold robes. He looked as if he'd swallowed a lantern. His hand went to his heart in acknowledgement of their stares. "I was able to manifest this bright flame of love during my last life as a human on Earth, when I learned that it is love which creates the vibration necessary to make photons. In that lifetime, I gained my mastery studying under Lord Himalaya, Manu of the Fourth Root Race, who taught me how to work with light energy. He showed me how to switch off my mind by activating my heart chakra. The mind slows down when the heart is activated. Ultimately, the ego will go once the heart stays permanently activated."

As Soonam listened to Lord Lanto's words, she unconsciously bowed her head in recognition of the truth he spoke. She felt as if he was speaking to them from an ancient time. Attivio shifted in his seat and accidentally brushed her arm. His fingers felt like flower petals on her skin.

"This state, where the head bows down before the heart, is normal for fifth dimensional beings, but it is not easy for humans, because the ego mind is a house they have lived in all their lives. And it is hard to give up one's familiar home. However, with guidance, humans can do it. They are also capable of union with God, for He is their creator, too, but, they must want this union as much as a drowning man wants air. In all the universe, there is nothing but the Lover and the Beloved. Humans have their beloveds, their true loves, their passions, and it is in this way that they prepare for the deepest love, the love of the Divine within each other and within their very selves. Love is the richest and most profound experience a human can have. Those humans who experience the depths of love share a profound gratitude, which raises their vibration and lifts them up to the gates of heaven." Here he sensed that Shoshimi, who stood beside him with the jaguar lying at her feet, wanted to add something. He turned to her and she spoke to the group.

"It is not only humans who love," she said. "The Creator also loves. He loves humans. They, too, are his beloveds. He is the maker of Souls. In every atom of every Soul, resides the Divine. Once human beings realize this, they will have no need for ego. Some humans already know this truth, but you will be the way-showers, and many more will receive this knowledge. The Divine will work through you. He is the Doer."

Attivio considered this description of love, and of the human ego as a house which a person has lived in all his life, and he started to understand the third dimensional challenge of attachment in a new way. As his mind played with images of the ego as a house, he lost track of Shoshimi's voice and found himself in the middle of a daydream.

A small boy in a Star Wars t-shirt and shorts stood next to a woman with curly red hair, facing a wall. The woman was cramming a small piece of folded up paper into a crevice between the stones of the wall. Draped over the woman's arm was a basket containing fruit and vegetables. Several men in tall black hats, and black suits with white shirts, stood near them talking. The courtyard was full of people putting bits of paper into crevices in the wall. Some were wailing, their palms and faces pressed against the stones of the wall. The boy tugged the woman's hand. She gave the folded paper one last push into the crack and backed away from the wall.

Soonam noticed Attivio drooping forward, his eyes closed, and guessed that he was having a vision, just as she'd had when she saw the little girl and the man by the fountain eating ice cream, so she didn't disturb him. But the next moment he jerked back and opened his eyes. He looked at her, then closed his eyes for a moment, then looked at her again. She saw he was disassembled by his vision, and tenderness for him swept through her, making her violet eyes soft as water.

Shoshimi paused, and seemed herself to be lost in some reverie. She looked up toward the vaulted ceiling and the pink sky beyond. The black cougar stirred at her feet. Finally, sure of her direction, she drew her eyes downward and fixed them on her audience. "I would speak to you of the present condition of human beings, so you will understand them better. With Amerissis and El Morya, you participated in an exercise where you met various humans in New York City. Today we'll build on that knowledge. Understand that the humans of today are not as spiritually powerful as they once were. Part of their DNA was deactivated 12,000 years ago, shortly before the destruction of Lemuria. The Galactic Councils of Light responsible for Earth imposed this restriction because of the misuse of power by the citizens of Atlantis. As a result of this deactivation of part of their DNA, humans have only the seven major chakras open, instead of the original twelve. The five sacred extrinsic chakras have been shut down. The seven rays that were left activated within the body do help with human spiritual evolution, but closing the five extrinsic sacred chakras has slowed down their spiritual development, and they are far less spiritually powerful."

Here Shoshimi paused, and looked to Lord Lanto to see if he would add his thoughts. He acknowledged her with a bow of his head, and stepped forward to speak. "Until humanity wakes up and develops a level of consciousness which can once again be trusted with sacred energy, they will not have access to the five secret rays. You will be born with these five extrinsic chakras deactivated as well, and you must remember the existence of these secret rays once you incarnate, and reactivate them in your new human body. When you reactivate them, the dark lords will become aware of you and attempt to seduce you to their ways. Failing that, they will try to destroy you. Choose always to communicate from your heart and this will help to protect you, for love is the greatest protection in all worlds. Invoking the Flame of Illumination in your crown chakra will be an added protection. The thousand petals of this chakra will expand to connect you with the Mind of the Divine, and the dark side will not be able touch you."

Shoshimi's light grew more brilliant as Lord Lanto spoke of The Flame of Illumination and she added, "The flame is indeed a powerful protector, but you must invoke it. If you do, it will guide you away from erroneous beliefs and corrupted religions. For, The Flame of Illumination is the flame of wisdom, knowledge, and clear thinking." She looked out over the group assembled before her as she spoke. Her feelings were complicated. She respected them for their choice to help, but she felt for them, too, because of the risk they were taking. After they had worked so hard to evolve on the path home to the Creator, they could lose everything for untold eons before finding the path of light again. She bowed her head, then lifted her eyes and turned to Lord Lanto. He again addressed them.

"We cannot alter the human bodies which you will inhabit,

but we can prepare your light bodies and arm them with the knowledge of how to awaken in human form. All human bodies are connected to their etheric forms by a cord of light. This cord runs from the human body to the Higher Self and up to the I Am Presence. When the body dies, the cord is withdrawn back up into the Higher Self. Most humans are not aware of this. We hope that this cord of light will be so strong in each of you that your human form will have access to all the knowledge in your higher bodies as soon as you open your five extrinsic chakras. Today we will do an exercise in which you will, like humans, have only your seven lower chakras functioning. With your permission, we will shut down the five chakras above the crown chakra in each of you, so you can experience life as humans do, with only the seven main chakras in the body open. Your challenge will be to use the vibration of love to create enough photons to reopen your five extrinsic sacred chakras. You may go anywhere on Venus, and engage in any activity you like, alone or in groups, in order to create the vibration of love which will form enough photons for you to reopen your five higher chakras. Remember, it is love which creates light."

There was a general rustling in the group as they anticipated undergoing this powering down and loss of their consciousness. Maepleida felt a momentary panic, unusual for her. Heipleido gave her a reassuring look, which didn't reassure her.

"With your permission, we will begin now the process of closing your higher chakras, starting with your twelfth. Your twelfth chakra, of shimmering gold, which connects you with the cosmos, and with the monadic level of divinity, is now closed," Shoshimi and Lord Lanto said together.

Soonam felt a wave of pain so strong at the loss of this connection to the Divine that she let out a gasp.

"Yes," Lord Lanto said, "it is indeed painful to be cut off from the heart of the Divine. But remember, love can create the light necessary to restore this connection. Next, we will close your eleventh chakra, the pink-orange chakra. As we close your eleventh chakra, you will lose your ability for teleportation, bi-location and telekinesis."

Maepleida winced at this loss. Bi-location was a special strength of hers and she sagged inside as she felt the pink-orange light evaporate from her aura.

"Moving down to your tenth chakra of pearl-white, you will now lose the power of divine creativity. You are no longer able to create at will that which you desire."

This was a shock particularly to Toomeh, whose fanciful side was well developed and which he employed in a variety of creative ways, mostly to delight others. He felt a darkness creeping towards him with the closing of his tenth, pearl-white chakra.

"We are now closing your ninth chakra, the blue-green chakra of your Soul blueprint which registers all your abilities, learned in all your lifetimes."

Ederah felt a sudden emptiness as her ninth chakra closed, as if she'd been struck and then hollowed out. Her eyes sought Bereh's. But his eyes were closed as he withstood the pain of this loss.

"And lastly, we close your eighth chakra, the sea-foam-green chakra which activates your spiritual skills." Everyone present crumbled a bit in their shoulders and spines, feeling this diminishment.

"Fear not dear ones," Lord Lanto said seeing their apprehension. "Seek to create the vibration of love. It is the vibration of love which will create the photons necessary to re-open your higher chakras."

Shoshimi then spoke to them. "Try to make a good time of it. Experience this new human-like state and see what you can do with it. Remember, create the vibration of love and all will return to you. Go now to the grounds around the temple and begin your work."

The eight friends made their way out through the temple arch. Feeling insecure in this weakened state, they decided to work together. They sat under their favorite tree, but nothing felt right. They looked around at one another to see if they looked different with their higher chakras closed. Attivio voiced what they were all thinking. "We look a little less radiant, I'd say."

"A little?" Maepleida said. "We're positively drab."

"We'd better get to work straight away then," Bereh offered. As usual, Bereh was relentlessly positive, but this time it didn't help Ederah, who appeared somewhat shriveled up.

"But how?" Ederah asked.

"Our heart chakras are all still open," Soonam said, hoping to restore Ederah. "We should be able to use that energy to create the vibration of love to make enough photons to reopen our higher chakras."

"Of course, you're brilliant, Soonam," Laaroos said. Toomeh beamed at Laaroos.

"OK, we'll focus on our hearts and add our breath. I think the breath is important, and what else?" Heipleido asked.

"Breathing into our hearts with deep full breaths is good, but I think we need an intention, some gift of love, if we're to create real photons," Ederah said, beginning to engage in the task.

"Right, why not try to create something beautiful for all the human beings on Earth," Bereh suggested.

"Yes," Soonam said. "Let's send waves of love to shower the Earth, and lift up all those who are suffering in fear and pain, all the beings on Earth, not just the humans, but the animals and plants and crystals and rocks, everyone on Earth."

"Good plan," Heipleido said. "But how will we know if it's working?"

"Hopefully we'll start to feel our upper chakras opening again," Laaroos said. "And with all eight of us creating the vibration together, it'll be stronger than if we each do it alone."

"Should we send our intention on a sound wave or color

wave or both?" Toomeh asked.

"Both I think," Laaroos said. "We can each choose our own color and mantra."

"Eyes open or closed?" Maepleida asked. It was the first she's joined in on this exercise.

"Any preferences?" Heipleido asked.

"Eyes open, I think, and mantras silent," Soonam said, "then we can see if there are any visible signs that we're creating photons." Everyone nodded in agreement as they arranged themselves in a circle under their tree.

Other groups of various sizes were scattered here and there on the grounds, also working on the assignment. Shoshimi, accompanied by her jaguar, and Lord Lanto walked among the groups, discussing their strategies with them.

When Shoshimi reached Soonam's group she asked what their plan was. Ederah spoke first. "We're planning to use our intention to send love to Earth and all her beings."

"And we'll enhance our intention with light and sound waves," Laaroos added.

"And breath," Attivio said.

Shoshimi nodded her approval. "Yes, much can be carried on the breath. Breathe through the invisible tube which runs through your body from one apex of your star tetrahedral field to the other. Breathing this way will enhance the life force and the love steaming through you. Make your intentions clear and strong and a bit more specific," she told them.

Before she could move on to the next group, Soonam caught Shoshimi's eye and asked her why she was accompanied by the jaguar. Shoshimi explained. "In one lifetime, I was eaten by a jaguar, and so carried a fear of the creatures. At first his presence was to help me conquer that fear, later he helped to remind me to be compassionate toward the fears of others. Now that I see all as One, I see him as a part of me, and in truth, I have long since grown to love his company. He is a dear friend and ally."

Maepleida hadn't been listening to this explanation but had instead remained focused on their task. "Be more specific, what did she mean?" Maepleida asked after Shoshimi moved on.

"Well, our intention to send love to Earth is pretty general and might not be easy to focus on," Heipleido told her.

"Maybe we should each pick a group or a cause or an area of the Earth where we want to focus our intention," Laaroos suggested. "I'd like to focus on all the wanderers who haven't yet awakened."

Toomeh felt a pang on her behalf, knowing how it had been for her to leave her mother behind on Earth after El Morya's training exercise. Laaroos sensed his support and bowed her head just slightly toward him, a gesture which ignited a fire in his heart.

"I'd like to send my love and healing to all the children of the Earth who are handicapped or sick or hungry or homeless or refugees," Soonam said. Attivio knew she was thinking of the little girl in the wheelchair, watching the other children climb about on Alice in Wonderland. When they walked away from the child, Soonam had remarked that there are those who would be destroyed by this unfairness, but this little girl had not been.

"I prefer animals to humans," Maepleida said. "I'll send my love to all the animals on Earth who are unloved and suffering."

Ederah bit her lip before speaking. "I'll send love to beings suffering from discrimination because of their race, religion or sexual orientation."

Bereh, moved by the quiet civilization in her choice, inclined his head to her in a small bow.

None of the men had yet spoken. Toomeh went first. "I'll send my love to all the victims of war, soldiers, refugees and civilians alike."

"I'll add my energy to yours, Toomeh," Heipleido said.

"There are many humans who the dark side has enslaved through addiction to drugs and alcohol," Bereh said. "I'll direct my energy to help them. It's down to you, Attivio."

"Yes, I'm thinking of those humans who are subjected to hatred and abuse. I'll focus on helping them."

"So, that's it, we're set then." Soonam beamed. "Shall we join hands and breathe as one before we begin?"

Shoshimi and the jaguar joined Lanto who was standing near the temple arch observing the groups before him. They began to feel the energy in the groups build as they focused their intention on achieving the vibration of love. If they could generate enough love it would create the photons necessary to re-open their higher chakras. Each group had chosen a slightly different creative approach to the task. Fixing his gaze above their heads, at the upper apexes of their star tetrahedrons, Lord Lanto watched and waited for their love to create the light necessary to open their higher chakras. Shoshimi squatted down beside the jaguar and whispered something to him before she, too, turned her gaze to the sky above the groups.

Slowly at first, and then more and more quickly, sea-foam-green spinning orbs of light began to appear a few feet above the heads of some, signifying the opening of the eighth chakra of Divine love and spiritual skill. Shoshimi's heart smiled at the sight. As she and Lanto continued to watch, the blue-green of the ninth chakra became visible fifteen feet above a few heads, restoring their Soul blueprints. Next, about fifty feet above them, here and there, the pearl-white light of the tenth chakra of Divine creativity began to spin. Soon after, the pink orange of the eleventh chakra could be seen a hundred feet up over the heads of more and more of them. Maepleida breathed a sigh of relief as she felt her powers of teleportation, bilocation and telekinesis return to her. Within twenty minutes or so, as time is measured on Earth, most of the groups had opened all the scared chakras, save the highest.

Lord Lanto scanned the sky above the groups, looking for the shimmering gold light that would signify their reconnection to the cosmos and the Monadic level of Divinity. Nothing yet. He waited and watched. Would they be able to create enough photons with their love to break through to the twelfth chakra, the chakra of connection to the cosmos and to Divinity itself? The very air over Venus seemed to be humming as he watched the sky above them. Still nothing. Then, yes, there it was, hundreds of feet up the first shimmering, gold, spinning orb, high above Soonam's head. Lord Lanto exhaled with great joy as more and more shimmering gold orbs joined Soonam's. The volunteers had done it. They'd created enough photons using the vibration of love to re-open all five of their scared chakras. Lanto and Shoshimi exchanged a look. This mission to Earth might just succeed.

The concentration of the participants was so focused that although many eyes were open, few of them were aware of the light show above them. Lanto called their attention to the beauty of the spinning orbs in the sky above their heads, which were normally invisible, but for the purposes of this exercise, Shoshimi had altered that.

"Bravo, my beloveds, she said. "Well done. Using the vibration of love, you will create miracles on Earth. We will leave you now. But, a simple prayer from your heart will bring us into your field." With Shoshimi's last words, two brilliant yellow rays flowed out from Lord Lanto's chest and his crown, and spread over the entire gathering, bestowing such mental clarity and power of discernment as few there had ever before felt, and creating in them a feeling of the pure bliss of being held in the endlessness of love.

Lady Venus materialized beside Shoshimi and Lanto, and thanked them for their effort on behalf of the mission. Then she released them all to rest and process what they'd just experienced. The gong would call them back in two hours' time. That afternoon they would be addressed by the Maha Chohans: Lady Ruth and her twin flame, Paul the Venetian. As Chohans of the Third Ray, the Flame of Cosmic Love, they would speak about the nature of love on Earth. When Toomeh heard who would be addressing them he glanced at Laaroos, who gazed back directly into his eyes before slipping her hand into his. When her fingers closed around his palm, he felt sure she must know that his heart was about to burst with love for her.

Soonam was also pleased by this announcement. "I love the pink ray. And now we're to meet the Chohans. Isn't Lady Ruth also known as the Goddess of Beauty?"

Attivio brushed her lips with his. "Come, let's join the others for lunch," he said, reaching for her hand.

As their group gathered under their favorite tree to relax, Heipleido and Maepleida seemed to be waiting for everyone to settle. Heipleido sat in his usual pose, with one foot resting on the knee of the other leg. Once everyone was comfortable, he told them that Maepleida had an announcement. As all eyes turned to Maepleida, she hesitated, until Heipleido nodded to her with infinite tenderness.

"I've changed my mind about going to Earth. I can't bear the thought of being in a human body and not knowing my true identity as a being of light. I don't want to spend lifetimes trying to force open a hidden door."

No one spoke. In truth, they all had their moments of doubt about what they were about to undertake. Besides, they were all higher dimensional beings who did not judge others. To judge another is a negative behavior that no being beyond the third dimension would engage in. Judgment of another impinges on their free will, and any violation of the free will of another life stream is an activity of the dark side.

"What will you do instead?" Toomeh asked.

"My plan is to return to the Pleiades, unless Lady Venus gives me permission to stay here until Heipleido incarnates on Earth. I'd like to see him through the training. I've requested a meeting with her to ask permission to stay.

"We'll all be separated either way," Laaroos said. "Now that I've just met Toomeh, the last thing I want is to incarnate into a third dimensional body and perhaps be stuck for eons."

"Neither of you has to do it," Maepleida said, standing up to reveal the splendor of her being.

"Many of my people from Arcturus went on the last mission with Shoshimi, Lord Lanto and Lord Kumara, and got stuck there. As you know, my mother was one of them. I have to go on this mission. When the call came it was like the answer to a prayer. I can't give it up, even for Toomeh," Laaroos said.

Despite being advanced souls, for whom no situation is emotionally charged, Maepleida's announcement stirred up confusing feelings in Soonam and Attivio, and Ederah and Bereh, too. They rose and strolled off, hoping to coax one another away from the fields of their own doubt. Toomeh and Laaroos soon followed the others. Left on their own, Heipleido took Maepleida in his arms. Despite her unconquerable face, she felt like a wounded tree. "I'll find my way back to you, no matter what," he whispered into her hair. She rested her head on his heart in a tender gesture that was unlike her.

When the gong called them back to the temple, Lady Ruth and Paul the Venetian, Chohans of the Ray of Cosmic Love, were already there. They stood resplendent in rose colored robes adorned with aquamarine stones. If it were possible, they may even have had a drop too much beauty. Before addressing them, Lady Ruth fixed her sparkling blue eyes on the group assembled before her, put her hands together in front of her heart and bowed slightly, in acknowledgement of their divinity. "Beloveds, we greet you this afternoon in the name of love, and the threefold flame cradled in each of your hearts."

At these words from Lady Ruth, Paul the Venetian bowed to them from the waist, and slowly lifting his head beamed out a vibration of such radiant love that it lit a fire in every one of their hearts.

Soonam turned a lovely shade of pink all over her body. Toomeh reached for Laaroos's hand. Tears gathered in Bereh's eyes. Even Maepleida seemed to melt a little.

"It is this threefold flame in your heart which signifies that you are a divine being. But we must remember that humans, too, are divine beings, and harbor the same threefold flame in their hearts as does each of you. It is true that most humans haven't yet realized this. But it is the hope of all the chohans of the seven flames that your mission will spark this consciousness in the people of Earth, lighting the threefold flame in the heart of every one of them. You will not accomplish this on the mind level, but will rather *infuse* this love into their hearts. If you succeed, you will create a paradise on Earth."

Lady Ruth had such a way of talking to them, and so great was the love in her being, that they hung on her words like pearls of dew reluctant to drop from the tall grass. Soonam was captured by the idea of infusing love into the hearts of humans as a way to create paradise on Earth. Imaging this made her shiver with pleasure.

"I know that some of you are questioning your decision to sign on for this mission," Paul the Venetian said, stepping forward. Maepleida shifted in her sapphire chair. Of course, he had picked up on her fear, he was an ascended master.

"It's true. This mission will be challenging. But know this, there is a sure pathway back to your home dimension. If you throw your heart into the sea of fire, the threefold flame will light your way home. The threefold flame is also the energy which will draw your twin flame to your side once you are on Earth." Here he paused and closed his eyes as if envisioning that holiest of reunions between twin flames, and his face shimmered with radiant bliss.

Attivio looked at Soonam, who was still pink and even more soft looking than usual. What he felt for her was too sweet to describe.

Paul the Venetian opened his eyes and continued. "The threefold flame can also create miracles of healing and rejuvenation on Earth. Once you engage it, you will be unstoppable, but you must remember to awaken it once you reach the third dimension. The journey into the heaviness of the vibration in the third dimension will stifle and perhaps turn your flame to embers. Fan it dear ones, so it may spring to life again and light the world. Once you ignite it, you will experience a feeling of pure physical bliss in your human body. If you can relax within that feeling of the endlessness of love, life in the third dimension will offer more joy than sorrow. The challenge really is to hold the state of love for all beings as one. When you are human, live with this thought every day. Even when you are doing the simplest things, shopping, cleaning, walking, remember the presence of the Divine in you, and in all beings. The Divine is in every shape around. Live with this presence all day long and you will be free from fear." He paused to study them before continuing and his eyes lingered on Laaroos, then on Toomeh, and a look of radiant joy came over his countenance. Toomeh observed this, but Laaroos had closed her eyes as she listened to him speak, and had slipped into a reverie.

A young Japanese woman, with her black hair piled up high on her head, and held in place with two lacquer sticks, stood before a full-length mirror in a pale-blue kimono with a pattern of white irises on it. Satisfied that the obi was secure, she smoothed down her kimono and gave a final touch to her shiny black hair. Then she turned and extended her hand to the little girl playing at her feet. The child was dressing and undressing her doll, trying different kimonos on it. As she played, she talked to her doll, asking her which kimono she liked best.

Toomeh glanced at Laaroos to see if she'd noticed that Paul the Venetian had looked directly at them, but seeing her eyes moving behind her closed eyelids, knew at once that she was somewhere else. He turned his attention once again to the speakers.

Lady Ruth picked up the thread of the talk. "Once you awaken the threefold flame of Divinity in your hearts, you will again be able to see all things as love, even while residing in the density of your human body. And seeing all things as love is what will free you from reaction. Reactivity creates imbalances and the feeling of separation which blinds one to the true reality that all are One. When you are nonreactive you can be a co-creator on Earth, just as you are here, in the higher dimensions. Use the threefold flame to wake up on Earth and remember that all things, all life, all of creation, is part of the one original thought. You are part of the original thought. Now, you see all, and love all as Self and as the One. Put this thought in your pocket for when you are human."

Laaroos felt her orange diamond seat jiggle, and opened her eyes with a start. Who was the Japanese woman who had in a few gestures before her mirror allowed Laaroos to imagine a whole life?

Paul the Venetian was now speaking. "Once you can see all things as love in the third dimension, that consciousness will prevent you from creating negative reactions in your emotional body. It is challenging to avoid negative reactions in the third dimension. But it must be done in order to keep your human body healthy. Negative reactions create imbalances in the body. These imbalances lead to physical and emotional illness. It is the imbalances caused by negativity which the dark side hopes to exploit. The dark side looks for opportunities to stir up negativity, to unbalance humans. Once out of balance, the body can easily become ill. And in the third dimension, it will not be as easy for you to heal physical illness." Here he paused to make sure they got his point. Seeing that they were with him, he continued. "So, you see dear ones, emotional balance is necessary to stay healthy in a human body. Emotional balance prevents you from being blinded by feelings of separation and judgment. Balance allows you to be fully imbued with fearless love. And against fearless love, the power of the dark side is helpless, and melts away."

Ederah strayed again into the fields of doubt. How were they to stay emotionally balanced in the slow, heavy vibration of the third dimension? Maepleida's announcement had challenged the high battlements of what she had considered her incorruptible commitment to this mission. Her commitment no longer felt as durable as stone, but seemed to be crumbling like ash. Bereh read her thoughts. And at the touch of his mind, she relaxed and picked up the message he was sending her: *Against my fearless love for you, across all dimensions, and all eternity, the dark side will have no chance.* The touch of Bereh's mind, like cool leaves brushing her face, restored her. She flashed him a look of gratitude. Both turned their attention back to Lady Ruth and Master Paul the Venetian.

"There is a method to overcoming negative reactions like anger," Paul the Venetian explained. "Acknowledge your anger, accept it as a type of red ray energy, accept it as a part of yourself. The first acceptance is acceptance of self, especially negative aspects of your third dimensional self. Let your anger be understood, integrated and loved as part of yourself. Difficult situations which provoke human anger are catalysts which offer experience. Love and accept the catalyst as your teacher."

"Yes," Lady Ruth interjected, "when you are in human form, there will be many catalysts and it will be far more difficult to maintain your emotional balance and a state of fearless love. You will have to think before you act, or even feel, or you will destroy your balance and your state. If you remain calm and accepting, you will enable your Higher Self to reestablish your divine blueprint, and return your electrons to their natural orbit and frequency. Your human body will be made of electrons, just as your light body is. Everything on Earth is made of electrons, just as it is in the higher dimensions. In the fifth dimension, you consciously work with the unlimited supply of electrons at your disposal to create whatever you choose to create. As higher dimensional beings, you are conscious creators. You also understand that when the electrons that make up your body are moving in their natural orbit they enable your body to draw in large quantities of light. And you use that light, along with your intention, to qualify the electrons at your disposal to create whatever you want." Lady Ruth allowed her words to sink in before turning to Paul the Venetian, so he might add his thoughts.

"I would remind you," he began, "that light is not only for creative purposes. Light is also your protection. Light is the food of your inner bodies and the way to accelerate your vibration. All this you now take for granted, and may not even think of. But you will have to consciously think of it once you are in a human body. And once in a human form, you will need to consciously draw in light from the lower apex of your star tetrahedral field, into the soles of your feet, upward through your body, through your pineal gland, up to your crown and to the upper apex of your star tetrahedral field. You must do this daily in order to keep your electrons in the orbit of their divine blueprint. The magnetic fields about your human body will become stronger as you draw the spiraling energy up through the soles of your feet to meet the down flowing energy from within. As you meditate you will raise the level where the two energies meet. For most humans, the up-streaming and down-pouring light meet at the solar plexus chakra. But for many more now, the two streams have breached the heart chakra. This is good news. As Earth moves into the fourth dimension, those who operate from the heart chakra and above will be able to make the leap to the next dimension with the planet."

Maepleida tried to focus on the information she was receiving, but her mind kept going over the question of whether or not she was making the right decision. Heipleido felt the disorder in her normally ordered mind, but knew she was discovering herself. Inclining his head toward her, he inhaled her scent. She smelled of trees beside a mountain stream.

"As a human, you will need to be in a harmonious state, free of emotional reactivity, in order to utilize these streams of light energy. For a balanced entity, no situation is emotionally charged. A balanced entity is non-reactive. Since it has been many eons since you were reactive to potentially upsetting situations, you may not remember what a struggle it can be to hold your state in the face of upsetting situations." Here he paused and studied them for a moment. Satisfied that they were with him, he continued. "To remind you of how challenging it is to remain balanced in the third dimension we propose an exercise, during which you will re-experience the phenomenon of being gripped by an emotionally painful situation. Your challenge in this exercise will be to remain emotionally balanced despite the situation. This will best be accomplished by remembering that all are One. There are no others. Since that is the ultimate truth, there is no reason for anger at others. This realization will calm your painful reaction. The battle on Earth will be won person by person, soul by soul, as each being manages his anger. This is how the planet will be saved."

Soonam turned this over in her mind. Thinking of it this way, it seemed a more manageable task. If she could hold her state in the face of frustration, and not give in to anger and retaliation, then the battle might be won in each moment, day by day. Attivio picked up her thoughts, transmitted out from her hair, hair the color of pale wheat.

"It is emotional reactivity which leads to the nuclear wars which destroy planets," Paul the Venetian said. "We must, each of us, one by one, learn to control our reactivity. A wanderer who served on Earth in the last wave stated the challenge with clarity: 'The world hangs by a single thread, and that thread, is the psyche of man.' He was known in that lifetime as the psychologist, Carl Jung. He understood that the battle against the dark side would be won by the efforts of each individual taking responsibility for his emotional reactions. Jung rightly feared that the reactivity of the human psyche, with its tendency to blame others, and to project the shadow rather than to look within for the source of the problem, could cause a nuclear war. It is crucial that each of you, when you are human, control your emotional reactions and take responsibility for your own shadow, your own darkness, rather than projecting it.

We'll practice this control in an exercise for which we'll adjust your consciousness so that it will be that of a third dimensional being. As you know from exercises with the other chohans, this reduction in your light field will be a painful jolt. Be assured that we will restore your higher dimensional consciousness after the exercise."

Here lady Ruth said, "I would add a word. Third dimensional beings may intuit that all are One, but generally do not realize that to hurt another is to hurt oneself. The most frequent response of third dimensional being is to lash out when frustrated. Giving in to the impulse to lash out hurts the human body as well as the soul, but even worse, it draws the dark side into your field, to feed on your negative energy and grow stronger. Don't provide food for the dark side by giving in to anger." Having delivered this reminder, Lady Ruth bowed to her partner to continue.

"Once we have changed your consciousness to third dimensional, we will send thought forms tailored to each of you in order to provoke a reaction. You will experience this as a real situation, common in third dimensional life, but nothing catastrophic. The situations we'll place you in are the kind which would normally aggravate and unbalance a third dimensional consciousness. Attempt to maintain your state of calm, or at least, quickly regain it. Use your breath to help you.

To prepare, we ask you all to leave the temple and find a secluded spot where you can be alone. We have altered the landscape around the temple to resemble Earth, as well as to create more secluded spots. Once you are all situated we will remove your higher powers. After the exercise, when you have regained your state, return to the temple and you will be restored to your home vibration."

"Are you going to do the exercise?" Heipleido asked Maepleida as they walked outside.

"Yes. I want to share your experiences as long as I'm here on Venus."

Before they parted to find their secluded places, he pulled her into his arms and held her to his heart. When he let her go, Maepleida went off in the direction of their cottage and Heipleido walked in the other direction, until he came to what felt like a fairy circle in a forest. It was strange to see everyone walking alone in the changed, but wondrous landscape around the temple. Soonam danced on ahead of the others, past all the cottages, until she saw a hill in the distance. She ran up the hill and sat on the far side of a large tree. Attivio headed toward a woodland pond which he spotted in the distance. Once there, he sat down on the shore to watch the water birds. After walking a fair distance, Ederah spotted a tree house in a large old tree. Narrow wooden stairs circled the tree and led up to the little house set among the branches. Calling up, she found it unoccupied, so she climbed the stairs and settled inside, seating herself on a chair shaped from rustic, bent wood. Like Attivio, Bereh chose to be near water. Drawn by the sound of a babbling brook, he made his way into the woods. He spotted a large, flat rock in the middle of the shallow stream and waded over to it and sat down to listen to the holy sound of the water bubbling over the stones. As they turned, and set off in opposite directions, Toomeh and Laaroos looked back several times at one another. Quite soon, Laaroos found herself alone in a field of wild flowers. She laid down on her back and gazed upward at the sky, breathing in the freshness of the cool air.

After a short walk, Toomeh stood still. In front of him was a woodland cottage with the door ajar. Approaching it, he pushed the door all the way open. The warm darkness inside suddenly turned cold as something black swirled up and flew past him. He made a mental note to mention this to Venus and Kumara, in case security had been breached, allowing a spy from Orion to slip through. The now empty cottage held a lingering dark feeling, so Toomeh proceeded further on and found himself by the mouth of a cave, with a peaceful curve. "OK, then," he said to no one, "this'll be my place."

Sensing that everyone had found a secluded spot, Lady Ruth, reduced them all to a third dimensional vibration and Paul the Venetian released the thought forms. Toomeh shuddered as he experienced the reduction. It felt like a naked, night sky, in which suddenly, all the stars had been extinguished. Maepleida groaned when she felt the change. Then bang, the thought form hit, and she found herself face to face with two policemen, one of whom was about to handcuff her. The manager of the large book store had in his hands what he said was Maepleida's backpack, and was showing the police the stolen books inside it. The next moment her arms were yanked behind her and she felt the handcuffs lock over her wrists. This is so primitive, she thought, as she listened to the manager tell the police how he'd caught her.

"When she saw me approach her, she picked up a book of poetry and pretended she was reading it," the manager explained. "But I saw her backpack open on the floor beside her, with the stolen books inside, so she didn't fool me."

"But that isn't my backpack," Maepleida insisted, in an angry tone, her blood boiling at being handcuffed and falsely accused.

"Pipe down," the larger of the two officers told her, the spittle from his mouth hitting her lips and chin.

"Ugh," she said trying to wipe her mouth on her shoulder.

The manager continued excitedly, telling the police how he'd had enough of books being shoplifted. He was pleased he'd caught a thief at last, and joked that in the old days thieves were either branded or lost a hand for their crime. Maepleida caught her breath at this and realized she was in a serious situation. She wondered what they did now to thieves.

"But I'm not a thief! Look in the backpack. It isn't mine." No one was listening to her. She needed another strategy. "What am I supposed to remember to stop reacting to this," she asked herself. She fell silent and began to think and to breathe. The three men were obviously pleased to have apprehended someone. She wanted to hate them, but that wasn't the way through this tricky event. It wasn't going to be easy to acknowledge the divine in them, and to see them as one with herself. She tried to recall the instructions they'd been given. The instructions came back in pieces. *Accept your anger as a part of yourself, as a red ray energy which will dissipate if you accept it. Use your knowledge that all beings are one to pull those around you into a higher vibration and the situation will dissolve.*

Maepleida focused on her breath, using it to accept and calm her angry feelings and to send out to each of the three men the vibration of love. She began to relax and noticed one of the policemen glancing at the backpack. "Let me have a look in it," he said, "maybe there's some identification, since she claims it isn't hers." The manager handed over the navy-blue unisex-looking bag and the officer dumped it out on the manager's desk. Some loose change landed on the desk. A nickel and some pennies rolled off onto the floor. A box of condoms in a small paper bag also fell out onto the desk. The officer looked at the receipt. The condoms had been purchased earlier that day from the drugstore next to the book shop. Maepleida, calmer now, continued to breathe and send out loving vibes. She could feel the red ray energy of anger leaving her physical body. One of the policemen took her arm and headed for the drugstore followed by the store manager. The clerk behind the counter in the drugstore told them that he'd sold only one pack of condoms that day, and it was to a man. The police uncuffed Maepleida and apologized. She smiled kindly at them, wishing them well. Then, suddenly, she found herself standing in front of her own cottage on Venus. She breathed a sigh of relief. When she'd stopped reacting, she'd actually affected the consciousness of the officers. Third dimensional consciousness was challenging, very challenging, but it could be managed. Still, she didn't want to be stuck in it.

Even with only third dimensional consciousness, Heipleido was enjoying the fairy circle, when suddenly, the scene changed and he was on a track, in a huge stadium, running a race. As he flew over the ground, ahead of all the other runners, he knew this was the moment he'd been preparing for, for years. Feeling the wind beneath his feet, he felt joy at the ease and strength, with which his body performed as he sailed along over the track with an easy lead over everyone else. This was his race, and he exulted in the fact that all the months and years of effort had paid off. Then something caught his ankle and he stumbled, tried to regain his footing but couldn't, and crashed to the ground face down in the dirt. He rolled onto his back in pain. Anger and disappointment, even heartbreak, flooding through him. Who, or what, had tripped him? He looked around confused, trying to understand what had happened. Had a runner come up suddenly and sailed past him, tripping him intentionally? He attempted to stand, but the pain in his ankle was too much. He rolled back down onto the track and looked up at the sky. Rage and disappointment engulfed him as he looked for someone or something to blame. The rest of the runners flew by him. He stared up at the clouds moving above him, and a thought tickled his mind, creating a space in his anger. There was something he was supposed to remember. He tried to calm his breath and think. Why wasn't anyone coming to see if he was hurt? Where was he? A voice in his head told him to *breathe*. With each breath, he grew calmer until he began to accept his anger as a part of himself. *It doesn't matter who wins if we are all One. Acceptance is the key to end the pain.* This realization further calmed his anger and he began to draw in light from the soles of his feet up into his body, to regain a state of peacefulness. He pulled in so much light that it catapulted him back into the fairy circle. He stood there a moment, whole again, with nothing broken, able to stand, and very relieved to be free of his rage and disappointment. He also had a new respect for the emotional pain that beings in the third dimension had to endure. It had been eons since he'd had to wrangle an emotion as uncomfortable as rage. He looked around to determine in which direction the temple lay.

Ederah sat alone in her tree house waiting for the thought form. And while she waited she observed her mind as a third dimensional being. She saw that third dimensional consciousness was a more anxious state than she was used to. She was wondering how to help this, when suddenly, she found herself on a crowded metro platform. Everyone around was speaking French. The train pulled into the station and people squeezed past each other, some getting on and some getting off. She felt someone grab her bottom and squeeze. As the doors closed she reached for her shoulder bag. It was gone. It must have been a team, one groping her, while the other stole her bag. Anger welled up in her at her own stupidity for letting the distraction of being groped allow the robbery to happen. Then came a wave of hurt that someone would violate her in order to steal her things. "But I'm alright," she reminded herself. "This hurt is caused by my attachment to my material possessions and to my sense of my body as me, as the only aspect of myself. But I'm confused. Didn't I long ago relinquish attachment? What is happening? There's something I'm supposed to do." Then she remembered that this was an exercise, taking place in the third dimension, and her task was to hold her state in the emotional situation. "I can do this. This is as nothing, against the power of light," she said out loud, wondering where that thought had come from. She waited to see what effect these words would have on her state.

They were softening her pain somehow. She felt a little calmer. *Yes, my bag is lost, and my dignity temporarily assaulted. But am I lost? These losses are as nothing if I am not lost, if I know that I am Divine.* At these thoughts, she felt her breath grow deeper, and she rode it up and down the length of her body and out beyond it, above and below her. As she moved her breath through her body, it restored her state, the metro station disappeared, her anger and fear melted away, and she found herself once more in the tree house, seated in the rustic chair. Relieved, she hurried down the stairs and headed back to the temple.

Rivulets of clear water flowed around the rock on which Bereh sat reminding himself that whatever situation he was about to find himself in was an opportunity to practice non-reactivity. The next moment, the scene changed and he was red-faced and sweating, shouting at his cab driver. They were stuck in New York City traffic. "This is the most important job interview of my life. I can't be late. How could you miss the turn and land us in the middle of this traffic?" Bereh checked the time and realized he was never going to make it. He was fuming at the stupidity of the driver. Then, in the mirror, he caught the look of fear on the driver's face. Seeing the man's humanity, Bereh sat back and took a breath which opened a space in his consciousness so his anger wouldn't hold him so tightly. "What's the matter with me?" he said out loud and took another breath. "But I need this job." He felt his anger burn his blood as he tried to accept that the interview was lost. A phrase: *Accept your anger as you,* popped into his head. He acknowledged to himself that he was a ball of rage, but then what? But the acknowledgement had begun to work. He was calming down. The red ray energy was dissipating a bit. Yes, he thought, this interview is important, but is it more important than how I treat another human being? What am I supposed to remember? How do I get out of the grip of my own reaction. He felt sorry for losing his temper and frightening the cab driver, who barely understood English. From somewhere in him came the thought that to hurt another is to hurt yourself. *What you do to another is also done to the self, just as what you do to yourself is also done to the other.* Bereh apologized to the driver, who seemed surprised, and then grateful. Closing his eyes, he drew in another slow breath. When he opened them, he was no longer in the taxi, but was again staring at the sparkling water of the stream. The light glistening on the water, and the sound of it as it flowed over the rocks, filled him with delight. A moment ago, he'd been in a rage. Could anger be a choice in the third dimension? Could one choose to let it go, he wondered? It was definitely more difficult than in the sixth dimension, but it could be done. Relieved, Bereh stood up and waded back to shore.

Cool air flowed from the mouth of the cave and caressed the back of Toomeh's neck as he sat cross legged in the entrance of this seldom visited place, waiting. Suddenly, the scene changed, and he found himself sitting near a reception desk. He glanced at his watch, then approached the woman at the desk. "How much longer will it be?" She didn't look up at first, but continued typing and ignored him. "I've been waiting for the doctor for over an hour," he said.

"Have a seat, please. I'll tell you when we're ready for you." Her tone was rude and dismissive. The please wasn't really a please, it was a demand. He wanted to insult her back, but he checked his tongue. His blood boiling, he sat down again. One by one the other patients were called and still he waited. He wanted to leave and slam the door. But he needed to learn the results of his tests. Was he bothered more by the wait or the attitude of the receptionist or the fear that he had cancer? His eyes fell on a little book on the table beside him. Bound in leather and stitched with gold, it had probably been left by another patient. *To Refuse or to Yield: The Pain is in the Resistance.* He hadn't noticed it earlier. Whether it was serendipity or fate that this book had been left for him to find, it had its effect. Toomeh picked it up and flipped through it to a paragraph about acceptance. It said that if one

111

can accept a situation without resentment, and accept your own anger as yours, the suffering will stop. Yes, breathe, and try to see all as One, even cold, mean receptionists.

His vibration began to accelerate as he concentrated on accepting his present situation, and the receptionist. As he used his breath to draw in light through the soles of his feet, he became peaceful. A few moments later, he once again felt the cool air from the cave on the back of his neck. Relieved to be rid of the rage and fear, and back to himself, he bounded up and headed for the temple, and Laaroos.

Few things are as lovely as a field of wild flowers gently rippling in a summer breeze. Laaroos lay on her back in the midst of them. She heard the words before she could fully see where she was.

"No, no, our decision is final," the woman in the admission's office barked. "As I told you, your daughter has been rejected. Our school takes only the cream into its kindergarten class."

Judged, insulted and rejected, but mostly hurt for her child, Laaroos collapsed inside and dropped the rejection letter on the woman's desk. She'd hoped the letter had been a mistake.

"No, there's been no mistake," the woman had snapped at Laaroos. "Your daughter doesn't meet our standards. Now, if you don't mind, I have work to do."

Laaroos wanted to snap back, and tell the woman that her rudeness was unnecessary. She could feel the negative energy coming from the woman and hitting her, like a hard punch in the heart. Trying to regain her calm, she began silently talking to herself. "Am I less because she treats me like this? Why am I so bruised? It's of no importance at all. Only the ego gets hurt, the Soul is never injured. Maybe my daughter wasn't supposed to be in a school with so much negative judgment of others, especially small, young others. Maybe it's a lucky escape. What I want for my child is to love others, not judge them. The reputation of this school be dammed, and this cruel heartless woman can go to hell." Laaroos, still shaking with anger, turned on her heel and walked out without a word to the admission's director. Once outside in the fresh air, she breathed a little easier, but couldn't quite regain her center after the insults the mean, officious woman had hurled at her child. She could think of a few more words to describe her, too. "No, I shouldn't judge this woman. I feel dark doing it. I don't want to engage myself with thoughts of her, or how she got to be the way she is. How do I stop feeling bad? How do I stop reacting to her? Stop thinking of her? How do I free myself? What is it that I'm supposed to remember?" As she continued to talk to herself, Laaroos started to feel a little better, but she was still in the grip of hurt and anger. Another phrase popped into her mind. "Help is always a heartbeat away, but one must ask." Laaroos sent a prayer from her heart asking for help, and immediately heard the words: *Accept your anger as a part of you. This situation is a catalyst for your growth.* She struggled with herself to hold this thought in her heart and send it out through all her cells, and into every electron in her body, until she could almost feel her electrons speeding up, shifting her feeling toward the woman from anger to acceptance. Relief flooded her like cool water running over hot, tired feet. She was free from anger and hurt. As she exhaled, the sky above her was once more, pink and she was again surrounded by wild flowers. In a moment, she was on her feet, heading toward the temple, and Toomeh.

Soonam could feel the tree breathing as she sat with her back pressed against it. She closed her eyes and drifted into a shared consciousness with the tree being. She felt its acceptance and contentedness with all things. Soonam loved trees, and this tree knew it and returned her love. Then she felt a quick jerk pull her down to the third dimension, with a simultaneous loss of power as her vibration slowed, and she stiffened with shock to find herself in a wood paneled study. She was standing at a desk, reading a letter to her husband from a woman who claimed that he was the father of her child, a little boy. Her legs turned to stone. How had he not told her. There was no date on the letter. When had he received it? Where was the envelope? Who was this woman? She heard his steps behind her as he came into the room. She rounded on him, the hand holding the letter, shaking.

"You've seen the letter."

"Is it true?"

"I don't know. I knew this woman ten years ago, before I met you, but she never told me she was pregnant."

"When did you receive this letter?"

"A few days ago."

"And you didn't think to tell me?"

"I was afraid. I wanted to get to the truth of it first. I didn't want to hurt you, especially since you're in pain that we haven't conceived a child."

"But we promised, no lies, ever, and no deception, when we made our vows." In that moment, she hated him for not trusting her, for not telling her. She wanted to pound his chest or throw something heavy at his head. He saw the fire in her violet eyes. She saw him note it, and she was gratified at his fear. "You coward," she shouted. "You were afraid to trust me."

"No," he said. "I was afraid to lose you."

She saw the pain in his face, but she didn't want to succumb to it. She wanted to nurse her own pain a little longer, and to torture herself with the thought that he had no child with her, but might have one with another woman. All the time, she knew that her feelings of jealousy and betrayal were somehow a choice, and this choice was the rope that would keep her tied to the pier of pain and suffering. But how to untie the rope? She stood, stuck in her agony, wanting to look for a way to break through to some other state, but reluctant to let go of her pain at the same time. A little voice in her heart spoke to her. "You are choosing to hurt yourself and this man you love." She knew it was true, she was inflicting this pain on herself, and this knowing gave her a little space to maneuver away from her suffering. A little distance was enough for her to take in his suffering. Her compassion for him moved her even further from her anger, until she felt light filling the open space. Then she remembered what she was supposed to do to free herself from her third dimensional reaction: accept her anger as a part of herself. Judging her husband wouldn't help. That was the wrong path. She must look to herself and own her own reaction. Realizing this, she closed her violet eyes to better feel the light flowing through her. As she concentrated on the feeling of the light, and drew it upwards from the soles of her feet, she felt it enter her heart with the sweetness of Cupid's arrow. As she let go of her judgement of her husband, her pain vanished, and she once again found herself leaning against her tree.

Water lapped at Attivio's feet as he sat by the edge of the pond, watching the water birds. A breeze rippled the surface. Suddenly, the pond disappeared and he found himself behind the wheel of a car, heading down the highway toward a roundabout. His baby daughter was asleep in her car seat behind him. As he eased into the roundabout, a fast-moving car appeared out of nowhere and slammed into the side of his car, spinning it in a half circle so that he was facing on-coming traffic. In what felt like slow motion, he glanced behind him to see if his daughter was hurt, and then pulled off the road onto the shoulder, his car still facing the wrong way. He was gripping the steering wheel so tightly his hands hurt. The other driver hadn't even stopped. He got out and opened the back door to pick up his wailing infant. "You could have killed my child," he wanted to scream. Holding the baby and trying to calm her, Attivio leaned against the car door and tried to steady his shaking body. What he felt scared him. Overcome with rage, he wanted to find the other driver and kill him. He found a pacifier in the car seat and put it in the baby's mouth. She grew calmer as she sucked, but her eyelashes were wet with tears. He pressed her to his heart. He tried to breath to release his rage. The driver had just sped off, as though he had no regard for what he had done, or for what might have happened. Opening and closing his fists a few times, and breathing slowly, helped Attivio to regain a state of some calm. "I'm supposed to accept my rage and let it dissipate," he said out loud to his daughter, "and see that jerk as part of the One." But he couldn't. He knew if anything had happened to his daughter he would have found the guy and killed him. That thought terrified him. Then where would he be? Caught in a murderous reaction. His own reaction was what he was supposed to accept as a part of himself. Attivio struggled to acknowledge his murderous rage as belonging to him, as a part of himself, and as he did, light seemed to move up his legs from the soles of his feet, into his heart. He looked down into his daughter's violet eyes and felt an onrush of love so powerful it pushed out every other feeling. He felt an overwhelming gratitude. His feeling of gratitude increased the flow of the light energy in his body, speeding up his electrons and helping to release the red ray energy of anger. He closed his eyes to enjoy the feeling and when he opened them, the pond was once again before him. He sat in silence, absorbing what had just happened, gazing at the still surface of the water, and then he remembered something about the power of silence, that only in silence can things be assimilated. He sat in silence a little longer, until he felt he had fully assimilated all the light which the state of gratitude had created, and only then did he stand up and head for the temple. But he couldn't forget the baby with the violet eyes. He felt a longing to hold her again, and wondered if she was somewhere in his and Soonam's future.

Lady Ruth and Paul the Venetian were waiting for them as they all made their way back to the temple. Laaroos and Toomeh felt all the pleasure of reunion, even after so brief a separation. Bereh changed himself into a white bird and landed on Ederah's shoulder to whisper a secret in her ear. Heipleido did a flip fifty feet into the air on seeing Maepleida coming toward him. She responded by duplicating herself five times and all five of her applauded his feat. Attivio reached for Soonam's hand and held it in the warmth of his own. He wanted to hear her experience and share his own, but for now, touching her was enough. As they took their places on their various crystal seats, Paul the Venetian commended them for their ability to regain a harmonious state so quickly. "It is beyond the ability of third dimensional beings to never be angry, but they can learn to regain a state of peace, which, if done quickly enough, will deprive the dark forces of a vital source of energy. When you are in the third dimension, you must acknowledge your anger, and maintain your state of calm, no matter what comes at you, not only to avoid feeding the dark forces, but to protect your health. Do not allow your mind to be restless. Restlessness is a form of anger, and the restless mind picks up every current from the atmosphere."

Lady Ruth then spoke to them. "You can also protect yourself by focusing your attention on any master or on your own divine spark. Visualizing shapes and colors, like mandalas, can enhance your ability to focus. As you hold this focus and sweep your breath the length of your field, from top to bottom and bottom to top, you will charge your human body, much as a car battery is charged. It is not necessary to charge your body in your current higher dimension as you are able to hold sufficient light to allow divine energy to continually stream through you. You understand that love has no limit. But in the third dimension you will need to consciously recharge each day.

Giving thanks, for each moment you are alive on Earth, will also raise your vibration. But remember, the greatest source of protection will always be the ability to view both yourself and others as Creator and to see all as One." With these words, she closed her eyes in an infinitely tender manner. Gazing at her peaceful face, Soonam felt an indescribable rapture.

"This is all fine, but how are you to remember to do it once you're only third dimensional beings," Maepleida whispered to

Heipleido in a tone lacking all nuance.

"I'm packing my pockets full," he said, "like a squirrel burying lots of nuts for the winter ahead."

Lady Ruth continued. "As humans, you will experience loss and suffering. And loss and suffering are heartbreaking challenges for humans, and evoke many reactions in them. As you have just experienced, third dimensional consciousness is a most reactive vibration. But you must offer gratitude for these challenges. It is these experiences which will hollow you out, refine you, and hone your sense of purpose. Your awareness of the spiritual nature of reality will help you to maintain a balanced harmonious state in the face of whatever happens. Use your challenges as catalysts to awaken to your true nature as light beings. Love and accept these catalysts. Be grateful for them, for they are sent by your Higher Self. And, stay close to your gratitude. Gratitude is a high vibration. Don't forget, the source of the catalyst is always the Higher Self, that very consciousness in you which is listening to me right this moment. All is well."

All is well, Soonam thought. She was determined to hold onto that perspective. Attivio picked up her thought, and inclined his head ever so slightly toward her. Catching a fleeting glimpse of the peace in her violet eyes, he remembered the baby, and his heart gave a little leap.

"Before we leave you, we would speak to you of human love," said Paul the Venetian. "Although they can be violently reactive, humans have a great capacity for love, so you will not be without love even before you awaken. However, there is much confusion on Earth between love and the sexual exchange. Sex in the third dimension, as in the fifth, is meant to be a joyous energy exchange to benefit each partner. The male transfers physical energy and strength to refresh the female. The female transfers mental, emotional and spiritual energy to inspire the male. The fire of the male keeps the woman from stagnation, even as the cool waters of the female calm the fire of the male. Orgasm is the point of transfer. This is not well understood among humans. Orgasmic energy is pure love, ecstasy, the very vibration of the Creator. The universe dwells in a state of orgasm, a timeless ecstasy; therefore, orgasm can trigger contact with intelligent infinity, even from the third dimension. We ask the twin flame pairs among you, once you are on Earth, to direct your electrons to pull your twin flame into your field. The power of your sexual union will multiply many times the positive vibration on the planet, making it easier for all others to awaken. Seek one another. What you are seeking will be seeking you. Call to one another from the threefold flame in your heart. Your sexual union on Earth will be as God knowing God. Your sexual union will lift up the planet and free countless souls from the lower dimensions."

Here Lady Ruth added her thoughts. "If you call on us, we will do all we can to help you. Our legions of pink flame angels will be at your command in answer to your call. Know that when you call, yours will not be the first call to have been received and answered. Requests for help have been made before and have been answered in a variety of different ways. During one attempt to answer the call of humans, Master El Morya, and several of the other chohans, used esoteric architecture and thought forms to construct the pyramids as a tool to help humans awaken. Although the pyramids still stand, they can no longer be used for that purpose, as the alignments have shifted. They do, however, serve other purposes."

Heipleido wondered if that's why he'd been shown the vision of the little boy and his mother standing beside the great pyramid. Had he been given that vision to let him know there would be tools offered to help them once they incarnated? Or, was there some other reason? Maybe he was to incarnate in the land of the pyramids.

"Be assured," Paul the Venetian told them, "that our approach will be flexible and that we will be equally creative in answering your call, as the hope for humanity now lies in your hearts. Already, during the last few centuries, in preparation for this mission, we have placed monuments, statues and artifacts around the planet to remind you who you really are. For example, when you travel to Earth, some of you will see a famous sight in New York Harbor, a statue of the Goddess Liberty. She is a replica of the statue which once stood at the gates of Atlantis. Liberty is the goddess who protects the flame of freedom on planet Earth. Americans don't yet realize their statue represents a real being, an actual goddess. One day they will know."

As he heard these words, Toomeh remembered his visit to the statue of the Goddess Liberty. So, the man he had met, standing up in her crown, had been right, Lady Liberty was a replica of the goddess who had once stood at the gates of Atlantis.

"Use the Flame of Love. Throw your hearts into the sea of fire. Call on us and the chohans of each of the seven rays. You will never be without help a heartbeat away. Pray. Help is always there. I am Paul the Venetian, lover of your souls."

"And I am Lady Ruth, commending you for your courage."

They had no orbs or staffs or wands or swords, but as if from their hearts came a wave of pink light so blissful that Soonam mentally swooned in ecstasy. Ederah and Bereh glowed with pleasure and Toomeh found the courage to speak to Laaroos. The chohans had infused them with the pink ray of Divine love. Then they were gone. Where they had stood was now only a glow of rose-colored light and then nothing. They had dematerialized.

As Soonam and Attivio left the dome with their friends, they found the night air fragrant with the sweet scent of thousands of rose blossoms. Pink skies streaked with gold formed a canopy above them. The soft evening light kissed the trees and turned their leaves and branches into gold. Toomeh and Laaroos trailed behind the others. Toomeh spoke first. "You know what's in my heart, Laaroos, but I will speak the words aloud. I love you. You are my one, my twin flame, the one I have been seeking through worlds and lifetimes since we flew out from Source as one spark, and split into masculine and feminine, becoming two life streams from one."

"And you are my one, my twin flame," she said, moving into his waiting arms, which encircled her in a ring of light. They looked into one another's eyes in acknowledgement of who they were to one another. As their lips touched, a pink-gold flame shot up over a hundred feet above their heads before cascading down around them in a display of pink-gold light. Everyone recognized this as a twin flame reunion, and rejoiced in it. Ederah and Bereh, Attivio and Soonam, and Maepleida and Heipleido, who had all gone ahead, turned back now toward the light, knowing it was Toomeh and Laaroos. They had all been silently waiting for this sublime moment. Heipleido manifested a bottle of champagne, explaining that it was one way joyful moments were celebrated on Earth. Bereh manifested a silver tray with delicately cut crystal champagne flutes. Ederah and Soonam raised their glasses to Toomeh and Laaroos. When more of their fellow wanderers gathered, Attivio multiplied the number of glasses and Heipleido turned the champagne bottle into an endless fountain. Though everyone toasted, no one cared for the taste, so Heipleido changed the champagne fountain into a fountain of nectar. Twin flame reunions were always, everywhere, in all the universes, cause for great celebration. The sky above them, which moments before had been a sleeping roof, broke open revealing stars, from even far off galaxies, all echoing their joy.

Chapter 6

Embodied Discipline

The next morning Maepleida received a message from Lady Venus asking her to come to the palace during the midday break. Heipleido walked over and took her in his arms. Every atom in his body became a heart when he held her. Loving her, and desiring her, without attachment had been his greatest challenge as a higher dimensional being. "If you are after desire, you are not after God," his guides had told him again and again, "you are not after Oneness." At the time of their twin flame reunion he had thought, *what punishment love is, how will I bear the pain of so much tenderness*? But his trust had grown over the centuries, and he knew never to want anything too much, or even at all, but only to trust in the will of the Divine. Only there could true bliss be found. Nevertheless, holding her in his arms, he felt the sweetest peace, and the prospect of being separated from that wasn't a happy one.

"We should be heading to the temple," Maepleida said, pulling away, her face stretched between two emotions.

As they approached the dome for the morning session, they spotted a figure robbed in white, wearing a golden crown on his head. His long dark hair fell to his shoulders. A large, polished, snow quartz was set in his crown and centered over his third eye. Around his head a golden halo was visible. In his right hand he held a wand made of seven rays of light, representing the seven sacred flames. His sandals, too, were of gold. From each of his chakras streamed white light. Floating above his shoulders, and slightly behind him, were the archangels Gabriel and Hope. The two light-filled angels were huge and seemed suspended in space.

"It's Lord Serapis Bey," Attivio said, walking up to Heipleido.

Soonam stood still beside Attivio, captured by the splendor of the archangels. Something in her felt in perfect harmony with them.

"Yes, it's Serapis Bey," Bereh said, joining them. "He and his twin flame, Amutreya, have just arrived from their temple in Luxor, Egypt. They're going to speak to us this morning about ascension on Earth, and what it will require of each human, including us, once we're third dimensional."

"But I don't see Amutreya," Ederah said.

The six friends entered the temple. A few moments later, Toomeh and Laaroos floated in, looking radiant and expansive, like two oceans which had merged, swimming into one another's bones and skin, only to discover that all along they were one body. When they were all seated. Serapis Bey entered.

In a voice which rang out above them like a silver trumpet, he began. "We greet you with the great love. The Archangels Gabriel and Hope have come with me today to offer you their blessing for your mission."

The two archangels left his side and flew up to the vaulted ceiling, then, swooping down over the heads of all those assembled, sprinkled them with tiny golden crystals. The crystals dissolved on contact with their bodies, but set running in them feelings of fearless joy, and endless love. Their blessing bestowed, the angels departed, moving right through the roof as if it was only air. Soonam's heart followed them up and out of the temple. She knew Serapis Bey was speaking, but it was beyond her power to concentrate.

"I know your fears," Serapis Bey told them, "and I would say to you, be assured that there is a path to take in order to awaken and ascend while on Earth. But on that path, each of you, while human, will have to once again pass the seven major initiations required for ascension. These are initiations you have long ago undergone, but you will not remember them once you take a human incarnation. Ah, but here is Amutreya."

Amutreya, Goddess of Purity, stood under the arched entrance at the back of the temple with Lady Venus beside her. As Serapis Bey called attention to their arrival, the two goddesses bowed to one another and Lady Venus took her leave. Amutreya came forward to join Serapis Bey, her long white robes brushing the marble floor. Like Serapis, Amutreya wore a golden crown over long, dark hair which reached down to her waist. Serapis extended his hand to her as she approached.

"Amutreya and I will remind you of the seven initiations required for humans to ascend from the third to the fourth dimension. As you listen, set them in your unconscious so you can work through them more easily once you are in your earthly form, for the unconscious is accessible to humans with a little effort. These initiations will sound very simple to you in your present state, but they will be a challenge when you are a third dimensional human. Let us begin."

Amutreya spoke first. "You will have to relearn how to control all thoughts and feelings that are not aligned with your Higher Self. As you are now, you naturally do this. It is second nature to you. It will not be as easy when you are a third dimensional human. You experienced this challenge in the exercise you did yesterday with Lady Ruth and Paul the Venetian. As you attempted to be nonreactive to situations which ordinarily frustrate those of a third dimensional consciousness, you experienced a bit of struggle to regain your state. If one knows how to decipher which thoughts are their own, and which are picked up from the atmosphere around them, from other humans, or from negative thought forms, some of which will be sent to you from the dark lords of Orion, thought control can be mastered. Negative thought forms in particular must be recognized, and thrown out. When complete control of the mind has been achieved, you will be able to discard any thoughts which you don't want, any which destroy your state and disturb your bliss. Then nothing will agitate or frustrate you. Ultimately, your mind will be merged into the Greater Mind."

Ederah found herself staring back and forth from the quartz above Amutreya's third eye to the quartz above Serapis Bey's third eye. She fixed her gaze on Amutreya's quartz, and as she listened more to the music of her voice than to the meaning of her words, she lost track of the message. Bereh turned to look at her, but Ederah's chair was empty. She had vanished. He spoke her name softly, remembering that invisibility was one of her powers. Again he called her name, hoping to draw her back into a visible realm. After several seconds, she reappeared. Impulsively he kissed her lips. They tasted like sea water.

"Sorry," she said. "I was staring at Amutreya's quartz and I slipped over into invisibility. Ederah could easily make herself vanish from sight. But this was the first time it had ever happened without her intending it, and that troubled her. They were all slipping into reveries without willing it, and now, without her intending it, she'd become invisible. She sat up straight and refocused her attention. Serapis was now speaking.

"Once you have gained control of your thoughts and feelings, the second initiation you must undergo will be to relearn the universal laws of cause and effect. If you understand the laws of cause and effect, you can avoid creating karma which would bind you to the third dimension. As humans, you may elect to do anything you choose. But every choice comes with consequences. By the actions you engage in, you will create your life, dispense your own glory and gloom, and decree your own punishment. In this sense, every human is a creator."

Hearing the law of cause and effect related so directly to one's choices gave Maepleida a start. What would her choice not to go on this mission create? Was her unconquerable confidence in herself succumbing to doubt? She closed her eyes to try and escape the grip of her mind, and found herself drifting into an unfamiliar scene.

Several large white swans swam across a pond toward a little girl of two or three years. The little girl wore a light-blue dress covered with a pattern of tiny flowers in a darker blue, and a hand-knit white sweater. She was tossing pieces of bread from a paper bag, which she held in her small hand, into the water, and watching as the swans stretched their long necks toward the bread and deftly ate it. A tall, elegant woman stood beside her, preventing her from getting too close to the swans.

Heipleido touched her hand and she jerked back from her reverie. He looked at her to see if she was alright. Momentarily disoriented, she sat frozen, perhaps annoyed at his interference. Heipleido telegraphed to her *I'm sorry if I startled you. You know I have only and ever loved you.* They both turned their attention back to Serapis Bey, Maepleida wondering what she'd just seen.

"The third initiation which you must undergo is the practice of unconditional love for all forms of life. Whether you agree with their politics, or their religion, their dress, the way they raise their children, whether they are mineral, vegetable, animal or human, all are to be loved unconditionally. Never hurt the feelings, or body, of another. When you hurt another, you hurt yourself. Do not think of anyone as other. There are no others. All are One. Even the dark lords serve the Creator in their own way." Serapis paused to let that sink in, and Amutreya then addressed them.

"Once you are able to have unconditional love for all beings, then you are ready for the fourth level of initiation. To achieve the fourth level, you must be able to hold enough radiance to be capable of seeing your Higher Self, and eventually, your Divine I Am Presence. Service to others, meditation and the practice of gratitude will increase your radiance, as will the practice of drawing in light from the lower apex of your star tetrahedron, through the soles of the feet, and pulling it up to the heart. Without this radiance, you will be incapable of withstanding the light of the higher dimensions. As you meditate, remember that the heart of all things is bliss. Do not be distracted by the doors of Maya – money, power, drugs, lust and property. Happiness is within only."

Toomeh stole a glance at Laaroos. She looked younger, purer even than a newborn. If he ever lost her again, he would rip open the sky to find her. He tore his eyes from her and forced himself to focus on Amutreya, who was reminding them of the fifth initiation which humans must achieve to ascend into the fourth dimension.

"You must hold enough radiance to accept the consecration of your hands, feet, lips and eyes, so they may be infused with the power to heal. Again, drawing light energy up through the soles of your feet and down from your crown, and raising the point at which they meet, will prepare you for these consecrations. By age twenty, in Earth years, if you have awakened, you will be capable of healing yourself, as well as all who come to you for healing. When you achieve the sixth initiation," Amutreya told them, "you will not only be able to heal, but you will be a ministering servant, nurturing all life. As such, you will naturally bow to the God in all beings. When you are surrendered to the will of the Divine, it becomes your will. This is possible as a third dimensional being. Don't think it is not. With the help of previous wanderers, some Earth beings are already achieving this consciousness. Your presence will add to the numbers of the awakened. Finally, you must undergo the purification of every cell, atom and electron in your body until you are in perfect alignment with the will of God. Under the sponsorship of the Lady Portia, Goddess of Justice, and the Master Saint Germain, you will be purified by the action of the Violet Flame until you become like a window through which God flows. Refrain from taking into your human body those substances which will alter your natural vibration and separate you from the harmony of the Divine spheres."

"These seven initiations are a lot to expect of a third dimensional being," Toomeh whispered to Laaroos.

"Yes, but remember, we passed through all these same

initiations before, when we were first evolving from the third dimension to the fourth," Laaroos said.

"You're right, we know we can do it," he said. He looked at her, and felt her presence like a fire in his heart. *I will break the oceans in half to find her again on Earth*, he thought. Their gold-orange eyes locked for a moment before they turned their attention to Serapis Bey, who now addressed them.

"Amutreya and I stand ready to assist you on your path. And it will be your reward to become an ascended master, if you succeed in awakening to your true identity once on Earth in the heaviness of the third dimension. Your awakening will lift up all beings. If you are sincerely committed to this mission, all heaven will be at your beck and call to assist you. We will match your efforts. Come to our temple at Luxor in Egypt during your sleep time, and we will renew your energies and restore you for your task. Heed these words. Plant them in the eternal aspect of your innermost being. From our hearts, we give you our blessing for your victory." With those words, Lord Serapis Bey lifted his wand and held it over them. Waves of light of astonishing beauty ushered from it and bathed the entire temple in lustrous white light, then violet, and shimmering gold, followed by waves of pink, and light in many shades of blue and green, and finally, the brightest yellow, turning again to pearly-white. Each color carried with it the vibration of its ray. As one vibration after another flowed over them, everyone in the temple experienced a transformation enabling them to hold more radiance than they had ever before experienced. The feeling was one of expansion and ecstasy. As they looked at one another they saw an incandescence so radiant that none could speak.

When they left the temple after the morning session, Heipleido accompanied Maepleida to the steps of Lord Kumara and Lady Venus's palace. He watched while she ascended the white stone stairs and disappeared.

Maepleida entered an interior courtyard garden, in the center of which was a large pool of clear water.

"Shall we sit in the garden?" Lady Venus said, as she approached Maepleida. The garden was full of the soft fragrance of flowering trees. They sat together on a bench, facing the water. In a branch above them a bird was singing. He was a magnificent fellow with a sweet voice, a yellow chest and wings of velvet black. In contrast to the sweet sound of their winged accompanist, Maepleida's words felt sharper than she intended as she told Lady Venus of her decision not to go on the mission to Earth. Lady Venus listened in silence until Maepleida had finished.

"Are you at peace with your decision, my dear?" Lady Venus could see into her heart, and knew that she was not at peace, but she also knew that Maepleida hadn't yet acknowledged this.

"I would ask you only one thing," Lady Venus said. "Go to see Amerissis and El Morya at their temple at Darjeeling, in the Himalayas on Earth. You will be escorted through the quarantine surrounding Earth. Sit before the blue flame diamond. Look out over the snow covered peaks of the Himalayas, and feel into your own heart. The palace altar at Darjeeling holds the fire of the Blue Ray, the Ray of the Will of God. It is not a God somewhere outside of you, but the God within you who must guide your choice. Listen until you hear what your own I Am Presence desires of you. Let the answer come casually toward you as you sit in the vibration of the blue flame. Travel in your merkaba. You'll be there instantly."

"I'd like to speak to Heipleido first," Maepleida said.

"Yes, of course."

"Thank you, Lady Venus," Maepleida bowed deeply. On her way out, she passed Lord Kumara and bowed also to him before hurrying down the palace steps.

She resolved to tell Heipleido, and leave at once for the Himalayas.

After lunch the friends gathered, without Maepleida, under

their favorite tree, and attempted to soothe Heipleido's swollen heart. He felt as if she had been carved out of his body. And to all of them, it was like one of their arms or legs was missing. But each of them, even Heipleido, would accept whatever choice she made, with no judgement. Acceptance of what is, even giving up one's longed for life, was something each of them had mastered many eons ago. If Maepleida told them that her choice was aligned with the will of her I Am Presence, they would all support her, no matter what.

Chapter 7

How Healing Works

No one felt like learning more about their mission to Earth so soon after Maepleida left. It felt as if her name had been erased, but the gong rang for the afternoon session, and they walked through the arch, and allowed the feeling of peace in the temple to envelope them. Moments after they were all seated, an oval of light appeared in front of them, and before their eyes it transformed into a beautiful youth with green eyes the color of emeralds.

"It is my great joy to be here on Venus to address you my beloveds," Master Hilarion began. "I come to you from my temple on Crete where I serve as Chohan of the Green Ray, the Flame of Healing." Hilarion wore a voluminous cape of bright green over a shirt woven of light of many colors. The splendor of his being was matched by that of his voice which rang with equal notes of tenderness and strength, youth and wisdom, humility and power. Light gleamed off his whole being, but was particularly bright on his forehead, between his emerald eyes. When one stared at it, this light from his third eye seemed to grow to a hundred stories high.

Seeing that Soonam had fixed her violet orbs on Hilarion's eyes and forehead, Attivio leaned over and whispered to her, "Emerald eyes signify that he's able to wield great spirals of light for healing."

Soonam turned her gaze to Attivio.

As she opened her mouth to answer him, he leaned toward her and caught the fragrance of wild violets on her breath.

"Many lifetimes ago," Master Hilarion told them, "you all learned the secrets of healing. They are automatic to you now as fifth dimensional beings, but they won't be once you are human.

This afternoon we'll consciously retrace the steps for healing, so you can implant them in your unconscious for retrieval on Earth. With a little effort, all humans can have access to the unconscious, where much knowledge is stored. Foremost, I would remind you that, *the healer does not heal*. The healer merely offers an opportunity for realignment, by channeling intelligent energy as focused light. Healing must be chosen by the etheric body of the one to be healed. It is the will of the entity which allows his indigo body to heal his physical body. This can happen in an instant if the seeker is sincere in his desire to heal. Many wanderers to Earth have helped humans by offering energy spirals of light to those seeking a cure. Perhaps the one most well-known on Earth for this practice, is Jesus, who is known to us, his fellow chohans, as Lord Sananda, and he, too, will be coming to Venus to speak with you. Jesus viewed the person to be healed as whole, and offered him the opportunity to realign himself with this image of wholeness. But it was up to the seeker himself to choose the realignment and permit his own indigo body to heal him. Not only Jesus, but all wanderers are capable of offering realignment to those desiring healing, as in fact, are all humans if they align with the Divine in themselves. But humans, for the most part, don't realize their power to heal. They cannot yet create any type of body they desire. That is a gift that arrives only in the fifth dimension. However, they can heal themselves and others if they are shown how."

Heipleido was having trouble concentrating on Hilarion's words, and his mind drifted off to thoughts of Maepleida. He thought of the vision she had shared with him, of the child feeding bread crumbs to swans. Bowing his head, he smelled swans on the skin of his chest, and he felt like weeping. How was it for her to be on Earth, high up in the Himalayas? Had she even arrived safely, avoiding any interference from the dark lords? She had said that she would travel alone in her own merkaba. A shiver ran through him. Ederah, who was sitting next to him felt it, and wrapped him violet light.

"From my retreat on Crete," Hilarion continued, "I have been observing humans for a long time. Nearly all their health problems, diseases and illnesses are caused by disharmony in their emotional bodies. This lack of harmony comes from unresolved emotional issues, which when not brought to consciousness and processed download into the physical body as pain and illness. All unprocessed negative emotions cause illness in humans but anger is perhaps the most problematic. Anger is a particular challenge for many humans who may have repressed their anger and be unaware of it. They don't realize that anger affects their bodies and can cause their cells to go out of control, and their electrons to spin in a counter clockwise direction. One cause of cancer in humans is repressed, unresolved anger. Cancer is a frightening word for humans, but even cancer can be amenable to self-healing if the entity grasps that the mechanism for the cancer's growth is the anger which has altered his cells. I would add that sometimes cancer is sent as a catalyst from the Higher Self for another purpose, and in some instances may not be related to an entity's anger. But take care dear ones when you incarnate as human to acknowledge and process your anger, releasing it from the body."

Despite Ederah showering him with violet light, Heipleido's thoughts were still of Maepleida. He saw her blue, silk nightgown fall to the floor about her feet revealing her naked splendor, the remembrance of her destroying his peace. And, what of their still undreamed dreams? They would require a thousand more lifetimes together. Heipleido pulled his mind back to Hilarion's words.

"Thoughts can become things in the third dimension," Hilarion reminded them, "just as they can in the higher dimensions. Look to your thoughts when you are human. For, when you are human, you must not only observe the thoughts you feed yourself, as you do now, but you must be careful to process the emotions which your thoughts provoke, so that they don't alter the cells of your physical body. In your recent exercise, you had a chance to feel the power of human emotional reactivity. You each found a way to bring that reactivity under control and to free yourself from the pain of the reaction. Ongoing negative emotional reactivity reverses the flow of electrons in a third dimensional being. This reversal, and slowing down of electrons, within the human body damages it, destroying the internal harmony and alignment. The result is illness. However, once an entity faces the emotional issue, and stops reacting negatively to it, it becomes possible to restore harmony in the body. The greatest harmony comes, always, from the awareness of the Divine resting within you. This awareness heals all emotional issues, and it is emotional balance which keeps your cells from going out of control. Once you restore harmony in your emotional body, then your physical body will naturally heal."

Heipleido caught these last words, and knew they were meant for him. He needed to accept Maepleida's departure in order to restore harmony in his emotional body. He also knew Hilarion's next words would remind them all of the best method to achieve this.

"Some diseases are of karmic origin. Some are deemed necessary by the Higher Self, as a catalyst for the entity's growth. All catalysts come from the Higher Self. Awareness of the Divine within will heal even these diseases. Other diseases, as I said, are caused by unprocessed emotional reactions."

Remember the Divine resting within, that was the key Heipleido needed. *Focus your awareness on the Divine resting within*. That will ease the pain in your heart. He breathed a sigh of relief at this simple, but profound, realization.

"At this time on Earth, most humans do not understand the need to restore emotional harmony for healing, and most use only the medical approach. Many so-called medicines are too strong for the human body. And many treatments are barbaric in their attempt to heal by poisoning, cutting or burning the body with radiation. Some humans do meditate, and do what they call therapy, or the talking cure. Talk therapy is helpful in getting people to feel their emotions, rather than download them into the body. But in order for it to be completely successful the therapeutic process must continue until there is recognition of the Divine resting within each being. Meditation and talk therapy are more enlightened methods than much of what traditional medicine offers, but their use is not yet common practice in the general population."

Ederah, like Soonam, found herself entranced by Hilarion's eyes, from which his soul poured forth. He was so innocent, so young, so wise. His voice flowed out to them like a gentle brook, and they swallowed his words like water offered to them from his cupped hands.

"It is our hope that when you are incarnate as humans, with a little prodding from your dreams, and by using the thought forms which we'll send to you, that you will be able to recover the memory of how to heal yourselves. In your current higher dimensional bodies, you know that healing is effected through realization of the Divine resting within you. Your awareness of Intelligent Infinity makes self-healing possible. However, once you enter the third dimension you will need to become consciously aware of the spiritual nature of reality in order to fully practice self-healing. This is one reason meditation will be so important for you. Meditation is your daily appointment with Intelligent Infinity. Meditation creates the pipes through which grace and healing flow. As a human being, you will still be able to go deep into the stillness within, and to find a place to rest immersed in divine love. When you reach this still place within yourself, you will feel sheltered and secure as your whole being will be contained in love. Thoughts and memories will float by, and you will merge them into the feeling of love. Nothing will disturb your serenity. This state of *Samadhi* is possible for all humans who seek it."

Soonam delighted in this description of meditation as *the pipes through which grace flows*. "It makes it so clear," she whispered to Attivio. "This is how we'll meditate when we're human. We'll picture the pipes with divine grace flowing through them."

Attivio leaned toward her, again seduced by the fragrance of violets on her lips.

"We in the etheric realm have tried to introduce spiritual truths, but much of humanity remains in spiritual slumber. If you succeed in piercing this slumber, you will become masters of light. And it will be of great help to you if you can remember how to heal, and how to meditate using light. In addition to the green flame of healing, you will also use the same flame that Lord Sananda used when he walked on Earth as Jesus. I speak here of the Resurrection Flame. All the flames will be beneficial, but the Green Flame is intended for healing, and the Resurrection Flame, for restoring life. To heal yourself, and others, while on Earth, call on the power of both these flames. Wield them with love, in the full consciousness of the Divine resting within you."

Toomeh and Laaroos, after their twin flame reunion of the previous evening, were still swimming in their own oceanic world, wild with tenderness, and the scent of one another's limbs. But the mention of the Resurrection Flame recalled them, and they tried mightily, as if turning an ocean liner around on the high sea, to attune themselves to Hilarion's words.

"Spiritual law requires that before calling on the flames for healing, you ask the permission of your Higher Self and your I Am Presence, as well as the permission of the Higher Self of the person you wish to heal. Once permission is granted, you may call on the flames, which flow continually to the Earth, much as does sunlight. A simple prayer from your heart will bring them into your field. Draw the flames upward from the soles of your feet into your heart, then down through your left arm, out to your left hand. Use your left hand to deliver the spirals of light. Direct the spiral flames as needed, remembering to offer gratitude for their assistance. In a few moments, we'll practice this technique of drawing the flames upward into your body in order that you may wield them for healing. But first, with your permission, for the purposes of this exercise I will return you to your third dimensional level of healing ability. This way you can experience what it will be like to use the flames as a third dimensional human being, which you will be when you incarnate on Earth. Having experienced this reduction in your light energy during previous training exercises, you know that it is not pleasant. Therefore, I beg your indulgence. Chose a partner or partners, as you wish, but not your twin flame, and then find one of the healing tables I have placed around the temple grounds. You may work in groups of two or three or four. First one of you will be the healer, and then you'll switch. You will have to discover the imbalance in your patient, then use the Green Flame of Healing and the Golden Flame of Resurrection to restore harmony in the body so that your patient may heal. I will create the ailments in each of you that are most common on Earth. Let's begin."

Ederah, Laaroos and Soonam partnered, and Heipleido, Attivio, Toomeh and Bereh decided to work as a group. They chose the two tables set up under either side of their favorite tree. All of them suddenly felt the now familiar painful regression to the third dimensional vibration. It was as if half of their light energy was being sucked out of them, as in fact, it was.

"Do we start by asking permission of our higher selves to do the healing?" Ederah said, looking at Soonam and Laaroos, as the three of them gathered around their healing table.

"Yes, I think so, and permission from our I Am Presence as well," Laaroos said.

"I feel a sharp pain in my abdomen," Soonam said. "I must be meant to be the patient first."

She stretched out on the table and laid her hands on her belly and closed her violet eyes.

All three women asked permissions of their higher selves and their I Am Presence. Then Laaroos stepped up to the table and looked across Soonam's body at Ederah, who nodded for her to begin.

Laaroos gently lifted Soonam's hands off her abdomen, and placed her own where Soonam's had been. Concentrating on the soles of her feet, Laaroos sent down shoots deep into Venus. She rocked Soonam's abdomen back and forth with a gentle motion. At the sweetness of the touch, Soonam exhaled, but her face was tight with pain. Visualizing the shoots extending from the soles of her feet into the ground, Laaroos drew up spirals of emerald green light. She watched with her consciousness as the underground shoots, deep in planet Venus, filled up with radiant emerald energy, then traveled upward, and entered her body. Drawing the light up to heart, then up into her head, she directed the emerald energy to flow over her head and back down to her heart and out her arms into her palms, which rested on Soonam. Laaroos concentrated on increasing the spirals and intensity of the light which poured out of her hands into Soonam's abdomen. Ederah reminded them all to acknowledge the Divine resting within. As Laaroos wielded the Green Flame, Ederah began to call on the Resurrection Flame, drawing the golden and purple light in through the soles of her own feet and up her body. She placed her hands beside Laaroos's hands on Soonam's abdomen, and let the purple-gold flame pour out of her palms into Soonam, calling on the flame to restore a perfect balance in Soonam's internal organs and in her etheric body blueprint. Ederah reminded herself that the healer does not heal, but offers light spirals to create a condition of harmony which rebalances the patient. Once rebalanced, the patient can then choose to accept the altered, now healthy blueprint, and heal herself. Soonam's breathing became less labored as Laaroos and Ederah drew up the spirals of emerald, gold and purple light, and directed them out their palms into her, to rebalance her. Ederah reminded Soonam to focus on the Divine resting within her. With this direction, Soonam's face relaxed a bit, and her breathing became smoother. Ederah and Laaroos watched and waited for further signs that Soonam's distress was easing. She looked better, but she was still in some pain. They began again to channel the light spirals, and started to feel the energy flowing more rapidly through them, and out their palms into Soonam. Laaroos reminded Soonam that she must choose to accept her rebalanced state and to see herself as whole in order to heal herself. All three women concentrated on the light energy from the flames, reminding themselves that it came ultimately from Source.

"The pain is gone," Soonam said, sitting up. "Things began to turn around when you reminded me to focus on the Divine resting within me. But that last round of light spirals completely rejuvenated me, and I was able to heal."

Ederah and Laaroos broke out in big smiles. Perhaps more could be done with third dimensional consciousness than they'd realized. That boded well for their mission. All three of them thanked the flames and bowed to the Divine in one another, bringing their hands together in front of their hearts.

Ederah felt her left knee buckle and realized she was meant to be next on the table. After permissions from their Higher Selves, Soonam placed one hand on Ederah's left knee and one on her right elbow and began sending in the spirals of healing light. Laaroos held Ederah's feet and sent the purple-gold Resurrection Flame out of her own palms into the sole of Ederah's foot and up her leg to her knee. But Ederah still felt the pain.

"Remind me again. How did Hilarion describe the task of the healer?" Soonam asked.

"I think he said that the healer doesn't heal, he merely offers an opportunity for realignment by channeling intelligent energy as focused light," Laaroos said.

"So, then we have to focus our intention more on channeling Divine energy as light," Soonam said.

"Yes," Laaroos agreed, "let's remind ourselves again that we are each Divine."

With renewed focus, they transmitted more light for Ederah's body to use to rebalance itself. The pain and swelling in Ederah's knee began to subside as she continued to breathe deeply and to focus on absorbing the light energy. In just a few minutes, she sat up, smiled and hopped off the table.

"That was fast," Laaroos said.

"Apparently healing can happen in an instant, even in the third dimension, with the realization of the Divine," Soonam reminded them. "Jesus did healings in an instant when he walked on Earth, making the blind see just by placing his palms over the eyes and channeling divine light into them."

"He wasn't a third dimensional being in that lifetime though," Ederah said.

"But he was. He had to leave his home dimension and become third dimensional to incarnate on Earth, just like we have to," Soonam said. They all smiled, realizing the truth of Soonam's words.

Laaroos stretched out on the table next. "It must be my turn, but I feel fine."

With the permissions granted, Soonam and Ederah placed their palms a few inches over Laaroos and scanned her body, imagining that they had cameras in their fingertips. They turned up nothing until they got up to Laaroos's head. Then they both picked up, through their intuition, that several arteries in Laaroos's brain were blocked, and that the blockages could cause her third dimensional self to have a stroke. They called on the Green Ray, and sent spirals of it flowing into Laaroos's arteries so that her body could use the spirals to rebalance her and clear her arteries. Then they called on the Resurrection Flame, drawing it up through the soles of their feet and directing it out of their palms and into the arteries in Laaroos's brain so her body could use it to break up the blockages and clear her arteries, restoring them to perfect functioning. As they wielded the flames, Soonam reminded both Laaroos and Ederah to acknowledge the Divine resting within them. When the color in Laaroos's face and neck became bright pink, they took it as evidence that the blockages had broken up.

The three women hugged one another.

"At this moment we're only third dimensional, but we were capable of healing. Suddenly I feel happy, as a human must feel happy," Soonam said.

"I feel it, too," said Laaroos. "Not as the bliss of our higher state, but a kind of strong childlike happiness at accomplishing something. Human emotions are different from what we feel, but they are powerful, and somehow sweet."

Soonam had the urge to dance around. I am flawed as a human, she thought, but my flaws are beautiful to me.

Meanwhile, on the other side of the tree, Heipleido lay on the table with a crushing pain in his chest. "It feels like a heavy weight is sitting on my heart," he told them.

The other three men, Toomeh, Attivio and Bereh gathered around three sides of the table. Each of them asked permission of their own, and Heipleido's Higher Self, to use the flames and to direct them into Heipleido so they could rebalance his body and restore his health. Arranging their hands on Heipleido's chest they began drawing in spirals of light up through the soles of their feet. Heipleido felt a lethal stabbing pain in his chest. The pain radiated down his left arm with tremendous force. His body jolted and went limp. His breath stopped. Master Hilarion, who had been walking under the trees, stopping at various healings stations, came closer to watch. Toomeh felt for a pulse. There was none. Hilarion took another step closer and spoke to them.

"Healing requires the realization of the Divine resting within you," he reminded them. "Focus on that consciousness and use the Resurrection Flame to restore him to life."

Toomeh looked across the table at the tension on Bereh's forehead. As their third dimensional selves, they were terrified. Attivio looked to Master Hilarion for help.

"Focus on the Divine resting within," Hilarion spoke gently. "Draw the Resurrection Flame up through the soles of your feet. Direct the spirals of light out through your palms into his body. All three of them did as Hilarion directed them. "Concentrate. See the flames. Offer your patient the opportunity to heal himself."

Finally, Heipleido's chest began to move up and down.

"Well done." Hilarion smiled at them.

Heipleido opened his eyes and sat up.

"Why do you all look so relieved?" he asked.

Next, Attivio lay on the table, with a high fever, followed by Toomeh with a brain tumor and, finally, Bereh, with a paralysis of his right side. By wielding the Resurrection Flame and the Emerald Ray, they rebalanced one another and each was able to heal.

When Hilarion called them back to the temple and restored them to their higher dimensional consciousness, they all had a new appreciation of the stress that third dimensional humans face when they become ill and try to heal. But they also had new hope and faith in the capability of their future third dimensional selves.

"Implant this technique in your pineal gland, so that you can use it once you walk on Earth. But most important of all, remember that healing occurs when one realizes that there is no imperfection, no disharmony, that all is complete and whole, that all are One and the Divine resides in every cell of our bodies. All is Divine. Call on me for assistance. Come to my retreat on Crete during your sleep time. It will be my pleasure to give you further teaching and to share my knowledge with you."

Master Hilarion lifted his gentle eyes and gazed out over them. In his left hand, a jeweled goblet set with emeralds appeared. He raised it up. "I hold my cup of healing out to you, dear ones." As he said these words, a golden goblet, encrusted with emeralds, and filled with the sweetest of healing nectars appeared in the left hand of each of them.

"Call on the Green Ray whenever you are in need, and my legions of Green Flame angels will instantly be in your field. Prepare your hearts diligently for your mission, my beloveds. I am Hilarion, offering my cup of love." Hilarion raised his goblet and drank to them. All did the same. As the last drop was swallowed, all the goblets disappeared. The nectar filled them with a blissful warmth. Master Hilarion bowed to them, and straightening up, he took his leave with these words, "Feel me in the vibration of your third eye. You are never alone. Keep your feet upon the path of light. Godspeed valiant ones."

As he turned and vanished, he sent a beam of emerald light from his third eye into the third eye of everyone present, charging them with energy so that all felt perfectly balanced, uplifted and refreshed.

The six friends gathered around Heipleido as they left the temple for the day.

"Without her, I feel myself to be a small thing, like a giant star stuffed into a black hole or a little gray mouse rattling around in what was once the body of a majestic elephant."

They all felt his loneliness without Maepleida. She had sliced herself away from them. But each understood that this was right, and that all would be well in the end. Ederah and Bereh walked Heipleido to his cottage, now an empty nightingale's nest. Soonam and Attivio, and Toomeh and Laaroos sat under their tree, mostly in silence, watching the sky change from pink to a blaze of gold. When night was finally in the sky, they rose.

Chapter 8

A Day of Rest

Soonam lay asleep, curled up around Attivio, still busy with her dreams. Lying still, eyes closed, he listened to her breathing. When it changed, he knew she had awakened and he turned to face her. She opened her eyes and light fell out of them. None of the volunteers had slept since becoming fifth dimensional, but all had returned to the sleep-wake cycle in preparation for this mission.

"I'd forgotten how much I like sleeping," Soonam said. Especially the delicious feeling of falling into sleep."

"You're what's delicious. Come closer so I can drown in your violet scented mouth." Attivio pulled her into his arms and undressed her heart. Their love was now like full ripened grain, an experience beyond thought. Eons ago they had been shy travelers in the fields of love, exploring slowly the holiness of the heart's affections.

At the same moment, Bereh was sitting up in bed making plans to delight Ederah. To this end, he manifested a breakfast tray for two, with tea, scones, jam and clotted cream. Then he woke her with the words, "Breakfast in bed, my sweet one, like the ladies in England do it."

Ederah, with her eyes still closed, smiled a sleepy smile when he held a warm scone under her nose and whispered the softest words into the seashell of her ear.

"Hmmm, lovely," she said, luxuriating in the sensations. *Touch has a memory*, she thought. *I will tuck these touches in a safe corner of my heart.* When she finally opened her grey-gold eyes, Ederah saw a beautiful, flowered porcelain tea pot and cups, set out on a breakfast tray next to silver spoons and snowy-white, cloth napkins.

"What a good idea this is, Bereh. Did you choose it because we had an English dinner the other night?"

"Perhaps without realizing it," Bereh said.

Along with getting used to sleeping again, they were all eating food again, too. They could easily survive on light as fifth dimensional beings, but once born they would need food. She bit into a scone with delight. "Hmmm," she said again, "the perfect confection. Is that cinnamon I taste in the scone."

"Yes, but I can change it to blueberry or orange cranberry if you prefer."

"No, cinnamon is perfect. And I propose we have breakfast from a different country each morning we're here in training. How about an American breakfast tomorrow," Ederah said, while pouring the tea, "and the day after, a Japanese one, and then a Russian, and then a Persian, and an Indian, and a Mexican, and a Moroccan, a Nigerian, and a Chinese and a Japanese — until we know all about breakfast on Earth."

"Steady on, darling. I'm not sure about raw fish for breakfast, or chicken feet either."

A few cottages across the hillside from Ederah and Bereh, Heipleido lay on his back in bed, one arm folded behind his head, thinking of Maepleida. He lingered on a vision of her eyelashes. They were like soft feathers, so thick a tiny nightingale could have nested in them. He longed to pillow his head on the gentle swelling of her breast. Waking up beside her each morning was one of the times he had loved best since coming to Venus. He never tired of looking into her mysterious eyes, or of laughing at some witty remark she tossed out so easily. Her mother had warned him that she'd inherited a drop too much of the family contrariness. He disagreed, he knew she could be tough, but he liked that about her. *If we must cut the threads for now, it will be alright,* he rationalized. *All eternity stretches before us, so a lifetime or two apart while I'm on Earth will be as nothing.* But he didn't convince himself. The truth was, he ached for her. Nothing felt right. Half himself was missing. As he lay brooding over her loveliness, he felt a prisoner, remembrance of her destroying his freedom. He threw the covers off and got up.

Laaroos was still asleep when Toomeh awoke. He lay there gazing at the splendor of her, feeling more content than he could ever remember being. *To feel such devotion to so fair a form completes me*, he thought. *We complete one another. But now we're about to part for a time, maybe for eons, if we fail in this mission.* As he gazed at her sleeping face, he felt his motivation to find her on Earth and reunite grow implacable. Feeling his gaze, she opened her eyes and felt her soul pour forth into him. It was still new, waking up next to him and trembling at his masculine beauty, knowing him as herself, the other half of her soul's body.

It was to be a day of rest for all of them, to metabolize the information and teachings they had received so far. Because Maepleida's departure had subdued them all, they'd made no special plan for their whole group for the day, so they were all on their own.

Ederah and Bereh decided to visit the part of the Akashic records where the history of Earth was recorded, hoping that learning about Earth's history would help to prepare them for their mission. As they didn't have a crystal like Ederah's father's, which could access the records remotely, they would have to transport themselves to Saturn's rings, where the records were stored. But this was easy enough to do using their intention. By focusing on the vibratory rate of the hall containing the records, and then adjusting their own vibration to match that of the hall, and then activating their merkabas, they could arrive there instantly. For beings who view all of creation as One, tele-transportation is easily accomplished. In a moment's time, they were in Saturn's rings, standing before a magnificent shimmering sphere with wide, white stone steps leading to an open archway. Inside, they were greeted by a living tapestry, which was weaving itself with threads of many colored light.

The tapestry hung on long ropes of braided gold, so that both sides were visible. They stopped to observe it creating itself. It looked as if it was being woven by invisible hands. As they stood before it, a guide approached them and offered to be of service. By his manner and appearance, they recognized him as a fellow Venusian, and asked him what was being written in the tapestry. He told them that the planned mission to Earth, now in preparation on Venus, was at that moment being recorded in the tapestry. Ederah asked the guide who, or what, determined what was to be written.

"The tapestry is a living being, sensitive to all events in this part of the galaxy. No one outside of itself directs it. It picks up currents from the atmosphere, and weaves them in as it sees fit."

"But how do you know what it's writing?" Bereh asked the guide.

"It requires training to read directly from the tapestry," he explained. "I'm here, in Saturn's rings, studying that now."

Ederah saw that a profusion of pink light, the color of the sky on Venus, stood out from the other colors of light that were at that moment being woven into the tapestry, and she thought the tapestry must still be writing about the training taking place.

After admiring it a little longer, they asked the guide for directions to the light tablets which held the history of Earth. He accompanied them through several large, vaulted chambers before pointing them to the tablets they had requested. He then bowed and left them to their research.

"Look at this," Bereh said, pointing to a section of the light tablet he was reading. "It says that the Earth was created by the Elohim."

"Yes, the Elohim are part of the Godhead, the builders of form," Ederah said. "They create universes, galaxies, solar systems and planets, and sustain all creation with their light."

Bereh read further. "The light of the Elohim is of such a magnitude that even fifth dimensional beings cannot comprehend it."

"That's all fascinating, but I want to read about something I've just come across, about Camelot," Ederah said. "I remember both my mother and El Morya talking about it. It looks so magical and romantic. Camelot is where Master El Morya was incarnated as King Arthur, the leader of the Great White Brotherhood, during the fifth century on Earth."

"Yes, I remember your mother talking about Camelot over dinner when we all visited."

"And Master Saint Germain was known as Merlin in that lifetime. He was the wizard who taught King Arthur."

"I can see we each have to do our own thing," Bereh said. "I want to look up when the quarantine around Earth began, and why it was thought necessary to quarantine Earth. Wait a minute. Here it is. You have to hear this. 'The quarantine was put in place 75,000 years ago, after the beings from Mars were brought to Earth in their light bodies once Mars became uninhabitable due to nuclear war.'"

"But that doesn't explain the reason for the quarantine," Ederah said.

"Because the third dimensional beings on Mars were too warlike," Bereh read, "they were genetically manipulated to be more peace loving before being seeded on Earth. However, after it was done, the genetic manipulation was declared, by the council of nine and the twenty-four guardians of Earth, to be a violation of the free will of those beings from Mars. Therefore, going forward, the council decreed that there would be no more interference with any being incarnate on Earth. The quarantine was established to ensure it." Bereh sat pondering this and wondering how the genetic manipulation had been carried out on the Martians that were moved to Earth. The thought of manipulating any being, even warlike beings, was abhorrent to him. To his mind, free will was one of the most precious gifts an entity could possess. While Bereh contemplated the desirability of free will, Ederah moved on to researching the history of wanderers on Earth. She learned that there were currently more than 65,000,000 wanderers from higher dimensions now living on Earth as humans in the third dimension. Each of them had volunteered, motivated by the desire to be of service to others, and had agreed to pass through the veil of forgetting, just as she and her friends were doing. Unfortunately, most of them had not yet awakened in the third dimension. Many had become karmically involved on Earth, and gotten swept into the maelstrom. Ederah recalled Laaroos's mother, stuck on Earth, drawing mandalas in Washington Square Park, and felt grateful for the preparation and training her own group was receiving. Each wanderer from a higher dimension who remembered her mission made it easier for all other wanderers to awaken. Ederah paused in her reading, bowed her head, and offered a prayer for all the wanderers who had not yet awakened. The day passed quickly, and by the time they reset their frequencies to match those of Venus, for their return home, both Ederah and Bereh had learned much, and were falling in love with the little blue-green planet called Earth.

Soonam and Attivio had a different idea for their day. Because Soonam loved boats, row boats, sail boats, motor boats, big boats, small boats, all boats, and because they had enjoyed the sight of people boating in Central Park during the exercise in New York City, before they were even out of bed, and still snuggling, Attivio suggested a day on the nearby lake.

"Yes! Shall we sail or row or motor or glide along using only our intention?" Soonam asked.

"Row, I think," Attivio said. "I'm in a rowing kind of mood since seeing the row boats in Central Park. Then we can rest and drift along on the water, too, if we like."

Soonam created a sheer, pastel, flowered dress for herself, like one she'd seen a lady wearing at a nearby table at the Boathouse in Central Park. Next, she pulled on stockings, slipped into lavender shoes and buckled them across her slender feet. Attivio manifested a white summer suit and a gentleman's straw hat with a white hat band. "Smashing," they said in unison, looking at one another, and set off through the woods, hand in hand, Soonam's dress dancing and floating about her legs as she walked. When they reached the lake, they saw that it was a clear blue, and as calm as glass. Attivio manifested a wooden rowboat and two oars. He offered Soonam his hand to help her in. She settled in the back of the boat, facing him, and using her intention placed a bright-blue padded cushion under each of them, and one behind her back. She reclined on her cushion and dribbled her fingers in the water, sighing with pleasure at the feeling of the soft water on her fingertips. As they glided along, neither of them spoke, or even sent a telepathic message. But silently, Soonam was enjoying the sight of Attivio with his jacket off, his shirt sleeves rolled up, his manly arms, strong and steady on the oars. He was divine, in his half-human, half-light body. She stored this picture of him deep in her memory, for a time when she might need it. Then she closed her eyes and let her mind become a still reflection of the lake. After a while, Attivio lifted the dripping oars out of the water to let them rest on the sides of the boat. Feeling the change in motion as they drifted in the water, Soonam opened her violet eyes, and smiling, suggested they create a picnic like people had on Earth. Attivio needed no coaxing to warm to the plan. And reminded her that in Central Park, people were sitting on the grass eating something called sandwiches, with pickles and potato salad and chocolate cake and lemonade and watermelon. Delighted with his memory, Soonam ordered picnic sandwiches a la America, for two. Instantly, assorted little sandwiches, accompanied by pickles and potato salad appeared on white plates in their laps, on top of red and white checkered cotton napkins.

"Shall we?" Soonam said, inclining her head toward the plate on her lap.

"Absolutely, eating food is nice," Attivio said.

"Do humans have to eat, or do they just do it for pleasure?" Soonam asked.

"Both, I think. They have to eat food because they don't yet know how to use light as energy," Attivio reminded her.

"I keep forgetting that. Well I like eating food," Soonam said.

After they had enjoyed their first course, Soonam created water melon cut into little round globes, and chocolate cake with chocolate icing.

"Oh, where did the strawberry ice cream come from, I didn't create that," Soonam said.

"I added that touch," Attivio said.

"Perfect." Soonam beamed at him as she tasted the pink ice cream. "This is what the little girl I saw by the fountain in New York was eating when her father helped her with the drips."

Attivio smiled at her, as he so often did.

"I hope one day, on Earth, we will float together on a lake, and have a picnic just like this, awakened in the third dimension, with the full knowledge of who we are," Soonam said.

Finished with their picnic, the pair floated along the smooth surface of the lake, first carried by an invisible current to one side, to pause under some hanging tree fronds, then drifting out again into the sunlight before being ferried by the breeze to the other side of the lake, to rest in the shade under a large tree branch. After letting the boat drift here and there for a while, Attivio suggested a swim. They slipped out of their clothes and dove into the water naked. Soonam resurfaced with a radiant smile.

"Delicious, silky water," she said. Luxuriating in the sensation of the water was an experience beyond thought for her, and she reveled in it, rolling over onto her back and floating, her lovely naked form visible just beneath the water, her eyelashes heavy with water droplets.

Attivio beheld her as one staring at a goddess. But before his pleasure could turn to brooding over their imminent separation, he said, "Come on, race you across." And they were off.

Laaroos and Toomeh slept late. When she awoke, Laaroos looked around their cottage and said to Toomeh, "Lie to me. Tell me this is our home, and we will never be parted."

"Then let's make it live the song in our hearts," Toomeh said.

"I hear the architectural notes of arches and vaulted ceilings," Laaroos said.

"Yes, they're shapes which intensify the spiraling of light," Toomeh added.

"I love the way spiraling light feels when it touches our magnetic fields, but also, there's the soft way they look and sound compared to the severity of right angled walls," Laaroos said.

"At one time on Earth, in the Americas, some groups of advanced humans, being aware of the spiraling of energy, created structures called tipis. And the pyramids, too, supposedly help light energy to spiral," Toomeh told her.

"But for today," Laaroos reminded him, "there is no Earth mission looming." And she brushed his lips with such sweetness from her own, that she drew his mind completely back to their present moment.

"Right," he said, "ready to commence?"

Moments later they were sitting under a vaulted ceiling. Four arches created a perimeter to the space. Next, they surrounded the structure with delights on each side. On the east side, Laaroos created a reflection pool with floating, white lotus blossoms. On the west side of their arched temple, Toomeh added a terrace with a fountain from which water swirled under the feet of a sculpture of Eros and Psyche. To the south, they made an orchard of fruit trees, including one with golden pears. Through the arch on the fourth side, beyond the wild flowers, off in the distance, a sea of the palest turquoise sparkled in the sun. Next, they turned their attention to the interior, covering the vaulted ceiling with murals of twin flame pairs from across time and space. Laaroos paid special attention to creating the image of Jesus and Mary Magdalene, known to them as Lord Sananda and Lady Nada.

Their creation complete, they played. Laaroos looked to Toomeh like a fairy child dipping her toes in the fountain, her feet light, her eyes wild as she danced off to pick a golden pear. She brought it to him where he lounged on a Persian carpet covered with pillows. Laaroos sighed as he covered her naked body with wild flowers, placing each one carefully so it adorned all the parts of her he worshipped. After they had shared the ecstasy of love making, she turned on her side and asked him, "What do you suppose sex will be like as a human in the third dimension? I have no recollection of what it was like from when I was a third dimensional being."

"It will most likely have a purpose beyond just pleasure, just as it does for us in the higher dimensions," Toomeh said. "But I don't know if third dimensional beings can use sex as a gateway to the Divine, as we do.

"I remember Paul the Venetian saying that humans could use sex as a bridge to the Divine."

"I don't remember that," Toomeh said, "but I did hear Kumara explaining the other evening that 'the ultimate moment of sexual ecstasy is the only real moment of Ananda in the third dimension.' He also said that, 'orgasm is the sweetest thing on earth, and is given to humans for pleasure and procreation. And that seminal fluid in men is the actual creative energy of God as it manifests on the physical plane, while in women, the creative energy of God is preserved in the chakras.'"

Laaroos casually rolled over onto her back and Toomeh's heart missed a beat seeing the gentle edifice of her breasts. She pretended not to notice his reaction and continued the conversation.

"Even in the third dimension, sexual union is an exchange where the female is refreshed by the strength of the male, and the male is blessed with inspiration and healing by the female," she said smiling.

Toomeh could wait no longer. "Come here," he said pulling her close and placing his palm over her mound of Venus before entering her. *Oh, to feel forever its swell,* his heart sighed.

Laaroos felt his touch like a whisper and poured forth her soul in ecstasy. Their minds, bodies and spirits united in sexual fusion, they were one flesh and one light, riding the orgasmic wave of the universe.

"You have absorbed me," Toomeh breathed. "I am dissolving into bliss."

The day was less orgasmic for Heipleido. He descended into the daylight darkness of the meditation cave beneath the temple. Being rounded, not unlike a vaulted ceiling or a tipi, the cave was a place of power which would intensify his meditation. In deep communion with his Higher Self and his I Am Presence, Heipleido sat cross legged and straight backed throughout the day. When he emerged, at day's end, he wore his serenity within and without, his fifth dimensional self, his Higher Self and his I Am Presence in alignment. He felt no anguish over Maepleida's absence. He knew that for the balanced entity, no situation is emotionally charged. He felt the peace of having faith in another, and the even greater peace of having faith in oneself. Walking up the hill to his cottage alone to retire for the night, he was free from the prison of his longing.

Chapter 9

Lord Sananda and Lady Nada

"Good morning, my beloveds." Lord Sananda's voice rang through the temple like the sound of a clear bell. "My twin flame, Nada, and I have come to help prepare you for your mission to Earth."

Heipleido slipped into his seat next to Toomeh, who noted how clear Heipleido's eyes looked, and smiled at him before turning his attention back to Lord Sananda.

"You will be joining more than sixty million wanderers from higher dimensions already on Earth, who are there attempting to raise the planetary vibration. As you know, our plan is for your group to provide the tipping point, allowing enlightenment to sweep the planet."

Soonam stared at Lady Nada's loveliness. Red hair fell to Nada's waist. Her slender arms, throat and oval face were milky white against her flowing violet robes. She looked as if she had been soaked in flowers. Soonam had heard many stories about Lady Nada, but loved most the one of her first meeting with Lord Sananda. At the time of their meeting, he was known as Jesus, and she, as Mary Magdalene. He was standing in the square in the midst of a group, speaking to them, when she chanced to pass by. Held by the sound of his voice, Mary stayed to listen. Jesus felt her presence, and his eyes sought her in the crowd, as if he knew who he was seeking, and when he found her, he locked his gaze on her eyes, binding them together across the distance. The experience of the light pouring from his eyes into her own was so overpowering, that she instantly awakened. In that trembling moment, her thought almost became a whisper, *he comes to me with all my faults, and knows me as his own*. Today, Jesus and Nada stood side by side, wearing separate bodies, but all knew them to be one Soul.

Soonam turned her gaze from Nada to Jesus. In contrast to Nada's milky whiteness, Lord Sananda's skin was a deep bronze. His shoulder length brown hair and rich bronze skin were alive with light, and from his palms an even greater light flowed out in rivers of gold. Lady Nada, too, radiated light from every electron in her being as she stood before them shimmering in her violet robes.

"Two thousand years ago Nada and I incarnated on Earth, as you are about to do, as wanderers. In that life, we were known as Mary Magdalene and Jesus. Our mission, like yours, was to find one another and to heal the effects of planetary disharmony. We were not attempting to create a religion, but to bring the message that we are, each one of us, Divine, and that all are One. We wanted to tell the humans that there is nothing outside of themselves that can satisfy their deepest longings, that happiness is within only. It is an illusion that humans are separate from the Highest. We tried to infuse the knowledge that God is a resonance inside each of us which can be felt, especially in the heart and throat. By teaching how to live in the now moment, how to focus on the Presence within, we tried to activate the Divine Presence in the hearts of human beings. But things did not go as planned in that incarnation. The Dark Lords were then, as now, abroad in the land, disguised as humans, and occupying many places of power. When I was arrested and brought before Pontius Pilot, I saw him as a large, black reptile covered with scales, standing up on his hind legs, with short, claw-like arms, about fourteen feet tall. Most humans did not see through his disguise and mistook him for a human. Creatures of the dark side still operate on Earth. Though their numbers are fewer, they remain in positions of power in finance and in many governments. And, they are still in league with the Orion group, fighting to win the souls of humans for the dark side."

Heipleido recalled the creepy feeling he had during their

training exercise in New York, when he and Maepleida had passed the bankers' box at the ball game in Yankee Stadium. Seeing those men had given him the shivers as he sensed their true dark forms hidden by their human disguise. He shuddered at the memory and turned his attention back to Sananda.

"Much of what I attempted to teach in that lifetime was distorted by the dark lords in their hope of using it to control the humans. That is how the dark side works. They start with a truth, and twist it so that it seems like a truth, but it no longer is. *The Ten Commandments* are an example of this. No true God would say — *thou shalt not.* Free will is God's law. God does not dictate. *The Ten Commandments* in the form of dictates are a distortion by the dark side, used to control and frighten people into submission. Humans are meant to have free will. No one is meant to command them."

Bereh's whole being resonated with this, and he repeated Sananda's words to himself – "no one is meant to command humans. They are meant to have free will." So completely entranced by Sananda and Nada was he, that he made a mental note to call on them specifically for help, should he need it once on Earth. He tucked this mental note deep into the pituitary of his light body.

"Despite not everything going as planned in that lifetime," Sananda continued, "I was able to demonstrate one truth – and that was that there is no death. Yes, the body can die, but the soul, does not die. In that lifetime, I was able to bring my body back from the dead after the crucifixion, because I was given a powerful affirmation. And it was that affirmation which allowed me to resurrect my physical body. As you know, words and prayer have power. Nada and I will give you that affirmation now.

I am the resurrection and the life.

Say it in your heart three times and feel the Resurrection Flame kindle within you. Carry this affirmation with you to Earth. Use these words to invoke the Resurrection Flame daily so you may restore yourself to wholeness whenever you have a need. In a moment, we'll do some practice with this affirmation. But first, Nada will talk to you about how the human body works."

Lady Nada bowed her head just a bit toward Sananda in acknowledgement of his invitation to speak. Then she turned her eyes to the group before her. When she started to talk, the light emanating from her heart and throat glowed an even brighter gold. She swept her violet robes to one side and took a step closer to them. "The mechanical concept of the human body is incorrect," she began. "For those in the third dimension on Earth, even as for you who sit before me in the fifth dimensions, the body is, in fact, the creature of the mind which controls it. As such, it is very malleable and open to suggestion. As you know, in the fifth dimension, and beyond, you can freely create the body you desire. Those in the third dimension cannot create the form they desire, but they can still affect their physical bodies, though to a more limited extent. The limitation exists mainly because most third dimensional beings are unaware of the possibilities. And as yet, most humans don't know how to use affirmations to help their bodies. Many doubt that affirmations actually work, because they don't perceive the mechanism through which they create their effect.

"*Affirmations work by instructing the body about what the mind desires.* The mind in harmony with the will of the Higher Self can manifest with unlimited possibility. Even the third dimensional being can learn to manifest with unlimited possibility once they align their minds with the Higher Self. As you will be third dimensional beings once you incarnate, you will need to open the door of your mind to be able to protect, restore and preserve your bodies. Once your mind is open, you will be able use the Resurrection Flame, along with affirmations, to restore others as well as yourself. You had some experience of this flame when Hilarion came to work with you and you practiced healing one another. Today we'll again work with the Resurrection Flame. Sananda and I have devised an exercise so that you can practice using the flame along with affirmations." Nada turned to Sananda, who took up the task of explaining the exercise.

"For our exercise," he began, "we've created what is called on Earth, a hospital. It contains lots of rooms with beds. Many people on Earth die in hospitals, and the energy in hospitals is often negative and frightening, which is why we've chosen to create this setting for your work today. To be of help on Earth, you will need to be at ease in many kinds of places, including hospitals. Once enlightenment sweeps the planet there will be no need for hospitals. But until everyone has the power to heal, hospitals will continue to exist. Today we will ask you to work in groups of three or more. Choose a hospital room and designate one of your group to be the patient. With your permission, once you enter the hospital I will regress your vibration to the third dimension. Again, as with Hilarion's exercise, your challenge will be to heal using only the powers of a third dimensional being. But this time, you will add an affirmation. To remind you, third dimensional beings do have the ability to work with light, and to use affirmations to heal, but only once they become conscious of this power. Third dimensional power is not as concentrated as that of a fifth dimensional being, so you will have to work together to wield the Resurrection Flame to restore life." Sananda paused, and Nada said, "If your twin flame is the group member who volunteers to die for this exercise, it will be especially difficult for you. Remind your third dimensional self that there is no death."

"Shall we all form one group?" Soonam asked as they left the temple.

"Yes, that feels right," Ederah said, "because we'll need our combined energy."

With everyone agreed, they entered the hospital and immediately felt themselves sink into the third dimension. The loss of contact with the Divine, as their five extrinsic higher chakras shut down, was excruciating. Then the smell of strong disinfectant and sickness assaulted their senses, repulsing them. Despite this, they pushed on and found a hospital room. The room was painted a dull, institutional green and unfamiliar equipment stood beside the bed and in the stainless-steel bathroom. The whole effect was cold and most unwelcoming.

"Never mind it," Soonam counseled. "If we succeed on Earth, these places will be obsolete."

"Right then, let's get on with it," Bereh said. "I'll be the patient."

Ederah squeezed his hand while he stretched out on the bed, and smiled up at her. She reminded him to keep repeating, *I am the resurrection and the life.* But a moment later, he fell silent, his quiet breath ceased and he no longer moved. He was physically dead. Ederah stopped breathing without realizing it. Her third dimensional self was terrified. Sananda entered the room and placed his hand on Ederah's heart, and she remembered to breathe again. He and Nada had multiplied themselves, so one or the other of them was with each group.

"Place your palms on him and call on the Resurrection Flame," Sananda instructed them. "Use the invocation. Concentrate on drawing the flame up through the soles of your feet."

"Into our hearts?" Ederah asked, her voice trembling.

"Yes, and then up to your crown and back to your heart and down your arms into your palms," Sananda told her. "Your intention is what wields the flame."

Ederah clenched and unclenched her hands and placed them over Bereh's heart. Everyone did as Sananda instructed and gathered around the bed with their palms on Bereh, who remained lifeless.

Laaroos began the affirmation, *"Bereh is the resurrection and the life."*

Toomeh joined her, then Soonam and Attivio and Heipleido

added their voices and intention. They drew the purple-gold flame up through the soles of their feet into their hearts and out through their hands, directing it into Bereh's body. As they continued to work, the power in the room built. Once or twice Ederah glanced at Sananda, who nodded his assurance.

"Use your intention. See the flame and wield it," he instructed.

For several minutes, nothing happened. Ederah began to weep, which was strange to her, as she had forgotten about crying. But of course, third dimensional beings cried when they were scared or sad.

"Open the door of your mind," Sananda instructed her. "Work with the flame. Use your intention. Remember that God is a resonance inside each of you. Each of you holds God's power to restore life."

They all renewed their intention and focused again on the affirmation, and on drawing the flame upward through the soles of their feet and out through their palms into Bereh's heart. As fifth dimensional, any one of them could have done this alone, but as third dimensional they were struggling.

"Work together to build enough power," Sananda directed them.

And again they refocused and strengthened their intention. Heipleido felt the energy growing stronger. Laaroos, too, felt it, and gave an involuntary shiver. When Bereh's chest began to rise and fall, Ederah let out a gasp. Bereh opened his eyes and turned his head to look at her.

"I was watching you all from just above as you sent the flame into my body," he said.

Lord Sananda raised his hand and restored them to their fifth dimensional consciousness. As their higher chakras re-opened and contact with the Divine was restored, a feeling of bliss swept through them.

"Well done. Come back to the temple now," Sananda said.

When they were all comfortable back in the fifth dimension,

Sananda addressed them.

"You have all successfully used the mantra and wielded the Resurrection Flame to restore life. As the guardians of the Resurrection Flame, Nada and I offer you the gift of it. Use the unlimited aspect of yourselves to wield it and create miracles on Earth." Sananda bowed to them and turned to Nada, who then spoke to them.

"Beloveds, you've done well today using only your third dimensional powers. I am certain of your victory. Remember always that in each infinitesimal part of yourself, in every cell, in every electron, resides the One, in all of Its power."

Lady Nada bowed to them, then lifting her left hand released from her palm a shower of golden beams which floated out over them and gently fell upon each head, initiating a feeling of profound well-being. She opened her mind to them, and allowed them to touch it with their own. As Soonam touched Nada's mind with hers, the feeling of bliss was so sublime that she gasped out loud. Through Lady Nada's gift, each of them experienced new depths of the endlessness of love possible in enlightened beings existing beyond the fifth dimension. Soonam floated more than walked out of the temple, Attivio at her side.

Sananda and Nada were standing under the trees with Lord Kumara when Ederah and Bereh approached. They were discussing Earth's web of electromagnetic energy fields. Sananda turned to include Ederah and Bereh as he spoke.

"Humans, like their planet, are also electromagnetic energy fields with energy centers. As you all just experienced, humans have only the seven lower chakras open. In order to achieve enlightenment and to ascend, every human must balance all seven of these chakras."

"This balancing will be made easier for everyone by your presence on Earth," Nada added.

"Are you saying that ascension and full enlightenment will be possible from the third dimension?" Bereh asked her.

"Yes, enlightenment as an opening to Intelligent Infinity, in whatever degree is possible for each being," Nada said.

Up close she was even more beautiful. Ederah observed her in awed silence. Native to Venus, Ederah and Bereh, like all Venusians, were themselves beautiful, tall, elegant, golden beings of gentle character. But Lady Nada, it seemed to Ederah, possessed another order of beauty altogether.

"During your lifetime as Jesus, at what age did you realize that you were a wanderer from a higher dimension?" Bereh asked, turning to Sananda.

"Some surprising things happened when I was a child, but really, not until my early teenage years did I have the full realization that I had come on a mission," Lord Sananda told him.

Bereh turned to Lady Nada.

"For me, it was when I met Sananda, at age sixteen, after I had escaped from slavery and prostitution. I went to hear him speak, not knowing who he actually was to me. I was hiding in the crowd, afraid to be seen and feeling unworthy to be there. But his eyes found mine, and I was powerless under his gaze to look anywhere except back into those burning eyes. It was the power transmitted by his gaze that awakened me. I knew at that moment that he was my twin flame. All twin flames can instantly spark an awakening when they meet on Earth. The recognition, for me, was immediate," Lady Nada said. "We're pleased that there are so many twin flame pairs in your group. It will lighten the task."

Ederah found her voice. "Will twin flame pairs be special targets for the Orion group?"

Lord Sananda smiled at her. "Generally the Orion group prefers to make contact with the weaker-minded entity as their goal is to enslave, but in the case of twin flames, your suspicion is correct, they will make an exception, and target them. Twin flame pairs are considered by those of Orion to be a great prize when led to the dark side," Sananda added, "but be not afraid. Help is always available if you call on it."

As they prepared to leave, Lady Nada extended an invitation. "Come to our retreat outside Jerusalem. We have much to share. You can travel in your light bodies during your body's sleep time once you incarnate."

Lord Sananda raised his hand in blessing. Then they were gone. They simply turned and vanished. Ederah and Bereh felt a sudden emptiness at their departure, as if the sun had passed behind a cloud.

Chapter 10

Maepleida in the Himalayas

Maepleida stood on the marble steps, and gazed out over the snow-covered peaks of the majestic Himalayas. When she turned around to face the palace, she saw El Morya standing above her at the entrance. With a warmth and graciousness which Maepleida had not expected, he came down the steps to greet her. He looked every inch the king from Arthurian legend, strong and regal, compassionate and wise. He bowed. A gold-white dawn broke in the sky. It was morning on Earth.

Together they climbed the steps and walked through a large archway, where El Morya's twin flame, Amerissis, awaited them. Walking on either side of her, the couple led Maepleida deeper into the entrance hall, toward a blue flame a hundred feet high. The flame occupied the center of the hall. All around the walls burned smaller blue flames in golden sconces. The smaller flames lit tapestries depicting the past lives of the ascended masters responsible for Earth: Merlin teaching King Arthur as a boy, Arthur and Guinevere, Sir Lancelot and the Knights of the round table, Jesus and the three wise men. Amerissis and El Morya escorted Maepleida through the great hall, past the tapestries, into the temple room.

The first thing Maepleida noticed upon entering the room was the altar, which was made of sapphires and diamonds, and covered with burning beeswax candles. The candles lent a soft fragrance to the air and warmed the jewels. Amerissis directed her attention to an enormous diamond in the center of the room. It stood fifteen feet tall and had thousands of facets.

"Each facet represents an aspect of the Divine Will," she explained.

Maepleida made a slight bow to the large crystal,

acknowledging its divine consciousness.

"In the presence of this diamond being, the facets of your own diamond heart will come into alignment with the Will of God in you," Amerissis told her. "When you surrender to the will of the Divine within you, you will know which path to choose."

Royal-blue, velvet cushions surrounded the large diamond. El Morya extended his arm toward them. "We'll leave you now," he said. "Someone will show you to your room when you're ready." Their presence felt like that of two loving parents and Maepleida wished they wouldn't leave her so soon. She arranged the folds of her dove-grey gown and sat down on one of the cushions facing the diamond. Instantly, she felt the power of the diamond engulf her. Thoughts of Heipleido, Venus, their friends, the mission, moved through her mind as she tried to clear it to meditate. What was she resisting, she wondered, hadn't she come for answers? After some struggle, her mind released its grip, and she merged with the incorruptible energy of the diamond. Maepleida didn't know how long she had sat by the diamond when she finally rose, and bowed to it, in gratitude. The candles cast elongated shadows on the temple walls and on the now dark, arched medieval windows. She glanced out the window to see the final rays of the setting sun paint the Himalayas gold, then crimson, and finally lavender.

When she left the temple room, she was met by a young woman in white who led her to a hallway high up in the castle. The arched ceiling in the passage was a light sky-blue. Several arched doorways lined the passage. The woman opened one, and showed Maepleida into a spacious candlelit room with a tapestry depicting an elegant woman, who appeared to be studying the heavenly bodies in what looked like medieval times on Earth. It hung over the bed. A single arm chair was drawn up to the crackling fire, and a wooden table, laden with nectar, ambrosia, and holding a small bouquet of wild flowers, was next to the chair. When the young woman left, Maepleida said out loud to no one, "I miss Heipleido." She blew out all the candles which were set in sconces along the walls, and sat in the firelight, its flickering warmth feeling more harmonious. Not wanting to brood overlong on Heipleido, she allowed herself one indulgence, and luxuriated in the memory of the velvet softness of his black skin. In his light body, she had never felt his skin, but on Venus they were all embodied in hybrid forms in preparation for the mission. It had been a delight to both of them to touch one another in this new form. It is something holy to be devoted to so fair a form, she thought as she rose to go to bed, her eyelashes heavy with love's tears.

The next morning Maepleida went again to sit before the large diamond, praying that it would pull her into alignment with the Will of the Divine in her. That afternoon, she had an audience with Amerissis and El Morya. Amerissis directed her to focus on knowing and loving her innermost being, reminding her to welcome and accept her confusion as part of her path. Then El Morya invited her to a gathering that evening, and explained that incarnated wanderers would be coming, traveling in their light bodies, for support and instruction. Maepleida felt excited at the prospect of seeing actual wanderers, and imagined that one day Heipleido and their friends might attend such a gathering. This was indeed an unexpected boon, almost a look into the future. Some of them would be awakened and know their mission, El Morya said, but some would not yet understand what they were doing in the third dimension. He hoped tonight's talk would stir remembering in those who had not yet realized that their true home was in a higher dimension. Maepleida's heart lightened at the prospect of seeing these wanderers, who had risked all to come to Earth. Perhaps it would strengthen her own resolve, one way or the other.

That evening the palace was a town vibrating with anticipation as it filled with wanderers and their guides from all over the globe. Maepleida felt the excitement as she entered the great hall and looked up at the vaulted ceiling at least a hundred feet above her. Thousands of guests had traveled in their light bodies to be here this evening. Amerissis and El Morya strode through the throng, their sapphire robes sailing out behind them, until they reached the center of the group. The guests formed a circle around them, at least sixty-deep.

"Welcome beloveds. You are so very welcome here," El Morya began. "We have invited you tonight to stir you to awakening to the knowledge of who you truly are. In your light bodies, accompanied by your guides, you know full well that you are Divine beings, temporarily housed in a flesh and blood human body. Your human bodies are asleep now, back in your earthly homes, but your true self is here with us, listening to my words. When you leave tonight, you will take our message back and download it into your human consciousness so you may wake up in the third dimension to the reality that you are a light being, a being who has come to serve planet Earth and her people. Use the information we will impart this night to create heaven on Earth. Yes, it is possible," he said, lifting his arms as if to embrace all those before him, then turning around to face those who stood behind him.

"You are creators. Tonight, I will speak to you about the source of your creative energy, about the unlimited supply of electrons at your disposal every day, electrons with which you can create your reality. Know that each of you receives from Source an unlimited supply of electrons with which to work in order to create what you wish. You can use your thoughts, intentions or emotions to create your experience. Some of you here tonight are aware of this power, and some of you do not yet remember it when you are in your human bodies during the daytime. Let me jog your memory."

Maepleida felt for a moment that she could be back on Venus with her friends, sitting in the temple listening to a master. It heartened her to know that there would be further reminders and teachings when Heipleido and the other wanderers came to Earth.

"Once you understand the power of the electrons at your disposal, you will be able to create paradise," El Morya told them. "When you do not realize that you are the creator, by default you create much pain and suffering for yourselves, and for the planet. Electrons respond to your intention, whether it is positive or negative. Electrons want to respond to love, but if that is not the intention with which you direct them, they have no choice but to respond to what they receive, even if they are used to create hate and destruction. This was the case with the electrons used to create the atom bomb. They had to serve the intention of those qualifying them and become a bomb. Imagine how those electrons felt to be used to kill thousands of beings. Use your own unlimited supply of electrons wisely, qualify them with love to create consciously. Hold onto the awareness that your intention is, in fact, creating reality."

Maepleida looked around at the beings listening to El Morya. She wondered if among them were any old friends of Ederah's parents who had gotten stuck on Earth. Perhaps even Laaroos's mother was in this group of wanderers, listening to El Morya. She turned her attention back to El Morya, who was now bowing to Amerissis, inviting her to speak.

"My beloveds," she began. "You can create paradise on Earth if you qualify your electrons with the vibrations of love and peace. Make your choice in each moment, with full awareness and responsibility. Take care not to qualify your electrons with negative emotions or intentions. If you erupt in negative outbursts, you will distort the electrons in your own body, and open yourself to invasion by the dark side, which feeds on negative energy. In the human third dimensional body, in which most of you now find yourselves during your waking hours, the frustration is great, and negative outbursts are not uncommon. But it is dangerous to give in to negative outbursts. They make the body ill. Negative outbursts will draw the dark lords into your field, to feed on your negative energy and grow stronger as you weaken. Take care of the electrons at your disposal and create consciously. We do not want Earth to become another Maldek. For 200,000 years after the destruction, the entire population, in soul form, without bodies, remained in such a tight knot that no one of the confederation could reach them. You have come to Earth, now, at this time, to prevent that from happening to this beautiful planet and her people." Amerissis paused, and studied those surrounding her. The blue silk of her gown rustled as she made a half turn to include those behind her. "Be careful, my beloveds, electrons are a powerful business. They can be used for any purpose. Mind what you intend, dear ones, and you will create a paradise on this blue-green planet." Amerissis looked to El Morya to see if he would add a word before releasing them.

"Return now to your sleeping human bodies, and awaken to the true knowledge of who you are," El Morya told them. "We give you our blessing. Be at peace. All is well. Until we meet again, beloved light warriors, we bid you Godspeed." Then, as the wanderers cleared a path, Amerissis and El Morya walked through the throng and out of the hall.

After the gathering, Maepleida returned to her room and sat alone by the fire, her feet up on a green wooden trunk on which a garden scene was painted. She replayed all she had seen and heard that evening, and was relieved to see, close up, one of the ways in which wanderers were guided and helped once they incarnated. But she now had even more questions. She wondered how many in the group that evening would be able to stir their human bodies to awareness of their true identity, and remember their reason for being on Earth. Calmer, but still undecided about the mission, Maepleida questioned why there had to be a quarantine around Earth. Why couldn't light workers just help from their own higher dimensions? Why did they have to incarnate as third dimensional humans to help? Had she been told this already? In her confusion, had she forgotten? She stood up and walked over to the window, and stared out at the snow-capped peaks of the Himalayas, now lit by Earth's moon, only a crescent of which was visible tonight. Somewhere out beyond the moon was Venus. *There is a holiness in longing*, she thought. After staring into the sky for a long time, she climbed into bed and lay her head on her pillow, which had been brushed with wild lavender, and fell asleep with a hunger for the sound of Heipleido's breath.

Maepleida didn't see either Amerissis or El Morya the next day, or the next. She kept to her meditation schedule, her love of solitude growing as she felt herself coming into greater alignment with her Higher Self. And as she did, she seemed to grow softer and more beautiful to all those in the palace who silently observed her. On the third day, El Morya sent for her and she was shown to his area of the castle. It was a large room with a big circular fireplace in the middle surrounded by different levels on which were strewn rich carpets and pillows, covered in textiles from around the Earth. El Morya gestured for her to take a seat. She picked up a black and ivory print pillow and placing it on a rich Persian carpet, not unlike those she had seen at Ederah's parents' home, settled herself on it.

El Morya sat down near her and asked, "Has your path become any clearer?"

"I don't know, but I do have a question?"

El Morya nodded.

"Why was the quarantine put around Earth? I don't know of any other planet where this is the case."

"You are correct. Earth is the only planet in any galaxy with a quarantine."

"So why was it done?"

"Because, Earth is a planet where free will is meant to be the rule. No one from any galaxy was supposed to interfere with the progression of the humans here. The experiment was to see if once separated from the Creator, beings could find their way back home without assistance, unless that assistance was requested by them. Those who volunteered were aware of the conditions."

"But something happened?" Maepleida asked.

"Yes, something happened. Seventy-five thousand years ago the atmosphere of Mars became inhospitable due to a nuclear war which killed the entire population, but, unlike in the case of Maldek, the planet itself wasn't blown apart, it simply became uninhabitable. Mars, like Earth, was home to third dimensional beings. The guardians of this solar system met in their seat of government, in Saturn's rings, and decided to bring all the souls from Mars, to Earth, and to have them incarnate, through birth, as humans." At that point, the Martians had only their light bodies, as all their physical bodies had been obliterated in the blast."

"So, they had all been wiped out in the conflagration on Mars, and were not incarnate at the time of the transfer?" Maepleida asked.

"That's correct, as far as their physical bodies were concerned. Their souls, of course, had not been destroyed. But, it was felt by the guardians of Earth, that the beings from Mars, even in their light bodies, were too predatory and warlike, and would possibly destroy Earth if they were allowed to incarnate as they were.

"And altering them violated their free will?" Maepleida asked.

"According to the Council of Nine responsible for this solar system, yes, it violated the law that all beings on Earth have free will. And it disrupted the original Earth experiment, which was to see if beings, wiped of all memory of their origins, could find their way back to Source without help."

Maepleida absorbed all this in silence, then spoke slowly as she put the piees together. "So, in order to insure free will, going forward, the council placed a quarantine around Earth, so there could be no further manipulations or alterations of any being living on this planet, and that's why we have to incarnate as human, in order to be of help?"

"Precisely. Since wanderers have not been genetically manipulated, and freely volunteer to be ordinary third dimensional humans, with all memory of their Divine origin wiped, they aren't in violation of the rules governing incarnation on Earth."

"Then some of the Earth beings are from Mars. Where did the rest of Earth's population come from?"

"Two billion of the Earth's population are descended from those of Maldek, who were eventually brought here when contact with them finally became possible, about 500,000 years ago. For the prior 200,000 years they had been unreachable due to the shock of the nuclear blast. However, as karmic retribution, they were not permitted to incarnate as third dimensional humans. They were given second dimensional animal bodies, similar to bigfoot, and they lived in the interior of the Earth while they evolved again toward the third dimension."

"Are they still living there, inside the planet?"

"They are not. The majority have now evolved at least into the third dimension, their karmic debt having been repaid."

"So, most of those from Maldek are now in third dimensional human bodies?"

"Many, yes. And some of them have evolved past the third dimension into the fourth, and have transcended, and no longer incarnate on Earth."

"I understand you to be saying that a large number of present day humans are the original volunteers for the Earth experiment from either Maldek or Mars. Are there also groups from other planets?"

"About two billion are entities from other galaxies, who sought a third dimensional experience for their progression back to Source. And there are also currently sixty-five million wanderers from higher dimensions. The remainder of the population evolved on Earth from first to second to third dimensional beings. For example, from a rock or crystal, to a plant or tree, then to an animal, and finally a human."

"How many of the sixty-five million wanderers currently on Earth are aware that they come from a higher dimension?"

"About nine per cent are fully awake. Half know they are not of this time on Earth. All know there is something different about them."

"Only nine per cent are fully awake?"

"Yes, it's very challenging to wake up in the heaviness of Earth's current vibration.

"Did many of those present for your talk the other night awaken as a result of it?"

"It was a step closer for all those not yet aware of their true identity and purpose, and a catalyst to full awareness for about a quarter of them."

Maepleida left El Morya with her head throbbing. She went to her room and flung herself down on her bed, only to jump up again, and pace, settling finally on the window seat. She felt the cold through the glass, but unlatched it any way, and leaned out toward the Himalayas. She wondered if her friends back on Venus had yet discovered all this. She still wasn't clear whether or not this mission was the right path for her. Shivering, she pulled the window shut and latched it. Her pale-grey cashmere shawl was draped over the chair by the fire. She wrapped it around her shoulders and made her way through the castle to the great diamond. Now more than ever, she wanted to hear the voice of her Higher Self. Maepleida had a full knowledge of all her past lives. But the perspective of the Higher Self includes all future lives as well. And while she would not be shown if she would succeed and awaken as a wanderer, she could learn if this mission was the will of the Divine within her. She seated herself on a cushion before the large diamond, determined to remain however long it took to know.

Chapter 11

Where Are We Going?

The minute Soonam saw that Attivio was awake, she said, "Today's the day we're going to learn the name of the country where each of us will be born for our mission." Attivio reached out and took her in his arms, kissing first one corner of her mouth and then the other, before touching his lips to hers.

"The question is," Attivio said, "will twin flame pairs be assigned to the same country?"

"I don't see why not," Soonam said. "That wouldn't be a violation of anything, and we won't remember that we're twin flames."

Attivio shivered when she said that.

"No, but each of our gifts is to be matched with a situation where it will be most helpful," he said, shaking off the shiver.

"But our gifts will only come into play once we've awakened," Soonam said. "And when awakened, we're all telepathic, and capable of healing and materialization and able to travel anywhere in our light bodies."

Attivio couldn't help himself, he smiled into those violet eyes which he loved so well, and kissed her again. "Darling Soonam, you know that each of us has a unique gift as well."

The energy in the great temple was electric with anticipation. Ederah and Bereh took their seats next to Laaroos and Toomeh. Soonam, Attivio and Heipleido hadn't yet arrived. In fact, the three of them were still standing outside Heipleido's cottage. They'd been about to walk over to the temple, when Heipleido spotted what looked like Maepleida, approaching from the direction of Lady Venus and Lord Kumara's palace. They all knew that Maepleida's special power was the ability to instantly physically duplicate herself across time and space. So, was it her, or was she sending a messenger?

"It's me. I'm back," she telegraphed, as she moved toward them with a stride a little more expansive than usual. I've just told Lady Venus and Lord Kumara that I'm going on the mission after all."

Heipleido did three flips in the air up to the height of forty feet.

"Show off," Maepleida teased, tugging his earlobe when he landed. In case they'd forgotten it, Soonam and Attivio were reminded by Heipleido's display that his superpower was incredible agility and strength. Amid bouncing and jumping for joy, the four of them proceeded to the temple and took their seats with their friends, to the general delight of all eight of them. "I'll explain later," Maepleida telegraphed to the group. After some playful fidgeting, they all settled down.

"We thought we'd make this a little fun," Lord Kumara said strolling up toward the front of the temple with Lady Venus beside him. He looked up and commanded the temple roof to open to the sky. "You'll each receive an actual paper envelope, like they use on Earth for mail delivered by the post office. In the envelope will be the name of the place you will incarnate. When you open your envelopes a hologram of your future parents will appear. You may view this hologram as often as you like. And, after you receive your envelope, you're to have the rest of the day off."

Lady Venus raised her arms toward the open dome, and at her gesture the dome filled with birds, each with an envelope in its beak. There were birds of orange and blue, and yellow and black, and green and pink, tiny birds and singing birds and quiet birds. The winged messengers descended, and each found its way to the being whose name was on the envelope it carried, and dropped the envelope on the lap of the one to whom it belonged. Kumara and Venus gazed at the scene before them, enjoying the sight, and the pleasure of the wanderers when they received the paper envelopes from their feathered postmen. Soonam, in particular, delighted in her bird and stroked his small lavender head in gratitude for his gift. Perched on her knee, he looked up into her violet eyes, and she returned his gaze, communicating to him her pleasure in meeting him. Attivio drank in the look of joy on her face while she and the tiny lavender bird gazed at one another. He made a mental photo of the image to hold in his heart forever. Then the birds, one after another, took flight and departed through the open roof into the pink Venusian sky.

When the last bird had gone, the friends made their way outside and gathered under their tree to open their envelopes.

"How shall we do this?" Bereh asked.

"Let's go around the circle," Toomeh said. "I'll start if you like."

"Go on then," Maepleida said.

"Dublin," he said out loud. As soon as Toomeh spoke the words, a holograph-like scene of a young couple, on a green hillside, appeared before them.

A salty breeze blew off the Irish Sea, and whistled up the hillside, ruffling the tall grass at the feet of a young couple. The breeze caressed their hair, and made the woman's skirt billow out, as she turned to make her way over the moor and further up the hill, through the bright yellow gorse. Rose-lipped and pink-cheeked, with thick brown hair and smiling grey eyes, she held fast to the man's hand. Though young, he was well upholstered, but not heavy, and not too tall. They paused, and stood still to inhale the scent of the heather and bracken which covered the heath. The man raised her hand to his lips, kissed the fingers, then let it go, and knelt to retie one of his hiking boots. When he finished, he remained on one knee, gazing up into the woman's face, and recited something to her. As she listened, she looked down into his eyes with a look of infinite softness.

Then the scene vanished.

"Your future parents look quite romantic," Laaroos said to

Toomeh.

"We should have a look at all of them, then we can discuss," Maepleida suggested.

"She's back alright," Heipleido said, a warm feeling suffusing his whole being.

Toomeh nodded to Laaroos, who sat beside him, to go next.

"Tokyo," she read out, and a scene appeared before them.

A young, elegantly dressed Japanese couple, seated on a wooden bench, with a high carved back, gazed intently at one another. The bench was nestled under a plum tree, in a corner of a large and sprawling oriental garden. The woman was dressed in a formal kimono. She spoke with breathless happiness, sharing something with the man. He wore a white, summer suit and an expression of compassion as he listened to her. A sudden shower peppered them with raindrops. They appeared to take it as a blessing, and gazed upward through the plum blossoms at the spring rain.

Ederah was seated next to Laaroos, so she opened her envelope next. "Moscow." Immediately a winter scene opened before them.

A graceful woman in a long green full skirted coat, which swirled about her legs, skated over the ice holding a little girl by the hand. The little girl wobbled a bit and dropped one of her red mittens on the ice without noticing. The pair crossed a rough patch near the edge of the rink, and skated up to a man and a small boy. Just at that moment lights of many colors came on under the ice, delighting the children. The man and woman exchanged a few words, while the boy retrieved his little sister's mitten. Then all four joined hands and skated together over the rainbow-colored ice.

"You'll already have a brother and a sister when you're born," Bereh said to Ederah. Maepleida silenced him with a look.

Bereh, used to Maepleida's forthright ways, smiled at her, and opened his envelope. "Mumbai," he said, his heart throbbing at learning he would be born so far from Ederah.

Several intent monkeys walked beside an Indian couple, as they made their way along the path to the ferry landing. The couple were no longer young, but they weren't old either. The man wore a good, but well-used suit, and the woman, a sari of deep rose-pink, which complimented her light-brown skin. The man was enjoying the antics of the pesky monkeys, who were attempting to relieve his wife of the parcel of food she was carrying. Sunlight flashed off the gold bangles on the woman's arm as she reached up to hand the parcel of food to her husband. He opened the bag and tossed small bits of pakora to the happy monkeys. The woman protested, but with laughter.

"I hope you like monkeys, Bereh," Maepleida said, laughing, and breaking her own rule.

Soonam was sitting beside Bereh, so it was her turn next. She tore open her envelope and read: "New York City."

A beautiful, but cold looking young woman sat on the edge of a bed, peeling off her sheer stockings. A handsome, kind looking man in a tuxedo entered the room and spoke to her. She dropped her stockings on the floor and gave him a bored look before removing her rings and carelessly tossing them on the nightstand. The man approached and sat beside her on the bed. He reached up to brush her hair back from her forehead, but she grabbed his wrist to stop him. He got up and walked out of the room.

Attivio couldn't help himself and blurted out, "Your future mother looks challenging. Hopefully your dad will protect you." Soonam smiled at him gratefully.

Then Maepleida chimed in. "There's certainly no breathless happiness in that scene."

Heipleido gave her a look. It was the first negative image of their future parents that they'd yet seen. But, they were going to earth to make a difference, and to balance negativity, so they must welcome it, Bereh reminded them.

Attivio was next. He opened his envelop. "Jerusalem."

A girl in a red bathing suit and a turquoise t-shirt walked along the beach kicking the sand. She held the hand of a tall young man. They moved closer to the water's edge, stopped and stood still for a moment, to let the sea wash over their feet. The girl looked up at the man with a tear stained face. He wiped her tears with the edge of his t-shirt. A wave came in and rolled over their feet up to their calves. He kissed the top of her head and looked out at the sea.

No one commented and Maepleida went ahead and opened her envelope. "London."

At least a dozen white swans floated over the water toward a tall young woman in a trench coat, who was tossing food to them. When her paper bag was empty, and she had nothing more to offer, she strolled away from the water's edge. She crossed several lawns before reaching a statue of a boy playing a flute. There she stopped and gazed up at the statue, as if she would speak with the stone boy. But then, feeling something wet, she looked down at her legs and saw blood running down the inside of her knees and into her shoes.

Heipleido was the last one to open his envelope. "Cairo."

A large bouquet of bright orange poppies was centered on a glass coffee table, between two love curved seats. A tall slender man in his early thirties sat on one of the love seats. Opposite him, on the other, was a petite young woman, holding a beautiful green-eyed cat curled up in her lap. She was explaining something to him, about the book she had just been reading. After listening attentively for a few minutes, he said something which made her laugh, revealing perfect white teeth behind bow-shaped red lips.

"I like this couple," Maepleida said, "although she looks like little more than a child, she's so self-contained and lovely. Even her flowers are perfect."

"I'm glad you approve of my future mother," Heipleido said.

Since Maepleida didn't mention that her own future mother had been alone, and dripping blood into her shoes, no one else did either.

"We're all in major cities," Bereh observed.

"Of course," Maepleida said, "that's where all the stress is, with people packed in like sardines, everyone's thoughts flying about their heads, bumping into everyone else's."

"It's also where the religious zealots strike in order to do the most damage," Bereh said, "so it's where we can make the most difference." Bereh could generally be counted on to see the positive. Ederah looked at him with such sweetness that he blushed crimson right up to the roots of his hair.

"Your mother looks like a tough character," Maepleida said to Soonam.

"At least my father looks like a gentle soul," she answered, "and I'm delighted to be incarnating in New York City, even though Attivio will be a world away in Jerusalem and his future mom was so sad walking by the sea."

"I hope it doesn't mean that she was unhappy to be pregnant," Attivio said.

"I didn't get that feeling. She seemed more frightened than sad to me," Laaroos said.

"I agree," Ederah chimed in. "I think I'm the only one who was shown siblings," she added.

"That was a lovely scene of the family ice skating together in Moscow," Bereh remarked.

His bravery in the face of this separation touched Ederah. Looking at the compassion on his face, her heart broke even further open. Wherever they were sent, their connection was eternal, they were immortal beings, she reminded herself, and a most angelic look came over her face. It did not go unnoticed by Bereh.

"And you're going to be Japanese," Toomeh said to Laaroos.

"I like that idea," she said, "except that Japan is a long way from Ireland." Toomeh looked back at her as if she was not only the fairest star in the sky, but the only one.

Heipleido had been silent up to this point, still absorbing the information that he would incarnate in Cairo and Maepleida in London. Was it a miscarriage that they'd seen, he wondered, caused when Maepleida had temporarily decided not to incarnate on Earth? And what had been the outcome?

Then the conversation turned to Maepleida's time with Amerissis and El Morya in the Himalayas.

"What was it like?" Ederah asked.

"The Himalayas fill you with strength and purity," Maepleida said, "and the Blue Flame Temple has such power, that just sitting before the blue flame diamond activates your heart chakra and pulls you into alignment with the will of your Higher Self."

"And is it the will of the Divine for you to go on this mission?" Attivio asked in a playful voice.

She ignored him. "And another thing. I attended a meeting where Master El Morya addressed wanderers from all over the planet. They were brought to his palace in their light bodies, by their guides, while their physical bodies were asleep."

"Are you saying that it's possible that although we're to be in different countries, we might still all meet at one of the meetings led by the chohans of the different rays?" Heipleido asked.

"Yes, but we may not remember it the next day, when we awake in the morning, in our human forms again," Maepleida said.

"What are these meetings for?" Toomeh asked.

"To stimulate the awakening of the wanderers to their true identity," Maepleida answered.

"Then this is the kind of help we'll receive, too, once we're on Earth," Bereh said.

Maepleida nodded. She could feel that Heipleido wanted to be alone with her, so she added, "we can talk about all this later."

Heipleido leapt up and pulled Maepleida to her feet with his two strong hands. When they'd gotten a little distance from their friends, he said, "I think you know what it means to me that you've chosen to go on this mission after all."

"Just following the will of my Higher Self," Maepleida teased.

"And I didn't enter into the equation at all?" he asked, reaching for her and pulling her toward him. Over the centuries, love had assumed many forms for them, sometimes joy and bliss, sometimes peace, at times sorrow and longing. Like a tree, their love had many branches, but always the root was love.

"I will admit I missed you while I was away," she said, "but no, I'm proud to say I submitted to the Will of the Divine in me, completely. Now, tell me, what did I miss while I was in the Himalayas?"

"We'll get to all that later," he said, "but now, I'm taking you on a magic carpet ride for two," and he tilted her head up and kissed her open lips for a long time.

Soonam watched Maepleida and Heipleido walk off, and sighed.

Toomeh smiled at her sigh and said, "I quite agree."

"I suppose people can move around on Earth from one city to another," Soonam said. "How else will we be able to reunite with our twin flames? How will I meet Attivio if he's in Jerusalem and I'm in New York?"

We saw in the Akashic records that people on Earth travel everywhere now by airplane," Bereh said.

"Well, I'll definitely take as many airplane trips to New York as possible," Attivio said, with a smile in his voice, at least until I'm once again able to activate my merkaba.

"Or you could be an exchange student," Ederah said. "According to what we saw, that's another way young people experience countries other than their own."

"With Bereh in Mumbai, and you in Moscow, you'll learn firsthand about two very different cultures," Toomeh told Ederah."

"Conditions in any of these cities could change over the next twenty years," Ederah said.

"If we're successful, lots of things could change on Earth," Bereh said.

Toomeh looked over at Laaroos, who had been very quiet.

"Dublin and Tokyo are so far from one another," she said.

"We'll manage," Toomeh said. He said it with such infinite

softness that her heart gave a little leap, as if it wanted to jump out of her body to touch him.

Just before dusk, the sky lit up with a blaze of gold. *Only love is real,* Laaroos thought.

As fifth dimensional beings, each of them would accept whatever came with grace and calm. But their mission had just become very real. The physical distance separating them from one another, and from their twin flames, was now quantifiable. But what they'd viewed had further opened their hearts toward humanity. The holograms had planted seeds of love in them for their future parents. The roots binding them to Earth had been planted. With their hearts full of another world, they made their way to their cottages, walking slowly, under the shimmering stars.

Part Two

Meanwhile on Earth

Chapter 12

Dublin

"Dinner's almost ready. Where are you?" Caitlin texted.

"Deep in the machinery of my own mind," Aiden texted back.

"And where might your mind be located?"

"I'm in the Long Room at Trinity College Library."

"Looking at the *Book of Kells* again?"

"No, today I'm contemplating the bust of Cicero, and trying to come up with an angle for an article I'm writing." Aiden loved the peace in the Long Room. No one spoke above a whisper. Even joyous first year students managed to respect the etiquette of silent behavior.

"Well, you're going to be late for lamb stew with onions, potatoes and pearly barley. *The Irish Times* can wait while you dine with your wife."

"Jumping on my bike now."

"Good, because I have a surprise for you."

As his bike bumped over the medieval cobblestones of their bohemian Temple Bar neighborhood, Aiden thought of warm bread smothered in butter. Caitlin always baked fresh bread for Irish stew. You could count on it. And what was her surprise? Their banter, as much as their conversation, while hiking on Howth Hill or over the Dublin Mountains never failed to surprise him. She was his delight, his compensation for all the hard parts of life. And she, she loved that he could still be surprised at something in her. Aiden opened their wrought iron gate, walked his bike through it, and listened for it to clang shut behind him before leaning his bike against the stone wall and climbing the twelve stone steps up to their flat.

"Smells delicious," he called from the front door.

"You're just in time," Caitlin told him from the kitchen.

Walking up behind her, he put his arms around her, and kissed her neck as she set the steaming bowls on the table.

"Wine or Guinness?" he asked her, crossing to the sink to wash his hands.

"I'll pass, but you go ahead."

Caitlin placed the warm bread on the cutting board next to the serrated knife, and covered it with a cotton cloth. Then she lit the candles and turned down the lights.

"Ah, the candlelit world of the soul," Aiden said, as he paused to observe her before pouring himself a glass of red wine and sitting down at the table with it.

"So, what's this surprise that requires candlelight?"

"Eat first."

He could read her well after three years of marriage, and he knew it was a good surprise, so he ate contentedly. Caitlin smiled to herself as she too dipped her spoon in the fragrant stew.

When he had eaten his stew, and had seconds, he took a sip of wine, wiped his mouth on the white cotton napkin, leaving the faintest rouge stain on it, and looked at her in anticipation.

"Do you want to guess?" she asked him.

"No, I don't want to guess," he said, playfulness in his voice.

"OK," she said, matching his mirthful tone.

"Go on then," he urged.

"I'm pregnant."

"We're having a baby?"

"We most definitely are," she said, her voice all smiles.

The next moment his arms were around her. "I could dance a jig," he said, laughing.

"Let's hold off on the jigs until this little one's safely in our arms. There's many a slip between the cup and the lip."

That night as they lay in bed together, Aiden asked her, "Where is our little one at this moment, here in bed with us, inside your belly, or far off somewhere in another galaxy?"

"Maybe he's in another realm preparing for his journey to

Earth."

"He?"

"Don't know why I said he."

"But do you think it's a he?"

"Does it matter to you?"

"I don't think so. How about you?"

"I've always imagined having a daughter," Caitlin said in a dreamy voice.

"You'd prefer a daughter?" Aiden asked.

"I did, but now that I said 'he,' I do think it'll be a boy, and I will love him madly."

Aiden took her into his arms and kissed the corners of her lips and then her open mouth, her ears, her throat, his passion igniting a fire in them both as their burning senses guided them deeper and deeper, until they dissolved into one another, becoming one transcendent soul. Making love with Aiden had been for Caitlin, since that first time, a gateway, a bridge, the way into the inner world of the eternal, an experience beyond thought, beyond even the luxurious sensations which moved through her flesh when he touched her.

Before he fell asleep, he whispered to her, "Do you think there'll be some ancient act of recognition the moment he's born, so that we'll know him instantly?"

But Caitlin was already fast asleep, dreaming her own dreams.

"Sweet dreams, my fairy girl," he said, as he, too, drifted off.

The next morning, she drew back the drapes in the bedroom to veils of grey rain. Standing on the threshold of the day, she gazed out at the grey brick and the grey stone and the grey air, and imagined the River Liffey swirling with grey water, bumping along on its journey to the Irish Sea. As a child, standing on the Ha'penny Bridge with her mother, she'd fallen in love with the River Liffey. It's where she still went to do her thinking, imagining that the water could conjure up her deepest thoughts and feelings and lead her to a solution for any problem. It was different for Aiden. When he had a problem to solve, he sought Dublin's parks. His first choice was often Phoenix Park, where the wild deer had run free in the huge, walled oasis since 1662. Though in spring, he would forsake it, in favor of Saint Anne's Park, with its riot of daffodils and tulips.

"The noise just disappears when you step into a park," he told Caitlin the first time he took her to feed the ducks in Saint Stephen's Green. Caitlin knew what he meant. She'd grown up walking the family Labrador/ Retriever in Harold's Cross Park, an organized little park, a kind of perfect Victorian oasis, awash in blooms all through the spring and summer.

As she gazed out at the silver morning, she didn't hear Aiden come up behind her. He put his arms around her still slender waist, and rested his chin on her shoulder. At five feet nine, he was only two inches taller than she.

"Penny for your thoughts," he said.

"I'm wondering if the rain will nix our walk on Howth Hill?"

"Let's have breakfast and see if it melts away into an Irish mist," he said.

"Good, let's make boxty? That should sustain us for a long walk in the mist," she said.

Caitlin prepared the potato pancakes and Aiden the bacon, eggs and tomato.

"Do you feel up to taking the bikes to Howth or should we drive?" he asked her as he placed the hot bacon on a paper towel and blotted it.

"It's only fifteen kilometers. We can bike, if the rain lets up," she said.

"I meant, now that you're pregnant..."

"I can bike. Once I reach the beached whale stage it may be another story, but for now, I'm good." She poured oil into the frying pan and let it warm up before spooning the batter out.

"Hand me the paper towels, will you?" Aiden tossed the towels into her waiting hands and turned off the whistling tea kettle.

While she waited for the potato pancakes to fry, Caitlin imagined what it would be like having a highchair pulled up to the breakfast table and a baby dining with them. Who would this baby be, and where was he now? A smile formed on her lips as she laid the sizzling potato pancakes on the paper towel. Aiden sat down, poured their tea, and passed her a cup. Caitlin rolled the warm cup in her palms before taking a sip.

"You're far away," he said, looking across the table into her grey eyes, which perfectly matched the grey jumper she wore over a pale-pink blouse. He'd told her once that her eyes were the color of Dublin stone itself. She caught him looking at her, smiled and brushed a lock of her thick brown hair off her forehead. Aiden returned his attention to his plate, and piled up on his fork a layered mouthful, with a piece each of potato pancake, bacon, egg and tomato. "Delish," he said.

After breakfast he cleared up, while Caitlin dug their hiking boots out of the closet. Luck was with them. By the time they were ready to leave, the veils of rain had become only an Irish mist, and they pedaled toward Howth Village with ease. By the time they reached Howth the sun was breaking through in patches, staining the ground here and there with that other worldly Irish light they both loved. They threaded their way through the bustling village, then stowed their bikes at the base of Howth Hill. As they made their way over the moors and through the bright-yellow gorse on the heath a sea breeze blew through their hair. Caitlin stopped to inhale the scents, and gaze at the heather and bracken, decorated with clusters of wild flowers. Savoring the feast of seeing, they fell silent, and hiked for some time without speaking. After a steady climb, they arrived at Balscadden, which had once been Yeats' home. Caitlin stood at the door through which Yeats had passed, and her eyes rested on a chink in the wooden frame. A sweet phrase from Yeats himself drifted across her mind: 'A little space for the rose breath to fill.'

Aiden felt her reverie. "You're feeling the imprint of Yeats' presence on this place?"

"Yes, I do sense his passion in the ether around this house," she said.

Aiden nodded. "I feel it, too. To be a poet and use words as Yeats did, what glory."

"Do you suppose it was some divine being he channeled to help him write as he did, or was he himself some divinity, come to Earth to grace us with his words?"

"Since you raise the question, what do you think? Aiden asked her.

"I like to think he was a man, who when he sat down to write opened himself to a higher consciousness, which poured honeyed words into his ears, and he stirred those sweetened sounds into his own ideas, to humanize them before offering them to us."

They walked on, each in the silent territory of his own interior world, climbing steadily upward, until the whole sky flew in to meet them. There were views in every direction. The Bailey lighthouse became clearly visible out on its point of land, jutting into the Irish Sea. They looked down far below them, and watched grey seals diving for fish, and guillemots, fulmars, gulls and gannets circling over the emerald hillside which rolled down to meet the bay. The holiness of it almost hurt. Aiden broke the silence. "This place always makes me want to pray. Standing here, I dwell in eternity, no more a servant of my hour. I understand why in ancient times, the land of Ireland itself was reverenced as the body of the goddess."

"Yes," Caitlin said, smiling at him for waxing so poetic.

"What?" He cocked his head the tiniest bit.

"Nothing, just you. Shall we sit and offer devotion to the ancient goddess?" Caitlin said.

Aiden took off his jacket and spread it on the ground for her. Absorbed by the numinous quality of the Irish landscape they sat still, and each slipped into their own reverie. The land felt to Caitlin like another presence, a separate being, full of its own silent memories, with nothing of its mystery forgotten. Aiden lay back and imagined he was being held in the lap of the goddess.

Walking along the coast on the way back down, they passed the 15th century ruins of Saint Mary's Abbey and paused to wonder about the lives spent there. Continuing on, Aiden checked the distance on his watch computer. "We've hiked six and a half kilometers. I think we've earned a pint. What do you say to The Bloody Stream?"

Caitlin smiled to herself. When she didn't answer right away, he remembered that she was pregnant.

"Right then," he said. "Bad idea."

"Of course we can stop. There are plenty of drinks without alcohol, and the Bloody Stream does have good pub food," she reminded him, catching his swinging hand in her own and closing her fingers around it. They got their favorite table, the one with the high back wooden seats next to the fireplace. Penumbral light cast by ten ivory candles held in a large, wrought iron candle holder played across Caitlin's brow, and the fire beside her warmed her body. Firelight danced in Aiden's eyes, too. Had she ever been happier than at this moment, Caitlin wondered, as a jolly, pink-cheeked waitress, new to The Bloody Stream, walked up to take their order.

"Seafood chowder for my wife, and a Guinness and a beef pie for me."

Caitlin turned to Aiden. "So, what's the problem with the article you're working on for *The Irish Times*?"

"Did I say there was a problem?"

"You went to the Long Room yesterday. I know what that means."

"I'm so transparent?"

"I wouldn't say transparent, exactly."

He nodded at her in admission, and then let a smile break

across his face when he saw her amused look.

"It's only that I want to do more, more than just cover the same old territory which keeps the world stuck. I want to do more than just help it go around? When I write something, I want it to help the world go forward?"

"A tall but worthy mission, my darling. Sounds like you want to do nothing short of changing people's consciousness."

"How do you get people to be more conscious, for example, even about the choices they make?

"Look at the violent emotion, venom really, being uncovered and stirred up as the result of the American election. It seems that people will overlook a lot in a candidate to protect their own interests. Even the United States congressional leaders are overlooking the new president's character, refusal to relinquish his personal business interests, and possible ties to the Russian hacking of the presidential election. How does the fact that his party is turning a blind eye serve the greater good? How does that help the working man? What happened to the understanding that I am in everything, and everything is in me?"

Caitlin smiled across the table at him.

"You're an idealist, Aiden. You don't subscribe to the competitive model, where if others have more, you have less. That's the advantage of working from your Soul, you understand that there's more than enough to go around if it's distributed equitably."

"But isn't it the job of journalists not only to inform, but to uncover unfairness and lies, and even to raise consciousness?"

"Ideally, yes, but for many, I'm afraid that there's no passion stronger than the desire to convince others to believe as they do," Caitlin said. "And isn't that what cable news and slanted newspapers are about, trying to get people to believe as they do, rather than just reporting?"

Aiden nodded his agreement. "That's what's so frustrating. If the ego always wants to be right, and tries to get others to agree with it, how does one get anybody to listen at a deeper level?"

"That's your challenge my love," Caitlin said. "And as my mother used to tell me, 'a difficult challenge makes a good friend for the soul.'"

The waitress set Aiden's Guinness in front of him and he lifted the glass to his lips with relish. Caitlin ordered a tea.

"Are you chilled?"

"No, but I like the feel of the warm cup in my hands."

The waitress returned with a steaming bowl of chowder, which she set before Caitlin, and a hot beef pie which she placed in front of Aiden. They looked down at their food in anticipation of the pleasure, and ate with gratitude.

If Toomeh could have heard this conversation between his future human parents, he would have undoubtedly felt affection for them, and perhaps even viewed them as kindred spirits. For they were among those humans, who, if not already fourth dimensional beings, were edging very close to that consciousness. Their understanding, *that I am in everything, and everything is in me,* was a knowing closer to the heart of fourth dimensional consciousness than to third. Their understanding that we are all part of the Oneness, that there are no *others,* and that, what you do for another is also done for the self would certainly have resonated with Toomeh. Caitlin and Aiden had made their choice between service only to self, and service to others. This would be a great joy to Toomeh once he grew up enough to see his human parents for who they were. He might have been tickled, too, by Aiden's question to Caitlin, about whether their baby was presently in her belly, or in some other universe, preparing for his Earth life?

Chapter 13

Tokyo

Umeko shifted the phone to her opposite ear. "Shall we meet at the Nakajima Teahouse?"

"Perfect." Kosuke was direct, but as usual, sparse with his words, especially for a romantic man. Umeko smiled to herself. Precise in all things herself, she turned off her phone and carefully placed it in her bag, in the pocket which had been designed for it. She glanced in their bedroom mirror to check her thick, black hair, which was swept up in a knot and held in place with two, glossy, lacquer sticks. She turned to leave, but in a moment of self-consciousness, turned back to the mirror and put her hands over her obi. She could still wear an obi over her kimonos, but she'd had to loosen it a bit. At four months pregnant, she was blooming.

Kosuke entered the Oteman Gate to Hama-Rikyu Onshi Park, and strolled over the bridge spanning the moat. Halfway across the bridge, his eyes already sought his favorite tree, the three-hundred-year-old pine, whose sprawling arms greeted visitors to the park. Out of respect for the tree, he drew himself up to his full height, which was nearly six feet, tall for a Japanese man, and bowed in homage to the ancient being. His bow complete, Kosuke began to whistle as he continued on to the next bridge, which led to the peony gardens. Though he appreciated all horticulture, these moated gardens with their saltwater ponds were a particular favorite of his. He sniffed the air and inhaled the scent of sea salt mingled with peony and iris.

Nakajima teahouse sat on an island in the middle of the garden's only tidal pond. Umeko arrived first, and was gazing out at the purple Siberian irises when she saw Kosuke coming over the long wooden footbridge to the island. Slender, and a little tanned, Kosuke looked handsome in his white, linen summer suit and tie. He raised a hand in greeting as he walked over the bridge toward her. From the first, his elegance, gentility and easy sophistication had seemed to her to be from another era. No wonder his parents had named him Kosuke, which means rising sun. Umeko smiled at him across the distance. Even from thirty feet, Kosuke felt her smile, like sunlight, pour over him.

Kosuke was a linen merchant, with a particular appreciation, even a passion, for Chijimi linen. The very impracticality, and the close relationship with nature which was necessary for the creation of Chijimi grass linen was what had drawn him to it. The grass thread was spun in the snow, because the moisture which the snow produced eased the task of working with such a delicate thread. After the spinning, the thread was then also woven in the snow, to take advantage of the natural humidity. After the spinning and weaving, the linen was soaked overnight in ash water before being rinsed repeatedly the next day. Finally, it was laid out over the snow to bleach. Kosuke loved and admired the delicate care and romance embodied in this process. To add to the romance, the process was undertaken only by young maidens.

When they were first dating, Kosuke had taken Umeko by train to see the linen laid across the breast of the snowy mountainside. On the journey there, they'd barely escaped an avalanche, which covered the train tracks only minutes after their train had passed. But they'd arrived safely that February evening just as the setting sun showered a soft, red glow on the snow and over the Chijimi linen stretched out on the breast of the mountain.

"Chijimi is made in the snowiest region of Japan," Kosuke had explained to her on that trip. "In that land which lies just to the west of the mountains on the main island. Siberian winds blowing across the Sea of Japan fill with moisture as they blow over the water, toward the Japanese coast. From the coast, the winds howl inward through the land until they strike the mountains, where they drop their moisture as snow. Sometimes the snow grows to fifteen feet deep. This is where Chijimi is woven by maidens in the winter months. It's an ancient art, but it's practiced less now, as fewer maidens will devote their youth to the laborious process. That's why Chijimi linen has become scarce."

Umeko was fascinated by all that Kosuke taught her of Chijmi linen and fell a little in love with the linen herself. Kosuke's affection for the linen, too, had grown after that trip to Chijimi country. He credited both the linen, and the avalanche, with helping Umeko fall in love with him. He appreciated what a heady combination danger and beauty could be. Trapped by the avalanche, they stayed in the only inn the small village offered. Before bed they took a midnight stroll. The mountain, no longer bathed in the red light of sunset as it had been when they arrived, was, at midnight, starlit. Gazing up into the night sky, Kosuke felt the whole firmament wrapping them in its embrace. It was there on the mountain that he asked her to be his wife. That was four years ago, and it seemed he could still touch the moment, even now, as he walked across the foot bridge to the tea house to join his wife.

A young woman in a pale-blue kimono adorned with a pattern of irises, and with the traditional long sleeves worn by maidens, approached their table carrying two, small, black, lacquer trays, each tray held a sweet cake, centered on a green leaf, a pointed wooden stick for cutting the cake, and a bowl of steaming green tea. Umeko picked up the cake with her right hand and placed it on her left palm, where she cut it with the wooden stick. She then speared each small sweet, piece in turn, and ate them one by one. Kosuke did the same, offering his palate the sweetness of the cake to prepare it for the bitterness of the tea to follow.

"There's something of a mountain feel to this cup," Umeko said on finishing her cake and picking up her tea bowl. Kosuke cast his eyes over her bowl, then at his own. Umeko's was the softest, green Oribe, splashed with tiny black speckles. His own was white Shino, and had a more controlled pattern of bracken shoots. Kosuke lifted his bowl, and placing it in his left hand, turned it two quick clockwise turns, before drinking it all in three sips. Umeko did the same, but with four sips.

He placed his tea bowl back on the lacquer tray and looked up at her. "Are you ready for a stroll?"

Umeko nodded and he summoned the young serving girl and paid for their tea, bowing elegantly to her, as they rose to leave the teahouse. Kosuke took Umeko's elbow as they crossed the footbridge, and asked her, "Now, are you going to tell me what your psychic said?"

"When we reach the Plum Grove. Are you so impatient?" she teased.

"You know me, ever anxious to see behind the veil."

"And I fell in love with you because I thought you imperturbable," she teased again.

"Yes, I'm a vessel of quiet restraint," he joked, "but here's the Plum Grove and I shall have satisfaction."

They sat down side by side on a bench in the shelter of a plum tree. Umeko had chosen this spot because it was her lucky place, and because of the meaning of her name, child of the plum.

"Now don't make fun of me, just listen," Umeko began.

"I promise." He had no intention of making fun of her. After three miscarriages, his daily mission had been to envelop her in soft affection. He hoped the psychic had shone even a vein of light into the well of her pain. He would have driven out the pain entirely, demanding that it leave no trace, were that possible. Umeko moved close to him, as if imparting secrets that must not be overheard. "The baby is a girl, and she will live to be born."

Kosuke took her hand and kissed it. He didn't trust himself to speak, lest he reveal his lack of faith in psychics. If Umeko could believe, who was he to question her. For himself, consulting a psychic seemed to be just shifting the uncertainty from not knowing an outcome, to not knowing if one could trust the psychic's answer.

"The child is a wise being, from a higher dimension, who comes by choice to bring love to our planet. Her own home is the star Arcturus," Umeko continued. "And we knew her in a past life, where we were together in another galaxy. But she won't remember any of this when she is born to us as a baby."

"Is that all, nothing out of the ordinary to add?" Kosuke smiled, attempting a lightheartedness which he didn't feel. Umeko's naivety, her willingness to believe farfetched tales, troubled him, not because he minded fantasy. He quite enjoyed it. But because he feared that the information would give her false hope. He took her hand and asked, "Do you believe this literally?"

"I do, and we can at least easily check the sex of the baby, instead of waiting until it's born as we planned."

"But, my darling, that won't prove anything. There's at least a fifty-fifty chance that the baby is a girl." He knew he was trying to protect her, and that it was impossible. His position was weak. Pain came to every life and must be born, he reminded himself. Perhaps pain should be welcomed as a teacher. So instead of trying to save her, he listened, and let her happiness flow over him.

"Ever since that February night, after the avalanche, on the starlit mountain in Chijimi country," Umeko said, "I've had dreams of a red star and a light being. As I looked up into that night sky, it was as if each star was speaking, but one was trying to give me a message."

Kosuke didn't tell her that Arcturus wasn't visible from the Northern Hemisphere in winter, but only in late spring.

"You're quiet," Umeko said.

"I have an idea," he said. "Let's take the train this Sunday to visit the great Buddha of Kamakura. We can offer thanks for this message, and ask for his protection for our daughter as she journeys to us." He realized he was still trying to wrap her in blessings and protections.

Umeko smiled at him, her eyes full of joy and gratitude. "I'll wear my silk kimono with the pattern of phoenixes ascending to the clouds," she said, "to honor the great Buddha." For the first time in many moons, Umeko could feel, and almost see, silver threads of light breaking through the darkness of her fear. They would place their unborn child under the protective eyes of the Great Kamakura Buddha, and at last her heart would be at rest. How well Kosuke understands me, she thought. A sudden shower danced on the plum leaves overhead. The raindrops felt like a blessing to Umeko, who lifted her lips and eyes to welcome it. Reluctant to rise and leave the sweet shelter of the plum tree, they sat with upturned faces, feeling the spring rain through the branches.

Umeko and Kosuke would have been astounded to know that on far away Venus, their little daughter to be would witness this very scene of the two of them, sitting on this bench, under the branches of the plum tree, looking up into the raindrops. And Kosuke, in particular, would have been further amazed to know that at this moment, his daughter actually was a being of the fifth dimension, capable of creating with her intention alone, but more than that, she was a being with a heart as big as the sky, who saw all beings as God. But, perhaps what he would have been most stunned by was that she had not only seen a statue of the Planetary Buddha, but had met him in person.

Chapter 14

New York City

They'd been out partying all night, and dawn was in the sky when the taxi let them out in front of their Greenwich Village townhouse. Jackie preceded Hunter through the front door, dropped her coat on a chair, tossed her clutch on the side table and climbed the wide curving staircase to the second floor. Hunter locked up. He didn't like partying all night. But he allowed that marriage demanded some concessions. He climbed the stairs and entered their bedroom.

Without looking at him, Jackie said, "I don't want to be pregnant. I don't want this baby." She was lying on her back across the bed, her feet still on the floor.

He felt her words like a sudden a punch to the gut. His face drained of color, he crumpled into a chair by the cold fireplace. There was no hint of playfulness in her tone to give him relief from the sharpness of her declaration. The amorphous dread he'd been feeling for weeks now had a clear shape. So, this is it. This is how she'll defeat me, he thought. She's miserable being pregnant, afraid all the fun will be over, so she lashes out and stings me. How selfish she is, concerned only with her own looks, pleasure and desires. What he had taken for good character when they first met had turned out to be nothing more than design. He resisted the urge to glare at her, and instead walked over and looked out the window, down at the quiet street below.

Hunter was a self-contained sort of man, not given to judging others. He'd been tolerant, had made excuses for her, and had said nothing to her about her decadent habits. From the beginning, he'd tried to simply love her, without commenting on or criticizing her behavior. He'd lavished her with gifts and houses and money in place of more verbal demonstrations of his affection. Now he felt that he was to blame for the type of wife she'd become. Reluctantly, he withdrew his eyes from the street below, and glanced across the room at her. She pulled off her rings and tossed them on the bedside table. Her gesture was so abrupt that her arm bumped the table, toppling a photograph, sending it to the floor with a crash. She kicked it out of her way and folded over to peel off her stockings. Even her father had warned him that perhaps Jacqueline had inherited a drop too much self-importance. But she had been beautiful and feisty and fun, so he'd married her despite the warning. He sat still staring at her without seeing her.

"Are you going to say anything or have you turned to stone?"

There was no gentleness in her tone, nor even any friendship, and certainly no affection. Despite this, he gathered his courage together and found his voice. "You haven't yet succeeded in turning me to stone, darling, though tonight's effort is rather valiant."

Hunter stood up, intending to walk out of the room after delivering these words. Instead, he crossed the room, sat down on the bed next to her, and stroked back the hair which had fallen over one eye.

She grabbed his wrist. "Don't."

Her cold distain increased his fear. Why did she instinctively reject his attempts to soothe her? "Let's talk about this tomorrow," he said, in a pleasant and straightforward tone as an attempt to disguise the appeal in his eyes. When she ignored him, he walked into his dressing room in the sure knowledge of her hatred. *She doesn't like me. In fact, she despises me.* How many times had he concluded this in the past few months? Dressed in his pajamas, robe and slippers, Hunter padded downstairs to his library, poured himself a scotch, and sat sipping it in the dark, oppressed by his own weakness. If she meant this, there would be a finality to their marriage, and with finality, would at least come peace, which would be preferable to living everyday with the fear of the end. And there would be no more nights of sitting in solitude, wondering about their dubious future together. Swimming in the riptide of her love, and hate, was tearing him apart. Already he suspected the beginnings of an ulcer. An hour later, when he climbed the stairs, she was asleep. He slipped into bed beside her and tried to push away the stark realization that he'd made a terrible mistake.

They'd been introduced at a weekend house party on Long Island. The month was June, and it was one of the first delicious weekends of the summer. At the time, he'd been working at his father's investment banking firm, managing the arm which handled charitable contributions. And she, as she put it, was "engaged in the high battlements of thought," at a publishing company. Although he found her language and tone showy, he'd excused it, reminding himself that young, educated, high spirited women, and men, were often susceptible to pride, which could be tempered with time. Because he found her sassy, self-assured attitude so intoxicating, he'd made all manner of excuses for her from the moment he met her. That first night, after dinner, they'd left the rest of the house party in the drawing room, and walked down to the beach alone. It seemed to him that the sea breeze that evening was more fragrant than ever before in all his years of summering on Long Island. As they strolled along the water's edge, sidestepping clumps of seaweed in their path, he listened to her more intently with each step. Only much later did he realize that she had begun that very night to weave him into her own design. The stars had seemed brighter that first night, too, brighter than ever in all his childhood summers. She talked of the books she was editing, and of politics, art, and reincarnation and India, where she was dying to go. At the touch of her mind, the world seemed reborn. Her dark, Dionysian tenacity excited him as the perfect foil to his own Apollonian humanism. She created in him such a sublime fever that he hadn't slept the whole of that first night, but instead, sat by his open window, leaning out, watching the sky turn from violet to lavender, to palest yellow. By the end of that summer, infected with her passionate nature, he'd believed himself madly in love with her, and asked her to marry him. He convinced himself that he loved her, and that he alone knew her true soul. It was no matter if others couldn't see it. But even then, when she first accepted his offer of marriage, and he felt he had gained the moon, he was already defenseless against her ability to inflict pain on him. His friends saw that he had deceived himself, of course, and a few of them put aside niceties and spoke directly to him. But he would not have cold water poured on his passion. They had tried to warn him that with a creature like Jacqueline, suffering was inevitable. Over time he'd seen his folly, and had learned to survive by pretending to be less sensitive than he was. Did she realize this streak of deception?

It was midday when Jackie came downstairs. She appeared in the doorway of his library wearing a white, silk robe. He felt his chest tighten at her presence. When she seated herself on his leather sofa, he folded his newspaper and set it on the table beside him.

"Come here," she said patting the place next to her. Though it irritated him to be ordered about like a puppy, he crossed the room with as much dignity as he could muster. Her coquettish manners no longer excited anything in him. He understood now that she was incapable of grasping the subtleties of his nature. Even her extravagant beauty had worn itself thin and he saw that her classic face was nothing but a façade for her insensitivity.

"So. Perhaps I spoke too harshly last night." She paused to gauge the effect of her words. "It's not that I don't want this baby, though I do hate being pregnant. It's such an interference."

Though he tried to mask it, relief flooded his countenance, and the tension in his muscles started to dissolve. Observing both his relief, and his attempt at deception, Jackie savored her victory, which had been easily achieved with a mere few words.

He knew she wasn't finished, and he sat silently waiting for the needle under the silk. His foreboding ended with her next move, which caught him off balance. She leaned toward him and kissed his lips. Despite himself, he absorbed the warmth of her mouth like a tiny promise, and reaching for her, returned the kiss with equal pressure. She was pliant as he slipped his hand into her robe and closed his fingers over her breast. Their kiss deepened as he pressed her back on the sofa, excited by her naked body under the silk robe. Her thighs opened for him and he slid inside her, seeking the deep well within her, all the while continuing the kiss. In that moment, he was ready to overlook anything, even though part of him understood that he was driving straight toward tragedy. After, when he sat up, and looked out the window, already regretting his weakness, he saw that snow was falling steadily, laying a soft blanket of white over the ground.

She followed his eyes to the window and jumped ahead of his thought. "Let's take a walk in the snow," she said, turning her face up to him.

By the time they were dressed and bundled up, the afternoon light was already fading to a soft lavender. As they walked toward Washington Square Park, he watched snowflakes gather on her dark eyelashes and melt onto her cheeks. Am I a fool to make her the source of my happiness, he wondered? An old phrase of his mother's drifted through his mind: 'If you have to ask...'

Children were making snowmen in the park, using small branches, fallen from the trees, for arms. Hunter smiled at them. He and Jackie paused to watch as parents pulled buttons and carrots from their pockets to serve as eyes and noses for the snowmen. One child stuck a bunch of celery leaves on her snowman's head for hair, and made red lips from an apple peel. Some older children made a snow couple sitting side by side, with their stick arms wrapped around one another. A flock of pigeons took flight from the snow-covered lawn. Hunter followed their path with his eyes as they ascended into the sky, shifted their direction, and changed color from black to silver as they circled the fountain, and landed on the top of Washington Square Arch. Jackie shivered and Hunter took her arm. "You need a warm fire," he said, not thinking of her, but of the small being inside her. On the walk home she was friendly, suggesting that they dine in front of the fire. "Myrna made cornbread yesterday and left some chili in the fridge," she told him.

It was nearly dark by the time they reached their front steps. Their handy man had not yet cleared the snow and it was piled up on the stairs like thick white icing on a cake. Hunter wiped the snow from the railing with his gloved hand. Jackie grasped the railing and climbed the steps to their front door, leaving footprints in the white frosting. Inside, they shook the snow off their coats in their foyer, and stepped out of their wet boots, and left them sideways, dripping on the carpet. The fire was roaring when Jackie came in with a tray of hot chili and warm cornbread, and set it on the large, round, multicolored ottoman they'd bought on their honeymoon in India. Hunter was gracious enough to thank her for this effort, despite wondering what chili might do to his dodgy stomach.

"I thought we might talk about names for the baby," she said, kneeling next to him on the floor before the fire. "If it's a girl, I'd like to call her Rose."

How unruffled she was today, Hunter thought. To have Jackie in love with you was to be lifted to the gates of paradise, but when her mood turned and she lashed out, the poison sting cast you into hell, where you would languish, sick with disgrace at your own weakness for being her victim. Jackie's emotions and moods, so different from his own, were unfathomable to him. The stark realization that through this child, he was bound to her now created a sense of foreboding. Jackie buttered a piece of cornbread and handed it to him, smiling into his eyes, with what looked like love.

Had Soonam seen this look from the woman who was to be her human mother, she would not have been fooled by it. The manipulation in it would have been clear to her, and she would have realized that she was in for some challenges as the daughter of such a woman. Perhaps, however, she would have approved of the name, Rose, which the woman had chosen for her, as she was a great lover of flowers, particularly flowers with a heavenly scent. Had Hunter known, that even as he stood in Washington Square Park concerned with keeping the body of this baby safe and warm, the being who was to live in the baby's body was at that very moment on Venus, thinking of the man and little girl she had seen in a vision, sitting by the fountain eating strawberry ice cream cones, he would have not only been astounded, but would perhaps have taken heart for the road ahead. For Soonam was to be his daughter, and there could be no more wonderful being on Earth than this soul fashioned of love and joy.

Chapter 15

Jerusalem

Rachael lay on her side in the warm sand next to Daniel. While he slept, face down, she studied the constellation of moles on his back. She ran her finger lightly over a pair of two, small ones, hardly bigger than pieces of fresh ground pepper, just under his left shoulder blade. They must be stars from very far away to look so small, she decided, as she imagined his back as the Milky Way. For as long as she could remember, she had been fascinated by the stars, and by the possibility of life on other planets. Maybe this was because as a small child, she had often been visited by angels when she played alone. At least that's what she thought they were, as they told her that there was life in many places in the universe, and that one day, she would know a being from another world. She'd never mentioned the visits from the angels to anyone, not even Daniel.

Daniel turned over, wrinkling up their big, striped beach towel. He covered his eyes with his forearm to block out the sun. Even lying still, his body conveyed a sense of virile grace. Rachael followed the line from his shoulder to his hip, and down to his ankle, and all the way to the tips of his orderly toes. Lest he feel her staring at him and wake up, she pulled her eyes from his body, sat up and began pouring handfuls of sand back and forth from one hand to the other, watching as it drained through her fingers. But she was not thinking of the sand as she absentmindedly picked up another handful and watched until it, too, had all dribbled through her fingers. Anyone strolling along the beach observing her would have seen that she was distracted, maybe even that something was hurting her heart.

It had been her plan that morning, when they'd driven out from Jerusalem, to spend the day at the Dead Sea, that before they reached Neve Midbar Beach, she would tell Daniel that she was pregnant. But she hadn't managed to get the words out. And she didn't understand the reason for her paralysis. They'd been living together for two years and had even talked about getting married. They'd both completed their military service, and they both had jobs. Rachael was a midwife and she loved her work. The joy never diminished, no matter how many babies she delivered. Her baby would mean a temporary hiatus from work, but she'd go back as soon as she could. It wasn't that making her so fearful of speaking to Daniel. But what was? She couldn't fathom the source of her fear, or more truthfully, her terror, of telling him. This wasn't like her at all. She was competent and cool under pressure, but now all that was gone.

Daniel uncovered his eyes and looked at her. "Shall we walk over to the bar for a drink and a bite?"

Rachael nodded and picked up her shoes, pouring the sand out of each one before slipping it on. She stood up and pulled on her oversized turquoise t-shirt, which hung down to the bottom of her red bikini.

Daniel saw that her usually transparent face was clouded over. That had been happening a lot lately. She let him take her hand, but turned her face away from him to stare at the Dead Sea.

The beach bar was a casual outdoor place, with tables around it and the menu written on a blackboard. Daniel led her to a table, determined to talk to her. They both looked at the menu board. Rachael ordered the chicken shwarma wrap and a lemonade. Daniel chose the falafel, tahini, humus platter with pita, and a beer.

As soon as they'd ordered, Rachael felt his eyes questioning her. Should she plunge in now or wait until after they'd eaten? Indecisive, she ran her fingers through her curly red hair, as if to organize her thoughts, straighten them out, line them up, and conduct them into speech. But it was Daniel who spoke.

"What's the matter Rachael? You've hardly said a word since we set out this morning."

The fear of his anger at her news swam before her eyes and her paralysis deepened. But why would it send him into a rage?

"Come on, out with girl. I know something is on your mind. Your face has been a cloudy sky more often than not these last few weeks. That's not like you." He chose a deliberately playful tone, hoping to ease the tension furrowing her brow.

The waitress set their lunch down in front of them and walked away, her flip flops smacking her heels as she went. Rachel focused on the sound of them as the waitress retreated, and wished she had an excuse to call her back. Not trusting her voice, she stared at her plate, then across the table at him, but she couldn't find her voice.

They'd met while serving in the Israeli army. Rachael had been one of the toughest, most fearless soldiers in the company. So, what was this scared hesitation on her face today? Daniel didn't want to back her into a corner by grilling her, but something was eating her, and he wanted to know what. Would he have to pry it out of her? That wasn't his style.

"Hmm... the pita's warm," he said tearing off a piece and offering it to her. Rachael didn't say anything, but took it from his hand. Ripping off another piece of pita, he dipped it in the soft humus and took a bite. When he looked up, Rachael's large green eyes were brimming with tears which clung to her eyelashes, and spilled onto her cheeks, rolling down into the corners of her lips.

She didn't want this relationship to be over. She didn't want his reaction to her news to disappoint her in him or maybe even break her heart. She didn't want to die. What? Where had that last thought come from? I'm losing it, she thought.

"Enough. What is going on?" His voice was kind, but firm.

The damn in her broke and she blurted out, "I'm pregnant. I was afraid to tell you. I was afraid you'd be angry." Her eyes held the terrible look of a drowning woman, and his heart clenched at the sight.

"Why would you think that?" He was in disbelief that she could be so afraid of his reaction. "Don't you know me at all?"

"I don't understand my fear myself. It grips me and sweeps away my reason. Every time I planned to tell you, I buckled, put it off, took a nap and fell victim to further procrastination."

"How long have you known?"

"I did the home test two months ago. I'm almost four months pregnant."

Disparate feelings of bewilderment and happiness collided in Daniel. His joy at her news banged headlong into his confusion about her fear of his reaction. Her lack of trust pierced him. Neither of them had any interest in eating now. "Let's lose this place," he said. Rachael nodded. After signaling for the check, Daniel downed his beer, left the money on the table and grabbed her hand, giving it a squeeze.

They walked along the edge of the Dead Sea in silence. Rachael stared at the tips of her blue, striped, canvas shoes, then out across the water. Daniel kept hold of her hand. He was quiet as he turned things over in his mind. But all the while, there was a joy stirring deep inside him, building slowly, like a spring bubbling forth. He was going to be a father. They were going to have a baby. On the drive back to Jerusalem, he told her he was happy she was pregnant, but he needed to understand her fear of telling him. But she didn't understand it herself.

"I know it's irrational. And it's not that I don't trust you. My fear paralyzed me. I don't know where it came from."

"But you do want to have this baby with me, because I very much want it?"

At this, Rachael burst into tears, "Yes. Yes, I do, too, very much want to have this baby with you."

It seemed that out of nowhere, the scent of lilies wafted through the car, carried on the breeze through the open windows.

Rachael looked out, thinking they must have passed a garden. Then she let herself go and succumbed to their fragrance. Relief flooded her like a sudden spring rain after a drought. They drove in silence for some time before Daniel spoke.

"I want to figure out why you couldn't tell me for two months. I want to understand what was going on in your mind."

"You mean go to therapy?"

"My mother consults someone she swears by," he said.

"Isn't your mother's person a past life regression therapist?"

"Maybe, I don't know exactly, but he's a place to start."

"But do you even believe in reincarnation?"

"Hey, I'm a modern man, open to trying new things. He turned to look at her and saw that she was laughing.

"What?" he asked.

"You surprise me sometimes, that's all."

"Good, because this fear of talking to me can't happen again if we're going to be a family."

Rachel leaned back on the head rest, smiled, and closed her eyes.

Daniel called his mother that evening. Her therapist, Alan, was in fact a past life regression therapist as Rachael had thought. Daniel hung up from his mother and immediately emailed Alan.

"Did she ask you why you wanted the information? Rachael wanted to know.

"Nope, and I didn't volunteer. She knows I'll share that with her if I want her to know."

"God bless your mother. She has such good boundaries. I wish I could say the same for mine."

Before they went to bed, Daniel checked his email. Alan had answered, offering them an appointment for the following Thursday. "Great," Daniel said out loud, as he emailed back telling Alan that they'd definitely be there. He walked into their bedroom, told her the news, and kissed her on the tip of the nose. Until that moment, he hadn't realized how much Rachael's distance the last few weeks had affected him. But tonight, he could feel that she was back, and that made him playful.

While they sat in Alan's garden, waiting for their appointment, Daniel watched the sun spill through the tree branches, and make moving patterns on the ground each time the breeze ruffled the leaves. Rachael enjoyed the fragrance of Alan's many lilies as she went over again what he had explained to her on the phone. He would relax her, then regress her to a past life. He would ask her unconscious to show her the past life which had made her fearful of telling Daniel that she was pregnant. When the door from the office into the garden suddenly opened, they both jumped. Alan was a big, affable man, without the slightest touch of arrogance or ego. He introduced himself and welcomed them into his office. It was the color of warm sand, almost white. A large Buddha stood in one corner and a gurgling fountain in another. There was a chaise, with two comfortable chairs, one on either side of it. All the furniture was the color of sand, too. After asking them if they had any questions before they began, Alan directed Daniel to a chair and invited Rachael to recline on the chaise. The subdued light in the office, and the soft colors, felt pleasant. Rachel slipped off her sandals and lay down. Alan offered her a light blanket which she gratefully accepted for the sense of security it offered.

To begin the session, Alan hit the large gong standing next to his chair. It made a deep, low, calming sound. Trusting his feeling that they were in good hands, Daniel sat back in his chair. Alan explained that he would hit the gong again to bring Rachael back at the end of the regression. Directing her to focus her breath on her third eye, he relaxed her and suggested that with each breath her inner vision would increasingly slip the ego's constraints about time, and free her to view her past lives. He requested the permission and aid of her Higher Self, and his own Higher Self, to do this session. After some minutes, Daniel noticed that all muscle tension was gone from Rachel's body and she seemed to be in a kind of trance. Alan directed Rachel to see a bridge before her. When she said, in a whispery, faraway voice, that she could see the bridge, he instructed her to cross it, and view the lifetime which had caused her fear of telling Daniel that she was pregnant. He instructed her to describe what she saw.

It looks like North America, maybe New England, a long time ago. I'm dressed like a pilgrim girl. I'm maybe fourteen or fifteen. I'm vomiting in the woods. I hear my father coming and I'm terrified. If he finds me vomiting, I will be killed. I know I'm pregnant, and that I've been raped by an older man, the town magistrate. My parents don't know this. I'm terrified. I hear my father getting closer, but I can't run. My father falls upon me, beating me and dragging me back to the house. He's berating me. I can't look at him or speak, but I know my father is Daniel. He barks questions at me, but I deny that I'm pregnant or that I've had sex. He tells me that people have started to notice my body and a rumor has started that I'm a witch. Somehow, I know that the magistrate's wife has started this rumor. Another girl has been accused and condemned before me. She was burned at the stake as a witch while the town watched, and her family was shunned. I'm terrified to admit to my parents that I've been raped by the same man and that I'm pregnant. I lose my voice in a kind of hysterical paralysis and fall to the ground. My father yells at me to get up. I can't move.

Alan stopped Rachael, and told her to step back from the scene. He instructed her to breathe in through the soles of her feet and draw the breath up to her heart. "I will begin counting backward from ten to one. When I get to one, I'll ring the gong, and you will be fully back in Jerusalem, in my office, in present day reality."

At the sound of the gong, Rachael fluttered her eyelids. Alan spoke softly, instructing her to lie still and breathe. Tears streamed down her face staining her cheeks. Daniel asked Alan if it was alright to take her hand.

"Give her a minute, touching her could shock her if she's not fully back. I want to explain something, and do a little breath work with both of you, to release the effects of this past life."

Sensing that Daniel was horrified that he had been Rachael's abusive father in a previous life, Alan explained. "As we go through our incarnations, we play different roles for the people in our soul group. In one lifetime, we may be the child, in the next the parent, lover, enemy, employer or best friend. All our experiences are designed by our Higher Self to help us awaken to the knowledge that we are divine light beings. Each of us has to play the bad guy sometimes, to help another member of our soul group evolve. When the experiences in a lifetime have been very traumatic, they can be carried into the next lifetime."

Rachael opened her eyes and looked at Daniel. "It's alright," she said.

"Let's do some breathing to release this trauma for both of you. Bring your attention to the soles of your feet, and imagine you are drawing in white light. Use your breath, draw the light up through each of your chakras to open them, and help them spin in a clockwise direction. Begin with your root chakra, which is at the base of your spine and work your way up to your crown. As your breath pulls the light through each chakra, the chakra will release any tension, trauma, or fear that it's holding. Once your breath reaches your crown, reverse direction, breathe in light through the top of your head and sweep the breath and light downward, instructing it to carry away all the trauma and fear from each chakra. Using your breath, sweep the effects of the trauma all the way out through the soles of your feet, and send it down to the center of Mother Earth to be purified."

When they'd finished several rounds of breathing and sweeping, Alan told them to do this exercise every day for the next week. Performing this will make you feel better. It will speed up the electrons in all of your cells. When our electrons are moving in a clockwise direction, and at a good speed, we feel strong and happy. Breathing and meditation help our electrons to work optimally.

As they left Alan's office, Rachel stopped and looked into Daniel's eyes.

"Thank you for that."

"You're thanking me for the beating you just got, seeing that life where I was your cruel father."

"Look at me. A burden has been lifted."

She was right. When he looked into her eyes they were full of a soft, gentle light. The fear had been replaced with understanding and love. He gazed at her as long as he could bear it, for to look into such light-filled eyes was almost too intense.

A week ago, they had been two people standing on either side of a chasm, now they stood together, their heads reaching toward the tip of heaven. Daniel reached for her hand. "Come on. I'm taking you out to dinner. I want to start this baby off right, with a banquet fit for the gods."

Rachael's full blue skirt floated up around her as she skipped down Alan's walk toward the car.

Had Attivio heard Alan, instructing his future human parents about how to speed up their electrons, he would have felt right at home. He understood full well, even before the training on Venus, that each being is not only made of electrons, but is also given an unlimited supply of electrons each day with which to create as he sees fit. And had Daniel and Rachael been able to see Attivio, sitting with Soonam on Venus, they would have gasped to see a most beautiful light being, with pale-violet eyes and golden hair, seated next to another light being, also with golden hair, and with eyes the color of drenched violets.

Chapter 16

Moscow

"But we have two children. Do you want more?" Igor asked.

"I wasn't planning it, but it's happened," Masha answered.

The dining room door swung and their pink-cheeked maid came in carrying their breakfast. Both Masha and Igor fell silent. Masha thanked her as she set a plate down before each of them.

"Ahh, syrniki, my favorite," Igor said, leaning forward and sniffing the plate before him, which held three, round, fried dumplings made of egg and cottage cheese, sprinkled with powdered sugar. Artfully arranged on the plate, next to the dumplings, were a small bowl of jam, a few fresh strawberries and a little dish of sour cream.

Masha refreshed their tea from the blue and white porcelain pot beside her before speaking again. "Now, about the baby," she reminded him, attempting to pull his attention back from his plate. "How do you feel about another child?"

Igor put his fork down, reluctantly, and looked at her. "The children are wonderful, and one more will be wonderful, too, but for me, it's always been about spending my life with you, Mashenka. But if you want this baby, then that's what we'll do."

"But are you happy about it?"

"I will be, when it's here. Will that do?"

Masha smiled at him in answer, and he reached out and covered her soft, smooth hand with his.

He'd fallen in love with her the first moment he saw her walk into the ball dressed in a pale, silvery-blue, velvet gown. On that snowy night, she had arrived accompanied by her mother. Her father, like Igor, was in the diplomatic corps. Even though she had been engaged to someone else at the time, she accepted a secret assignation with Igor. Foregoing both the thrill of forbidden fruit and the claustrophobia of an affair, Masha ended her engagement after just that one secret meeting with Igor. They married three months later.

"We promised the children we'd take them ice skating today," Masha reminded him. "I was thinking either Luzhniki or Gorky Park."

"Let's go to Gorky Park. The cafes there have such lovely food," Igor said, between bites of dumpling.

Masha smiled at him without a word.

It was snowing when the four of them descended the front steps of their three-story house, Igor carrying all their skates over his shoulder. Masha, graceful in her long, full-skirted, forest-green, wool coat, held four-year-old Clara by the hand. Ahead of them, Igor walked beside six-year-old Alexei, who was busy stretching out his tongue, catching snowflakes. Igor tried to pull Alexei's blue knitted cap down to cover his ears, but the child wriggled his head away to resume his activity. Clara dropped one of her red mittens in the snow, and Masha knelt to pick it up.

"Hurry up, Mama," Alexei called back to them.

They entered Gorky Park to discover a wonderland of trees and branches freshly decked with snow. Even before the rink came into view, they could hear the merry voices of children ringing through the frosty Moscow air. Igor sat Clara and Alexei on a bench at the edge of the rink and laced up their skates, then put on his own. Masha stood still on her blades for a moment before stepping over the rough ice at the edge to glide out onto the clear, smooth rink. Skating with grace, she took a turn around the ring, her full skirts flowing out about her legs, swaying first one way, then the other, as she circled back to her family. Alexei was up and moving easily over the ice. Clara stood, and waving her arms to keep from losing her balance, pushed off with one foot. Masha skated up beside her, took hold of her hand and skated along with her. Some older boys of twelve or thirteen were showing off with jumping turns. Igor could feel Alexei's desire to join in their fun, and told him, "Your turn will come, you're only six, and besides, I want to skate with you."

Full of pride, Alexei reached up for Igor's hand and together they raced along the ice, giving their bodies to the wind. Masha, meanwhile, instructed Clara in some of the finer points of making turns. The afternoon passed too quickly. The sun set early this time of year, and when it did, the colored lights under the ice came on, evoking a collective "ah…" from the skaters.

"Just a few more turns to enjoy the lights. Then we must go," Igor told the children.

As Igor removed the children's skates, Alexei asked, "Can we eat in the park?"

"Cook is making stroganoff for you," Masha reminded him.

"A snack then?" Alexei pressed, looking at his father, who he knew took good care of his stomach.

Masha and Igor exchanged looks and agreed.

"Honey cake," four-year-old Clara piped in.

"And a potato pirozhki for me," said Alexei, who loved mini pies of all kinds.

There were lots of good choices in the park for having a bite. Igor steered them to a cozy spot down a snow laden path. The children had hot coca with their snacks, Masha a tea, and Igor a mulled wine. "Sublime," he said, tasting his wine, "perfect thing, after an afternoon of skating."

Clara stuffed the light, fluffy, honey cake into her pink mouth with obvious pleasure, while Alexei absorbed himself in his mini pies, one each of meat, salmon and potato. Masha watched her children and wondered how having a baby sister, for, she was quite sure the baby would be a girl, would affect their lives.

It had started snowing again by the time they reached home. Masha turned the children over to their nanny, and went up to bathe and change. They were expected at the Ritz-Carlton for a party that evening, one of many diplomatic functions connected with Igor's position they attended each season. Masha slid down into her bath until the hot water, fragrant with rose oil, touched her earlobes. She exhaled. A time for meditation and recognition of the Divine within, her bath was a precious ritual which she looked forward to each evening. As part of her meditation tonight, she would send a message of welcome to the soul of the child who was growing within her.

How can I already love you as I do, and know that you'll be somehow different? Where are you now? Do you yet know we're to be your family on earth? Are you going to be a girl in this lifetime, as I suspect? I have seen you in my dreams, far off in another world, a young woman strolling under a pink-golden sky. You always seem to be made of light and to almost float along on your long limbs. Is it you I see in my dreams or is it just the sausage, I sometimes eat at dinner?

Masha didn't really think it was the sausage, but she was protecting herself from hoping too much that this vision of light could really be coming to Earth as her child. Masha had had a relationship with the Divine since her own childhood. From her nanny, she had learned, when she was barely six, and her four-year-old sister died, to take comfort from daily meditation and prayer. Her nanny had instructed her well, that there is no death, that the soul is eternal, and that she might still talk to her sister, and tell her of her daily exploits and trials, as she had ever done in life. She still prayed for her sister and shared her secrets with her. Shaking off thoughts of the light being walking under a pink-golden sky, Masha stepped out of the bath and shivered momentarily until she felt the warmth of the heated bath towel around her shoulders. After drying herself, she hung up her towel, slipped on a long, silk robe and massaged rose cream into her legs before they could completely dry, having discovered as a teenager that damp skin is more absorbent than dry skin.

Her gold, floor length gown was already laid out on the bed when she entered her room. She glanced at it with pleasure, realizing she wouldn't fit in it much longer. Sitting down at her dressing table, one by one, she pulled out the pins which held her hair up and let it fall about her shoulders. She shook her head to loosen her hair the rest of the way before brushing it back off her face so she could apply moisturizer and makeup. Since her eyes and eyebrows were naturally dark, makeup didn't amount to much more than light powder, a touch of rouge and mascara. Then she swept her hair up into a French twist and held it in place with pins. Satisfied with the result, she put a diamond earring in each ear and stood up. Igor had come in, handsome in his tux, and was sitting on the bed watching her. She dropped her robe unselfconsciously, and put on a sheer bra and panties before slipping her dress over her head and letting it drop down around her body to the floor. Igor stood to zip up the back of her gown.

"The zipper is already snug," he said, kissing the back of her neck.

The upstairs restaurant at the Ritz overlooked the Kremlin, and afforded magnificent views of Red Square. Masha always looked forward to this bird's eye view of Saint Basil's Cathedral. As a child, she'd imagined Saint Basil's to be a castle where fairy princesses lived. On her tenth Christmas, her parents had given her a beautiful replica of it, large enough to fit her dolls. But tonight, more than her delight in the fancifully colored domes, she was anxious to see the tall, tent roofed tower in the center which housed the Church of the Protecting Veil of the Mother of God. She wanted to offer a prayer to Mary, the mother of God, asking her to safely guide their unborn daughter on her journey to them.

In all her dreams, the baby always appeared as a young woman. She was tall with grey-gold eyes that looked deeply into Masha's own green orbs, and held them fast as if trying to communicate something from a far-off world. Once, in a dream, early in the morning, just before she awoke, Masha thought she heard her speak of a mission to help Earth. When she'd told Igor of the dream, he'd kissed her and told her that, of course, she would dream her child was coming to save the world, when she herself worked so tirelessly with all her charities to help mankind, especially the poor. She hadn't disputed him, but she knew the dream wasn't because of her work, but a real message coming from a being in some far-off world, who wanted to alert her that she was coming for a purpose.

As they pulled up in front of the Ritz, unlike Masha, Igor's thoughts were not on churches or the mother of God or their unborn child. He was anticipating the caviar and champagne as much as the conversation. With happy thoughts of imminent pleasure, he stepped out of the taxi and turned back to offer Masha his hand.

She felt the warmth of his fingers right through her long evening gloves as she stepped onto the pavement.

Since seeing the holograph-like scene of the family in Moscow, gathered around a new born, Ederah often thought of them. And in thinking of them, she naturally thought of what she would like to convey to them, if that were possible. She would most certainly have been pleased to know that her mother on Earth was a sensitive being, sensitive enough to have picked up some of her messages about her purpose in taking a human life. And it might have particularly pleased Ederah to know that Masha was eager to ask Mary, the mother of Jesus, or as Ederah knew him, Lord Sananda, to pray for her safe journey into the third dimension. For of all the masters who had come to Venus, Ederah loved Lord Sananda best. And perhaps she would have been delighted, too, to learn that her future mother had actually seen, in her dreams, images of her, in her light body, strolling on Venus under the pink-gold sky.

Chapter 17

Mumbai

"But I can't be pregnant. My husband is dead, and I'm forty-six years old. I thought it was menopause," Mrs. Singh said.

"It isn't menopause, you're four months pregnant," her gynecologist said. "Would you like to hear the heartbeat?"

Aastha nodded, and Dr. Bandekar placed the stethoscope in her ears. At the sound of the tiny heart, tears sprang to her eyes. "It's so strong and brave for one so small," Aastha said. In twenty-eight years of marriage, she'd never been able to conceive. Now, with her husband, Siddharth, dead less than three months, what she had longed for all her married life had finally happened. Along with feelings of disbelief, joy and fear collided inside her as she stood in the dressing room, trying to adjust her sari with shaking hands. Then a new thought struck her – *I knew my name couldn't mean 'faith and trust' for no reason.* It was pouring rain and windy when Aastha left Dr. Bandekar's office, carrying a bag with the big, fat, vitamin pills the nurse had given her. August was still monsoon season in Mumbai. Aastha hurried along the busy street, trying to avoid bumping into the young people, who, even in the wind and rain, stopped to look at the walls of street art.

When she reached home, Aastha's first thought was to perform puja. She set the pregnancy vitamins on the table, and took off her wet sari and sandals. Still in shock that she was pregnant, Aastha moved mechanically as she put on a dry sari, picked up the broom, and walked into the altar room. She swept every corner of the room several times, ruminating until she lost track of time, wandering down the years. She remembered how Siddharth had instructed her, as a mere girl of eighteen, in the early days of their marriage, on the importance of bringing one's attention and presence especially to simple tasks. Thinking of his words, she tried to settle her mind, and focus only on sweeping. But memories kept intruding. The news of this pregnancy had taken her right back to the early days of her marriage, when each month she had hoped for news of a baby beginning its life inside her. How many disappointments had she known before hope died?

It had been Siddharth's first task, when they married, to have the altar constructed. He'd insisted it be made of sandalwood. And he'd selected an east facing room and supervised everything himself, choosing a beautiful statue of Krishna for the center of the altar. For the selection of the flower vases, incense burner, candle holders and silk altar cloth, he arranged a special shopping day for Aastha with his mother. Though a mere girl, Aastha was allowed her preferences, and she chose a cloth woven in gold and purple. It still graced their altar today. She ran her fingers over the fine cloth, and tears squeezed out of the corners of her dark eyes and ran down her cheeks at the memory of laying the cloth with Siddharth for the first time as newlyweds. He had been so pleased with all the things she had chosen, especially the cloth. Aastha wiped her eyes on the corner of her sari, and picked up the broom again. It was dusk before Aastha realized that she was sweeping mindlessly, lost in her memories. Chastising herself for her lack of attention to her task, she put the broom aside and began concentrating on cleaning the altar and the statue of Krishna. Careful not to touch Krishna's face, she wiped the statue and the altar. That done, she gathered fresh flowers, mangoes, oranges and honey as an offering.

When she was a bride, she had not known how to perform daily puja, but Siddharth had explained to her that each small action should be a surrender to the Infinite. He taught her to breathe consciously as she worked, to imagine each in breath to be a receiving of the gift of life, and each out breath a surrender to the Infinite. Now, when she performed pujas, her breath naturally flowed in harmony with her task. The first offering she set before Krishna was raw honey, to represent the sweetness of life. Beside the honey, she arranged the mangoes and oranges, giving each piece of fruit a little wipe with a clean cloth before setting it down in front of Krishna. The same two porcelain vases that she had chosen as a bride still stood on either side of the statue of Krishna. With awareness that each humble action she performed was an act of creation, and therefore a step on the journey to salvation, Aastha removed the old flowers and carried the vases to the kitchen to rinse them out, and fill them with fresh water. Then she returned them to their places, and arranged fresh, pink oleander and jasmine from her garden in each vase. This done, she lit the candles, and a new stick of sandalwood incense, and only then did she sit cross-legged on her meditation cushion before the altar to give thanks for the blessing of the coming child. Since Siddharth's death, she had added one additional item to the altar, his copy of *The Bhagavad Gita*, the one which he had been reading the night before he died.

They spent that last day of Siddharth's life, though they didn't know it was to be the last, on Elephanta Island, exploring the caves. Then afterward, they stood together before the statue of the three-faced Shiva: creator, destroyer and preserver of the universe, and prayed to Brahman that Atman in them would lead them to him. Both Siddharth and Aastha believed the teaching of *The Upanishads*, that one who knows God, becomes God. Once during their meditation, Aastha had opened her eyes to gaze at the peaceful serenity of Siddharth's face, his head bowed before the six-meter high statue of Shiva, with its own eyes closed in eternal contemplation.

Aastha remembered, too, Siddharth's laughter at the pesky monkeys patrolling the path back to the boat in hopes of a piece of paratha or a samosa or some crusts from a Bombay sandwich. She had to stop him from feeding the monkeys all the batata vada bites that they were to enjoy during the hour boat ride back to Mumbai. They'd bought the bites on the way to the island that morning. Aastha had stood beside Siddharth, watching, and anticipating the pleasure to come as the street vendor dipped balls made of mashed potatoes, green chills, garlic, lime juice, turmeric and fresh coriander in batter and then dropped them into the deep fryer. The fried bites were still fragrant, hours later, when they bit into them on the boat ride home. After he finished his snack, Siddharth dosed off in the sun for the rest of the journey. Aastha sat beside him, enjoying the breeze from the sea, which carried the smell of salt.

When the boat docked in Mumbai, Siddharth opened his eyes, and suggested that they go up Malabar Hill on their way home, to watch the sunset over the Arabian Sea. They both loved the light on Malabar Hill at all times of day, but especially at sunset, when the red footpaths turned a deep crimson. It had been an especially beautiful evening, with a soft breeze, and a pink and lavender sky, streaked with orange, rising above the shimmering incandescence of the Arabian Sea. As they stood looking out, he'd taken her hand, which had pleased her. Then, gazing out over the sea and up to the heavens, he spoke to her of light.

"This light is free. You can't buy it in the marketplace. It is given to us to illuminate our path. Brahman is the light which shines beyond all darkness."

Though Siddharth was a devote Hindu, he didn't often speak out loud to her of Brahman. That he had done so on Malabar Hill pleased her.

As soon as they reached home, Aastha began grilling the chicken cubes which she had marinated overnight in yogurt, ginger, garlic and lime juice. While she made a sauce of butter, fresh cream, tomato puree and cumin, Siddharth washed up, and seated himself in the garden under the lime tree, with his well-worn copy of *The Bhagavad Gita*. A soft breeze carried the delicate fragrance of the flowering lime to her as she worked in their open kitchen. She paused, and inhaled the fragrance before arranging the rice and chicken on an oval platter. She carried the platter out to the garden, and placed it on the table.

"I see you're reading your bible of love again," she said.

"It is more a love song to God than a Bible," he told her. "A love song to both the darkness and the light."

Aastha went back to the kitchen for the warm paratha, which she wrapped in a cloth napkin. They gave thanks for their food and blessed the plants and animals who had given their lives for this meal. Though many Hindus are vegetarian, Siddharth and Aastha were flexible, and occasionally partook of chicken and fish. They ate their meal in silence, enjoying the fragrant bouquet of scents from their food, and the flowering lime, jasmine and oleander growing in their garden. When they finished, Siddharth again surprised her, by speaking of love.

"Brahman is love, but also Brahman is the end of love."

Aastha didn't question him, but listened quietly, pleased that he was speaking to her of love. When he fell silent, she sat gazing with pleasure at her many pots of herbs. Curry leaves in their large earthen pot stood next to cardamom and caraway. In a grouping of three pots nearby, she had planted cilantro, onion chives and garlic chives. Beyond the pots was a group of lime trees. All these growing things she thought of as her kingdom, and it gave her pleasure just to look at them.

Siddharth interrupted her reverie by yet again speaking of Brahman.

"Brahman has need of us, even as we have need of Him."

At these words, Aastha gave Siddharth a questioning look, to which he replied, *"He needs us, to have someone to give his love to. It is his Ananda, his great joy, to love us."*

As he said this, he smiled at her from his heart, giving her a feeling of warmth and joy.

Next morning, when she awoke, Siddharth wasn't in bed beside her. Aastha assumed he was performing pujas in their temple room and went to join him. But she found him lying on the floor in the hall, outside the bathroom. He was completely still, his eyes open but unseeing. She fell on her knees, crumpling up beside his body, which already seemed to be an empty shell. She knelt over him without touching him, and began to pray.

"All the universe has come from love, and to love may Siddharth return. Guide him on the path of light." She repeated this simple prayer over and over. After she didn't know how long a time, she became aware that she was chilled and cramped, and she unfolded her body and stood up to make her way to the phone. Her elder sister came to her at once. Then, soon after, both Siddharth's parents, and her own arrived with several men Aastha didn't know. They washed Siddharth's body and wrapped it for the pyre. She knew that before sunset he would be set upon it. Then, too suddenly, his body left their home for the last time. She followed the men outside. It was May when he died, and the monsoons had not yet started. That morning the sky was filled with pink, feathery clouds. *How could he not be here to see them? Does he see them from where he is?* How different the previous day had been, when together they had set off for Elephanta Island. "Only in God is there immortality," she murmured through her tears, as she watched the backs of the men carrying Siddharth down the path away from her. It was only at that moment that she fully realized how completely she loved him. Over the years of their marriage, he had become the essence of all life to her, the light in the sun and the moon, the fragrance of the flowers, the scent of the earth in her garden, because she had seen the Divine in him. Love had grown softly and bloomed in season for them both, but only now in this moment of loss, did she fully comprehend who he was to her. Images and phrases from his beloved Gita began to flow through her.

"I am the taste in water,

the light in the moon and sun
the sacred syllable *OM*
in the Vedas, the sound in air.

I am the fragrance in the earth,
the manliness in men, the brilliance
in fire, the life in living,
and the abstinence in ascetics."
The Bhagavad Gita (Stephen Mitchell translation)

In the weeks after his death, her love for him had taken on a new boldness. Even in the agony of his absence, and the belief that, henceforth, she would meet him only in dreams and meditation, her love for him had deepened. Theirs had been an arranged marriage. They had met only once before the first ceremony. When he was finally alone with her, he had been surprised and delighted by her beauty, the thickness of her long black hair, the smoothness of her skin, and the roundness of her hips. And she had been grateful for his kind and gentle ways. In all the years, he had not criticized her, or himself, for failing to conceive a child, but had accepted it as the will of God, and had instructed her, "Whatever may befall you, never fail to keep your heart calm in the tenderness of love." Now their earthly journey together was over. But she held his words to her heart, even as she held his child in the safety of her body, imagining the tiny being, with its little heart, beating so bravely.

After Siddharth's death, she had planned a life of meditation and contemplation, but now their child would draw her back into the world. *I was pregnant the day we went to Elephanta Island,* she thought, *but I didn't know it. How happy Siddharth would have been. If this child is a boy, I'll call him Arjuna, in honor of his father's reverence for the light.* And in the months since his death, she had discovered that she had been wrong about something. She did not meet Siddharth only in her dreams and meditations, but in each breath, and in the fragrance of the lime trees, and in the many-colored sunsets, and in the moonlight shining across her pillow. And she knew he would be there, too, shining in the eyes of their baby.

As she went about her household tasks, Aastha spoke to the baby, calling him Arjuna, telling him about his father, and about the home he would be born into. As she carried on this conversation with her baby, she grew more and more certain that the child would be a boy. One afternoon while working in her garden, she felt faint and stopped to rest under a lime tree. As usual, she told her baby what she was feeling, but this time she imagined that he answered her, not in words, but in images, which flashed before her mind. He sent her a vision of a pink sky above a pearly dome. The vision was so real that she had to open her eyes to make sure the sky above her was still blue. Letting her eyelids fall closed again, she saw a very tall, maybe even eleven or twelve feet tall, slender man with a long neck and grey-gold eyes smiling at her. He didn't look at all Indian, but he seemed as gentle and kind as the most noble and serene of Indian men. For many days, she couldn't get the image of this being out of her mind. After that, she spoke not only to the baby, but also to the beautiful man from the land with the pink sky.

When Bereh opened his envelope, the day the birds delivered them on Venus, he saw his future parents together on Elephanta Island, laughing at the antics of the monkeys which surrounded them. He'd liked them both. But after that, when he tried to picture them, he could see only his mother. "What does this mean," he'd asked Ederah.

"I don't know, but remember, what is, is right. All will be well, Bereh." Her words calmed him.

Aastha wondered, as she grew rounder and heavier, how she would help her son to grow up without his father. And often, as she worked in her garden, her hand would go to her belly to reassure Arjuna that she would love him enough for both of his parents. All through her pregnancy she continued to talk to him about his father, and to tell him of his father's love for *The Bhagavad Gita*. Then leaning forward over her belly, she would whisper to him the words which Krishna spoke to Arjuna on the battlefield.

"Now listen to my final words,
the deepest secret of all;
I am speaking for your own welfare,
Since you are precious to me.

If you focus on me
And revere me with all your heart,
You will surely come to me; this
I promise, because I love you."
The Bhagavad Gita (Stephen Mitchell translation)

Chapter 18

London

Charlotte leaned over the water and tossed her bread crusts to the gathering swans. One swan in particular was more aggressive than the others, quickly paddling in any direction in which she tossed the bread, and stretching his long neck out to swipe it out from under the nose of any of the others. He amused her, maybe because he reminded her of her mother-in-law. Kensington Gardens was one of her favorite London spots, not only because of the swans, but for all the greenery and peace. Her breadcrumbs gone, Charlotte left the swans to themselves. The sun felt warm on the back of her long, slim calves as she walked away from the water. Half thinking to visit it, but mainly deep in her own thoughts, Charlotte wandered in the direction of the Peter Pan statue. She was six months pregnant with her first child. The baby would mean lots of changes. Robert wanted her to stop working and be a full-time mother, but she loved her job as accessories editor at British Vogue. Still, all the work trips to Milan and Paris and New York wouldn't be as easy to manage with a baby.

Today was a rare Saturday alone for her. She usually spent Saturdays with Robert, but he had emergency committee meetings all day to discuss the demonstrations against the new American president's proposed visit to the United Kingdom. Because of the American president's vulgarity, lies, and unprincipled positions, many British people were opposed to inviting him to speak to parliament, let alone to meet with the Queen. Robert wouldn't be home until evening. He'd told her the meetings would be a waste of time, since the American president had such an out-sized ego that he would likely not risk coming to a country where there would be open demonstrations against him. Robert wished they could forget the American president, and discuss the Syrian refugee crisis instead. Nevertheless, he had to attend. "Party duty," he said.

And her mother-in-law, Maggie, too, was out of the picture today, as she was vacationing on the continent. So, for once, Charlotte was free of her suggestions and meddling. Still, before she left, Maggie had managed to lecture Charlotte yet again about the unsuitability of the wife of a member of the House of Lords working for a fashion magazine.

"Dreadful, as I've been telling you since you first became engaged to my son. Now that you're pregnant, I won't have it. You must give notice."

Robert had stood up for her, and told his mother that it was none of her business. Naturally Maggie bristled at this. "So, I'm to have no say, and to be treated like an outsider."

Thankfully, Robert had stood firm. It hadn't been that way in the past, when they were doing up their flat. Maggie had insisted that they use family heirlooms. Though the family seat in the country had been lost to taxes two generations before, the art and furnishings had been saved. What was not used in the London mansion had been stored for Robert. Charlotte wanted to design her own home, but Maggie had insisted that as a Lord, Robert would need to entertain in a certain style. Charlotte had lost the battle for the drawing room, the library and the dining room, but had held sway with her own office, their bedroom, the guest rooms and the kitchen. Now Maggie had ideas for the baby's room, but Charlotte was determined to keep her out of that planning.

Charlotte wandered through Kensington Gardens, paying no attention to where she was going, until she found herself face to face with the statue of Peter Pan. Gazing up, and marking his youthful countenance, she decided to pose a question to him. While she composed her thoughts, she moved her eyes over the rabbits at his feet. Then she said out loud, but softly, "What should I do about my job? I know it's a trivial problem in the grand scheme of things, and that I'm lucky to have a choice, but it is also about my identity. I don't want my mother-in-law to think she's won if I stop working," she told Peter. "That's petty, I know." Before she could converse further with Peter, she felt a warm trickle on the inside of her thighs. It ran down her long legs and into her shoes. Seeing that her legs were stained with red, she let out an involuntary, "Oh my God." Frozen by the sight of so much of her own blood, and the fear of what it could mean, she might have been a statue herself. Should she go to the emergency room or just go home and lie down? Somehow it occurred to her to call her doctor, and she moved her hand to reach into her pocket for her phone. The answering service picked up. Right. It was Saturday. She left a message explaining the urgency and asking for a call back.

As she made her way out of the park and hailed a cab, Charlotte realized she'd made the decision to go home. She bunched up her trench coat under her, hoping the blood wouldn't leak through it onto the taxi seat. By the time she was inside the flat, even her coat was stained red. Stripping off her clothes, she dropped them in a pile on the bathroom floor, and stepped into the hot shower, a prayer on her lips. Though they were Church of England, it was a Sunday relationship they had with religion, and possibly with God. Would he even listen? A trickle of blood was still running down her legs when she stepped out of the shower, and reached for her white terrycloth robe. Maybe not the best choice, but never mind that now. In the bathroom closet, she found an old box of sanitary napkins, stuffed two in her underwear, laid down on her bedroom floor, with her feet elevated, to google bleeding during the sixth month of pregnancy on her phone. It was probably not a good way to spend her time while she waited for the doctor to call her back, but she couldn't help herself. Sufficiently scared by what she was reading, she debated calling Robert, but then her phone rang. Dr. Gupta explained that the bleeding could be caused by a number of different things, but she'd need to examine her to know which. They arranged to meet at the clinic. Dr. Gupta's calm voice was reassuring, even though she'd offered no actual reassurance that Charlotte wasn't in fact having a miscarriage.

Charlotte had liked her from their first meeting and was glad to have a woman obstetrician. During their initial visit, she'd answered, without defensiveness, when Charlotte had asked her if she had herself gone through pregnancy and delivery. "No, not yet."

Charlotte guessed that she was in her early thirties. Not long after she began seeing Dr. Gupta, she and Robert had bumped into her at the theatre in the West End. She'd been with a handsome Indian man, who she introduced as her husband. Charlotte wondered if he was also a doctor. That evening, Dr. Gupta was wearing a gorgeous sari of deep turquoise and gold, and Robert had afterward remarked about how very feminine and elegant the sari was as a garment. When Charlotte mentioned to her mother that they'd bumped into Dr. Gupta at the theater, and repeated Robert's comment about saris, her mother, a Jungian analyst, had told her that after his trip to India, Jung had made the same observation about saris.

Charlotte changed the soaking pads, slipped on a pair of pants and a sweater, and decided she'd call Robert after she'd seen Dr. Gupta. Then she changed her mind. What if, for some reason, Robert got home early and saw all the bloody clothes soaking in the tub. She rang him and left a message explaining that she was on her way to see Dr. Gupta, and she'd phone him after the appointment. Dr. Gupta was already there when Charlotte arrived at the clinic. She listened for the baby's heartbeat and found it strong. Only then did Charlotte begin to weep with relief. She had been using all her energy to block the thought that her little daughter was dead inside her. She and Robert had both decided at the time of the first sonogram to learn the sex of the baby. Now they already had a relationship with baby Mary. At least that's what they were calling her between themselves. Robert's mother, Maggie, had of course insisted on knowing the sex, but they had held firm in keeping their secret between them. In the absence of information, Maggie decided that the baby was a boy, and that he should be named William after Robert's father, unless it was somehow a girl, then it could be called Margaret Elizabeth after her.

"Just ignore her," Robert told Charlotte. "Let her enjoy herself."

On examining Charlotte, Dr. Gupta found that the bleeding had stopped, but that Charlotte had a condition called placenta previa, in which the placenta partly detaches and migrates. It was now blocking Charlotte's cervix. She explained that with bed rest it could resolve by Charlotte's due date, which would allow for a normal vaginal delivery. If it didn't, Charlotte would need a C-section, something she had been very much against as she wanted her daughter to be able to choose her own moment to be born. Her phone rang while she was dressing.

"Darling, are you still at the clinic? I'm on my way. What did Dr. Gupta say?"

"Mary's alive, but I'll have to spend the rest of my pregnancy in bed. I'm about to leave. Let's meet at home."

Robert reluctantly agreed not to collect her from the clinic, and Charlotte hung up and put on her coat. Dr. Gupta's last words were, "Straight to bed."

Robert was in front of their building waiting for her when her taxi pulled up. His arms were around her before she was even all the way out of the cab. He paid the driver and tried to help her up to the front door.

"Darling, I'm not an invalid."

Charlotte undressed, put on her blue, silk pajamas over more pads and underwear, just in case the bleeding started up again, and climbed into bed under their soft, down comforter. The room itself made her feel good. She loved the generous, creamy, ivory colored drapes which fell all the way to the floor, the matching bedside lamps and white night tables piled with books, the duvet cover of the palest sea-green to match the lamp shades. She closed her eyes and opened them again to rest on the new, pale-green and white, striped chaise across the room, and the small, round, marble table beside it, also piled with books, atop which sat her eye glasses. The chaise had been Robert's idea, so she could read comfortably with her feet up once she was far along in her pregnancy.

"In case your ankles swell up," he'd said.

"And how do you know about swelling ankles in pregnancy," she'd asked him, laughing.

"I'm surprised you can ask. Don't you remember, we saw it on *Call the Midwife*?"

"So that's where you're getting your information about pregnancy," she teased.

That conversation had only been a month ago, when all was still well.

Robert made the tea and carried it into their room on a tray, along with a plate of chocolate covered biscuits. He set the tray down next to her, and seated himself on the edge of the bed to pour the tea. Sipping her tea, suddenly reminded Charlotte of the dream she'd had the night before, and she couldn't stop herself from blurting it out to Robert.

"I was having tea in my dream last night," she told him, "sitting up in bed, like I am now, when suddenly a large, hideous reptile about ten feet tall, with a long tail covered with black scales, appeared at the foot of our bed. He was standing on his hind legs, just glaring at my belly, giving me the evil eye. As I watched he flickered between a black shadow shaped like a man and his reptilian form. I knew, in my dream, that I wasn't supposed to be able to see him, and that he believed himself to be invisible to me, so I pretended I didn't see him. Hoping he would go away, I looked down into my tea cup, but I could feel his eyes boring into me, trying to hurt Mary. I froze in fear. I felt he wanted to kill her, and I alone stood in the way. Then he vanished, and I felt sick from the ugliness of him and his dark energy. I'd forgotten about it until you handed me this cup of tea."

"It's just a dream, darling," Robert said. "Have a chocolate biscuit."

"I know pregnancy hormones intensify dreams, but it felt so real. I was so certain that he wanted to harm Mary, to stop her from being born, and then today, the bleeding started."

"Let's not be superstitious, it's probably a coincidence that the dream was last night and today you've had a miscarriage scare."

"But, Robert, you know I was raised to see coincidences not simply as coincidences, but as meaningful synchronicity."

"I know your mother is a Jungian analyst, who filled you with all sorts of whimsy when you were growing up."

"That isn't fair, Robert. Jung's work is brilliant, but more importantly, it helps people make sense of their suffering. It isn't whimsy at all. I don't like you saying that. And I'm not out of the woods as far as a miscarriage is concerned."

"I'm sorry, darling it was cavalier and flippant of me to speak that way about Jung or your mother. You know I adore her."

"I know you find some of her ideas challenging."

Robert let her last comment drop and returned to the subject of the baby.

"I thought if you remained on bed rest the danger would pass. Are you saying a miscarriage is still a possibility?"

"Dr. Gupta couldn't absolutely promise that I wouldn't miscarry, even with bed rest."

For the second time since the bleeding had started, tears formed in the corners of Charlotte's eyes. Robert took her cup from her hands, set it on the nightstand and gathered her up in his arms. The strength and warmth in him reassured her and she attempted to make a joke.

"I know one person who'll be happy I'm on bed rest," Charlotte said, "it'll be your mother's best news this season, since I'll be a captive for the next three months."

Robert smiled at her and said, "Thank God you married me despite my mother."

"She was almost a deal breaker," Charlotte teased. "But I suppose we're made in a certain way, and can't help being what we are."

The truth was that nothing could have broken the deal for Charlotte, she had been smitten from the first moment she was introduced to Robert, at a friend's dinner party. On returning home from the party that night, she'd told her flat mate, "I met a man this evening, and I know already that he could break my heart."

It had taken Robert a little longer to realize what Charlotte would come to mean to him. For Robert, the fire of love ignited cautiously, but burned steadily until it filled his whole being. Early on, Charlotte had told her mother that Robert was like a dry lake bed, slowly filling with melting snow and spring rain, but once fully committed, he would be a steadfast partner. Her mother had smiled at her description. The lake bed was truly full now, so if they were going to lose Mary, at least Charlotte would have Robert's strength to lean on.

Since Charlotte and Robert were so firmly rooted in third dimensional reality, they would have been stunned to know that Maepleida, Heipleido, and their friends, on far off Venus, had witnessed Charlotte standing before the Peter Pan statue at the moment when she felt the blood running down her legs into her shoes. Maepleida, however, would not have been stunned to hear Charlotte's dream of the dark shadow flickering into a reptilian form. And she would have known it was no dream.

Chapter 19

Cairo

"What's that you're reading?" Adjo asked, walking into the room and finding Amisi absorbed in a book.

"A book about Sufism."

She lifted their cat, Nefretiti, off her lap and set her on the loveseat beside her.

"Sorry, Nefretiti, but my legs are falling asleep. I need to stretch them."

Nefretiti gave a little meow of protest.

"Give me a kiss," Adjo said, "and tell me why you're reading a book on Sufism."

She lifted her lips to his and gave him a soft kiss, which he returned with a half open mouth, reluctant to release her.

"Even though I was born a Moslem," Amisi began, "I've never understood how Sufism differs from Islam."

"But why the sudden interest now?" he asked. "We may have been born Moslem, but we don't practice."

Amisi sat down again and Nefretiti climbed back into her lap and curled up.

"I'm not sure why, maybe because of that recurrent dream I've been having."

"The one about the tall, black-skinned man emanating light?" Adjo asked.

"Yes, he's so luminous that I can't get him out of my mind. And in last night's dream, I saw him sitting in a temple with high vaulted ceilings, and a high roof open to a pink sky. There was a small, golden bird on his lap, and the bird had an envelope in its mouth which he seemed to be delivering to the luminous young man with the black marble brow. Both creatures were filled with so much love, it made me want to be closer to God myself."

"My sweet one, I still don't see how you got from your dream to Sufism?"

"I don't know myself, but I'm thinking about taking a class on Sufism at Al-Azhar."

Adjo smiled and sat down on the loveseat opposite hers. He looked at her over the large bouquet of deep-orange poppies. Their delicate, paper-like petals rose up on long stems from a vase on the low table between their two love seats. Amisi looked to him like a picture, sitting across from him behind the orange poppies. As always, she was elegantly dressed. "I dress for you and for myself," she'd told him early on in their relationship. Truth be told, she was a bit of a clothes horse, but Adjo didn't care. He enjoyed her beauty and taste. She created a sense of serenity around herself, and throughout their home, and he appreciated her for that, too. His sister said she was young to have such sophisticated taste. But her mother had told him that even as a child, Amisi had wanted to arrange flowers, and design clothes and furniture. As soon as they'd become engaged, she began selecting beautiful Egyptian textiles in black, burnt orange, and gold for their home. Cairo was a smoggy city, and Amisi made their home an oasis. "And, have you discovered how Islam and Sufism are related?"

"I've made a start. Scholars believe that Sufism began in the ninth century as an ascetic movement, an initiation into the mystical aspects of faith. Sufism looks beyond the external practices of a religion, like praying five times a day, and instead focuses on the interior experience of the mystic. Orthodox Islam teaches that to attain union with Allah, you must follow Sharia Law, and emulate the life of Mohammed. It's a religion which attempts to control people. Sufism appeals to me more because it's not about controlling people with laws. It's the mystical aspect of Sufism that appeals to me. I like the idea of practices which help you to merge with the source of Divine consciousness. According to Guru Maharaji, who's quoted in this book, Sufism is not a religion, it's a way of life. There can be Hindu Sufis, Muslim Sufis and Christian Sufis."

"And what does that way of life entail?"

"That's what I'm hoping to learn. Part of it seems to be a relationship with a guru, who is a man with the power to reveal something wonderful inside yourself, if you surrender to him, and rest in his bliss."

"Well, I hope it doesn't mean you'll have to give up your flower shop," he teased. "I'd miss all the beautiful flowers you bring home." He knew there was little danger of her choosing a way of life that threatened her work with flowers. She loved all flowers, but her favorite was the blue lotus, which grew along the banks of the Nile, rising from the mire of the river like a chalice, eager to reach the light. Its blossoms, the color of a lavender-blue sky, and green floating leaves and sweet fragrance had entranced Amisi, ever since she was a child playing by the river's edge. He knew she believed that the stronger the fragrance of a lotus, the more the flower held the presence of God. "Lotus flowers are like stars from heaven dropped into the Nile, so they can swim up to meet the light," she'd told him the first time he walked into her shop. Adjo had long understood that flowers were more than flowers to Amisi, but he was puzzled over this new interest in Sufism.

"So how does the power of the guru help one to find that something wonderful in oneself?"

"Through prana, which the guru directs into the heart chakra of the disciple to open the gates of grace. The transfer is from heart to heart. With his love and prana, the guru opens the heart chakra of the shishya.

"Shishya?" Adjo said.

"Shishya means disciple, or one who has surrendered to the guru. The guru stimulates the heart chakra of the shishya. The heart chakra is the focus, the leader of all the other chakras. And it's the heart chakra which gradually opens all the others. How it works beyond that is a mystery which I hope to discover."

"And what is prana?" Adjo asked her, aware of a deep feeling of sweetness in his whole body as he gazed at her. When she spoke, her voice, like a caress, affected his whole nervous system, creating a feeling of languor. A feeling of gratitude for this marriage washed over him as the sweetness of her voice flowed toward him over the poppies.

"I think prana means life force, but you can't see it. It's a force which is invisible to the physical eyes. It flows outward in both our waking and sleeping states, but in dhyana, deep peace, prana is reversed and flows inward and gets absorbed in the heart, creating a state of effortless calm, like a deep, still pool, full of silence. The guru creates this state in his disciple, but only after the disciple has completely surrendered to the will of God. The will of God is represented as the will of the guru."

"You never cease to surprise me, my little lotus," he said. "I want to hear more about dhyana. I think you must be my guru, for that's the state you create in me. But now I better get changed if we don't want to be late to my mother's dinner party.

They had been married only six months when Amisi discovered, much to her delight, that she was pregnant. Tonight, they were going to his parents' home to celebrate the news. Since she was in business for herself, Amisi planned to go on working as long as she could, and afterwards, she might even bring the baby to work with her. This idea, she hadn't yet mentioned to Adjo, or to either of their parents. She wasn't worried about convincing Adjo of her plans since they were extremely well suited to one another, and agreed about most things. They got each other's jokes, they enjoyed the same people, the same movies, the same games, and they especially liked one another's company and conversation. Neither of them could be considered an intellectual, or even particularly interested in a life of the mind, but they both appreciated music, art and good conversation. To that end, they kept up with world affairs and read popular new books. But this choice of Amisi's, to study Sufism, was a diversion from her usual pursuits, and it made Adjo wonder how it had come about. Had her pregnancy ignited this new interest? Adjo wasn't someone who thought much about God or religion. He was an engineer, who'd studied abroad in the United States at MIT, having opted not to join the family textile business. And he'd been lucky after he graduated to find work on the extension of the Suez Canal, a job which had set him up in his career. It had been when he was back home in Cairo, on summer vacation, before his last year at MIT, that he'd met Amisi. Walking into her newly opened shop to buy flowers for his mother's birthday, he'd seen a young girl of maybe twenty, arranging flowers for a customer. The girl's total concentration on her task, and respect for each blossom had captured his attention. Only when she was satisfied that the last flower was perfectly placed had she looked up smiling. She had been aware that he was watching her, and she had enjoyed the feeling. It hadn't felt like he wanted to hurry her at all, but only to appreciate her skill. She told him that she'd help him in moment, once her customer had paid. And she had. The arrangement of deep-purple irises and creamy jasmine, which Amisi created for him, had pleased his mother very much. Her shop was in the Khan Al-Khalili market, Cairo's largest market district, originally built in the 14th century. Adjo had originally been headed to the gold section of the market, to purchase a bracelet for his mother, but something had drawn him toward Amisi's shop, and when he saw her through the window, his heart made a helpless jump against his ribs.

Back at MIT the year following their meeting, her face had looked at him from the center of every flower, until he wrote to her, throwing his heart at her feet. When she answered that she had lost her heart to him, too, and never ever expected to get it back again, she set his soul aflame. But they had to wait out his time until graduation, and this they did with gentle longing, infinite sweetness and the help of "WhatsApp". They had touched one another's hearts, as if with magic wands, igniting sparks which then lived in them, connecting them despite the distance, like two stars signaling each other across a velvet firmament.

"Are you looking forward to tonight's dinner?" Adjo asked coming back into the living room in a casual shirt.

"Absolutely. Your mother has the best cook in Cairo, and I love fatta, besarah, baladi and basbousa."

"How do you know that's what we're having?"

"Because fatta is a soup made to celebrate a woman's first pregnancy."

"Oh. Why is that?"

"It's made with garlic and white vinegar. And both garlic and white vinegar are healthy for pregnant women. Besides, your mother knows I love it, even when I'm not pregnant. She also knows we're vegetarian and that you love besarah. It doesn't take a sleuth to know she'll be serving that, too, as you are her golden one."

It was true, Adjo did love besarah. A dish known since the time of the pharaohs, it was a celebration of vegetables, herbs and spices: parsley, dill, leak, crushed fava beans, green bell peppers, fresh coriander, cumin and caramelized onions.

"And," Amisi continued, "besarah is always accompanied by hot baladi bread made of whole wheat and bran. So, there you have our menu."

"And do you have the inside word that there'll also be basbousa?"

"Ah, yes. As it's your favorite cake, your mother won't miss an opportunity of having it set before you. She didn't give you a name which means treasure for no reason. Besides, since it's made with rose water, lemon and honey it will bring a special blessing for our child. And your mother is always ready to confer blessings."

"Come here, my clever one," he said, sitting down beside her and opening his arms. As she cuddled next to him on the love seat, he asked her another question. "Are you going to mention your new interest in Sufism tonight?"

"I wouldn't be surprised if your mother already knew something about it."

"What makes you think that?"

"You remember, when you were in America, I used to visit her. On one of those visits, she took my hands and told me, 'Amisi, in the whole of creation, there is nothing but the lover and the beloved.' Today I read that's what Sufis believe."

Adjo tilted his head and bit his lower lip, as if struggling with some thought.

"Don't think so hard, Adjo. Nothing is solved with the mind."

"What else did my mother tell you during those visits?"

"She said, 'One must live with the turmoil of life, even in the middle of it, and not react too much. And one must get rid of likes and dislikes and be accepting of what comes, forgetting oneself, only then can you drown in an ocean of love.'"

"I didn't know my mother was so wise," he half-joked. "Are you ready to go then?"

"In a minute, I want to put the fava beans I've been soaking on the stove to simmer overnight. And I have to feed Nefretiti."

"Are we taking these flowers by the door?" Adjo asked.

Yes, the blue lotus, not the white ones," Amisi called from the kitchen.

Adjo picked up the flowers and gazed out the window at a sunset of deep crimson and luminous gold. It's true, he thought, looking into the sky, *in the whole of creation there is nothing but the lover and the beloved.*

Had Heipleido, on far away Venus, heard these words from Adjo, about the lover and the beloved, it would have been music to his heart. For the understanding that there is nothing in all of creation but the lover and the beloved is a knowing which most third dimensional beings did not yet grasp. And, had Amisi known that her dreams of the luminous young man, with skin like black marble, were actually visions of her future son, who was even now training on Venus for his mission to Earth, she might have been less astonished than one would think. Amisi was more than she seemed, though she didn't yet know it.

Part Three

Final Preparation for Descent to Earth

Chapter 20

The Violet Flame

Everyone had spent the last few days learning more about the country where they would incarnate. This was more out of curiosity than for preparation, because once through the veil, they wouldn't consciously remember much, if any, of it. They also devoted a lot of time to discussing the Earth families they'd seen in their holograms, and trying to build stories around the vignettes they'd seen. Everyone thought Toomeh's parents, climbing the hill above the Irish Sea, very romantic and deeply in love with one another. Unfortunately, everyone was also in agreement about Soonam's mother. Maepleida summed her up in one word – 'nightmare.' Attivio said he preferred to think of her as a challenge, which would help Soonam to wake up faster. Soonam was glad that at least her father seemed loving.

"And they appear to be comfortably well off," Ederah told Soonam. "Which doesn't matter in the fifth dimension, where we can manifest anything we like, but in the third dimension it could be some sort of advantage, especially in New York City."

"Or it could be a hindrance, which is more likely," Maepleida piped in.

"Attivio's mother looks a bit challenging, too," Maepleida further observed, "walking along the Dead Sea, weeping. What was that about?"

"To me she looked frightened and sad," Soonam said, "like she was in the grip of something, but underneath that, she seemed kind and gentle. And the cute guy with her was trying to help."

"By 'that cute guy,' I assume you mean my father to be," Attivio teased her.

"I do like your Russian couple, Ederah," Maepleida said,

changing the subject from Attivio's mother, "they seem to have a lot of fun in life, and your future father certainly takes good care of his stomach."

"Yes, and I imagine I'll be ice skating with two older siblings," Ederah added. Bereh looked at her when she said this, and felt keenly her bravery and willingness to be positive, which made him love her all the more.

"You're going to be the most adorable Indian boy who ever grew up in Mumbai," Ederah teased Bereh. "I bet all the old people will be pinching your cheeks all day long."

"I do hope not. But I am pleased that the house has such a well-loved garden. Gardens make me happy. And I wouldn't mind meeting those playful monkeys we saw by the ferry."

"Speaking of adorable, how about Laaroos' mother, seated on the bench under the plum tree in the Japanese garden, all tidy in her kimono, turning her perfect oval face up to feel the raindrops falling through the plum blossoms. When I saw that scene, I felt like painting it, I was so moved by her beauty," Toomeh said, looking straight at Laaroos.

"I doubt anyone would want to paint my mother. By Earth standards she's positively a giraffe," Maepleida said, "a giraffe talking to a statue, with blood running down her long skinny legs."

"I found her quite attractive," Heipleido countered.

"You don't count. You're a well-known giraffe lover," Maepleida said, extending her lanky limbs.

"Speaking of painting, Heipleido, your parents made quite a picture themselves, sitting across from one another, gazing into each other's eyes over those orange poppies, your mother holding that beautiful Egyptian cat," Bereh said.

Heipleido nodded his agreement and added, "I do like the look of those two humans. In fact, I'd say there will be admirable things about each of these families."

No one disagreed, and talking it over felt good, because at

least for now, they knew where each other was going, and that was a comfort, even to a fifth dimensional being.

Their last Elysian days on Venus, before they must enter the rushing world were drawing to a close. Soon they would all separate, with some sadness, but also with faith in their mission, and a supreme desire to serve. Each of them would incarnate into a fetus. They would be able to enter and leave the fetus only until the moment of birth. Most souls can come and go, in and out of the infant's body, until age two. This privilege would not be granted to the wanderers, as it was considered too dangerous to leave the babies' bodies empty, without souls, since the dark lords would not hesitate to take any opportunity to kill the infants. And this could be accomplished more easily if the soul was absent.

The eight friends spent their final days on Venus in various ways. Soonam and Attivio chose sexual union. As immortal lovers, they entered the sacred vessel of the bridal chamber with complete transparency and total self-outpouring, emptying themselves, each unto the other, with the knowledge that they had not simply found one another, but had been in one another all along.

When he awoke on the third to the last day, after a night of passionate lovemaking, Attivio looked over at the sleeping Soonam, her hair, golden wheat in sweet disorder, and regarded her fair form. She opened her violet eyes to see his devotion. He leaned over and touched her lips with his own. *Touch has a memory*, he thought.

She snuggled into him like a warm puppy, and asked, "What's happening today?"

"I believe Lord Kumara and Lady Venus will address us this morning, followed by Master Saint Germain and Lady Portia, Chohans of the Violet Flame, this afternoon."

"Are they the last then?"

"The last, except for Earth's Planetary Buddha, who will come tomorrow or the next day to give us his blessing," Attivio told her.

"We better get up then," she said giving him a quick kiss on his lips.

As the gong in the temple campanile sounded for the third time, Maepleida and Heipleido took their seats next to Ederah and Bereh. Toomeh leaned forward to nod at them, but sat back when he heard Lord Kumara begin speaking. Attivio and Soonam slipped in beside Laaroos just at the last moment.

"Good morning radiant beings, for you are, each of you radiant with positive energy as we near the close of our time together on Venus, and disperse to Earth. Remember that separation is an illusion. Those who have penetrated this illusion know well that all are One."

Lord Kumara turned to Lady Venus who then spoke to them.

"When you enter the third dimension, try to live moment by moment," she said, "seeking always contact with, and guidance from, your Higher Self, that aspect of yourself which resides in the sixth dimension, and sees you in your totality. Your Higher Self is ready, at your call, to reach back into any dimension to offer you help and guidance."

Here, Lady Venus paused, and fell silent as she cast her eyes over them. The desire to wrap them in the wings of her love and protection was strong within her. She pulled herself back, and silently reminded herself that they must succeed or fail according to the Divine plan. But it was a struggle for her, as she deeply loved each of the beings before her. Whether they were bipeds like herself or quadrupeds or beings with eyes like hers or had tentacles with which they saw, she cherished them all. Before continuing to speak, she sent them the vibration of her love. It shimmered out over them and descended on each being in gently falling waves of grace.

"In each moment that you reside on Earth," she continued,

"try to seek the joy and bliss of the One Infinite Intelligence, remembering that both dark and light are part of the Divine. Earth is a planet with much duality. Where there is a dualistic way of thinking, there is judgment of those who do not think as we do. Take care not to judge others. You may discern differences in your thinking, but do not cross the line into judgment. To take that step will weaken you. All dualistic positions can be resolved if we accept the other also as an expression of the Divine. I include here those beings from Orion, who particularly tempt humans to choose the path of service only to self. Even they serve the creator in their own way. Do not fall into their trap, but also, do not judge them. Every being serves the Creator in their own way." Lady Venus spoke to them like this for some time, soothing their hearts and gently leading them a step closer to their departure for Earth. Finally, she released them for a rest. For the first time, the friends didn't gather under their tree. Instead, each twin flame pair wandered off in their own direction.

Toomeh was at the impatient stage of – *let's get on with it already*. Anticipation was beginning to weigh heavily on him. Laaroos tried to soothe him. "Think of your lovely, Irish, Earth mother and let her love you for a while," she told him, "until we're reunited in our immortal love after the success of this mission."

Toomeh was grateful for her wise words and her confidence. Laaroos didn't mention her own disappointment, that she wasn't to incarnate in New York City as she had hoped, to be near her own eternal mother from Arcturus, but was instead to be born in Tokyo.

Maepleida was now strong in her resolve to face the challenge of this incarnation on Earth. Supported by the knowledge that this mission was what her Higher Self intended for her, she wore an unconquerable face. Heipleido was of the exact same mind, but then, he had been gung-ho about this mission from the start. He was happy that they now thought as one, both anticipating a victorious mission.

Bereh, who loved Ederah with that all compassionate love which demands no return, reassured her repeatedly that he would penetrate the veil of forgetting, and find her in the third dimension. Somehow, he would wake up and remember that she was in Moscow, and find his way to her from Mumbai. Finally, laughing, she told him, "Enough, I know you will." She took him in her arms and pillowed his head on the swell of her soft breast.

Attivio and Soonam continued to spend their free time in the bliss of sexual magic, joining body, mind and spirit with the One Infinite Creator. Spirals of light arched and vaulted through them, and high above them up into the sky over Venus. In the nexus of each moment they sought the Creator, knowing that their seeking alone would dispel all illusion. After, they lay on their backs on the soft ground, staring up at the pink sky above them. Loathe to move after such a glorious union, they lay still and searched the sky for a glimpse of planet Earth. It was reluctantly that they rose and made their way to the temple when the gong sounded, calling them all back for the afternoon session.

Master Saint Germain, Chohan of the Violet Ray of Transmutation and Alchemy was already there, gleaming like a violet beacon. Beside him, stood his twin flame, Lady Portia, Goddess of Justice. Soonam and Attivio were the last to arrive. As she took her seat, Soonam could not take her eyes off the pair. Saint Germain's red hair was neatly combed straight back off his forehead. A pair of pale-violet eyes, a softer shade than her own, sat like two jewels below his arched eyebrows. His red beard, too, was neatly trimmed and combed around his lovely bow shaped lips. A long violet cape with a high collar fell from broad shoulders all the way down to sweep the ground. The whole impression was one of elegance and quiet composure.

"Beloved children of my heart, I clothe you in a cosmic mantle of violet fire. May it dissolve anything in your being but perfect harmony." With these words Saint Germain lifted his hands, and turning his palms toward them, released thousands of crushed violets, spun into streams of airy violet light. Soonam felt the effect immediately as bliss swept through her. Each of them delighted in this gift from the great alchemist. Ederah remembered that Saint Germain had been embodied on Earth in the fifth century as the magician, Merlin, in King Arthur's court. How different would Earth be now, in the twenty-first century, from how it was in the fifth century? Were humans still basically the same? Did they still believe in alchemists?

"The bliss that you are feeling now, at this moment," Saint Germain continued, "as I bathe you in violet light, is the true state of the unlimited aspect of yourselves. It is also the true state of the unlimited aspect of all the humans you are going to help. Their true form, like yours, is light and love. Unfortunately, they have been programmed by the dark side for centuries to forget this. The dark side has relentlessly implanted erroneous ideas in humans in order to create fear in them, so that they may be more easily controlled. Humans have been told they are sinners, and as such, that they are worthless. This is untrue. They are divine beings, who have only lost touch with the divinity that resides within them. Humans have had enough of this suffering and illusion. They are ready for your message. You will arrive on Earth like a band of alchemists to help them transmute their despair into knowledge of their true divinity. You will help them to open their eyes to the unlimited aspect of themselves and to the mystery-clad unity of creation."

Saint Germain turned to Lady Portia and bowed to her. She returned his bow, and stepped forward to address them. As she lifted her eyes, Soonam saw that they, too, like Saint Germain's, were a shade of violet a little lighter than her own. Portia's red hair rippled in waves and curls down her back to touch her waist. A necklace of amethysts gleamed on her slender neck, reflecting the light that touched it. "The great illusion of life on Earth," she began, "in which you are about to participate, 'like players upon a stage,' as one of Earth's great writers has described it, is girded underneath by majesty, the majesty of the One Infinite Creator. The One is the vessel in which all consciousness resides. Longing to be known, feeling like a hidden treasure, God brought the cosmos into being, creating worlds, visible and invisible. You are about to enter one of those visible worlds. Earth. It is a world of duality, a world where opposites abound, and are played out. Seek to see behind the veil of this duality for the true unity. Seek the One in the nexus of each moment. Your seeking alone will be enough to carry you through, so that you may awaken on Earth to the fullness of your true being."

Toomeh's ears perked up. The idea that *seeking* alone could be enough to carry one through, was a new thought for him, and he tried to grasp it with the archipelago of his deeper mind. If this was true, there was nothing to fear, because he would seek the One with all the strength in his heart. He became so excited that the orange topaz on which he sat gave him a little shake, to remind him to center himself. Laaroos also felt him stirring and read his mind. What she perceived delighted her. As much as she longed to be in a snowed-in cabin, alone with him, she was also excited for this mission. All this, Toomeh understood.

Ederah, too, reacted to the idea that seeking alone, could carry them through. Somehow, she hadn't realized this before, or hadn't explicitly stated it to herself. Even if they just remembered to seek the One and didn't remember that they had come from a higher dimension themselves, they could succeed. And maybe the seeking would jog their memories of who they were. With this understanding, she felt new hope, which helped her to coax herself away from that field of sorrow at parting from Bereh.

"Beloved children of my heart, before I leave you, I would offer you some little further advice for your incarnation. Many catalysts will assault your senses in your human body. All will be sent by your Higher Self for the purpose of your awakening.

Make use of them. Even make use of your sorrow, for sorrow is the supreme tool for awakening in the third dimension. It opens the human heart. Humans suffer over catalysts more than they need to. Don't let yourself be destroyed by the idea of unfairness. Instead, use the pain and sorrow which hardship creates to awaken. Your awakening will usher in a Golden Age upon Earth. You have prepared well. Your task is set. Take the path and you will find me there with you. The time is now at hand."

Lady Portia and Saint Germain looked out over the group assembled before them. Their violet eyes seemed to take in each of them individually and to acknowledge the gift that each was offering to Earth. Together they bowed deeply to the wanderers in acknowledgement of their courage, and sent a message into every heart: *All is well.* As this message reached the group, Lady Portia and Saint Germain became two pillars of violet light, and rose upward, exiting right through the top of the dome as if it was no more than air.

All is well, Soonam thought as she walked out into the soft evening light of Venus for one of the last times. She looked up into the sky, and said to Attivio, "I will miss the beauty of these pink-gold skies."

Chapter 21

The Planetary Buddha

Bereh and Ederah were subdued the next morning as they walked to the temple for their last day of training. There was a tenderness in their silence, but no sorrow. On the brink of giving everything, they both understood that through generosity, all sorrow is transformed into joy.

Maepleida and Heipleido were in a different state of mind. As they walked toward the temple, Maepleida teased Heipleido.

"Now who's the one having doubts about entering the realm of cyclical rebirths."

"I'm not having doubts. Why do you say that?"

"I say it because of your expression," Maepleida said.

"What expression?"

"The one where your marble brow furrows, and your chin rests nearly on your throat."

"A passing thought only, my sweetest love. I fully expect to sail the ship of freedom, bound for the port of liberation, and, I expect to bring many humans along with me. You heard Lady Portia and Saint Germain, 'Seeking alone is enough to carry one through to a state of oneness with the Divine.'"

With those words, he caught her hand and swung it up to his lips. While Maepleida and Heipleido were strolling toward the temple, Attivio and Soonam still cuddled in bed, reluctant to rise.

"I am too attached to you," he whispered into her ear, like it was a secret, "and that must be given up with all else, but oh, how my heart revolts."

"Everything that comes together, must also part, even twin flames," she reminded him. "That's the law in the third dimension, where we are bound."

He pulled her close and held her in his arms. "But to be torn from what I hold most dear."

"Our love for one another must expand on Earth to include all beings. That is the sure way to find one another again," she said, tugging his ear lobe between her teeth and igniting a fire in him. Toomeh and Laaroos were already approaching the temple when Soonam and Attivio were having this exchange. As they walked up they saw the Buddha laughing with Lord Kumara in front of the archway.

"What a sight to begin our day," Laaroos said.

Toomeh nodded. They watched as the Buddha and Kumara, with the remains of laughter still visible on their faces, turned and entered the temple ahead of them. Toomeh felt a new kind of serenity in the temple as he and Laaroos took their seats beside Maepleida and Heipleido. All eyes were fixed on Earth's planetary Buddha in anticipation. Soonam and Attivio slipped in just at the last minute.

"Greetings, my fellow Buddhas. Yes, you are all Buddhas," he said with laughter and music in his voice. "For what is a Buddha but one who gives up his own happiness, his own narrow self-concern, in order to free others from suffering." Pausing to observe them, he smiled perceiving the purity in their hearts. "Seeing all living beings as dear, you do not cling to your own solitary state of peace while others suffer. Without seeking reward, you voluntarily go into the realm of cyclic births. You part from your loved ones, and even from your own higher dimensional self, to plunge down into the third dimension, all for the sake of others. Your generosity in taking this action will, at the moment of your descent, relieve you of all sorrow at these losses, for through giving, sorrow is dissolved." The Buddha's words felt like gently falling snow. And the more softly it fell, the more deeply it sank into their minds. Bereh hoped it was so, that generosity of action relieved one of all sorrow, for he feared the pain of separation from Ederah, and he was ashamed of this fear, which he could not even admit to her.

"Tomorrow, when you depart for Earth, all the masters who came to Venus to train you will be present to see you off. Each will offer you a gift for the journey. The masters will line the light staircase. With each step downward you will become less and less dense, until finally, you are spun into the airy thinness of light. Within moments of stepping off from the bottom stair, you will find yourself in the womb of your earth mother, in the body of a human infant. Arriving in this tiny vehicle will be a shock. You may remain in the infant's body or hover near the mother until the moment of birth. Once the infant is born, you must stay within its body. Gradually you will become accustomed to the heaviness of the electro-chemical human body." The Buddha fell silent and stood still. It was his being, more than his words, which affected them, shifting them into a state in harmony with his own. "You have all the teaching you need. The time for words is past. I leave you with my blessing." He placed his palms together and bowed to them. With this gesture, his serenity spread through the temple and into each heart. No one moved or spoke, such was their state of bliss. The Buddha walked quietly from the temple.

Lady Venus and Lord Kumara came forward. "We will spend the rest of the day in meditation together, to prepare for the journey," Lady Venus said. "During this meditation, I ask you to make contact with your Higher Self, that unlimited aspect of you, who knows you in your totality, who knows all that you are, all that you have been, and all that you will be, including all that will befall you on Earth. But do not ask to be shown that. Instead, seek only guidance from your Higher Self. Bringing in your Higher Selves will create tremendous power in the temple. Use this power well my beloveds."

Ederah shifted a little in her crystal seat before falling into a concentrated silence. Sitting on the lotus shaped chair of rose quartz, which she had used since the first day of training, she asked the crystal for help in making contact with her Higher Self. The rose quartz and Ederah communicated by opening their minds and hearts to one another. Their mutual trust enabled Ederah to call down the shard of light connecting her to her Higher Self. Bereh was seated next to Ederah on the same large amethyst that he had chosen on the first day. All through the weeks of training, he had been thanking the amethyst for the positive energy and clarity of mind that she provided him. Now he turned to her again, and asked her to help him let go of all attachments, and rest in the One. He knew that once he achieved this state, he could invite his Higher Self into his field.

Maepleida's blue sapphire chair let her know immediately that she wanted to offer her gifts to help with this meditation. Chief among sapphire's gifts is the ability to open communication with higher beings. Since sapphire is also the crystal which aids one in aligning with the will of the Divine, Maepleida was happy to accept the offer. As soon as she accepted sapphire's offer, she felt both her throat chakra and her third eye expand to open her inner vision, readying her for contact with her Higher Self. Beside her, Heipleido sat on his amethyst and asked her for help contacting his Higher Self. A powerhouse of energy, amethyst was more than ready to assist him. As soon as the alliance was made, Heipleido felt his crown chakra spinning open. He inhaled and called down the shard of light which connected him to his Higher Self.

Toomeh had partnered with orange topaz all during the training. In the early days, before his twin flame reunion with Laaroos, he had sought companionship and comfort in the orange crystal, which she had generously provided. Topaz had also enhanced his courage and faith in the success of the mission to Earth. Now, before asking her for further service, he offered her his gratitude. A joyful, hopeful being, orange topaz readily united forces with Toomeh to open the pathway for the descent of his Higher Self. Beside orange topaz was the lovely orange diamond who Laaroos had chosen to help her make an incorruptible commitment to the mission. Orange diamond had from the first surprised Laaroos with the additional gifts of humor and joy. Now Laaroos asked her for help in connecting with her Higher Self.

Each day of the training Soonam had felt her rose quartz nurturing her and filling her with love. Their friendship had grown throughout the weeks until they looked forward to meeting each day. "I will miss you my sweet rose," Soonam whispered to the crystal. Together they entered a state of unconditional love for all beings, in which they were able to call down the shard of light connecting Soonam to her Higher Self. Beside them were Attivio and pink tourmaline. Known as the muse's stone, pink tourmaline inspires beauty and calm. But it also offers visions. Attivio assumed it was pink tourmaline who was the one responsible for showing him the scenes of life on Earth which had occasionally distracted him from their teachers. He smiled remembering her antics. Now he asked his muse for help in contacting his Higher Self. And this, she graciously provided, first by putting him into a state of complete calm, and then by adding her love to his in order to pull down the shard of light necessary for the contact.

Before entering their own meditative states, Lady Venus and Lord Kumara looked out over the beings seated in the temple. It was a sight most beautiful to behold. Every crystal seat was shimmering, and each being seated on a crystal was lit with an inner light, and from high in the sky over Venus poured down shards of white-golden light, one shaft entering each being seated below. Inside some of the shafts could already be seen, descending, a most glorious form of pure, transparent light in the identical shape of the one seated below it. Soonam's Higher Self was one of the first to descend and merge with her fifth dimensional aspect. Soonam felt the contact much as one might feel the warmth of the sun as one emerged from a chilly room.

Merging with the light energy of her Higher Self was a powering-up to a higher frequency of love. As Soonam basked in this love and peace, she felt as if she was being cradled and rocked in the arms of the Divine.

The experience for all the beings meditating in the temple was similar to Soonam's. Had any of them looked skyward, they would have seen many lovely, winged creatures peering in through the glass dome, having been drawn to the place by the purity of the energy and the beauty of the sight. And so, their last day of preparation ended in bliss.

Chapter 22

Into the Third Dimension

The next morning, the ordinarily pink Venusian sky was streaked with blue. As they walked toward the temple, Heipleido wondered if this was due to the space-time tunnel being opened for their transit to Earth. Both he and Maepleida wore deep, royal-blue robes with a dark-blue insignia, identifying them as natives of the Pleiades. The royal-blue, against their onyx skin, and their long flowing garments, which further accentuated their twelve-foot height, made them look like a king and queen. Seeing them, with their robes trailing the ground behind them as they walked, it was hard to imagine that this regal couple would soon be newborn human infants. Toomeh and Laaroos were already standing in front of the temple when Maepleida and Heipleido arrived. Their long, full, orange-gold robes identified them as Arcturian. The two couples bowed formally to one another as was the custom when beings were dressed in the garb of their home planet or star. The bows were meant, not only to acknowledge the Divine resting in each being, but also the Divine nature of each home planet and or star. Ederah and Bereh joined them next. Everyone again bowed deeply. As natives of Venus, they were dressed in robes of pale pink. All six of them turned in his direction when they heard Attivio's greeting. Both he and Soonam wore the soft, luxurious, deep-violet robes of the Violet planet. Attivio held onto Soonam's hand and only dropped it to bow to each of his fellow wanderers.

The many beings, who had come from all over the galaxy to train for this mission, gathered before the temple. All wore a bipedal body in preparation for this mission, though in reality, their native shapes differed in the numbers of legs and types of sense organs. They stood before the temple in robes of many different colors, each color signifying the home planet or star of the being wearing it. In robes of white, Lady Venus and Lord Kumara moved through the gathering toward the temple archway. When they reached it, they turned and Lady Venus spoke to them.

"Greetings my beloveds. I will not add, for the final time, because we will meet again in triumph at the hour of your victory. You have prepared well. Today you will not enter the temple, but instead will descend the golden stairs for your birth on Earth. You have all been born many times, in many different types of bodies, on numerous planets and stars. For most of you, this will be your first birth on Earth, and your first time voluntarily taking a lower form of consciousness. You will walk down each step and at the last step you will be swept into the space-time tunnel to Earth. You will emerge from the tunnel in the body of an infant. Take courage fair ones. Be at peace. All is well."

Toomeh whispered to Laaroos, "I don't see any golden stairs." But before she could answer him, Lord Kumara began directing them to the far side of the temple. Maepleida looked at her companions. "Are we ready to move forward?"

"Let's first join hands and offer our gratitude for this opportunity to serve," Soonam suggested.

Maepleida took Soonam's hand, and Ederah, Maepleida's, and Laaroos, Toomeh's and on, until they made a small circle of colored light, for their transformation into vehicles made entirely of light had begun. Soonam offered a prayer of gratitude, to which they all added their intentions.

We are grateful for this opportunity to serve, — Soonam
Let us be instruments of love for all beings, — Attivio
And let us bring joy into each life we touch, — Ederah
So that awakening may spread throughout the Earth, — Bereh
Lifting all beings to victory in the Light, — Laaroos

May we light the darkness for all in need, — Toomeh
May we all reunite in the third dimension, — Maepleida
And create a golden age on Earth, — Heipleido

When everyone had spoken, they stood together, with their heads bowed in silence. Heipleido was the first to speak. "So, we're off then. Courage my friends, until we meet again in victory."

Maepleida smiled at him, took his hand in hers, and they moved toward the line of pairs heading toward the golden stairs. The others followed close behind. The waiting wasn't long, and soon it was Maepleida and Heipleido's turn. Venus and Kumara bowed to them and motioned them forward. Maepleida glanced back over her shoulder at their friends before stepping forward onto the top step. A most beautiful golden light rose from the steps and Maepleida and Heipleido saw all the ascended masters responsible for Earth standing on the steps, like a parade of gods, radiating love and light. Still holding hands, Maepleida and Heipleido stepped forward to be greeted by Amerissis and El Morya, who stood side by side on the top step. "We shall follow you each step of the way, my beloveds, until the final day of your victory," El Morya told them. At the sight of him, Maepleida felt her throat chakra expand, and she silently expressed her gratitude to him for the help he had given her. He nodded slightly in recognition of her thought before turning to Amerissis, who said, "We give you the gift of the First Ray, the Blue Flame of the Will of God. Carry it with you in your hearts."

Maepleida's courage soared at these words, and holding tight to Heipleido's hand, she confidently stepped down to the next level where Lord Lanto, Shoshimi, and the black jaguar awaited them.

Soonam and Attivio followed Maepleida and Heipleido, and watched as their images became more and more light filled as they descended each step. Soonam and Attivio, too, received the gift of the Blue Flame from Amerissis and El Morya, and after leaving them were greeted on the second level down by Shoshimi and Lord Lanto, who said to them, "Go with the momentum of our love, wear it as a protection." As they spoke, they cast the golden yellow of the Illumination Flame over Soonam and Attivio, making them even more transparent. "Take with you the gift of the Second Ray, the Yellow Flame of Illumination, the flame of gaining wisdom through love. May the Illumination Flame expand God's Mind through all your thoughts." The two masters bowed deeply to the wanderers in acknowledgement of their service to humankind.

Ederah and Bereh followed Soonam and Attivio to Amerissis and El Morya and then to Lord Lanto and Shoshimi, then onto Paul the Venetian and Lady Ruth, who stood on the third level down, resplendent, holding the pink Flame of Cosmic Love. The great masters of the pink ray bowed to Ederah and Bereh, then placed their hands on the heads of both and blessed them. From the hands of the two masters poured the flame of love as Amerissis spoke. "We give you the gift of the Third Ray, the Pink Flame of Cosmic Love. May it flow through every cell of your new human body, so you may be a living stream of love. Offer this flame of unconditional love, brotherhood and compassion to all beings. Go my beloveds, and be love in action."

Toomeh and Laaroos were the last of the friends to step on the golden stairs. They followed Bereh and Ederah down each of the steps, stopping to receive gifts and blessings on each step, down to the fourth level, where they were greeted by Lord Serapis Bey and Amutreya. The pair were dressed in gold and white, and beamed the clear light of the Fourth Ray, the Ascension Flame into them, to remind them that they, and all the masters, stood ready to assist them at their first call. Raising a snow-white quartz over their heads, Serapis said, "We give you the gift of the Ascension Flame of Purification."

"May you awaken," Amutreya said, "and walk on Earth as a Master, in service to all beings."

Each twin flame pair continued down the golden stairs to be blessed also by Master Hilarion, guardian of the Fifth Ray, the Green Flame of Healing, then, by Lord Sananda and Lady Nada, guardians of the Sixth Ray, the Flame of Resurrection. On the last step stood Portia and Saint Germain, guardians of the Seventh Ray, the Violet Fire of Transmutation. At this stepping off place, these two great masters clothed each wanderer in the cosmic mantle of the Violet Fire, and released them into the light tunnel bound for Earth and the third dimension.

Attivio and Soonam were with Lord Sananda and Lady Nada as they watched Maepleida and Heipleido leave the last step and disappear from view. When Soonam gasped at their disappearance, Lady Nada reached for her hand, and told her to hold her focus on her *I Am Presence* as she traveled to her incarnation in the third dimension. Lord Sananda reminded Attivio that the mantra, *I am the resurrection and the life,* would always be there, simply for the asking. Then these four great souls bowed to one another, and Soonam and Attivio moved forward. Saint Germain and Portia greeted them on the final step. Portia told them that she rejoiced that they were part of this army of light, which would usher in the Seventh Golden Age on Earth. Saint Germain then infused them with the sacred Violet Fire. Filled with light, and feeling that their victory would be certain, they stepped off the last stair into the unknown. As they disappeared Saint Germain whispered, "My legions of Violet Flame angels go with you." Soonam and Attivio clasped hands they as they were pulled forward into the space-time tunnel, to be followed close behind by Ederah and Bereh, and then Toomeh and Laaroos.

Maepleida and Heipleido, who had been the first of their group to enter the tunnel of light, were holding fast to one another when they felt something pulling them in different directions. They locked eyes for a moment before they let go and disappeared from one another's view. Each twin flame pair experienced a similar pull as they were separated from one another to journey onward alone into the third dimension. Soonam and Attivio kept in mental touch as long as they could after they were pulled apart. Soonam's last message to Attivio was that even though she could feel her mind being wiped, she still knew her love for him. As the wrench came, Bereh told Ederah, "I will find you again." And Toomeh felt such sweet love for Laaroos that at the moment of parting he called out, "I am dying of tenderness."

Part Four

Birth on Earth

Chapter 23

Toomeh Becomes Ewen

Aiden walked into the kitchen and found Caitlin kneading a lump of dough.

"What are you doing, Cat. It's the middle of the night?"

"I'm making soda bread."

"I can see that, but why now?"

"I can't sleep – my stomach hurts. I must have indigestion. The pain comes and goes, so I'm distracting myself."

Aiden's eyes widened. "Cat, I don't think you have indigestion. I think you're in labor."

Aidan had often wondered these past few weeks if Cat was afraid of the birth, afraid of how the baby would safely get out of her body without being crushed or ripping her apart. Now the moment had come and she seemed to be in a kind of denial.

She looked at him in shock. "Labor? How could I not have thought of that?"

Aiden took her in his arms and reminded her that they had made a plan with her midwife to call when the contractions began and to time them. When they were ten minutes apart, it would be time to head to the hospital.

"Yes," Caitlin said, "but let me get this bread ready for the oven first, and you can time the pains so we have something to tell her."

Aiden put the kettle on, and went to pee. When he returned from the bathroom, Cat was doubled over in pain. He placed his hands on the small of her back and massaged her, then glanced at his watch to check the time. Once the pain had passed, he wrote down the time on the pad on the kitchen table. Caitlin put the bread in the oven and set the timer on the stove.

"How about a cup of tea?" Aiden asked.

"Yes, lovely." Caitlin sank into a chair at the table while Aiden made the tea.

As she drank her tea, Aiden took her left foot in both his strong hands and massaged it, upward toward her heart, as the midwife had shown him. Next, he lifted her right foot and did the same.

Their plan was for the baby to be born at Saint James Hospital, in the birthing center, with the help of Cat's midwife, Breanna. Dr. Donahue would only be called if she was needed. Another pain gripped Cat, and Aiden noted down the time. "Eleven minutes since the last one," he told her.

"That's about how it's been for the last hour," she said when the pain released her. He brought a warm wash cloth and wiped the beads of perspiration from her forehead. She looked up at him with that smile which she reserved only for him.

"I'm going to call Breanna, to alert her, and check if we should head over to the birthing center," Aiden said.

Cat nodded.

She looks so innocent and pure, he thought, and thought that her name which means *pure*, had never suited her more. "Do you want me to call your parents, too?" he asked.

"No, not yet, they'll be asleep."

Breanna told Aiden not to rush, but to head over to Saint James and she'd meet them.

The timer went off and Aiden took the steaming bread from the oven and set it on the window sill to cool. He glanced back at Caitlin and saw that she'd fallen asleep sitting up in her chair. He felt a rush of love for her. Caitlin startled and opened her eyes. Aiden noticed a faraway look in her eyes.

"I just had the strangest most beautiful dream," she said. But before she could tell him, another contraction shot through her body making it impossible to talk. Once it passed, she was anxious to share her dream, and it spilled out even before he could wipe the sweat from her face.

It was as if I was watching a movie, and in the movie, there was the most beautiful golden staircase, and on each step stood magnificent beings, full of light of different colors, and walking down the steps were couples, in robes of violet and blue and pink and orange. One being, looking like a young god, wearing a luxurious, long, flowing orange robe seemed to see me watching, and he smiled at me with such love and trust, I felt my heart would burst. He was with a woman, who also wore a long, sweeping, golden-orange robe. I couldn't take my eyes off them. But then they stepped off into a tunnel of light and I couldn't see either of them anymore.

Aiden listened spellbound. Was this a labor hallucination, or had Cat seen into the world behind the veil? Aiden himself had a vivid imagination, and like many Irishman, a strong belief in the invisible and magical realms. "Wow," was all he could say at first. Then, "Do you think you saw our son on his way to us from another dimension?"

"Yes, that's exactly what I think." Caitlin beamed. "Aiden, it was beyond any words I could find to describe it. I never want to forget it. And I will tell him every detail of what I saw when he's old enough to understand. I have to write it down now, so I won't forget any of it."

As she reached for the pad and pen another contraction took hold of her, and she breathed with it, knowing now that each contraction was bringing this beautiful being closer to this realm.

In fact, Toomeh had already arrived, and was in the kitchen with them, hovering near Caitlin's body. He knew he'd have to re-enter the fetus, from which he'd just released himself, at the moment the baby was born, but until then he was choosing to have a look around his new world. Soon all memories of his past, and who he was, would fade completely, but for now he could still hold onto shreds, and when he remembered walking down the golden staircase with Laaroos, he intentionally transmitted the vision to Caitlin, hoping she could see it.

While Caitlin wrote out her "dream," Aiden made more tea,

and cut them each a thick slice of warm bread and buttered it. He didn't want to rush her or alarm her, but he wanted to get moving to the birth center. Cat's story had ignited a fire in him. Aiden means fiery-one, he recalled. When they finished their bread and tea, he gently suggested they head to Saint James. They dressed and he called for a car. Aiden helped her down the stairs, and past their bicycles while carrying her bag, which had been ready by the door for the past week.

Breanna was waiting for them when they got upstairs to the birthing center at Saint James. After she examined Caitlin, she told them that Cat was only seven centimeters dilated, and suggested that they walk about, so gravity could help to move things along. Still in light form, Toomeh hovered over Caitlin's shoulder observing the hospital and the birthing center, and trying to remember where he had seen a hospital before. But his memory was becoming more and more dim. An hour later Caitlin was ten centimeters dilated and they decided to let their parents know that they were at Saint James. Cat's parents lived in Dublin, and Aiden's parents were stationed in Spain with the diplomatic corps. But Aiden's brothers were all local. Caitlin's two sisters were married and living in England. Aiden called them all.

Cat folded over with another contraction and he massaged her lower back. The contractions were coming faster now and she had less time to recover between them, but she was radiant and excited and anxious to meet this being who was coming to them. More walking, more measuring, more contractions, until exhausted, Cat said, "I have to lie down a minute."

Breanna took a look and said, "I see the baby's head! Reach down Caitlin and you can feel the crown." Instead, Cat bent her knees up, grabbed her thighs and pushed.

"OK then," Breanna said, "his head is almost out. Gentle pants now. Good. Pant gently, OK now, a big push." With that last push, the baby shot out into Breanna's waiting hands. "It's a boy!" she said, as she deftly wrapped him in a soft blanket and laid him on Cat's chest. She and Aiden stared in awe as he uncurled his tiny fingers and looked up into their eyes.

"Who are you and where have you come from?" Cat whispered to him. "I want to call him Ewen," she said. "Because Ewen means gift of God."

"Yes, perfect," was all Aiden could manage. With those words, Toomeh became Ewen, a gift from God. And the eternal being that was Toomeh fell into a kind of sleep, where he would remain until he managed to awaken in the third dimension.

Chapter 24

Laaroos Becomes Yosiko

The slender acupuncture needles which had been inserted during labor, to lower her blood pressure, were still in place when Ms. Kusuyama took the baby from Umeko's arms to wash and dress her. Umeko lay back on the tatami floor where she had given birth and breathed in the sweet scent of the mat. Kosuke was asleep nearby, on the futon which the Matsugaoku Birth Center had provided for him. It had been a long labor, despite all the walking – three to five hours a day – which Umeko had done in the weeks leading up to the birth. Her midwife had explained that walking and concentrating on the vibration in her heels while she walked would help her labor. Even so, her blood pressure had spiked and frightened them. Kosuke had remained with her throughout, massaging her belly and feet. After the birth he'd passed out, such had been the strain he felt during these past twenty hours.

Umeko closed her eyes and ran her mind over her body. It felt like a seed pod that had burst open giving forth its precious contents, and now lay split apart, spent, but proud to have fulfilled its purpose. Try as she had to concentrate on her breathing and pushing, there were times during labor that she had been gripped by powerful hallucinations, so strong that she felt she was not here, lying on this tatami mat at all, but far off in another world made of light. She tried to recall the world she had seen?

The sky was a translucent pink streaked with gold. A young couple stood facing one another. When their lips met, a fountain of light shot up from their heads, high into the sky above them. A kind of fireworks made of light and stars filled the sky and cascaded down around them in droplets of pink and gold and violet and blue and orange light. At

one moment, *the young woman turned and saw Umeko watching.*
She smiled the most beatific smile, as if she wanted Umeko to see this
particular scene. Was this the place my child had been before she came
to Earth Umeko wondered? Was this joyful being my daughter?

Umeko was right. It was the place her daughter had been
before incarnating. Laaroos' last thoughts, before the veil of
forgetting descended and she entered the body of the infant, had
been of her twin flame reunion with Toomeh on Venus. She had
relived the joy of connecting with him as she was being born on
Earth. So powerful was the memory, that Umeko had picked it
up. As she went over the vision again, to bask in the beauty of it,
Umeko stole another look at the sleeping Kosuke. Attending the
birth wasn't something she'd ever expected of him. He seemed
too elegant to get down into the primal, bloody, painful business
of giving birth. And yet, unasked, he'd simply assumed he would
be there to support her. She wanted to share her vision with him,
to see what he would say, but she let him rest.

The midwife came back to help her up to bathe, and to move
her onto a futon before she brought her daughter back to her.
When Umeko was bathed and resettled, the midwife placed the
baby in her arms, and Umeko offered her breast, which the infant
took easily with her rosebud lips. Had she ever known such joy?
They hadn't chosen a name, but at that moment she decided to
ask Kosuke if he liked the name, Yosiko, which means child of
joy. She gazed down into her baby's little face and asked her:
Where have you come from little one, from a very far off place made of
light? And have you left your true love there under the pink-gold sky?

Umeko would have been very surprised to know that the
baby in her arms was reading her mind and wishing she could
answer her questions. If she could have spoken, Laaroos would
have told her new mother, that, *Yes, I have come from a far-off*
place, the fifth dimension, and I was thinking of my true love, my twin
flame, Toomeh, as I was being born, and that's why you saw that scene.
But, already, I am forgetting where I came from. All knowledge of my

past is slipping away behind a veil, and I am struggling to hold onto it.

Kosuke stirred and opened his eyes to see his wife and child in sweet, peaceful communication. He picked up his kimono and slipping it on, reached into the pocket, and pulled out a small carefully wrapped package. Umeko smiled up at him as he sat down on the edge of her futon.

"I have something for you my darling, to mark this occasion of the birth of our daughter." He took the baby from her arms with surprising deftness, and handed her the meticulously wrapped box. Umeko undid the wrapping, and gasped when she saw the ring inside with its large, oval, orange stone.

"The jeweler said this stone was the closest he could get to the color of Arcturus. It's an orange diamond. I hope you will wear it with pleasure."

"Oh, Kosuke, this is the most glorious diamond I've ever seen. It reminds me of your name, rising sun. And all these months you remembered my interest in Arcturus." She bowed her head slightly to him before leaning forward to kiss him over their infant daughter. Lifting the orange diamond from the box she placed it on her finger. Umeko lifted her hand and showed her ring to the baby, who seemed to startle at the sight of it.

"I think she likes diamonds," Kosuke said smiling. "Rare, orange diamonds."

Laaroos listening to their words had perked up at the sound of the word, Arcturus, and when her new mother held up her hand and showed her the orange diamond, she stared at it intently, struggling to remember why it seemed so familiar to her.

"I've thought of a name for her," Umeko said. "What do you think of Yosiko?"

"*Child of joy*, yes. It's perfect for her," Kosuke agreed.

Chapter 25

Ederah Becomes Natasha

"Take us to the Perinatal Medical Center," Igor all but shouted through the car window at his sleepy driver. Before they could get in the car, another contraction sized Masha. The contractions were too close together now. Igor helped Masha into the back seat and slid in beside her, then dug his phone out of his coat pocket and rang Dr. Vladimirovna. Masha moaned.

"Breathe, Masha," he said, "and it will hurt less. Can't you go any faster?" he barked at Serge, who wisely said nothing. Serge had been his driver for ten years, and knew his employer well enough to know when to joke with him, when to listen, when was the best time to ask for a favor, and when to keep silent.

Masha was quiet. Igor wanted to ask her why she had waited so long to wake him, but he knew it was because she wanted to hold off until morning, rather than disturb everyone's sleep.

"I should have awakened you sooner, I'm sorry, Igor," she whispered. "Now I've caused more stress." This was her third child and she thought she could predict how things would go, but then, suddenly, the contractions were too close together.

"Don't fret, Masha. Let's just get there before this baby makes an entrance. It's not that far."

"Ahhh," Masha screamed, "the baby's coming now."

"Hold on, we're nearly there." The usually unflustered Igor began to sweat, beads of perspiration forming on his forehead.

"I can't!" Masha yelled.

"Pull over, Serge!" Igor barked. Serge swerved over to the side of the road, turned off the Volga and jumped out. He ran around the car and flung open the back door. Raised on a farm, he'd attended the birth of many farm animals, and luckily, wasn't squeamish. Igor got out of the car and looked at Serge. Masha was now lying on the back seat panting.

"Can I take a look?" Serge asked, uncomfortable with the etiquette of it.

"Please!" Igor spoke for them both.

Masha opened her coat and lifted her nightgown and the two men could see the crown of the baby's head between her legs.

"We need something clean and warm to wrap it in," Serge said.

Igor opened the small suitcase and pulled out several receiving blankets.

"I need to push now," Masha screamed.

Serge leaned down and said, "OK, but not too hard at first. Let your body guide you. It knows what to do."

"Good, good," Serge told her, "you're doing great. One big push now and the head will be out."

Masha screamed and gave a big push and out came the baby's head.

"Another push to free the baby's shoulders, and your baby will be born," Serge said, as he placed one cupped hand on the baby's head and the other under its neck. Masha exhaled and groaned as she gave a final push and the baby was out. Serge quickly wrapped up the baby to protect it from the cold, and set it on Masha's chest.

"Thank you, Serge, thank you so much," Masha gasped.

"Masha, are you alright?" Igor said.

"Yes, yes, but is it a girl or a boy? she asked. "I feel certain it's a girl."

Neither Igor nor Serge had looked, so absorbed were they in protecting the tiny being from the cold night air. Masha peaked into the blanket at the tiny creature. "It's a girl."

"We best get to the clinic now," Serge said. "The afterbirth must come out soon."

Igor seemed too shocked to move.

"Get in, and I'll drive you to the clinic."

Masha sat up enough to make room for Igor next to her, and Serge jumped back into the driver's seat and took them to the emergency entrance of the Perinatal Center. Somehow a stretcher appeared immediately, and Masha was placed on it, while a nurse took the baby. Igor stood there, still in shock, until Serge cleared his throat, as if to ask for instructions. Igor turned at the sound and remembered himself. "Serge, thank you for this. We are in your debt."

Serge nodded in acknowledgement and asked Igor if he'd like him to wait.

"No, no, you go. I'll stay with them and call when I'm ready to be picked up."

Igor walked into the center and asked where Masha and the baby were, and was told he'd have to wait to see them. He went to the cafeteria. What he wanted was a stiff drink, but that would have to wait. He ordered a double espresso and drank it in two sips. When he was allowed upstairs, Dr. Vladimirovna told him Masha and the baby were both fine and would be released the following day. The nurse took him to Masha's room, where he found her asleep, with the baby next to her bed in a bassinette. He crept in, closed the door behind him, and stared down into the bassinette at his baby daughter, who, to his surprise, opened her eyes and looked up at him. He picked her up and held her. She was swaddled in a pink blanket and looked all rosy-pink herself. He sat down in the armchair and gazed at her face. Overcome with emotion between the event of her birth and with just looking at her, tears flowed from his eyes and ran down his cheeks. "You certainly made a spectacular entrance little one," he whispered. He tried to recall holding Clara and Alexei as newborns, to see if the powerful feeling of love he felt looking at this baby was the same he'd felt holding them as newborns. It must have been, he told himself, tears still flowing from his eyes. Looking at her tiny face and into her deep grey-gold eyes, he felt the breadth of the whole universe, and it shook him in a way he hadn't experienced before, as if a doorway to the unknown had opened, beckoning him into the heart of love.

Masha opened her eyes and saw him weeping. She was quiet so as not to interrupt him. He seemed to be off in some reverie with the baby, and it was some time before he noticed that she was awake. When he finally looked up and saw her, he couldn't speak at first, and Masha wondered at the faraway look in his eyes. Finally, he said, "I'd like to call her Natasha."

"Yes, I like it, but is there any special reason for this name?"

"Looking at her, that's the name that came to me, and I think she wants us to call her that."

Masha smiled at him. "This doesn't sound like you talking, Igor. Did the trauma of the birth somehow change you into someone else?"

He knew she was teasing him. "Maybe, or maybe it's just her. Holding her, I've been fantasizing, and I even felt she was somehow directing my fantasy or at least sharing it."

"What were you seeing in this fantasy?" Masha asked, becoming very interested.

It was another world, like no place in Russia or even on Earth, some other planet maybe, where the sky was pink, not blue. A tall, young woman, maybe eleven feet high, slender and regal, like a princess or a goddess, with grey-gold eyes, was walking toward a large dome, made of what looked like pearl. The pearly surface reflected many colors of light. The whole atmosphere was full of such light as I had never seen before. And, Masha, many different types of beings were walking toward the arched entrance of this dome. Some were short and some tall, some seemed to reflect white light, some reflected other colors. They didn't all walk on two legs or even have eyes and ears and mouths as we do, but somehow, they still perceived their surroundings. None of the other beings, even the man by her side, seemed aware that I was watching them, only she alone paused, and turned and smiled at me before she walked under the archway into the temple. Her smile made me weep. Then I looked down and the baby opened her eyes, and they

*were the same grey-gold as those of the woman I'd seen in my fantasy.
Do you think I imagined all this?*

"No, Igor. I don't think you imagined it."

"Why is that, Masha? Because it is strange."

"Yes, for sure it is. But many times during my pregnancy,
I saw this land of the pink sky and I saw her moving over the
landscape. I didn't know if it was the pregnancy hormones or
the sausage I'd eaten. I confess, I wanted it to be real. I wanted
to believe she was somehow a special being coming to Earth, for
some purpose beyond herself, and that I was the vessel provided
for her."

Ever since that day back on Venus, when she had first opened
the envelope delivered to her lap by the sea-green bird, and
viewed the hologram of her future parent's ice skating in
Moscow, Ederah had frequently thought of them. Lord Kumara
told them that if they concentrated on their earthly parents, that
their parents might become aware of them, and even see them
in a dream. Ederah now knew this had happened, and she was
glad of it, because very quickly she was losing all her memories
of who she was and where she had come from. Soon they would
fade completely. She knew only that she had come for some
purpose, and she must try to remember what that was. She no
longer even knew her own name. From now on, in this lifetime,
she would be called Natasha.

Chapter 26

Heipleido Becomes Horus

The reason Amisi chose to give birth at Gohar Hospital is that it sits on the banks of the Nile. It even has balcony rooms where you can look down and see lotus flowers growing along the riverbank, reaching their faces up out of the mud toward the sun. Amisi liked to think of lotus flowers as stars which had fallen down from the sky, dropped into the river, and were striving to lift themselves heavenward again.

Sitting in bed, wearing a pale-blue, silk kimono, adorned with a pattern of lavender lotus flowers, Amisi held her newborn son. The robe had been a gift from Adjo when she told him she was pregnant. The baby's tiny face nestled against the soft silk, his little nose buried in a lotus blossom. Amisi looked up from his face, and turned her head to watch Adjo, who was out on the balcony, talking with his parents. She wanted to be out there, too, watching the Nile flow by, but she was on bed rest for another day.

It had been a difficult birth, as the baby had been born feet first. Dr. Ashmawy wanted to do a caesarean section, but Amisi had insisted on a vaginal birth. So her midwife had taken charge and employed an old-fashioned technique, which used gravity. By having Amisi sit up on the very edge of the bed, she pulled first one of the baby's feet, then the other, free from Amisi's body, and then let the baby hang, with the lower half of his body wrapped in a towel, for warmth, while his head and shoulders were still inside Amisi. This method used the weight of the baby's legs to help him drop out. There had been some tense moments, but in the end, Horus had come successfully into the world, feet first.

From just above his new mother's head, Heipleido had

watched this process, waiting for the right moment to enter the baby's body. In the fifth dimension, Heipleido was capable of great physical agility and strength. He wondered if he should enter the womb and turn the baby's body around. But he was unsure if once in the womb, inside the baby, he would remember that he had the gift of agility. So much had faded in the light tunnel, and he was forgetting more every second. He still recalled that he'd come on a mission, and that he was to enter this new body to serve, but he no longer remembered the details of even his own origin. So he waited and watched Amisi, and only entered the body of the baby when it was suspended half out of her. Then he instructed his infant body to drop out of his mother, and the tiny body had responded perfectly.

"It's lucky Dr. Ashmawy is a woman," Amisi's mother told her, "or you'd be recovering from surgery right now. You've always had your own ideas, but this time, I think you were right," she said, moving the glass bowl containing a single lavender-blue lotus just slightly on Amisi's bedside table to center it. Amisi smiled at her mother and said nothing, but she knew she'd been right to let her son choose the moment of his birth. With surgery, the baby doesn't choose when to be born, but is taken from his cozy shelter when the doctor is ready. Despite the pain, Amisi had insisted on letting Horus be in charge of the moment he would enter the world. Even Adjo had tried to convince her to have the surgery. But her strength had come from Horus himself, who she felt was communicating his need to her. She'd known practically from conception that the baby was a boy.

Amisi turned again toward the balcony to watch Adjo and his parents. She knew Adjo was discussing arrangements for the seventh day after Horus's birth. Amisi had insisted there was to be no slaughter of a sheep or goat. She and Adjo were vegetarian. But his parents felt the sacrifice was important, even though they were Moslem in name only. She and Adjo had agreed, however, to shave the baby's head, anoint it with saffron, and give the weight of the hair in silver coins to the poor. And, Horus would be circumcised. Amisi had continued to study Islam and Sufism throughout her pregnancy, and although she didn't pray five times a day, she had come to believe deeply in the power of prayer. In her own mind, she wasn't specific about who she prayed to, sometimes praying to the stars or planets or to the lotus blossoms, seeing the Divine in everything. She wondered now, looking down at Horus, asleep in her arms, if it had been he who had gotten her interested in prayer and devotion to the Divine. Her interest in prayer had certainly only awakened once she'd become pregnant.

"Shall I take him so you can try to sleep?" her mother asked.

"No, I'll rest after Adjo's parents leave. When is father coming to meet Horus?"

"He should return from Banha late tonight, so tomorrow," her mother said.

Adjo opened the balcony door and came into the room. "Alright, there'll be no animal sacrifice," he told them.

"Thank you darling," Amisi said. "One can honor the Divine and give thanks without harming an animal. They are an expression of God, too."

Adjo's parents came in also, and took one last long look at their grandson before saying goodbye.

"He's so full of light," Adjo's mother said. "It's hard to take one's eyes from his face." She leaned down and kissed the top of the baby's head.

When they'd gone, Amisi said she'd like to sit out on the balcony, on a chaise, and watch the Nile for a bit. Though it was against doctor's orders, she handed Horus to her mother and Adjo helped her out to the balcony and sat beside her.

"My mother's right about one thing," Adjo said, "Horus is very full of light. I wonder, do all babies hold so much light?"

"I expect they do," Amisi said, "how else can they inspire so much hope and love?" She gazed down at the Nile flowing along beneath them, and at the banks covered in lotus blossoms, and felt a peace she'd never known before. Adjo noticed her expression and asked her what she was feeling.

"I have loved my life and my family and you and my work with flowers, and graceful, silky Nefretiti. Oh, did you remember to feed her?"

Adjo nodded.

"But, this child, he is my real work, my service. Somehow life has more meaning now. I feel we're supposed to care for him so he can fulfill his mission."

"His mission, that sounds very serious," Adjo said. "And what is his mission?" His voice was playful.

"I don't know," Amisi said, keeping a serious tone. "But it's something to do with bringing light. All through my pregnancy I had dreams of light beings."

"Didn't Dr. Ashmawy tell you those dreams were caused by your hormones?"

Adjo hadn't yet acknowledged to himself that he was a little afraid of Amisi's growing preoccupation with these other worldly realms of light, afraid it would create a distance between them.

"Adjo, dreams come from the Divine aspect of ourselves, even if hormones do facilitate them. And the dreams were so real. I felt as if I was seeing into another world, a world of great power and beauty."

"And did you see Horus in this world?"

"I saw him leaping up to at least forty or fifty feet into a pink sky, with a single bound, right up to the top of a waterfall. Then diving back down into the shimmering water below."

"How did you know it was Horus? You've been telling me for months that we're all light beings."

"I knew. I just did. I don't know how," she insisted. "And I do believe that we're all light beings, only some of us know we are, and some of us don't know it, and think we're only our bodies."

"I don't like it when we don't think as one, Amisi."

They heard Horus start to fuss and Amisi said, "He must be hungry," and with Adjo's help, she rose to go to him. But she paused and stood a moment, for a last look at the lotus blossoms growing up from the Nile.

"Adjo, it is our task to help Horus, whatever he's come to do."

"I know, Amisi, and we will."

Chapter 27

Attivio Becomes Ephraim

Rachael hated the thought of the bris the next day. It seemed barbaric to her to cut off the foreskin of an eight-day-old baby. She looked down into Ephraim's little face, unsuspecting of the coming shock and pain. Everything in her wanted to protect him from all hurt. She opened her robe and offered him her breast. Despite twenty hours of labor, the birth had gone smoothly. Daniel had stayed with her throughout, and afterward he had been able to room in with her at the Hadassah Ein Kerem Birthing Center. But she'd been glad to get home the next day, and out of the medical atmosphere. Rachael sat in her new, white, rocking chair, resting her head against its blue and white striped cushions as she nursed Ephraim, and listened to the sound of her mother and her mother-in-law talking as they made challah for the next day's celebration. They were preparing many round shaped foods to symbolize the circle of life. When Daniel said he was going out to buy the wine, they'd handed him yet another shopping list. This one included chick peas, lentils, raisins, almonds, eggs and tomatoes, as well as white fish, smoked salmon, capers and dill. She and Daniel both felt their mothers were overdoing it, but it was useless to say anything.

Once he dozed off, Rachael wiped the dribbles of milk from Ephraim's cheek. Then she closed her own eyes to enjoy the moment. It was a time she relished, because it was when she saw the visions of the light realm with the pink sky, and the couple with the beautiful violet eyes. Something about the man's eyes reminded her of Ephraim. Today she was watching the violet-eyed couple drift around on a clear, calm lake in a blue row boat before enjoying a picnic. They made the food appear as if by magic. First sandwiches and potato salad, and then dark, rich, chocolate cake, watermelon and strawberry ice cream. It puzzled her that she only had these visions while holding Ephraim just after he fell asleep. Could he be seeing the same thing she saw, or even sending the visions to her? What Rachael didn't realize was that she was tuning in to Ephraim's memories, which still came to him in bits and pieces, especially as he crossed over from the waking to the sleep state. What he most enjoyed was seeing himself with the beautiful violet eyed woman, and he struggled to hold onto memories of her.

Realizing that this was her chance for a shower and a nap, while he slept, Rachael laid Ephraim in his cradle. But first she couldn't resist visiting the kitchen to see the preparations, and urge restraint. However, when she saw the lovely food, and realized all the effort it required, it was herself she restrained. On the table was a beautiful kanafeh, soaking in sweet syrup and sprinkled with pistachios. This cheese filled pastry was a favorite of Daniel's. Next to the kanafeh, was a platter piled high with warm bagels. Her mother-in-law dipped a knife into a bowl of soft cream cheese, spread it on a bagel and handed it to her. Rachel plunked into a kitchen chair and bit into the creamy warmth. Suddenly she was overcome with gratitude, for the food, for the two women preparing a celebration for her son, for Ephraim, for Daniel, and even, just to be alive. When she felt the tears welling up behind her eyes, she got up and headed to the bathroom for a shower and a good cry. Busy with their work, the two women didn't notice her tears of joy. But had they noticed, they would have understood completely.

While the hot water poured over her head and rolled down her back, relaxing all her muscles, the tears also rolled down her cheeks. "Tears are an upward release, a letting go, of pain and fear and tension," Alan, the past life regression therapist had told her, "but also of joy and happiness and gratitude."

The bathroom door opened and Daniel peaked in. "Shall I join you?"

Rachael nodded and he pulled off his clothes, dropped them on the floor, and stepped into the warm, steamy shower. He reached for the shampoo and squeezed a small amount into his palm and began massaging it into her scalp.

"Ah...delicious," she said. "Don't stop, I love having you wash my hair."

Daniel tilted her head back under the falling water and stroked the lather out of her long red hair. Then he washed it again, massaging even her neck and shoulders before rinsing her hair to a squeaky clean, and applying conditioner to just the ends, the way she liked.

"Now you," she said, reaching up for the shampoo to massage into his dark curly hair.

Ephraim was still asleep, when, wrapped in towels, they joined him in their bedroom and stood together over his cradle, still not quite believing he was their son. For his part, the baby was dreaming his own dreams, mostly of a beautiful, golden-haired lady with violet eyes, who called him Attivio. Ephraim enjoyed sleeping, because it allowed him to dream of a magical, light filled realm, and the violet-eyed creature he called Soonam. But the dreams were fading, and the need of his tiny body to be fed often awakened him, dragging him back from the light filled realm and from her, the one he most longed for. He vowed to himself that he would never forget her. But in this new realm, his parents called him Ephraim and he was already forgetting the name Attivio.

Chapter 28

Bereh Becomes Arjuna

Before she even cut the cord, Bhamini handed Aastha her newborn son. Through the tears and sweat covering her face, Aastha looked down at the baby in amazement, and prayed that Siddharth was seeing his little son from beyond the veil. Her sister, Mayra, tried to sponge her face with cool water, but Aastha, brushed her aside, and unable to find her voice, held up her arm and jingled the red bangles on her wrist, indicating that she wanted them removed and given to Bhamini as a thank you for bringing her son safely into the world. A gift from her sister, Aastha had worn the bangles from her seventh month of pregnancy on, believing that the sound of them jingling on her arm would comfort the baby inside her.

Bhamini brought her palms together and bowed in a gesture of gratitude for the bangles. Although giving the bangles worn during pregnancy to the midwife was a common practice, it nevertheless touched Bhamini, and her bow was genuine. Over the years as a midwife she had delivered hundreds of babies, but working with Aastha had been special. Perhaps because Aastha was older, and because her husband had died without knowing she was pregnant, or maybe it was the presence of the child she felt around her, even before he was born. Slipping the red bangles onto her own wrist, Bhamini said, "Now, let's get you and the baby cleaned up, so Jatakarma can be performed."

It had been arranged that Siddharth's father, Asish, would perform the ceremony of welcome for the baby, which would have been Siddharth's right, had he been alive.

"I'll go to the waiting area and tell our parents that the baby has been born," Mayra said.

The delivery rooms were on the seventh floor of the

Nowrosjeee Wadia Maternity Hospital, and the waiting area was on the first floor. Mayra walked to the elevators and pushed the down button. While she waited, her mind went back to the morning of Siddharth's death, and she saw him again, lying crumpled on the floor, with Aastha folded over him praying and weeping. Aastha hadn't even known then herself that she was pregnant. Atman would not yet have entered the baby's body at the time of Siddharth's death, Mayra thought. Mayra, like all Hindus, believed that it was not until the third trimester that the Soul enters the baby's body. The elevator doors opened and Dr. Bandekar stood before her. Mayra bowed slightly and he returned the gesture before asking how her sister's labor was progressing. "The baby's born," she said, "Bhamini is with them."

"I'll go to check on them," he answered moving past her to get out of the elevator before the doors closed.

Although the baby would not be formally named until the tenth day after his birth, Mayra couldn't help herself, and upon entering the waiting room burst forth with, "Arjuna is born and well, Aastha, too, is fine."

All four grandparents were on their feet at once, calling out prayers of gratitude and thanksgiving and whispering mantras for the health of the newborn.

"Bhamini is making them ready for Jatakarma," Mayra said, "so we should give them a moment before we go up."

Siddharth's mother picked up the small box she had left on her chair. It contained a delicate gold chain from which hung a tiny golden *OM*. She would place it around the baby's neck to symbolize the imperishable, the universe, the past, the future and the eternal now. Siddharth's father, too, had a gift. He held a bag containing a jar of honey and a small spoon, which he would use to awaken the baby's senses during the ceremony of Jatakarma, so he might taste the sweetness of life on his first day on Earth. Aastha's parents also had a gift. They had purchased a set of gold bangles, to replace the red ones which they knew Aastha would have given to Bhamini.

Having seen that all was well with Aastha and her infant, Dr. Bandekar came down to the waiting room to offer his congratulations to the family, and smiled genuinely when he felt their infectious joy. He appreciated, too, the beautiful saris worn by the women in Aastha's family. Dressed in orange and turquoise and fusia, they looked like walking flowers. When they could wait no longer, they gathered up their things, and crowded together in the small elevator to go up and greet Arjuna. They entered the room to find a blissful Aastha, holding her son. As they surrounded her, she held up Arjuna for them to better see him. Siddharth's father opened the jar of honey, dipped the small spoon into it, and dribbled the honey onto the baby's tongue. Then leaning down, he whispered God's name in Arjuna's tiny ear. He included the names of all three aspects of the Hindu Divinity: Brahma, the creator, Vishnu, the preserver, and Shiva, the destroyer. After this, he placed his hands on Arjuna's little shoulders and chanted as Aastha offered the baby her breast for the first time. He concluded with a verse from the *Bhagavad Gita.*

The presence that pervades the universe
Is imperishable, unchanging,
beyond both *is* and *is not*:
how could it ever vanish?
—Stephen Mitchell translation

Though it was a joyful family scene, each one present felt the absence of Siddharth, but they all accepted the will of God and did not let his absence mar their happiness. There would be more ceremonies soon. In ten days, they would have the naming ceremony, and in two weeks the ceremony to introduce Arjuna to the sun and the moon.

When everyone had left for the day, Aastha gazed at her son and told him about how his father had rejoiced in the welfare of all beings, even pesky monkeys, and how she had named him Arjuna because of his father's love for the *Bhagavad Gita*. Then she slid down in her bed and nestled him next to her, and fell asleep inhaling the sweet scent of his skin.

The sound of the nurse's voice startled her awake, calling her back from somewhere far away. Where had she been, what was it she had been shown, and by whom? Had she picked up the images from the mind of her baby son as he lay next to her? Were they his last fleeting memories of the world he had left behind? She wanted to hold onto them, but the nurse was asking her something. She couldn't focus on the words, so powerful were the images of the other worldly light-filled realm she had seen. Once the nurse had taken her blood pressure and temperature, and listened to the baby's heart rate, she left. Aastha tried to recall the world she had glimpsed in her dream.

A very tall, slender, fair-haired couple, with grey-gold eyes and white skin which seemed to be made of light, stood before a tapestry of many colored threads. The tapestry was hanging in a vast room, filled with shimmering light, and it appeared to be weaving itself. The couple stood before it and watched as pink and gold threads wove together in a wavelike pattern. They turned at the sound of someone approaching. After some conversation, they began walking away from the tapestry, toward tablets which were also made of light, and they read from the tablets with great interest, sharing with one another what they were reading.

Aastha looked down at her baby's warm brown skin, and wondered at the light-filled white skin of the couple, and at the meaning of the tapestry. Where had this vision come from? Had Arjuna shown her this scene? Her feeling that he had was very strong. Could this have been his world before he came to her? But these light beings looked nothing like him. And how could a tapestry weave itself?

Bereh, resting in the infant's body, was aware of her questions, and happy that she had seen his thoughts so clearly, for he had been thinking of the day he and Ederah had gone to Saturn's rings to read the Akashic records and learn about Earth. He wondered why this woman was calling him Arjuna when his name was Bereh. And where was Ederah? He had a vague memory of being in a space-time tunnel with her, but couldn't recall how he'd gotten into this tiny body, only that he must remain in it, because he had come for a purpose. What the purpose was, he couldn't remember. There was so much he couldn't recall, and what he did remember seemed to be fading away with each breath.

Chapter 29

Soonam Becomes Rose

The first thing Soonam felt when she emerged from the tunnel of light was warm water rushing toward her. First it hit her head, then covered her body. Strong hands caught her as she shot downward into the birthing pool. She tried to understand what was happening. Where was she? And where was Attivio? A moment ago, she'd been holding his hand.

"You have a beautiful daughter," the midwife told them.

Jacqueline rested her head against the back of the birthing pool. "Thank God that last push did it. I couldn't have gone on another moment," she said.

Hunter sat still next to the pool, staring at the baby. She was so perfect, so tiny, but so complete. The midwife tried to place the baby in Jacqueline's arms, while she cut the cord, but Jacqueline gestured her away. "Give her to Hunter. I'm exhausted."

Hunter knew better than to ask her if she'd at least like to see her daughter.

Reaching for a towel, the midwife wrapped up the baby in a cozy bundle, and handed her to Hunter's welcoming arms. He gazed down into the sweet face, offering enough love for both her parents. When he pulled her in closer to his heart, she opened her eyes. They were deep violet, the most beautiful eyes he had ever seen, and they were looking right at him. He wanted to weep.

Soonam was confused. She struggled to remember what had happened, but her memory was flickering. Moments ago, she had been in a light tunnel with someone special to her, whose name was Attivio. She had been calling out to him when she felt the water rush over her. She looked up to see who was holding her. The man was smiling at her, with his eyes full of tears, and calling her Rose. Was that her name now?

The afterbirth having been delivered, the midwife helped Jacqueline to her room and asked Hunter to follow with the baby. Once she'd settled Jacqueline, she took the baby from Hunter to bathe and weigh her. Hunter sat down on the chair next to the bed and reached for Jacqueline's hand, but she pulled it away. He wanted to tell her about Rose's violet eyes, and how she'd looked right at him, but he didn't want to risk being snapped at, especially when his heart was so full. Jacqueline turned away from him to stare at the wall. He'd hoped that seeing her baby and holding her would shift something in Jacqueline to soften her, now habitual, meanness. Before he met her, he'd been a happy man with many friends, free to manage his own life. Somehow, he'd come under her spell long enough to marry her. But it wasn't long before he realized he'd made himself a prisoner of her moods. He provided a more than comfortable life style for her, which she didn't appreciate, but assumed was her due. And he wasn't one of those husbands who for weeks fail to see the face of their wives. He was a man who noticed everything. He knew when the new moon was in the sky, as well as when the moon was full. But Jacqueline was too consumed with herself to see him at all. Hunter had discovered this about her too late. *How did I, how does anyone, let himself become the punching bag of another person? Why do I put up with it? How did she gain control of me? Why do I fear her? Am I still hoping she'll change and treat me with kindness and love. And what of this beautiful child, will Jacqueline's cruelty extend to her? How will I protect her?*

A nurse came in with Rose all diapered, dressed and swaddled, and offered her to Jacqueline.

"I don't want to hold her, take her to the nursery."

"Are you planning to breast feed her?" the nurse asked.

"Most certainly not."

"I'll hold her," Hunter said. And for the second time, Rose was placed in his arms. He looked down at her tiny, sleeping body. "No wonder you're tired," he whispered to her, "being born is quite an ordeal."

A food service person, wearing a uniform still labeled Roosevelt Hospital, even though the hospital had been taken over and renamed Mount Sinai West, came in and placed Jacqueline's dinner on her rolling bed table.

"Chicken pot pie for dinner," the server said in his cheery voice.

"Take it away," Jacqueline snapped.

The young man removed the tray and left without another word.

Shortly after, a nurse came in carrying the same tray, and urged Jacqueline to eat something. When Jacqueline ignored her, and continued to stare at the wall, the nurse looked sympathetically at Hunter. Out of conjugal loyalty, he said nothing to the nurse about Jacqueline's behavior. The nurse observed Jacqueline staring at the wall, and asked Hunter if she had held the baby.

"Not yet," he said, casually.

"I'm going to order a psych consultation. Sometimes after the birth, the mother experiences postpartum depression."

Jacqueline ignored this, too.

Hunter wished it was only postpartum depression, because terrible as that was, it could be treated and would pass. But habitual cruelty, and the absolute need to belittle and control others, only fed on itself and grew more monstrous. He walked out of the room and carried Rose to the nursery to ask if he might give her a bottle. As he sat in the nursery rocking chair feeding her, Hunter promised her that he would protect her from all harm. Her little sucking noises made him smile. He gazed at her face and watched as slowly her eyelids drooped and her violet eyes completely closed in slumber. If this wasn't the sweetest, most divine moment he'd ever experienced, he didn't know what was. From now on, the biggest job of his life would be to protect Rose from Jacqueline. Reluctant to put her down, Hunter set the empty bottle on the table beside him, and leaned back in the rocking chair to close his eyes for just a few seconds, to savor the moment. As he listened to Rose's gentle breathing, Hunter started to drift into a reverie. He was tired and afraid he might fall asleep holding her. He meant to put her in her bassinette, but his eyelids were so heavy that he let them drop closed, just for a moment, and the dream vision captured him.

Light beings cavorted with dolphins under a waterfall. And she was there, his little Rose, but all grown up, and exquisitely beautiful, with the same violet eyes that had so recently looked up at him from the face of the baby. She seemed to be made of light as she climbed onto the back of a dolphin for a ride. Hunter watched as the dolphin dove deep under the sparkling water, which looked like diamonds, then emerged to leap up high into the pink sky above, before diving back again into the water. All the while, the violet eyed, young light being held onto the dolphin as if she adored him. Then suddenly the dolphin became a man, also made of light, like her, and he had the same violet eyes, only a slightly lighter shade than Rose's. They were laughing and talking to other tall light beings as they emerged from the crystal water.

Soonam rested in Hunter's arms in a half-sleep state, feeling pleasantly full from the bottle, but fighting to stay awake to figure things out, to remember where she had come from and why she was here. She closed her eyes and scanned what still remained of her memory. A scene which delighted her came into view. She was swimming beneath a waterfall with friends. They were all wearing fanciful bathing costumes. One of them turned himself into a dolphin, then some of the others did the same. She climbed onto the back of her dolphin for a ride. She felt intense longing for this being and knew he was not only a dolphin. But who was he? And where had he gone? Where were they all now? And, where was she? Before she could consider her own question, she felt pulled against her will into a deeper sleep.

When he heard the nurse approaching, Hunter opened his eyes to the reality of the hospital nursery. He wanted to stay in that other world, with the light beings and the dolphins. The nurse suggested he go home and get some rest. He reluctantly handed Rose to her and peeked into Jacqueline's room to find her asleep. When he reached home, Hunter sat in his study, thinking, a long time, then he phoned his lawyer to discuss his chances for custody in the event of a divorce. And, for the first time since he'd married, he felt able to take charge, and slept the sleep of a young man again.

Chapter 30

Maepleida Becomes Mary

"More champagne?" Robert asked his mother.

"No, no it's quite enough."

Robert lifted the champagne bottle out of the silver ice bucket and poured himself another glass. It had been a long night, followed by a long day, but finally Mary had made her appearance. She and Charlotte were both asleep in the bedroom of their maternity suite, while Robert and his mother relaxed in the suite's well-appointed drawing room and enjoyed all the luxurious care the Lindo Maternity Wing of Saint Mary's Hospital could provide. And what they could provide was considerable, including chef prepared food, and afternoon tea and champagne.

Robert set his glass down and picked up the dinner menu on the table next to his comfortable armchair. "I think I'll order for Charlotte as well as myself. Are you staying for dinner, Mother? The chef here is top drawer."

"No. This is a special time for the three of you. And I'm tired, if you'll just see me out."

For once his mother seemed to be keeping a thoughtful boundary. Maybe Mary's birth would usher in a new relationship with her. Robert rose, offered his arm to his mother and walked her out of the hospital. She stood leaning on her elegant cane while he hailed one of the few remaining large, black, London cabs she favored. After helping her in, he returned to the Lindo Wing with a bounce in his step, and picked up the hospital phone to order dinner for two.

Walking into the bedroom, he found Charlotte awake, sitting up, holding Mary in her arms, and the nurse just leaving.

"What a picture you make," he said smiling at them. "But

how are you feeling, darling?"

"Happy," Charlotte answered, glancing down at the baby in her arms.

"Me, too. Happy, and hungry. I've ordered for us from the chef's menu."

"Lovely," Charlotte answered in a dreamy way, as if she hadn't registered his question. "Robert, do you suppose Mary remembers where she was before she came to Earth?"

"That's a funny question."

"I had the strangest dream just now."

"Oh?"

"There was a group of beings standing under a giant, ancient looking, tree. Not far from the tree was a beautiful temple which looked as if it was made of pearl. It's the same one I've seen before in my dreams. All the beings under the tree seemed to be made of light, rather than flesh and blood. Their group looked like it was made up of four pairs. Two of them had skin so black it was like onyx and they wore deep-blue robes which hung all the way to the ground, making them look like royalty. Their bearing was proud, in a good way, and they were very tall, maybe twelve or fourteen feet, with long necks. Beside them was a white skinned couple with violet eyes, wearing long, flowing robes the same color as their eyes. Another pair standing beside the black light beings, were almost as tall as them, but looked all golden, with grey-gold eyes and robes of the palest pink. The last pair were reddish-orange in color, with gold-orange eyes and orange robes. One girl, the onyx one, with the long, slender neck and perfectly balanced features looked directly at me, as if she wanted to say something, as if she wanted me to see her, especially. Then the whole group joined hands for what looked like some ritual."

The nurse must have come in then, because I woke up. I wanted to keep watching to see if the tall onyx girl would look at me again and say something. I can't get the scene out of my mind. They were all so beautiful and full of light. Do you think I could have somehow seen light beings from a higher dimension? Maybe it's something to do with Mary's birth. Maybe her birth opened a portal to another world."

Charlotte gazed at him with a faraway look. He could see that she had been affected by the dream. "You've had a lot of intense dreams during your pregnancy about the place with the pink sky and the pearl temple, and then there was your dream about the reptile. Didn't Dr. Gupta say it was because of the pregnancy hormones?"

"Yes, but this is the first time I felt someone was trying to show me something. And we both know dreams are about more than hormones."

"I know your mother thinks so."

"Of course she does, she's a Jungian analyst."

"Maybe you should speak to her about today's dream."

"I will, even though something about this one didn't even feel like a dream. I wish she was here."

"They weren't to know that Mary would arrive two weeks early."

"Have you reached them?"

"I left a message at their hotel in Rome."

"Good. But Robert, do you think I was being shown something? Or being given a message from beyond. Why did the tall, onyx light being look at me so intently? It felt like she was trying to communicate with me."

Robert squeezed her hand, unsure how to answer.

There was a knock at the door of the suite. A waiter in a white jacket and tie wheeled in a cart laden with silver covered dishes laid out on a white cloth.

"Shall I set the table, sir?"

"No, thank you, just leave everything."

Robert reached into his trouser pocket and gave the waiter ten pounds. Normally a generous man, Robert was even more so today.

"Can you take Mary and put her in the bassinette?"

Robert lifted Mary from Charlotte's arms. She didn't awaken and even appeared to be dreaming her own dreams behind fluttering eyelids. While she slept, her new parents tucked into warm shepherd's pie, baby spring peas, young carrots and, best of all, hot biscuits with sweet butter.

Maybe because she had spent time on Earth in the Himalayas with Master El Morya or maybe for some other reason, Maepleida retained, at least for the present, more consciousness of what was happening to her than did her friends. She remembered the moment she'd been pulled away from Heipleido in the space-time tunnel, and she still knew that they had all agreed to come on a mission to Earth to help humans remember their own Divinity. She thought of Heipleido, and Soonam and Attivio, and Laaroos and Toomeh, and Ederah and Bereh, and pictured them all on Venus, lounging under their tree, happily relaxing, as they had so many times. Then she pictured them all on their last day, dressed in their robes, standing together outside the temple before moving toward the golden stairs. She tried to send this image to her new mother. Despite the tiny human vehicle she now found herself in, Maepleida was hopeful. She'd have to get used to being called Mary, but that was nothing. If only she could hold onto the memory of what she had come to do. She would try to telegraph as much as she could remember to her new parents, in the hope of showing them something of who she was, and where she had come from, in case her own memory became completely veiled. She sensed that the woman had caught some of the vision she had sent, because for a moment, her vision eyes had met Maepleida's own. She fought sleep for fear that when she awoke all memory would be gone. But it was comfortable and warm being held in the woman's arms, and she finally succumbed, and was only dimly aware of being placed in a bassinette.

Chapter 31

The Dark Side

"Greetings Slaves. I have commanded your presence here on Orion to inform you of a new mission on which you will serve me. My spies inform me that a large group of positively polarized light beings have been training on Venus for a mission to Earth. This group does not take pleasure in the wailful choir of the suffering of others which so pleases me. They follow instead the path of service to others, in their attempt to find the gateway to Intelligent Infinity. Your mission will be to thwart. You will infiltrate the quarantine around Earth and create fear and terror in these wanderers, and in their human families, gaining control over them. You will make them doubt everything they once held dear, and you will draw them to the Dark Side. When you do, they will then serve you, as your slaves. The more slaves you have, the stronger your polarization to the Dark Side will become. So, make your picnic of suffering a filling one."

Darpith sneered as he looked out over them. He relished their fear and feasted on it. As a fifth dimensional being, he could create his form at will. For today's gathering he appeared in a reptile-like bipedal body. To instill the most discomfort possible in his slaves, he stood sixteen feet tall, and was covered with black scales. He had claw-like hands, a long, scale covered tail, and burning black coals in the place where eyes would have been had he been human. He could have chosen to appear fair, for like all fifth dimensional beings, he was capable of great elegance, as well as subtly of thought and action. But today it didn't suit his purpose to be subtle. In fact, it rarely did. He desired to crush his slaves and bend them to his will. If he was to achieve the necessary power on the dark path in order to become sixth dimensional, he must cause others the utmost misery possible.

Darpith grinned with pleasure at the memory of the pain he had inflicted on one of his spies who had accidentally been perceived on Venus. "I recently enjoyed the pleasure of putting one of you to death because he carelessly emerged from a cottage on Venus and his presence was felt by one of the light beings. Take heed slaves. I never tolerate sloppy work." Darpith feasted again, on the memory of the painful death he'd created for that slave.

"But to continue, the light beings who have recently been preparing on Venus for a mission to Earth have now incarnated as human babies. Their purpose is to awaken the humans to the knowledge that they are Divine. Humans must not gain this knowledge. Your mission will be to prevent their awakening and to turn them to the Dark Side. To do this you will employ trickery, mental telepathy, hostile thought forms and mind control. Should you fail to corrupt them, you will take ultimate power over them by putting them to death. Just as we of Orion planted the thought in the mind of John Wilkes Booth to assassinate Abraham Lincoln, and just as we planted and fed the thoughts to kill Sadat, John F. Kennedy, Robert Kennedy, Martin Luther King, Malcolm X and other beings who lived lives of service to others, so, too, will we destroy any being who will not bow to us. Search out the location of these wanderers from Venus and find your opportunity to plant negative thoughts of self-hatred, and jealousy of others in them, and in those near to them. Set them at odds with themselves and those they hold dear. Some will fall into our hands, others will resist. Take care, the wanderers are advanced beings of the fifth dimension. Our advantage is that the confederation had to adhere to the laws governing incarnation on Earth, and the wanderers will have passed through the veil of forgetting, and no longer know that their true home is in the fifth dimension. They will think that they are ordinary humans. As they grow up, the confederation forces will try to help them awaken. And the wanderers themselves possess an armor of light in their spirit complex which could alert them to your purpose, so beware. But for some years, they will be almost completely creatures of the third dimension. This is your opportunity. I order you to make plans to enslave these beings who have trained on Venus. Watch for opportunities to slip through the quarantine around Earth. Pollute whatever positive messages you can, even as you polluted many of the teachings of Earth's religions. Plant unease, mistrust and fear. Along with mental telepathy and mind control, you may use two types of entities to do your biding: thought forms, like the Men in Black, who we have used before, and who can materialize and dematerialize, and also robots who look like human beings, but have no soul. Remember, your first purpose is to enslave. That failing, you may enjoy the ultimate power over another by putting them to death. Do not fail, for if you do, you will receive the ultimate punishment, and it will not be swift.

Now, to other business. Our work with religious and political fanatics on Earth is proceeding well. You have incited rage in many white elitist groups in the United States and Europe. Continue to feed them negative thought forms. You have also infiltrated many minds in the Middle East. Much fear has been stirred up by the beheadings of journalists, and by the treatment of women as second-class beings in many countries. I would have you continue to create hostility between Israel and the Palestinians by feeding thoughts to the Israelis that they must take more land to be secure. Keep it up. Their wars and misery are our feast.

And your most recent focus, the feeding of the unstable president of the United States with thoughts of his unlimited power, and with ideas of how to create an elite which will incarcerate and enslave others whom he sees as not elite has been most gratifying to me. Keep planting bellicose rhetoric in him so that he will further destabilize international relations. He creates much fear, which makes our task easier. It is indeed a juicy picnic of misery, with this American president as the fat cherry on top, on which I can feast, for he is already under my control. Continue also to feed him thoughts of how to terrify many people in the United States by threatening them, rounding them up, separating families, and incarcerating or killing them. He already sees many as non-elite, while seeing himself as elite, so it will be child's play for you to manipulate him through mind control." Darpith grinned at the thought of the American president's stupidity. "Go now, do my bidding or face my wrath." The slaves prostrated themselves before Darpith, and he walked on them as he left the gathering, crushing those he stepped on under his claw-like feet.

Darpith was pleased with the fear he had created in his slaves, and rewarded himself by transforming into a handsome youth with a lean, fit body, and calling for a harem of beautiful slave girls to humiliate and torture. As he admired himself, he relished the picnic of pain he would unleash on Earth. Darpith's self-involvement was so complete that he failed to notice the confederation forces gathering in Saturn's rings to plan his defeat. He failed also to realize that there were other fifth dimensional entities on his own path who were planning his destruction, to gain all his slaves for themselves. Some of these beings were capable of far more subtly than Darpith. But for the moment, in ignorance of his enemies, he indulged himself in the pleasure of abusing his slave girls.

As Darpith fed his lust, Venus and Kumara arrived in Saturn's rings to meet with the Council of Nine, the Masters of the Seven Rays, and representatives from the Inner Cities of Light. Venus reported that all of the wanderers had been born alive and healthy. Lord Lanto shared information about Darpith's meeting, and also of his enemies within the Dark Side, who were plotting against him. After the reports, the head of the Council of Nine opened the session to plan for the coming battle with the dark side over the souls of humanity, and for the soul of planet Earth herself.

COSMIC EGG
BOOKS

FANTASY, SCI-FI, HORROR & PARANORMAL

If you prefer to spend your nights with Vampires and Werewolves rather than the mundane then we publish the books for you. If your preference is for Dragons and Faeries or Angels and Demons – we should be your first stop. Perhaps your perfect partner has artificial skin or comes from another planet – step right this way. If your passion is Fantasy (including magical realism and spiritual fantasy), Metaphysical Cosmology, Horror or Science Fiction (including Steampunk), Cosmic Egg books will feed your hunger. Our curiosity shop contains treasures you will enjoy unearthing. If you have enjoyed this book, why not tell other readers by posting a review on your preferred book site. Recent bestsellers from Cosmic Egg Books are:

The Zombie Rule Book
A Zombie Apocalypse Survival Guide
Tony Newton
The book the living-dead don't want you to have!
Paperback: 978-1-78279-334-2 ebook: 978-1-78279-333-5

Cryptogram
Because the Past is Never Past
Michael Tobert
Welcome to the dystopian world of 2050, where three lovers are haunted by echoes from eight-hundred years ago.
Paperback: 978-1-78279-681-7 ebook: 978-1-78279-680-0

Purefinder

Ben Gwalchmai

London, 1858. A child is dead; a man is blamed and dragged through hell in this Dantean tale of loss, mystery and fraternity.

Paperback: 978-1-78279-098-3 ebook: 978-1-78279-097-6

600ppm

A Novel of Climate Change

Clarke W. Owens

Nature is collapsing. The government doesn't want you to know why. Welcome to 2051 and 600ppm.

Paperback: 978-1-78279-992-4 ebook: 978-1-78279-993-1

Creations

William Mitchell

Earth 2040 is on the brink of disaster. Can Max Lowrie stop the self-replicating machines before it's too late?

Paperback: 978-1-78279-186-7 ebook: 978-1-78279-161-4

The Gawain Legacy

Jon Mackley

If you try to control every secret, secrets may end up controlling you.

Paperback: 978-1-78279-485-1 ebook: 978-1-78279-484-4

Readers of ebooks can buy or view any of these bestsellers by clicking on the live link in the title. Most titles are published in paperback and as an ebook. Paperbacks are available in traditional bookshops. Both print and ebook formats are available online.

Find more titles and sign up to our readers' newsletter at http://www.johnhuntpublishing.com/fiction

Follow us on Facebook at https://www.facebook.com/JHPfiction and Twitter at https://twitter.com/JHPFiction